Castle Dangerous
by
Sir Walter Scott

CASTLE DANGEROUS

As I stood by yon roofless tower,
  Where the wa'flower scents the dewy air,
Where the howlet mourns in her ivy bower,
  And tells the midnight moon her care:
The winds were laid, the air was still,
  The stars they shot along the sky;
The Fox was howling on the hill,
  And the distant echoing glens reply.

ROBERT BURNS.

INTRODUCTION.—(1832.)

[The following Introduction to "Castle Dangerous" was forwarded by Sir Walter Scott from Naples in February 1832, together with some corrections of the text, and notes on localities mentioned in the Novel.

The materials for the Introduction must have been collected before he left Scotland in September 1831; but in the hurry of preparing for his voyage, he had not been able to arrange them so as to accompany the first edition of this Romance. A few notes, supplied by the Editor, are placed within brackets.]

The incidents on which the ensuing Novel mainly turns, are derived from the ancient Metrical Chronicle of "The Brace," by Archdeacon Barbour, and from the "History of the Houses of Douglas and Angus," by David Hume of Godscroft; and are sustained by the immemorial tradition of the western parts of Scotland. They are so much in consonance with the spirit and manners of the troubled age to which they are referred, that I can see no reason for doubting their being founded in fact; the names, indeed, of numberless localities in the vicinity of Douglas Castle, appear to attest, beyond suspicion, many even of the smallest circumstances embraced in the story of Godscroft.

Among all the associates of Robert the Brace, in his great enterprise of rescuing Scotland from the power of Edward, the first place is universally conceded to James, the eighth Lord Douglas, to this day venerated by his countrymen as "the Good Sir James:"

"The Gud Schyr James of Douglas,
That in his time sa worthy was,
That off his price and his bounte,
In far landis renownyt was he."

BARBOUR.

"The Good Sir James, the dreadful blacke Douglas,
That in his dayes so wise and worthie was,
Wha here, and on the infidels of Spain,

Such honour, praise, and triumphs did obtain."
GORDON.

From the time when the King of England refused to reinstate him, on his return from France, where he had received the education of chivalry, in the extensive possessions of his family,—which had been held forfeited by the exertions of his father, William the Hardy—the young knight of Douglas appears to have embraced the cause of Bruce with enthusiastic ardour, and to have adhered to the fortunes of his sovereign with unwearied fidelity and devotion. "The Douglasse," says Hollinshed, "was right joyfully received of King Robert, in whose service he faithfully continued, both in peace and war, to his life's end. Though the surname and familie of the Douglasses was in some estimation of nobilitie before those daies, yet the rising thereof to honour chanced through this James Douglasse; for, by meanes of his advancement, others of that lineage tooke occasion, by their singular manhood and noble prowess, shewed at sundrie times in defence of the realme, to grow to such height in authoritie and estimation, that their mightie puissance in mainrent, [Footnote: Vassalage.] lands, and great possessions, at length was (through suspicion conceived by the kings that succeeded) the cause in part of their ruinous decay."

In every narrative of the Scottish war of independence, a considerable space is devoted to those years of perilous adventure and suffering which were spent by the illustrious friend of Bruce, in harassing the English detachments successively occupying his paternal territory, and in repeated and successful attempts to wrest the formidable fortress of Douglas Castle itself from their possession. In the English, as well as Scotch Chronicles, and in Rymer's Foedera, occur frequent notices of the different officers intrusted by Edward with the keeping of this renowned stronghold; especially Sir Robert de Clifford, ancestor of the heroic race of the Cliffords, Earls of Cumberland; his lieutenant, Sir Richard de Thurlewalle, (written sometimes Thruswall,) of Thirwall Castle, on the Tippal, in Northumberland; and Sir John de Walton, the romantic story of whose love pledge, to hold the Castle of Douglas for a year and day, or surrender all hope of obtaining his mistress's favour, with the tragic consequences, softened in the Novel, is given at length in Godscroft, and has often been pointed out as one of the affecting passages in the chronicles of chivalry. [Footnote: [The reader will find both this story, and that of Robert of Paris, in Sir W. Scott's Essay on Chivalry, published in 1818, in the Supplement to the Encyclopaedia Britannica.—E.]]

The Author, before he had made much progress in this, probably the last of his Novels, undertook a journey to Douglasdale, for the purpose of examining the remains of the famous Castle, the Kirk of St. Bride of

4

Douglas, the patron saint of that great family, and the various localities alluded to by Godscroft, in his account of the early adventures of good Sir James; but though he was fortunate enough to find a zealous and well-informed *cicerone* in Mr. Thomas Haddow, and had every assistance from the kindness of Mr. Alexander Finlay, the resident Chamberlain of his friend Lord Douglas, the state of his health at the time was so feeble, that he found himself incapable of pursuing his researches, as in better days he would have delighted to do, and was obliged to be contented with such a cursory view of scenes, in themselves most interesting, as could be snatched in a single morning, when any bodily exertion was painful. Mr. Haddow was attentive enough to forward subsequently some notes on the points which the Author had seemed desirous of investigating; but these did not reach him until, being obliged to prepare matters for a foreign excursion in quest of health and strength, he had been compelled to bring his work, such as it is, to a conclusion.

The remains of the old Castle of Douglas are inconsiderable. They consist indeed of but one ruined tower, standing at a short distance from the modern mansion, which itself is only a fragment of the design on which the Duke of Douglas meant to reconstruct the edifice, after its last accidental destruction by fire. [Footnote: [The following notice of Douglas Castle, &c., is from the Description of the Sheriffdom of Lanark, by William Hamilton of Wishaw, written in the beginning of the last century, and printed by the Maitland Club of Glasgow in 1831:]—

"Douglass parish, and baronie and lordship, heth very long appertained to the family of Douglass, and continued with the Earles of Douglass untill their fatall forfeiture, anno 1455; during which tyme there are many noble and important actions recorded in histories performed by them, by the lords and earls of that great family. It was thereafter given to Douglass, Earle of Anguse, and continued with them untill William, Earle of Anguse, was created Marquess of Douglass, anno 1633; and is now the principal seat, of the Marquess of Douglass his family. It is a large baronie and parish, and ane laick patronage; and the Marquess is both titular and patron. He heth there, near to the church, a very considerable great house, called the Castle of Douglas; and near the church is a fyne village called the town of Douglass, long since erected in a burgh of baronie. It heth ane handsome church, with many ancient monuments and inscriptions on the old, interments of the Earles of this place.

"The water of Douglas runs quyte through the whole length of this parish, and upon either side of the water it is called Douglasdale. It toucheth Clyde towards the north, and is bounded by Lesmahagow to the west, Kyle to the southwest, Crawford John and Carmichaell to the south and southeast. It is a pleasant strath, plentifull in grass and corn, and coal; and the minister is well provided.

"The lands of Heysleside belonging to Samuel Douglass, has a good house and pleasant seat, close by wood," &c.—P. 65.] His Grace had kept in view the ancient prophecy, that as often as Douglas Castle might be destroyed, it should rise again in enlarged dimensions and improved splendour, and projected a pile of building, which, if it had been completed, would have much exceeded any nobleman's residence then existing in Scotland—as, indeed, what has been finished, amounting to about one-eighth part of the plan, is sufficiently extensive for the accommodation of a large establishment, and contains some apartments the dimensions of which are magnificent. The situation is commanding; and though the Duke's successors have allowed the mansion to continue as he left it, great expense has been lavished on the environs, which now present a vast sweep of richly undulated woodland, stretching to the borders of the Cairntable mountains, repeatedly mentioned as the favourite retreat of the great ancestor of the family in the days of his hardship and persecution. There remains at the head of the adjoining *bourg*, the choir of the ancient church of St. Bride, having beneath it the vault which was used till lately as the burial-place of this princely race, and only abandoned when their stone and leaden coffins had accumulated, in the course of five or six hundred years, in such a way that it could accommodate no more. Here a silver case, containing the dust of what was once the brave heart of Good Sir James, is still pointed out; and in the dilapidated choir above appears, though in a sorely ruinous state, the once magnificent tomb of the warrior himself. After detailing the well-known circumstances of Sir James's death in Spain, 20th August, 1330, where he fell, assisting the King of Arragon in an expedition against the Moors, when on his way back to Scotland from Jerusalem, to which he had conveyed the heart of Bruce,—the old poet Barbour tells us that—

"Quhen his men lang had mad murnyn,
Thai debowalyt him, and syne
Gert scher him swa, that mycht be tane
The flesch all haly frae the bane.
And the carioune thar in haly place
Erdyt, with rycht gret worschip, was.
"The banys haue thai with them tane;
And syne ar to thair schippis gane;
Syne towart Scotland held thair way,
And thar ar cummyn in full gret hy.
And the banys honbrabilly

In till the Kyrk of Douglas war
Erdyt, with dule and mekill car.
Schyr Archebald his sone gert syn
Off alabastre, bath fair and fyne,
Ordane a tumbe sa richly
As it behowyt to swa worthy."

The monument is supposed to have been wantonly mutilated and defaced by a detachment of Cromwell's troops, who, as was their custom, converted the kirk of St. Bride of Douglas into a stable for their horses. Enough, however, remains to identify the resting-place of the great Sir James. The effigy, of dark stone, is crossed-legged, marking his character as one who had died after performing the pilgrimage to the Holy Sepulchre, and in actual conflict with the infidels of Spain; and the introduction of the HEART, adopted as an addition to the old arms of Douglas, in consequence of the knight's fulfilment of Bruce's dying injunction, appears, when taken in connexion with the posture of the figure, to set the question at rest. The monument, in its original state, must have been not inferior in any respect to the best of the same period in Westminster Abbey; and the curious reader is referred for farther particulars of it to "The Sepulchral Antiquities of Great Britain, by Edward Blore, F.S.A." London, 4to, 1826: where may also be found interesting details of some of the other tombs and effigies in the cemetery of the first house of Douglas.

As considerable liberties have been taken, with the historical incidents on which this novel is founded, it is due to the reader to place before him such extracts from Godscroft and Barbour as may enable him to correct any mis-impression. The passages introduced in the Appendix, from the ancient poem of "The Bruce," will moreover gratify those who have not in their possession a copy of the text of Barbour, as given in the valuable quarto edition of my learned friend Dr. Jamieson, as furnishing on the whole a favourable specimen of the style and manner of a venerable classic, who wrote when Scotland was still full of the fame and glory of her liberators from the yoke of Plantagenet, and especially of Sir James Douglas, "of whom," says Godscroft, "we will not omit here, (to shut up all,) the judgment of those times concerning him, in a rude verse indeed, yet such as beareth witness of his true magnanimity and invincible mind in either fortune:—

"Good Sir James Douglas (who wise, and wight, and worthy was,)
Was never over glad in no winning, nor yet oversad for no lineing;
Good fortune and evil chance he weighed both in one balance."

W. S.

7

No. I.

EXTRACTS FROM "THE HISTORY OF THE HOUSES OF DOUGLAS AND ANGUS. BY MASTER DAVID HUME OF GODSCROFT." FOL. EDIT.

* * * And here indeed the course of the King's misfortunes begins to make some halt and stay by thus much prosperous successe in his own person; but more in the person of Sir James, by the reconquests of his owne castles and countries. From hence he went into Douglasdale, where, by the means of his father's old servant, Thomas Dickson, he took in the Castle of Douglas, and not being able to keep it, he caused burn it, contenting himself with this, that his enemies had one strength fewer in that country than before. The manner of his taking of it is said to have beene thus:—Sir James taking only with him two of his servants, went to Thomas Dickson, of whom he was received with tears, after he had revealed himself to him, for the good old man knew him not at first, being in mean and homely apparel. There he kept him secretly in a quiet chamber, and brought unto him such as had been trusty servants to his father, not all at, once, but apart by one and one, for fear of discoverie. Their advice was, that on Palm-Sunday, when the English would come forth to the church, and his partners were conveened, that then he should give the word, and cry the Douglas slogan, and presently set upon them that should happen to be there, who being despatched, the Castle might be taken easily. This being concluded, and they come, so soon as the English were entered into the church with palms in their hands, (according to the costume of that day,) little suspecting or fearing any such thing, Sir James, according to their appointment, cryed too soon (a Douglas, a Douglas!) which being heard in the church, (this was Saint Bride's church of Douglas,) Thomas Dickson, supposing he had beene hard at hand, drew out his sword, and ran upon them, having none to second him but another man, so that, oppressed by the number of his enemies, he was beaten downe and slaine. In the meantime, Sir James being come, the English that were in the chancel kept off the Scots, and having the advantage of the strait and narrow entrie, defended themselves manfully. But Sir James encouraging his men, not so much by words as by deeds and good example, and having slain the boldest resisters, prevailed at last, and entring the place, slew some twenty-six of their number, and took the rest, about ten or twelve persons, intending by them to get the Castle upon composition, or to enter with them when the gates should be opened to let them in: but it needed not, for they of the Castle were so secure, that there was none left to keep it save the porter and the cooke, who knowing nothing of what had hapned at the church, which stood a large quarter of a mile from thence, had left the gate wide open, the porter standing without,

and the cooke dressing the dinner within. They entered without resistance, and meat being ready, and the cloth laid, they shut the gates, and tooke their refection at good leasure.

Now that he had gotten the Castle into his hands, considering with himselfe (as he was a man no lesse advised than valiant) that it was hard for him to keep it, the English being as yet the stronger in that countrey, who if they should besiege him, he knewe of no reliefe, he thought better to carry away such things as be most easily transported, gold, silver, and apparell, with ammunition and armour, whereof he had greatest use and need, and to destroy the rest of the provision, together with the Castle itselfe, then to diminish the number of his followers for a garrison there where it could do no good. And so he caused carrie the meale and malt, and other cornes and graine, into the cellar, and laid altogether in one heape: then he took the prisoners and slew them, to revenge the death of his trustie and valiant servant, Thomas Dickson, mingling the victuals with their bloud, and burying their carkasses in the heap of corne: after that he struck out the heads of the barrells and puncheons, and let the drink runn through all; and then he cast the carkasses of dead horses and other carrion amongst it, throwing the salt above all, so as to make altogether unuseful to the enemie; and this cellar is called yet the Douglas Lairder. Last of all, he set the house on fire, and burnt all the timber, and what else the fire could overcome, leaving nothing but the scorched walls behind him. And this seemes to be the first taking of the Castle of Douglas, for it is supposed that he took it twice. For this service, and others done to Lord William his father, Sir James gave unto Thomas Dickson the lands of Hisleside, which hath beene given him before the Castle was taken as an encouragement to whet him on, and not after, for he was slain in the church; which was both liberally and wisely done of him, thus to hearten and draw men to his service by such a noble beginning. The Castle being burnt, Sir James retired, and parting his men into divers companies, so as they might be most secret, he caused cure such as were wounded in the fight, and he himselfe kept as close as he could, waiting ever for an occasion to enterprise something against the enemie. So soone as he was gone, the Lord Clifford being advertised of what had happened, came himselfe in person to Douglas, and caused re-edifie and repair the Castle in a very short time, unto which he also added a Tower, which is yet called Harries Tower from him, and so returned into England, leaving one Thurswall to be Captain thereof.—Pp. 26-28.

* * * * * * *

He (Sir James Douglas) getting him again into Douglasdale, did use this stratagem against Thurswall, Captain of the Castle, under the said Lord

Clifford. He caused some of his folk drive away the cattle that fed near unto the Castle, and when the Captain of the garrison followed to rescue, gave orders to his men to leave them and to flee away. Thus he did often to make the Captain slight such frays, and to make him secure, that he might not suspect any further end to be on it; which when he had wrought sufficiently (as he thought), he laid some men in ambuscado, and sent others away to drive such beasts as they should find in the view of the Castle, as if they had been thieves and robbers, as they had done often before. The Captain hearing of it, and supposing there was no greater danger now than had been before, issued forth of the Castle, and followed after them with such haste that his men (running who should be first) were disordered and out of their ranks. The drivers also fled as fast as they could till they had drawn the Captain a little way beyond the place of ambuscado, which when they perceived, rising quickly out of their covert, they set fiercely upon him and his company, and so slew himself and chased his men back to the Castle, some of whom were overtaken and slain, others got into the Castle and so were saved. Sir James, not being able to force the house, took what booty he could get without in the fields, and so departed. By this means, and such other exploits, he so affrighted the enemy, that it was counted a matter of such great jeopardy to keep this Castle, that it began to be called the adventurous (or hazardous) Castle of Douglas: Whereupon Sir John Walton being in suit of an English lady, she wrote to him that when he had kept the adventurous Castle of Douglas seven years, then, he might think himself worthy to be a suitor to her. Upon this occasion Walton took upon him the keeping of it, and succeeded to Thurswall; but he ran the same fortune with the rest that were before him.

For, Sir James having first dressed an ambuscado near unto the place, he made fourteen of his men take so many sacks, and fill them with grass, as though it had been corn, which they carried in the way toward Lanark, the chief market town in that county: so hoping to draw forth the Captain by that bait, and either to take him or the Castle, or both.

Neither was this expectation frustrate, for the Captain did bite, and came forth to have taken this victual (as he supposed). But ere he could reach these carriers, Sir James, with his company, had gotten between the Castle and him; and these disguised carriers, seeing the Captain following after them, did quickly cast off their upper garments, wherein they had masked themselves, and throwing off their sacks, mounted themselves on horseback, and met the Captain with a sharp encounter, he being so much the more amazed that it was unlooked for: wherefore, when he saw these carriers metamorphosed into warriors, and ready to assault him, fearing (that which was) that there was some train laid for them, he turned about to have retired into the Castle; but there also he met with his enemies; between which two companies he and his followers were slain, so that none escaped; the Captain afterwards being searched, they found (as it is reported) his mistress's letters about him. Then he went and took in the Castle, but it is uncertain (say our writers) whether by force or composition; but it seems that the Constable, and those that were within, have yielded it up without force; in regard that he used them so gently, which he would not have done if he had taken it at utterance. For he sent them all safe home to the Lord Clifford, and gave them also provision and money for their entertainment by the way. The Castle, which he had burnt only before, now he razeth, and casts down the walls thereof to the ground. By these and the like proceedings, within a short while he freed Douglasdale, Attrict Forest, and Jedward Forest, of the English garrisons and subjection.—*Ibid.* p. 29.

No. II.

[Extracts from THE BRUCE.—"Liber compositus per Magistrum Johannem
Barber Archidiaeonum Abyrdonensem, de gestis, bellis, et vertutibus,
Domini Roberti Brwyes, Regis Scocie illustrissimi, et de conquestu
regni Scocie per eundem, et de Domino Jacobo de Douglas."—Edited by
John Jamieson, D.D. F.R.S.F. &c. &c. Edinburgh, 1820.]

Now takis James his waige Towart Dowglas, his heretage, With twa yemen, for his owtyn ma; That wes a symple stuff to ta, A land or a castell to win. The quhethir he yarnyt to begyn Till bring purposs till ending; For gud help is in gud begynnyng, For gud begynning, and hardy, Gyff it be folwit wittily, May ger oftsyss unlikly thing Cum to full conabill ending. Swa did it here: but he wes wyss And saw he mycht, on nakyn wyss, Werray his fa with evyn mycht; Tharfur he thocht to wyrk with slycht. And in Dowglas daile, his countre, Upon an evymiyng entryt he. And than a man wonnyt tharby. That was off freyndis weill mychty, And ryche of moble, and off cateill; And had bene till his fadyr leyll; And till him selff in his yowthed. He haid done mony a thankfull deid. Thom Dicson wes his name perlay. Till him he send; and gan him pray, That he wald cum all anerly For to spek with him priuely. And he but daunger till him gais: Bot fra he tauld him quhat he wais, He gret for joy, and for pite; And him rycht till his houss had he; Quhar in a chambre priuely He held him, and his cumpany, That nane had off him persaving. Off mete, and drynk, and othyr thing, That mycht thuim eyss, thai had plente. Sa wrocht he thorow sutelte, That all the lele men off that land, That with his fadyr war duelland, This gud man gert cum, ane and ane, And mak him manrent cuir ilkane; And he him selff fyrst homage maid. Dowglas in part gret glaidschip haid, That the gud men off his cuntre Wald swagate till him bundyn be. He speryt the conwyne off the land, And quha the castell had in hand. And thai him tauld all halily; And syne amang them priuely Thai ordanyt, that he still suld be In hiddillis, and in priwete, Till Palme Sonday, that wes ner hand, The thrid day eftyr folowand. For than the folk off that countre Assemblyt at the kyrk wald be; And thai, that in the castell wer, Wald als be thar, thar palmys to ber, As folk that had na dreid off ill; For thai thoucht all wes at thair will. Than suld he cum with his twa men. Bot, for that men suld nocht him ken, He suld ane mantill haiff auld and bar, And a flaill, as he a thresscher war. Undyr the mantill nocht for thi He suld be armyt priuely. And quhen the men off his countre, That suld all boune befor him be, His ensenye mycht her hym cry. Then suld thai, full enforcely, Rycht ymyddys the kyrk assaill The Ingliss men with hard bataill Swa that nane mycht eschap them fra; For thar throwch trowyt thai to ta The castell, that besid wes ner And quhen this, that I tell you her, Wes diuisyt and undertane, Ilkane till his howss hame is gane; And held this spek in priuete, Till the day off thar assembly.

The folk upon the Sonounday Held to Saynct Bridis kyrk thair way, And tha that in the castell war Ischyt owt, bath les and mar, And went thair palmys for to her; Owtane a cuk and a porter. James off Dowglas off thair cummyng, And quhat thai war, had witting; And sped him till the kyrk in hy Bot or he come, too hastily Ane off his criyt, "Dowglas! Dowglas!" Thomas Dicson, that nerrest was Till thaim that war off the castell, That war all innouth the chancell, Quhen he "Dowglas!" swa hey herd cry, Drew owt his swerd; and felly Ruschyt amang thaim to and fra. Bot ane or twa, for owtyn ma, Than in hy war left lyand Quhill Dowglas come rycht at hand. And then enforcyt on thaim the cry. Bot thai the chansell sturdely Held, and thaim defendyt wele, Till off thair men war slayne sumdell. Bot the Dowglace sa weill him bar, That all the men, that with him war, Had comfort off his wele doyng; And he him sparyt nakyn thing. Bot provyt swa his force in fycht, That throw his worschip, and his mycht, His men sa keynly helpyt than, That thai the chansell on thaim wan. Than dang thai on swa hardyly, That in schort tyme men mycht se ly The twa part dede, or then deand. The lave war sesyt sone in hand, Swa that off thretty levyt nane, That thai ne war slayne ilkan, or tane.

James off Dowglas, quhen this wes done, The presoneris has he tane alsone; And, with thaim off his cumpany, Towart the castell went in hy, Or noyiss, or cry, suld ryss. And for he wald thaim sone suppriss, That levyt in the castell war, That war but twa for owtyn mar, Fyve men or sex befor send he, That fand all opyn the entre; And entryt, and the porter tuk Rycht at the gate, and syne the cuk. With that Dowglas come to the gat, And entryt in for owtyn debate; And fand the mete all ready grathit, With burdys set, and clathis layit. The gaitis then he gert sper, And sat, and eyt all at layser. Syne all the gudis turssyt thai That thaim thocht thai mycht haiff away; And namly wapnys, and armyng, Siluer, and tresour, and clethyng. Vyctallis, that, mycht nocht tursyt be, On this manner destroyit he. All the vrctalis, owtane salt, Als quheyt, and flour, and meill, and malt In the wyne sellar gert he bring; And samyn on the flur all flyng. And the presoneris that he had tane Rycht thar in gert he heid ilkane; Syne off the townnys he hedis outstrak: A foule melle thar gane he mak. For meile, and malt, and bluid, and wyne Ran all to gidder in a mellyne, That was unsemly for to se. Tharfor the men of that countre, For swa fele thar mellyt wer, Callit it the "Dowglas Lardner." Syne tuk he salt, as Ic hard tell, And ded horss, and sordid the well. And brynt all, owtakyn stane; And is forth, with his menye, gayne Till his resett; for him thoucht weill, Giff he had haldyn the caslell, It had bene assegyt raith; And that him thoucht to mekill waith. For he ne had hop of reskewyng. And it is to peralous thing In castell assegyt to be, Quhar want is off thir thingis thre; Victaill, or men with their armyng, Or than gud hop off rescuyng. And for he dred thir thingis suld faile, He chesyt furthwart to trawaill, Quhar he mycht at his larges be; And swa dryve furth his destane.

On this wise wes the castell tan, And slayne that war tharin ilkan. The Dowglas syne all his menye Gert in ser placis depertyt be; For men suld wyt quhar thai war, That yeid depertyt her and thar. Thim that war woundyt gert he ly In till hiddillis, all priuely; And gert gud leechis till thaim bring Quhill that thai war in till heling. And him selff, with a few menye, Quhile ane, quhile twa and quhile thre, And umqumll all him allane. In hiddillis throw the land is gane. Sa dred he Inglis men his mycht, That he durst nocht wele cum in sycht. For thai war that tyme all weldand As maist lordis, our all the land.

Bot tythandis, that scalis sone, Off this deid that Dowglas has done, Come to the Cliffurd his ere, in hy, That for his tynsaill wes sary; And menyt his men that thai had slayne, And syne has to purpos tane, To big the castell up agayne. Thar for, as man of mekill mayne, He assemblit grret cumpany, And till Dowglas he went in hy. And biggyt wp the castell swyth; And maid it rycht stalwart and styth And put tharin victallis and men Ane off the Thyrwallys then He left behind him Capitane, And syne till Ingland went agayne. Book IV. v. 255-460.

Bot yeit than Janvss of Dowglas In Dowglas Daile travailland was; Or ellys weill ner hand tharby, In hyddillys sumdeill priuely. For he wald se his gouernyng, That had the castell in keping: And gert mak mony juperty, To se quhethyr he wald ische blythly. And quhen he persavyt that he Wald blythly ische with his menye, He maid a gadringr priuely Off thaim that war on his party; That war sa fele, that thai durst fych With Thyrwall, and all the mycht Off thaim that in the castell war. He schupe him in the nycht so far To Sandylandis: and thar ner by He him enbuschyt priuely, And send a few a trane to ma; That sone in the mornyng gan ga, And tuk catell, that wes the castell by, And syne withdrew thaim hastely Towart thaim that enbuschit war. Than Thyrwall, for owtyn mar, Gert arme his men, forowtyn baid; Aud ischyt with all the men he haid: And foiowyt fast eftir the cry. He wes armyt at poynt clenly, Owtane [that] his hede wes bar. Than, with the men that with him war, The catell folowit he gud speid, Rycht as a man that had na dreid, Till that he gat off thaim a sycht. Than prekyt thai with all thar mycht, Folowand thaim owt off aray And thai sped thaim fleand, quhill thai Fer by thair buschement war past: And Thyrwall ay chassyt fast. And than thai that enbuschyt war Ischyt till him, bath les and mar And rayssyt sudanly the cry. And thai that saw sa sudanly That folk come egyrly prikand Rycht betuix thairn and thair warank, Thai war in to full gret effray. And, for thai war owt off aray, Sum off thaim fled, and some abad. And Dowglas, that thar with him had A gret mengye, full egrely Assaylyt, and scalyt thaim hastyly: And in schort tyme ourraid thaim swa, That weile nane eschapyt thaim fra. Thyrwall, that wes thair capitane, Wes thar in the bargane slane: And off his men the mast party. The lave fled full effraytly. Book V. v. 10-60

CASTLE DANGEROUS.

CHAPTER THE FIRST.

Hosts have been known at that dread sound to yield,
And, Douglas dead, his name hath won the field.

JOHN HOME.

It was at the close of an early spring day, when nature, in a cold province of Scotland, was reviving from her winter's sleep, and the air at least, though not the vegetation, gave promise of an abatement of the rigour of the season, that two travellers, whose appearance at that early period sufficiently announced their wandering character, which, in general, secured a free passage even through a dangerous country, were seen coming from the south-westward, within a few miles of the Castle of Douglas, and seemed to be holding their course in the direction of the river of that name, whose dale afforded a species of approach to that memorable feudal fortress. The stream, small in comparison to the extent of its fame, served as a kind of drain to the country in its neighbourhood, and at the same time afforded the means of a rough road to the castle and village. The high lords to whom the castle had for ages belonged, might, had they chosen, have made this access a great deal smoother and more convenient; but there had been as yet little or no exercise for those geniuses, who have taught all the world that it is better to take the more circuitous road round the base of a hill, than the direct course of ascending it on the one side, and descending it directly on the other, without yielding a single step to render the passage more easy to the traveller; still less were those mysteries dreamed of which M'Adam has of late days expounded. But, indeed, to what purpose should the ancient Douglasses have employed his principles, even if they had known them in ever so much perfection? Wheel-carriages, except of the most clumsy description, and for the most simple operations of agriculture, were totally unknown. Even the most delicate female had no resource save a horse, or, in case of sore infirmity, a litter. The men used their own sturdy limbs, or hardy horses, to transport themselves from place to place; and travellers, females in particular, experienced no small inconvenience from the rugged nature of the country. A swollen torrent sometimes crossed their path, and compelled them to wait until the waters had abated their frenzy. The bank of a small river was occasionally torn away by the effects of a thunder-storm, a recent inundation, or the like convulsions of nature; and the wayfarer relied upon his knowledge of the district, or obtained the best local information in his power, how to direct his path so as to surmount such untoward obstacles.

The Douglas issues from an amphitheatre of mountains which bounds the valley to the south-west, from whose contributions, and the aid of sudden storms, it receives its scanty supplies. The general aspect of the country is that of the pastoral hills of the south of Scotland, forming, as is usual, bleak and wild farms, many of which had, at no great length of time from the date of the story, been covered with trees; as some of them still attest by bearing the name of *shaw*, that is, wild natural wood. The neighbourhood of the Douglas water itself was flat land, capable of bearing strong crops of oats and rye, supplying the inhabitants with what they required of these productions. At no great distance from the edge of the river, a few special spots excepted, the soil capable of agriculture was more and more mixed with the pastoral and woodland country, till both terminated in desolate and partly inaccessible moorlands.

Above all, it was war-time, and of necessity all circumstances of mere convenience were obliged to give way to a paramount sense of danger; the inhabitants, therefore, instead of trying to amend the paths which connected them with other districts, were thankful that the natural difficulties which surrounded them rendered it unnecessary to break up or to fortify the access from more open countries. Their wants, with a very few exceptions, were completely supplied, as we have already said, by the rude and scanty produce of their own mountains and *holms*, [Footnote: Holms, or flat plains, by the sides of the brooks and rivers, termed in the south, *Ings*.] the last of which served for the exercise of their limited agriculture, while the better part of the mountains and forest glens produced pasture for their herds and flocks. The recesses of the unexplored depths of these sylvan retreats being seldom disturbed, especially since the lords of the district had laid aside, during this time of strife, their constant occupation of hunting, the various kinds of game had increased of late very considerably; so that not only in crossing the rougher parts of the hilly and desolate country we are describing, different varieties of deer were occasionally seen, but even the wild cattle peculiar to Scotland sometimes showed themselves, and other animals, which indicated the irregular and disordered state of the period. The wild-cat was frequently surprised in the dark ravines or the swampy thickets; and the wolf, already a stranger to the more populous districts of the Lothians, here maintained his ground against the encroachments of man, and was still himself a terror to those by whom he was finally to be extirpated. In winter especially, and winter was hardly yet past, these savage animals were wont to be driven to extremity for lack of food, and used to frequent, in dangerous numbers, the battle-field, the deserted churchyard—nay, sometimes the abodes of living men, there to watch for children, their defenceless prey, with as much familiarity as the fox now-a-days will venture to prowl near the mistress's [Footnote: The good dame, or wife of a respectable farmer, is almost universally thus designated in Scotland.] poultry-yard.

From what we have said, our readers, if they have made—as who in these days has not—the Scottish tour, will be able to form a tolerably just idea of the wilder and upper part of Douglas Dale, during the earlier period of the fourteenth century. The setting sun cast his gleams along a moorland country, which to the westward broke into larger swells, terminating in the mountains called the Larger and Lesser Cairntable. The first of these is, as it were, the father of the hills in the neighbourhood, the source of an hundred streams, and by far the largest of the ridge, still holding in his dark bosom, and in the ravines with which his sides are ploughed, considerable remnants of those ancient forests with which all the high grounds of that quarter were once covered, and particularly the hills, in which the rivers—both those which run to the east, and those which seek the west to discharge themselves into the Solway—hide, like so many hermits, their original and scanty sources.

The landscape was still illuminated by the reflection of the evening sun, sometimes thrown back from pool or stream; sometimes resting on grey rocks, huge cumberers of the soil, which labour and agriculture have since removed, and sometimes contenting itself with gilding the banks of the stream, tinged, alternately grey, green, or ruddy, as the ground itself consisted of rock, or grassy turf, or bare earthen mound, or looked at a distance like a rampart of dark red porphyry. Occasionally, too, the eye rested on the steep brown extent of moorland as the sunbeam glanced back from the little tarn or mountain pool, whose lustre, like that of the eye in the human countenance, gives a life and vivacity to every feature around.

The elder and stouter of the two travellers whom we have mentioned, was a person well, and even showily dressed, according to the finery of the times, and bore at his back, as wandering minstrels were wont, a case, containing a small harp, rote or viol, or some such species of musical instrument for accompanying the voice. The leathern case announced so much, although it proclaimed not the exact nature of the instrument. The colour of the traveller's doublet was blue, and that of his hose violet, with slashes which showed a lining of the same colour with the jerkin. A mantle ought, according to ordinary custom, to have covered this dress; but the heat of the sun, though the season was so early, had induced the wearer to fold up his cloak in small compass, and form it into a bundle, attached to the shoulders like the military greatcoat of the infantry soldier of the present day. The neatness with which it was made up, argued the precision of a practised traveller, who had been long accustomed to every resource which change of weather required. A great profusion of narrow ribands or points, constituting the loops with which our ancestors connected their doublet and hose, formed a kind of cordon, composed of knots of blue or violet, which surrounded the traveller's person, and thus assimilated in colour with the two garments which it was the office of these strings to combine. The bonnet usually worn with this showy dress, was of that kind with which Henry the Eighth and his son, Edward the Sixth, are usually represented. It was more fitted, from the gay stuff of which it was composed, to appear in a public place, than to encounter a storm of rain. It was party-coloured, being made of different stripes of blue and violet; and the wearer arrogated a certain degree of gentility to himself, by wearing a plume of considerable dimensions of the same favourite colours. The features over which this feather drooped were in no degree remarkable for peculiarity of expression. Yet in so desolate a country as the west of Scotland, it would, not have been easy to pass the man without more minute attention than he would have met with where there was more in the character of the scenery to arrest the gaze of the passengers.

A quick eye, a sociable look, seeming to say, "Ay, look at me, I am a man worth noticing, and not unworthy your attention," carried with it, nevertheless, an interpretation which might be thought favourable or otherwise, according to the character of the person whom the traveller met. A knight or soldier would merely have thought that he had met a merry fellow, who could sing a wild song, or tell a wild tale, and help to empty a flagon, with all the accomplishments necessary for a boon companion at an hostelry, except perhaps an alacrity at defraying his share of the reckoning. A churchman, on the other hand, might have thought he of the blue and violet was of too loose habits, and accustomed too little to limit himself within the boundaries of beseeming mirth, to be fit society for one of his sacred calling. Yet the Man of Song had a certain steadiness of countenance, which seemed fitted to hold place in scenes of serious business as well as of gaiety. A wayfaring passenger of wealth (not at that time a numerous class) might have feared in him a professional robber, or one whom opportunity was very likely to convert into such; a female might have been apprehensive of uncivil treatment; and a youth, or timid person, might have thought of murder, or such direful doings. Unless privately armed, however, the minstrel was ill-accoutred for any dangerous occupation. His only visible weapon was a small crooked sword, like what we now call a hanger; and the state of the times would have justified any man, however peaceful his intentions, in being so far armed against the perils of the road.

If a glance at this man had in any respect prejudiced him in the opinion of those whom he met on his journey, a look at his companion would, so far as his character could be guessed at—for he was closely muffled up—have passed for an apology and warrant for his associate. The younger traveller was apparently in early youth, a soft and gentle boy, whose Sclavonic gown, the appropriate dress of the pilgrim, he wore more closely drawn about him than the coldness of the weather seemed to authorize or recommend. His features, imperfectly seen under the hood of his pilgrim's dress, were prepossessing in a high degree; and though he wore a walking sword, it seemed rather to be in compliance with general fashion than from any violent purpose he did so. There were traces of sadness upon his brow, and of tears upon his cheeks; and his weariness was such, as even his rougher companion seemed to sympathize with, while he privately participated also in the sorrow which left its marks upon a countenance so lovely. They spoke together, and the elder of the two, while he assumed the deferential air proper to a man of inferior rank addressing a superior, showed in tone and gesture, something that amounted to interest and affection.

"Bertram, my friend," said the younger of the two, "how far are we still from Douglas Castle? We have already come farther than the twenty miles, which thou didst say was the distance from Cammock—or how didst thou call the last hostelry which we left by daybreak?"

"Cummock, my dearest lady—I beg ten thousand excuses—my gracious young lord."

"Call me Augustine," replied his comrade, "if you mean to speak as is fittest for the time."

"Nay, as for that," said Bertram, "if your ladyship can condescend to lay aside your quality, my own good breeding is not so firmly sewed to me but that I can doff it, and resume it again without its losing a stitch; and since your ladyship, to whom I am sworn in obedience, is pleased to command that I should treat you as my own son, shame it were to me if I were not to show you the affection of a father, more especially as I may well swear my great oath, that I owe you the duty of such, though well I wot it has, in our case, been the lot of the parent to be maintained by the kindness and liberality of the child; for when was it that I hungered or thirsted, and the black stock[Footnote: The table dormant, which stood in a baron's hall, was often so designated.] of Berkley did not relieve my wants?"

"I would have it so," answered the young pilgrim; "I would have it so. What use of the mountains of beef, and the oceans of beer, which they say our domains produce, if there is a hungry heart among our vassalage, or especially if thou, Bertram, who hast served as the minstrel of our house for more than twenty years, shouldst experience such a feeling?"

"Certes, lady," answered Bertram, "it would be like the catastrophe which is told of the Baron of Fastenough, when his last mouse was starved to death in the very pantry; and if I escape this journey without such a calamity, I shall think myself out of reach of thirst or famine for the whole of my life."

"Thou hast suffered already once or twice by these attacks, my poor friend," said the lady.

"It is little," answered Bertram, "any thing that I have suffered; and I were ungrateful to give the inconvenience of missing a breakfast, or making an untimely dinner, so serious a name. But then I hardly see how your ladyship can endure this gear much longer. You must yourself feel, that the plodding along these high lands, of which the Scots give us such good measure in their miles, is no jesting matter; and as for Douglas Castle, why it is still three good miles off."

"The question then is," quoth the lady, heaving a sigh, "what we are to do when we have so far to travel, and when the castle gates must be locked long before we arrive there?"

"For that I will pledge my word," answered Bertram. "The gates of Douglas, under the care of Sir John de Walton, do not open so easily as those of the buttery hatch at our own castle, when it is well oiled; and if your ladyship take my advice, you will turn southward ho! and in two days at farthest, we shall be in a land where men's wants are provided for, as the inns proclaim it, with the least possible delay, and the secret of this little journey shall never be known to living mortal but ourselves, as sure as I am

19

sworn minstrel, and man of faith."

"I thank thee for thy advice, mine honest Bertram," said the lady, "but I cannot profit by it. Should thy knowledge of these parts possess thee with an acquaintance with any decent house, whether it belong to rich or poor, I would willingly take quarters there, if I could obtain them from this time until to-morrow morning. The gates of Douglas Castle will then be open to guests of so peaceful an appearance as we carry with us, and—and—it will out—we might have time to make such applications to our toilet as might ensure us a good reception, by drawing a comb through our locks, or such like foppery."

"Ah, madam!" said Bertram, "were not Sir John de Walton in question, methinks I should venture to reply, that an unwashed brow, an unkempt head of hair, and a look far more saucy than your ladyship ever wears, or can wear, were the proper disguise to trick out that minstrel's boy, whom, you wish to represent in the present pageant."

"Do you suffer your youthful pupils to be indeed so slovenly and so saucy, Bertram?" answered the lady. "I for one will not imitate them in that particular; and whether Sir John be now in the Castle of Douglas or not, I will treat the soldiers who hold so honourable a charge with a washed brow, and a head of hair somewhat ordered. As for going back without seeing a castle which has mingled even with my very dreams—at a word, Bertram, thou mayst go that way, but I will not."

"And if I part with your ladyship on such terms," responded the minstrel, "now your frolic is so nearly accomplished, it shall be the foul fiend himself, and nothing more comely or less dangerous, that shall tear me from your side; and for lodging, there is not far from hence the house of one Tom Dickson of Hazelside, one of the most honest fellows of the Dale, and who, although a labouring man, ranked as high as a warrior, when I was in this country, as any noble gentleman that rode in the band of the Douglas."

"He is then a soldier?" said the lady.

"When his country or his lord need his sword," replied Bertram—"and, to say the truth, they are seldom at peace; but otherwise, he is no enemy, save to the wolf which plunders his herds."

"But forget not, my trusty guide," replied the lady, "that the blood in our veins is English, and consequently, that we are in danger from all who call themselves foes to the ruddy Cross."

"Do not fear this man's faith," answered Bertram. "You may trust to him as to the best knight or gentleman of the land. We may make good our lodging by a tune or a song; and it may remember you that I undertook (provided it pleased your ladyship) to temporize a little with the Scots, who, poor souls, love minstrelsy, and when they have but a silver penny, will willingly bestow it to encourage the *gay science*—I promised you, I say, that we should be as welcome to them as if we had been born amidst their own wild hills; and for the best that such a house as Dickson's affords, the glee-man's son, fair lady, shall not breathe a wish in vain. And now, will you speak your mind to your devoted friend and adopted father, or rather your sworn servant and guide, Bertram the Minstrel, what it is your pleasure to do in this matter?"

"O, we will certainly accept of the Scot's hospitality," said the lady, "your minstrel word being plighted that he is a true man. Tom Dickson, call you him?"

"Yes," replied Bertram, "such is his name; and by looking on these sheep, I am assured that we are now upon his land."

"Indeed?" said the lady, with some surprise; "and how is your wisdom aware of that?"

"I see the first letter of his name marked upon this flock," answered the guide. "Ah, learning is what carries a man through the world, as well as if he had the ring by virtue of which old minstrels tell that Adam understood the language of the beasts in paradise. Ah, madam! there is more wit taught in the shepherd's shieling than the lady thinks of, who sews her painted seam in her summer bower."

"Be it so, good Bertram. And although not so deeply skilled in the knowledge of written language as you are, it is impossible for me to esteem its value more than I actually do; so hold we on the nearest road to this Tom Dickson's, whose very sheep tell of his whereabout. I trust we have not very far to go, although the knowledge that our journey is shortened by a few miles has so much recovered my fatigue, that methinks I could dance all the rest of the way."

CHAPTER THE SECOND.

> *Rosalind.* Well, this is the Forest of Arden.
> *Touchstone.* Ay, now am I in Arden; the more fool I. When I was at
> home I was in a better place; but travellers must be content.
> *Rosalind.* Ay, be so, good Touchstone. Look you, who comes here; a
> young man and an old, in solemn talk.
> As You Like It. *Scene IV. Act 2.*

As the travellers spoke together, they reached a turn of the path which presented a more extensive prospect than the broken face of the country had yet shown them. A valley, through which flowed a small tributary stream, exhibited the wild, but not unpleasant, features of "a lone vale of green braken;" here and there besprinkled with groups of alder-trees, of hazels, and of copse-oakwood, which had maintained their stations in the recesses of the valley, although they had vanished from the loftier and more exposed sides of the hills. The farm-house or mansion-house, (for, from its size and appearance, it might have been the one or the other,) was a large but low building, and the walls of the out-houses were sufficiently strong to resist any band of casual depredators. There was nothing, however, which could withstand a more powerful force; for, in a country laid waste by war, the farmer was then, as now, obliged to take his chance of the great evils attendant upon that state of things; and his condition, never a very eligible one, was rendered considerably worse by the insecurity attending it. About half a mile farther was seen a Gothic building of very small extent, having a half dismantled chapel, which the minstrel pronounced to be the Abbey of Saint Bride. "The place," he said, "I understand, is allowed to subsist, as two or three old monks and as many nuns, whom it contains, are permitted by the English to serve God there, and sometimes to give relief to Scottish travellers; and who have accordingly taken assurance with Sir John de Walton, and accepted as their superior a churchman on whom he thinks he can depend. But if these guests happen to reveal any secrets, they are, by some means or other, believed to fly towards the English governor; and therefore, unless your ladyship's commands be positive, I think we had best not trust ourselves to their hospitality."

"Of a surety, no," said the lady, "if thou canst provide me with lodgings where we shall have more prudent hosts."

At this moment, two human forms were seen to approach the farm-house in a different direction from the travellers, and speaking so high, in a tone apparently of dispute, that the minstrel and his companion could distinguish their voices though the distance was considerable. Having screened his eyes with his hand for some minutes, Bertram at length exclaimed, "By our Lady, it is my old friend, Tom Dickson, sure enough!— What can make him in such bad humour with the lad, who, I think, may be the little wild boy, his son Charles, who used to run about and plait rushes some twenty years ago? It is lucky, however, we have found our friends astir; for I warrant, Tom hath a hearty piece of beef in the pot ere he goes to bed, and he must have changed his wont if an old friend hath not his share; and who knows, had we come later, at what hour they may now find it convenient to drop latch and draw bolt so near a hostile garrison; for if we call things by their right names, such is the proper term for an English garrison in the castle of a Scottish nobleman."

"Foolish man," answered the lady, "thou judgest of Sir John de Walton as

22

thou wouldst of some rude boor, to whom the opportunity of doing what he wills is a temptation and license to exercise cruelty and oppression. Now, I could plight you my word, that, setting apart the quarrel of the kingdoms, which, of course, will be fought out in fair battles on both sides, you will find that English and Scottish, within this domain, and within the reach of Sir John de Walton's influence, live together as that same flock of sheep and goats do with the shepherd's dog; a foe from whom they fly upon certain occasions, but around whom they nevertheless eagerly gather for protection should a wolf happen to show himself."

"It is not to your ladyship," answered Bertram, "that I should venture to state my opinion of such matters; but the young knight, when he is sheathed in armour, is a different being from him who feasts in halls among press of ladies; and he that feeds by another man's fireside, and when his landlord, of all men in the world, chances to be the Black Douglas, has reason to keep his eyes about him as he makes his meal:—but it were better I looked after our own evening refreshment, than that I stood here gaping and talking about other folk's matters." So saying, he called out in a thundering tone of voice, "Dickson!—what ho, Thomas Dickson!—will you not acknowledge an old friend who is much disposed to trust his supper and night's lodging to your hospitality?"

The Scotchman, attracted by the call, looked first along the banks of the river, then upward to the bare side of the hill, and at length cast his eyes upon the two figures who were descending from it.

As if he felt the night colder while he advanced from the more sheltered part of the valley to meet them, the Douglas Dale farmer wrapped closer around him the grey plaid, which, from an early period, has been used by the shepherds of the south of Scotland, and the appearance of which gives a romantic air to the peasantry and middle classes; and which, although less brilliant and gaudy in its colours, is as picturesque in its arrangement as the more military tartan mantle of the Highlands. When they approached near to each other, the lady might observe that this friend of her guide was a stout athletic man, somewhat past the middle of life, and already showing marks of the approach, but none of the infirmities, of age, upon a countenance which had been exposed to many a storm. Sharp eyes, too, and a quick observation, exhibited signs of vigilance, acquired by one who had lived long in a country where he had constant occasion for looking around him with caution. His features were still swollen with displeasure; and the handsome young man who attended him seemed to be discontented, like one who had undergone no gentle marks of his father's indignation, and who, from the sullen expression which mingled with an appearance of shame on his countenance, seemed at once affected by anger

23

and remorse.

"Do you not remember me, old friend?" said Bertram, as they approached within a distance for communing; "or have the twenty years which have marched over us since we met, carried along with them all remembrance of Bertram, the English minstrel?"

"In troth," answered the Scot, "it is not for want of plenty of your countrymen to keep you in my remembrance, and I have hardly heard one of them so much as whistle

'Hey, now the day dawns,'

but it has recalled some note of your blythe rebeck; and yet, such animals are we, that I had forgot the mien of my old friend, and scarcely knew him at a distance. But we have had trouble lately; there are a thousand of your countrymen that keep garrison in the Perilous Castle of Douglas yonder, as well as in other places through the vale, and that is but a woful sight for a true Scotchman—even my own poor house has not escaped the dignity of a garrison of a man-at-arms, besides two or three archer knaves, and one or two slips of mischievous boys called pages, and so forth, who will not let a man say, 'this is my own,' by his own fireside. Do not, therefore, think hardly of me, old comrade, if I show you a welcome something colder than you might expect from a friend of other days; for, by Saint Bride of Douglas, I have scarcely anything left to which I can say welcome."

"Small welcome will serve," said Bertram. "My son, make thy reverence to thy father's old friend. Augustine is learning my joyous trade, but he will need some practice ere he can endure its fatigues. If you could give him some little matter of food, and a quiet bed for the night, there's no fear but that we shall both do well enough; for I dare say, when you travel with my friend Charles there,—if that tall youth chance to be my old acquaintance Charles,—you will find yourself accommodated when his wants are once well provided for."

"Nay, the foul fiend take me if I do," answered the Scottish husbandman. "I know not what the lads of this day are made of—not of the same clay as their fathers, to be sure—not sprung from their heather, which fears neither wind nor rain, but from some delicate plant of a foreign country, which will not thrive unless it be nourished under glass, with a murrain to it. The good Lord of Douglas—I have been his henchman, and can vouch for it—did not in his pagehood desire such food and lodging as, in the present day, will hardly satisfy such a lad as your friend Charles."

"Nay," said Bertram, "it is not that my Augustine is over nice; but, for other reasons, I must request of you a bed to himself; he hath of late been unwell."

"Ay, I understand," said Dickson, "your son hath had a touch of that illness which terminates so frequently in the black death you English folk die of? We hear much of the havoc it has made to the southward. Comes it hitherward?"

Bertram nodded.

"Well, my father's house," continued the farmer, "hath more rooms than one, and your son shall have one well-aired and comfortable; and for supper, ye shall have a part of what is prepared for your countrymen, though I would rather have their room than their company. Since I am bound to feed a score of them, they will not dispute the claim of such a skilful minstrel as thou art to a night's hospitality. I am ashamed to say that I must do their bidding even in my own house, Well-a-day, if my good lord were in possession of his own, I have heart and hand enough to turn the whole of them out of my house, like—like"——

"To speak plainly," said Bertram, "like a southern strolling gang from Redesdale, whom I have seen you fling out of your house like a litter of blind puppies, when not one of them looked behind to see who had done him the courtesy until he was half-way to Cairntable."

"Ay," answered the Scotchman, drawing himself up at least six inches taller than before; "then I had a house of my own, and a cause and an arm to keep it. Now I am—what signifies it what I am?—the noblest lord in Scotland is little better."

"Truly, friend," said Bertram, "now you view this matter in a rational light. I do not say that the wisest, the richest, or the strongest man in this world has any right to tyrannize over his neighbour, because he is the more weak, ignorant, and the poorer; but yet if he does enter into such a controversy, he must submit to the course of nature, and that will always give the advantage in the tide of battle to wealth, strength, and health."

"With permission, however," answered Dickson, "the weaker party, if he use his facilities to the utmost, may, in the long run, obtain revenge upon the author of his sufferings, which would be at least compensation for his temporary submission; and he acts simply as a man, and most foolishly as a Scotchman, whether he sustain these wrongs with the insensibility of an idiot, or whether he endeavour to revenge them before Heaven's appointed time has arrived.—But if I talk thus I shall scare you, as I have scared some of your countrymen, from accepting a meal of meat and a night's lodging, in a house where you might be called with the morning to a bloody settlement of a national quarrel."

"Never mind," said Bertram, "we have been known to each other of old; and I am no more afraid of meeting unkindness in your house, than you expect me to come here for the purpose of adding to the injuries of which you complain."

"So be it," said Dickson; "and you, my old friend, are as welcome to my abode as when it never held any guest, save of my own inviting.—And you, my young friend, Master Augustine, shall be looked after as well as if you came with a gay brow and a light cheek, such as best becomes the *gay science*."

"But wherefore, may I ask," said Bertram, "so much displeased but now at my young friend Charles?"

The youth answered before his father had time to speak. "My father, good sir, may put what show upon it he will, but shrewd and wise men wax weak in the brain these troublous times. He saw two or three wolves seize upon three of our choicest wethers; and because I shouted to give the alarm to the English garrison, he was angry as if he could have murdered me—-just for saving the sheep from the jaws that would have devoured them."

"This is a strange account of thee, old friend," said Bertram. "Dost thou connive with the wolves in robbing thine own fold?"

"Why, let it pass, if thou lovest me," answered the countryman; "Charles could tell thee something nearer the truth if he had a mind; but for the present let it pass."

The minstrel, perceiving that the Scotchman was fretted and embarrassed with the subject, pressed it no farther.

At this moment, in crossing the threshold of Thomas Dickson's house, they were greeted with sounds from two English soldiers within. "Quiet, Anthony," said one voice,—"quiet, man!—for the sake of common sense, if not common manners;—Robin Hood himself never sat down to his board ere the roast was ready."

"Ready!" quoth another rough voice; "It is roasting to rags, and small had been the knave Dickson's share, even of these rags, had it not been the express orders of the worshipful Sir John de Walton, that the soldiers who lie at outposts should afford to the inmates such provisions as are not necessary for their own subsistence."

"Hush, Anthony,—hush, for shame!" replied his fellow-soldier, "if ever I heard our host's step, I heard it this instant; so give over thy grumbling, since our captain, as we all know, hath prohibited, under strict penalties, all quarrels between his followers and the people of the country."

"I am sure," replied Anthony, "that I have ministered occasion to none; but I would I were equally certain of the good meaning of this sullen-browed Thomas Dickson towards the English soldiers, for I seldom go to bed in this dungeon of a house, but I expect my throat will gape as wide as a thirsty oyster before I awaken. Here he comes, however," added Anthony, sinking his sharp tones as he spoke; "and I hope to be excommunicated if he has not brought with him that mad animal, his son Charles, and two other strangers, hungry enough, I'll be sworn, to eat up the whole supper, if they do us no other injury."

"Shame of thyself, Anthony," repeated his comrade; "a good archer thou as ever wore Kendal green, and yet affect to be frightened for two tired travellers, and alarmed for the inroad their hunger may make on the night's meal. There are four or five of us here—we have our bows and our bills within reach, and scorn to be chased from our supper, or cheated out of our share of it by a dozen Scotchmen, whether stationary or strollers. How say'st thou?" he added, turning to Dickson—"How say ye, quartermaster? it is no secret, that by the directions given to our post, we must enquire into the occupations of such guests as you may receive besides ourselves, your unwilling inmates; you are as ready for supper, I warrant, as supper is for you, and I will only delay you and my friend Anthony,—who becomes dreadfully impatient, until you answer two or three questions which you wot of."

"Bend-the-Bow," answered Dickson, "thou art a civil fellow; and although it is something hard to be constrained to give an account of one's friends, because they chance to quarter in one's own house for a night or two, yet I must submit to the times, and make no vain opposition. You may mark down in your breviary there, that upon the fourteenth day before Palm Sunday, Thomas Dickson brought to his house of Hazelside, in which you hold garrison, by orders from the English governor, Sir John de Walton, two strangers, to whom the said Thomas Dickson had promised refreshment, and a bed for the evening, if it be lawful at this time and place."

"But what are they, these strangers?" said Anthony, somewhat sharply.

"A fine world the while," murmured Thomas Dickson, "that an honest man should be forced to answer the questions of every paltry companion!"—But he mitigated his voice and proceeded. "The eldest of my guests is Bertram, an ancient English minstrel, who is bound on his own errand to the Castle of Douglas, and will communicate what he has to say of news to Sir John de Walton himself. I have known him for twenty years, and never heard any thing of him save that he was good man and true. The younger stranger is his son, a lad recovering from the English disorder, which has been raging far and wide in Westmoreland and Cumberland."

"Tell me," said Bend-the-Bow, "this same Bertram,—was he not about a year since in the service of some noble lady in our own country?"

"I have heard so," answered Dickson.

"We shall, in that case, I think, incur little danger," replied Bend-the-Bow, "by allowing this old man and his son to proceed on their journey to the castle."

"You are my elder and my better," answered Anthony; "but I may remind

27

you that it is not so clearly our duty to give free passage, into a garrison of a thousand men of all ranks, to a youth who has been so lately attacked by a contagious disorder; and I question if our commander would not rather hear that the Black Douglas, with a hundred devils as black as himself, since such is his colour, had taken possession of the outposts of Hazelside with sword and battle-axe, than that one person suffering under this fell sickness had entered peaceably, and by the open wicket of the castle."

"There is something in what thou sayest, Anthony," replied his comrade; "and considering that our governor, since he has undertaken the troublesome job of keeping a castle which is esteemed so much more dangerous than any other within Scotland, has become one of the most cautious and jealous men in the world, we had better, I think, inform him of the circumstance, and take his commands how the stripling is to be dealt with."

"Content am I," said the archer; "and first, methinks, I would just, in order to show that we know what belongs to such a case, ask the stripling a few questions, as how long he has been ill, by what physicians he has been attended, when he was cured, and how his cure is certified, &e."

"True, brother," said Bend-the-Bow. "Thou hearest, minstrel, we would ask thy son some questions—What has become of him?—he was in this apartment but now."

"So please you," answered Bertram, "he did but pass through the apartment. Mr. Thomas Dickson, at my entreaty, as well as in respectful reverence to your honour's health, carried him through the room without tarriance, judging his own bed-chamber the fittest place for a young man recovering from a severe illness, and after a day of no small fatigue."

"Well," answered the elder archer, "though it is uncommon for men who, like us, live by bow-string and quiver, to meddle with interrogations and examinations; yet, as the case stands, we must make some enquiries of your son, ere we permit him to set forth to the Castle of Douglas, where you say his errand leads him."

"Rather my errand, noble sir," said the minstrel, "than that of the young man himself."

"If such be the case," answered Bend-the-Bow, "we may sufficiently do our duty by sending yourself, with the first grey light of dawn, to the castle, and letting your son remain in bed, which I warrant is the fittest place for him, until we shall receive Sir John de Walton's commands whether he is to be brought onward or not."

"And we may as well," said Anthony, "since we are to have this man's company at supper, make him acquainted with the rules of the out-garrison stationed here for the time." So saying, he pulled a scroll from his leathern pouch, and said, "Minstrel, canst thou read?"

"It becomes my calling," said the minstrel.

"It has nothing to do with mine, though," answered the archer, "and therefore do thou read these regulations aloud; for since I do not comprehend these characters by sight, I lose no chance of having them read over to me as often as I can, that I may fix their sense in my memory. So beware that thou readest the words letter for letter as they are set down; for thou dost so at thy peril, Sir Minstrel, if thou readest not like a true man."

"On my minstrel word," said Bertram, and began to read excessively slow; for he wished to gain a little time for consideration, which he foresaw would be necessary to prevent his being separated from his mistress, which was likely to occasion her much anxiety and distress. He therefore began thus:—"'Outpost at Hazelside, the steading of Goodman Thomas Dickson'— Ay, Thomas, and is thy house so called?"

"It is the ancient name of the steading," said the Scot, "being surrounded by a hazel-shaw, or thicket."

"Hold your chattering tongue, minstrel," said Anthony, "and proceed, as you value your ears, which you seem disposed to make less use of."

"'His garrison'" proceeded the minstrel, reading, "'consists of a lance with its furniture.' What, then, a lance, in other words, a belted knight, commands this party?"

"'Tis no concern of thine," said the archer.

"But it is," answered the minstrel; "we have a right to be examined by the highest person in presence."

"I will show thee, thou rascal," said the archer, starting up, "that I am lance enough for thee to reply to, and I will break thy head if thou say'st a word more."

"Take care, brother Anthony," said his comrade, "we are to use travellers courteously—and, with your leave, those travellers best who come from our native land."

"It is even so stated here," said the minstrel, and he proceeded to read: —"'The watch at this outpost of Hazelside [Footnote: Hazelside Place, the fief granted to Thomas Dickson by William the Hardy, seventh Lord Douglas, is still pointed out about two miles to the southwest of the Castle Dangerous. Dickson was sixty years of age at the time when Lord James first appeared in Douglasdale. His heirs kept possession of the fief for centuries; and some respectable gentlemen's families in Lanarkshire still trace themselves to this ancestor.—From Notes by Mr. Haddow.] shall stop and examine all travellers passing by the said station, suffering such to pass onward to the town of Douglas or to Douglas Castle, always interrogating them with civility, and detaining and turning them back if there arise matter of suspicion; but conducting themselves in all matters civilly and courteously to the people of the country, and to those who travel in it.' You see, most excellent and valiant archer," added the commentator Bertram, "that courtesy and civility are, above all, recommended to your worship in your conduct towards the inhabitants, and those passengers who, like us, may chance to fall under your rules in such matters."

"I am not to be told at this time of day," said the archer, "how to conduct myself in the discharge of my duties. Let me advise you, Sir Minstrel, to be frank and open in your answers to our enquiries, and you shall have no reason to complain."

"I hope at all events," said the minstrel, "to have your favour for my son, who is a delicate stripling, and not accustomed to play his part among the crew which inhabit this wild world."

"Well," continued the elder and more civil of the two archers, "if thy son be a novice in this terrestrial navigation, I warrant that thou, my friend, from thy look and manner of speech, hast enough of skill to use thy compass. To comfort thee, although thou must thyself answer the questions of our governor or deputy-governor, in order that he may see there is no offence in thee, I think there may be permission granted for thy son's residing here in the convent hard by, (where the nuns, by the way, are as old as the monks, and have nearly as long beards, so thou mayst be easy about thy son's morals,) until thou hast done thy business at Douglas Castle, and art ready to resume thy journey."

"If such permission," said the minstrel, "can be obtained, I should be better pleased to leave him at the abbey, and go myself, in the first place, to take the directions of your commanding officer."

"Certainly," answered the archer, "that will be the safest and best way; and with a piece or two of money, thou mayst secure the protection of the abbot."

"Thou say'st well," answered the minstrel; "I have known life, I have known every stile, gap, pathway, and pass of this wilderness of ours for some thirty years; and he that cannot steer his course fairly through it like an able seaman, after having served such an apprenticeship, can hardly ever be taught, were a century to be given him to learn it in."

"Since thou art so expert a mariner," answered the archer Anthony, "thou hast, I warrant me, met in thy wanderings a potation called a morning's draught, which they who are conducted by others, where they themselves lack experience, are used to bestow upon those who undertake the task of guide upon such an occasion?"

"I understand you, sir," quoth the minstrel; "and although money, or *drink-geld*, as the Fleming calls it, is rather a scarce commodity in the purse of one of my calling, yet according to my feeble ability, thou shalt have no cause to complain that thine eyes or those of thy comrades have been damaged by a Scottish mist, while we can find an English coin to pay for the good liquor which would wash them clear."

"Content," said the archer; "we now understand each other; and if difficulties arise on the road, thou shalt not want the countenance of Anthony to sail triumphantly through them. But thou hadst better let thy son know soon of the early visit to the abbot to-morrow, for thou mayst guess that we cannot and dare not delay our departure for the convent a minute after the eastern sky is ruddy; and, with other infirmities, young men often are prone to laziness and a love of ease."

"Thou shalt have no reason to think so," answered the minstrel; "not the lark himself, when waked by the first ray peeping over the black cloud, springs more lightly to the sky, than will my Augustine answer the same brilliant summons. And now we understand each other, I would only further pray you to forbear light talk while my son is in your company,—a boy of innocent life, and timid in conversation."

"Nay, jolly minstrel," said the elder archer, "thou givest us here too gross an example of Satan reproving sin. If thou hast followed thy craft for twenty years, as thou pretendest, thy son, having kept thee company since childhood, must by this time be fit to open a school to teach even devils the practice of the seven deadly sins, of which none know the theory if those of the *gay science* are lacking."

"Truly, comrade, thou speakest well," answered Bertram, "and I acknowledge that we minstrels are too much to blame in this matter. Nevertheless, in good sooth, the fault is not one of which I myself am particularly guilty; on the contrary, I think that he who would wish to have his own hair honoured when time has strewed it with silver, should so rein his mirth when in the presence of the young, as may show in what respect he holds innocence. I will, therefore, with your permission, speak a word to Augustine, that to-morrow we must be on foot early."

"Do so, my friend," said the English soldier; "and do the same the more speedily that our poor supper is still awaiting until thou art ready to partake of it."

"To which, I promise thee," said Bertram, "I am disposed to entertain, no delay."

"Follow me, then," said Dickson, "and I will show thee where this young bird of thine has his nest."

Their host accordingly tripped up the wooden stair, and tapped at a door, which he thus indicated was that of his younger guest.

31

"Your father," continued he, as the door opened, "would speak with you, Master Augustine."

"Excuse me, my host," answered Augustine, "the truth is, that this room being directly above your eating-chamber, and the flooring not in the best possible repair, I have been compelled to the unhandsome practice of eavesdropping, and not a word has escaped me that passed concerning my proposed residence at the abbey, our journey to-morrow, and the somewhat early hour at which I must shake off sloth, and, according to thy expression, fly down from the roost."

"And how dost thou relish," said Dickson, "being left with the Abbot of Saint Bride's little flock here."

"Why, well," said the youth, "if the abbot is a man of respectability becoming his vocation, and not one of those swaggering churchmen, who stretch out the sword, and bear themselves like rank soldiers in these troublous times."

"For that, young master," said Dickson, "if you let him put his hand deep enough into your purse, he will hardly quarrel with any thing." "Then I will leave him to my father," replied Augustine, "who will not grudge him any thing he asks in reason."

"In that case," replied the Scotchman, "you may trust to our abbot for good accommodation—and so both sides are pleased."

"It is well, my son," said Bertram, who now joined in the conversation; "and that thou mayst be ready for early travelling, I shall presently get our host to send thee some food, after partaking of which thou shouldst go to bed and sleep off the fatigue of to-day, since to-morrow will bring work for itself."

"And as for thy engagement to these honest archers," answered Augustine, "I hope you will be able to do what will give pleasure to our guides, if they are disposed to be civil and true men."

"God bless thee, my child!" answered Bertram; "thou knowest already what would drag after thy beck all the English archers that were ever on this side of the Solway. There is no fear of a grey goose shaft, if you sing a *reveillez* like to that which chimed even now from that silken nest of dainty young goldfinches."

"Hold me as in readiness, then," said the seeming youth, "when you depart to-morrow morning. I am within hearing, I suppose, of the bells of Saint Bride's chapel, and have no fear, through my sloth, of keeping you or your company waiting."

"Good night, and God bless thee, my child!" again said the minstrel; "remember that your father sleeps not far distant, and on the slightest alarm will not fail to be with you. I need scarce bid thee recommend thyself, meantime, to the great Being, who is the friend and father of us all."

The pilgrim thanked his supposed father for his evening blessing, and the visitors withdrew without farther speech at the time, leaving the young lady to those engrossing fears, which, the novelty of her situation, and the native delicacy of her sex being considered, naturally thronged upon her.

The tramp of a horse's foot was not long after heard at the house of Hazelside, and the rider was welcomed by its garrison with marks of respect. Bertram understood so much as to discover from the conversation of the warders that this late arrival was Aymer de Valence, the knight who commanded the little party, and to the furniture of whose lance, as it was technically called, belonged the archers with whom we have already been acquainted, a man-at-arms or two, a certain proportion of pages or grooms, and, in short, the command and guidance of the garrison at Thomas Dickson's, while in rank he was Deputy-governor of Douglas Castle.

To prevent all suspicion respecting himself and his companion, as well as the risk of the latter being disturbed, the minstrel thought it proper to present himself to the inspection of this knight, the great authority of the little place. He found him with as little scruple as the archers heretofore, making a supper of the relics of the roast beef.

Before this young knight Bertram underwent an examination, while an old soldier took down in writing such items of information as the examinate thought proper to express in his replies, both with regard to the minutiae of his present journey, his business at Castle Douglas, and his route when that business should be accomplished; a much more minute examination, in a word, than he had hitherto undergone by the archers, or perhaps than was quite agreeable to him, being encumbered with at least the knowledge of one secret, whatever more. Not that this new examinator had any thing stern or severe in his looks or his questions. As to the first, he was mild, gentle, and "meek as a maid," and possessed exactly of the courteous manners ascribed by our father Chaucer to the pattern of chivalry whom he describes upon his pilgrimage to Canterbury. But with all his gentleness, De Valence showed a great degree of acuteness and accuracy in his queries; and well pleased was Bertram that the young knight did not insist upon seeing his supposed son, although even in that case his ready wit had resolved, like a seaman in a tempest, to sacrifice one part to preserve the rest. He was not, however, driven to this extremity, being treated by Sir Aymer with that degree of courtesy which in that age men of song were in general thought entitled to. The knight kindly and liberally consented to the lad's remaining in the convent, as a fit and quiet residence for a stripling and an invalid, until Sir John de Walton should express his pleasure on the subject; and Sir Aymer consented to this arrangement the more willingly, as it averted all possible danger of bringing disease into the English garrison.

By the young knight's order, all in Dickson's house were despatched earlier to rest than usual; the matin bell of the neighbouring chapel being the signal for their assembly by daybreak. They rendezvoused accordingly, and proceeded to Saint Bride's, where they heard mass, after which an interview took place between the abbot Jerome and the minstrel, in which the former undertook, with the permission of De Valence, to receive Augustine into his abbey as a guest for a few days, less or more, and for which Bertram promised an acknowledgment in name of alms, which was amply satisfactory.

"So be it," said Bertram, taking leave of his supposed son; "rely on it I will not tarry a day longer at Douglas Castle than shall suffice for transacting my business there, which is to look after the old books you wot of, and I will speedily return for thee to the Abbey of Saint Bride, to resume in company our journey homeward."

"O father," replied the youth, with a smile, "I fear if you get among romances and chronicles, you will be so earnest in your researches, that you will forget poor Augustine and his concerns."

"Never fear me, Augustine," said the old man, making the motion of throwing a kiss towards the boy; "thou art good and virtuous, and Heaven will not neglect thee, were thy father unnatural enough to do so. Believe me, all the old songs since Merlin's day shall not make me forget thee."

Thus they separated, the minstrel, with the English knight and his retinue, to move towards the castle, and the youth in dutiful attendance on the venerable abbot, who was delighted to find that his guest's thoughts turned rather upon spiritual things than on the morning repast, of the approach of which he could not help being himself sensible.

CHAPTER THE THIRD.

This night, methinks, is but the daylight sick.
It looks a little paler; 'tis a day
Such as the day is when the sun is hid.
MERCHANT OF VENICE.

To facilitate the progress of the party on its way to Douglas Castle, the Knight of Valence offered the minstrel the convenience of a horse, which the fatigues of yesterday made him gladly accept. Any one acquainted with equestrian exercise, is aware that no means of refreshment carries away the sense of fatigue from over walking so easily, as the exchange to riding, which calls into play another set of muscles, and leaves those which have been over exerted an opportunity of resting through change of motion, more completely than they could in absolute repose. Sir Aymer de Valence was sheathed in armour, and mounted on his charger, two of the archers, a groom of mean rank, and a squire, who looked in his day for the honour of knighthood, completed the detachment, which seemed so disposed as to secure the minstrel from escape, and to protect him against violence. "Not," said the young knight, addressing himself to Bertram, "that there is usually danger in travelling in this country any more than in the most quiet districts of England; but some disturbances, as you may have learnt, have broken out here within this last year, and have caused the garrison of Castle Douglas to maintain a stricter watch. But let us move on, for the complexion of the day is congenial with the original derivation of the name of the country, and the description of the chiefs to whom it belonged— *Sholto Dhu Glass*—(see yon dark grey man,) and dark grey will our route prove this morning, though by good luck it is not long."

The morning was indeed what the original Gaelic words implied, a drizzly, dark, moist day; the mist had settled upon the hills, and unrolled itself upon brook, glade, and tarn, and the spring breeze was not powerful enough to raise the veil, though from the wild sounds which were heard occasionally on the ridges, and through the glens, it might be supposed to wail at a sense of its own inability. The route of the travellers was directed by the course which the river had ploughed for itself down the valley, the banks of which bore in general that dark grey livery which Sir Aymer de Valence had intimated to be the prevalent tint of the country. Some ineffectual struggles of the sun shot a ray here and there to salute the peaks of the hills; yet these were unable to surmount the dulness of a March morning, and, at so early an hour, produced a variety of shades, rather than a gleam of brightness upon the eastern horizon. The view was monotonous and depressing, and apparently the good knight Aymer sought some amusement in occasional talk with Bertram, who, as was usual with his craft, possessed a fund of knowledge, and a power of conversation, well suited to pass away a dull morning. The minstrel, well pleased to pick up such information as he might be able concerning the present state of the country, embraced every opportunity of sustaining the dialogue.

"I would speak with you, Sir Minstrel," said the young knight. "If thou dost not find the air of this morning too harsh for thine organs, heartily do I wish thou wouldst fairly tell me what can have induced thee, being, as thou seemst, a man of sense, to thrust thyself into a wild country like this, at such a time.—And you, my masters," addressing the archers and the rest of the party, "methinks it would be as fitting and seeming if you reined back your steeds for a horse's length or so, since I apprehend you can travel on your way without the pastime of minstrelsy." The bowmen took the hint, and fell back, but, as was expressed by their grumbling observations, by no means pleased that there seemed little chance of their overhearing what conversation should pass between the young knight and the minstrel, which proceeded as follows—

"I am, then, to understand, good minstrel," said the knight, "that you, who have in your time borne arms, and even followed Saint George's red-cross banner to the Holy Sepulchre, are so little tired of the danger attending our profession, that you feel yourself attracted unnecessarily to regions where the sword, for ever loose in its scabbard, is ready to start on the slightest provocation?"

"It would be hard," replied the minstrel bluntly, "to answer such a question in the affirmative; and yet, when you consider how nearly allied is his profession who celebrates deeds of arms with that of the knight who performs them, your honour, I think, will hold it advisable that a minstrel desirous of doing his devoir, should, like a young knight, seek the truth of adventures where it is to be found, and rather visit countries where the knowledge is preserved of high and noble deeds, than those lazy and quiet realms, in which men live indolently, and die ignobly in peace, or by sentence of law. You yourself, sir, and those like you, who hold life cheap in respect of glory, guide your course through this world on the very same principle which brings your poor rhyming servant Bertram from a far province of merry England, to this dark country of rugged Scotland called Douglas Dale. You long to see adventures worthy of notice, and I (under favour for naming us two in the same breath) seek a scanty and precarious, but not a dishonourable living, by preparing for immortality, as well as I can, the particulars of such exploits, especially the names of those who were the heroes of these actions. Each, therefore, labours in his vocation; nor can the one be justly wondered at more than the other, seeing that if there be any difference in the degrees of danger to which both the hero and the poet are exposed, the courage, strength, arms, and address of the valiant knight, render it safer for him to venture into scenes of peril, than for the poor man of rhyme."

"You say well," answered the warrior; "and although it is something of novelty to me to hear your craft represented as upon a level with my own mode of life, yet shame were it to say that the minstrel who toils so much to keep in memory the feats of gallant knights should not himself prefer fame to existence, and a single achievement of valour to a whole age without a name, or to affirm that he follows a mean and unworthy profession."

"Your worship will then acknowledge," said the minstrel, "that it is a legitimate object in such as myself, who, simple as I am, have taken my regular degrees among the professors of the *gay science* at the capital town of Aigues-Mortos, to struggle forward into this northern district, where I am well assured many things have happened which have been adapted to the harp by minstrels of great fame in ancient days, and have become the subject of lays which lie deposited in the library of Castle Douglas, where, unless copied over by some one who understands the old British characters and language, they must, with whatever they may contain, whether of entertainment or edification, be speedily lost to posterity. If these hidden treasures were preserved and recorded by the minstrel art of my poor self and others, it might be held well to compensate for the risk of a chance blow of a broadsword, or the sweep of a brown bill, while I am engaged in collecting them; and I were unworthy of the name of a man, much more of an inventor or finder, [Footnote: The name of Maker stands for *Poet* (with the original sense of which word it exactly corresponds) in the old Scottish language. That of *Trouveur* or Troubadour—Finder, in short—has a similar meaning, and almost in every country the poetical tribes have been graced with the same epithets, inferring the property of those who employ invention or creation.] should I weigh the loss of life, a commodity always so uncertain, against the chance of that immortality which will survive in my lay after my broken voice and shivered harp shall no longer be able either to express tune or accompany tale."

"Certainly," said Sir Aymer, "having a heart to feel such a motive, you have an undoubted right to express it; nor should I have been in any degree disposed to question it had I found many minstrels prepared, like yourself, to prefer renown even to life itself, which most men think of greatly more consequence."

"There are, indeed, noble sir," replied Bertram, "minstrels, and, with your reverence, even belted knights themselves, who do not sufficiently value that renown which is acquired at the risk of life. To such ignoble men we must leave their own reward—let us abandon to them earth, and the things of earth, since they cannot aspire to that glory which is the *best* reward of others."

The minstrel uttered these last words with such enthusiasm, that the knight drew his bridle, and stood fronting Bertram, with his countenance kindling at the same theme, on which, after a short silence, he expressed himself with a like vivacity.

"Well fare thy heart, gay companion! I am happy to see there is still so much enthusiasm surviving in the world. Thou hast fairly won the minstrel groat; and if I do not pay it in conformity to my sense of thy merit, it shall be the fault of dame Fortune, who has graced my labours in these Scottish wars with the niggard pay of Scottish money. A gold piece or two there must be remaining of the ransom of one French knight, whom chance threw into my hands, and that, my friend, shall surely be thine own; and hark thee, I, Aymer de Valence, who now speak to thee, am born of the noble House of Pembroke; and though now landless, shall, by the grace of Our Lady, have in time a fitting establishment, wherein I will find room for a minstrel like thee, if thy talents have not by that time found thee a better patron."

"Thank thee, noble knight," said the minstrel, "as well for thy present intentions, as I hope I shall for thy future performance; but I may say, with truth, that I have not the sordid inclination of many of my brethren."

"He who partakes the true thirst of noble fame," said the young knight, "can have little room in his heart for the love of gold. But thou hast not yet told me, friend minstrel, what are the motives, in particular which have attracted thy wandering steps to this wild country?"

"Were I to do so," replied Bertram, rather desirous to avoid the question, as in some respects too nearly bordering on the secret purpose of his journey, "it might sound like a studied panegyric on thine own bold deeds, Sir Knight, and those of your companions in arms; and such adulation, minstrel as I am, I hate like an empty cup at a companion's lips. But let me say in few words, that Douglas Castle, and the deeds of valour which it has witnessed, have sounded wide through England; nor is there a gallant knight or trusty minstrel, whose heart does not throb at the name of the stronghold, which, in former days, the foot of an Englishman never entered, except in hospitality. There is a magic in the very names of Sir John de Walton and Sir Aymer de Valence, the gallant defenders of a place so often won back by its ancient lords, and with such circumstances of valour and cruelty, that it bears, in England, the name of the Dangerous Castle."

"Yet I would fain hear," answered the knight, "your own minstrel account of those legends which have induced you, for the amusement of future times, to visit a country which, at this period, is so distracted and perilous."

"If you can endure the length of a minstrel tale," said Bertram—"I for one am always amused by the exercise of my vocation, and have no objection to tell my story, provided you do not prove an impatient listener."

"Nay, for that matter," said the young knight, "a fair listener thou shalt have of me; and if my reward be not great, my attention at least shall be remarkable."

"And he," said the minstrel, "must be a poor gleeman who does not hold himself better paid with that, than with gold or silver, were the pieces English rose-nobles. On this condition, then, I begin a long story, which may, in one or other of its details, find subject for better minstrels than myself, and be listened to by such warriors as you hundreds of years hence."

CHAPTER THE FOURTH.

While many a merry lay and many a song
Cheer'd the rough road, we wish'd the rough road long;
The rough road then returning in a round,
Mark'd their impatient steps, for all was fairy ground.

DR. JOHNSON.

"It was about the year of redemption one thousand two hundred and eighty-five years," began, the minstrel, "when King Alexander the Third of Scotland lost his daughter Margaret, whose only child of the same name, called the Maiden of Norway, (as her father was king of that country,) became the heiress of this kingdom of Scotland, as well as of her father's crown. An unhappy death was this for Alexander, who had no nearer heirs left of his own body than this grandchild. She indeed might claim his kingdom by birthright; but the difficulty of establishing such a claim of inheritance must have been anticipated by all who bestowed a thought upon the subject. The Scottish king, therefore, endeavoured to make up for his loss by replacing his late Queen, who was an English princess, sister of our Edward the First, with Juletta, daughter of the Count de Dreux. The solemnities at the nuptial ceremony, which took place in the town of Jedburgh, were very great and remarkable, and particularly when, amidst the display of a pageant which was exhibited on the occasion, a ghastly spectre made its appearance in the form of a skeleton, as the King of Terrors is said to be represented.—Your worship is free to laugh at this, if you think it a proper subject for mirth; but men are alive who viewed it with their own eyes, and the event showed too well of what misfortunes this apparition was the singular prognostication."

"I have heard the story," said the knight; "but the monk who told it me, suggested that the figure, though unhappily chosen, was perhaps purposely introduced as a part of the pageant."

"I know not that," said the minstrel, dryly; "but there is no doubt that shortly after this apparition King Alexander died, to the great sorrow of his people. The Maid of Norway, his heiress, speedily followed her grandfather to the grave, and our English king, Sir Knight, raked up a claim of dependency and homage due, he said, by Scotland, which neither the lawyers, nobles, priests, nor the very minstrels of Scotland, had ever before heard of."

"Now, beshrew me," interrupted Sir Aymer de Valence, "this is beyond bargain. I agreed to hear your tale with patience, but I did not pledge myself that it should contain matter to the reproach of Edward the First, of blessed memory; nor will I permit his name to be mentioned in my hearing

39

without the respect due his high rank and noble qualities."

"Nay," said the minstrel, "I am no highland bagpiper or genealogist, to carry respect for my art so far as to quarrel with a man of worship who stops me at the beginning of a pibroch. I am an Englishman, and wish dearly well to my country; and, above all, I must speak the truth. But I will avoid disputable topics. Your age, sir, though none of the ripest, authorizes me to suppose you may have seen the battle of Falkirk, and other onslaughts in which the competition of Bruce and Baliol has been fiercely agitated, and you will permit me to say, that if the Scottish have not had the right upon their side, they have at least defended the wrong with the efforts of brave men and true."

"Of brave men I grant you," said the knight, "for I have seen no cowards amongst them; but as for truth, they can best judge of it who know how often they have sworn faith to England, and how repeatedly they have broken their vow."

"I shall not stir the question," said the minstrel, "leaving it to your worship to determine which has most falsehood—he who compels a weaker person to take an unjust path, or he who, compelled by necessity, takes the imposed oath without the intention of keeping his word."

"Nay, nay," said De Valence, "let us keep our opinions, for we are not likely to force each other from the faith we have adopted on this subject. But take my advice, and whilst thou travellest under an English pennon, take heed that thou keepest off this conversation in the hall and kitchen, where perhaps the soldier may be less tolerant than the officer; and now, in a word, what is thy legend of this Dangerous Castle?"

"For that," replied Bertram, "methinks your worship is most likely to have a better edition than I, who have not been in this country for many years; but it is not for me to bandy opinions with your knightship. I will even proceed with the tale as I have heard it. I need not, I presume, inform your worship that the Lords of Douglas, who founded this castle, are second to no lineage in Scotland in the antiquity of their descent. Nay, they have themselves boasted that their family is not to be seen or distinguished, like other great houses, until it is found at once in a certain degree of eminence. 'You may see us in the tree,' they say, 'you cannot discover us in the twig; you may see us in the stream, you cannot trace us to the fountain.' In a word, they deny that historians or genealogists can point out the first mean man named Douglas, who originally elevated the family; and true it is, that so far back as we have known this race, they have always been renowned for valour and enterprise, accompanied with the power which made that enterprise effectual."

"Enough," said the knight, "I have heard of the pride and power of that great family, nor does it interest me in the least to deny or detract from their bold claims to consideration in this respect."

"Without doubt you must also have heard, noble sir," replied the minstrel, "many things of James, the present heir of the house of Douglas?" "More than enough," answered the English knight; "he is known to have been a stout supporter of that outlawed traitor, William Wallace; and again, upon the first raising of the banner by this Robert Bruce, who pretends to be King of Scotland, this young springald, James Douglas, must needs start into rebellion anew. He plunders his uncle, the Archbishop of St. Andrews, of a considerable sum of money, to fill the Scottish Usurper's not over-burdened treasury, debauches the servants of his relation, takes arms, and though repeatedly chastised in the field, still keeps his vaunt, and threatens mischief to those, who, in the name of his rightful sovereign, defend the Castle of Douglasdale."

"It is your pleasure to say so, Sir Knight," replied Bertram; "yet I am sure, were you a Scot, you would with patience hear me tell over what has been said of this young man by those who have known him, and whose account of his adventures shows how differently the same tale may be told. These men talk of the present heir of this ancient family as fully adequate to maintain and augment its reputation; ready, indeed, to undergo every peril in the cause of Robert the Bruce, because the Bruce is esteemed by him his lawful king; and sworn and devoted, with such small strength as he can muster, to revenge himself on those Southrons who have, for several years, as he thinks, unjustly, possessed themselves of his father's abode."

"O," replied Sir Aymer de Valence, "we have heard much of his achievements in this respect, and of his threats against our governor and ourselves; yet we think it scarce likely that Sir John de Walton will move from Douglasdale without the King's order, although this James Douglas, a mere chicken, take upon himself to crack his voice by crowing like a cock of the game."

"Sir," answered Bertram, "our acquaintance is but brief, and yet I feel it has been so beneficial to me, that I trust there is no harm, in hoping that James Douglas and you may never meet in bodily presence till the state of the two countries shall admit of peace being between you."

"Thou art obliging, friend," answered Sir Aymer, "and, I doubt not, sincere; and truly thou seemest to have a wholesome sense of the respect due to this young knight, when men talk of him in his native valley of Douglas. For me, I am only poor Aymer of Valence, without an acre of land, or much hope of acquiring any, unless I cut something huge with my broadsword out of the middle of these hills. Only this, good minstrel, if thou livest to tell my story, may I pray thee to use thy scrupulous custom of

41

searching out the verity, and whether I live or die thou shalt not, I think, discover that thy late acquaintance of a spring morning hath added more to the laurels of James of Douglas, than any man's death must give to him by whose stronger arm, or more lucky chance, it is his lot to fall."

"I nothing fear you, Sir Knight," said the minstrel, "for yours is that happy brain, which, bold in youth as beseems a young knight, is in more advanced life the happy source of prudent counsel, of which I would not, by an early death, wish thy country to be deprived."

"Thou art so candid, then, as to wish Old England the benefit of good advice" said Sir Aymer, "though thou leanest to the side of Scotland in the controversy?"

"Assuredly, Sir Knight," said the minstrel, "since in wishing that Scotland and England each knew their own true interest, I am bound to wish them both alike well; and they should, I think, desire to live in friendship together. Occupying each their own portion of the same island, and living under the same laws, and being at peace with each other, they might without fear, face the enmity of the whole world."

"If thy faith be so liberal," answered the Knight, "as becomes a good man, thou must certainly pray, Sir Minstrel, for the success of England in the war, by which alone these murderous hostilities of the northern nation can end in a solid peace. The rebellions of this obstinate country are but the struggles of the stag when he is mortally wounded; the animal grows weaker and weaker with every struggle, till his resistance is effectually tamed by the hand of death."

"Not so, Sir Knight," said the minstrel; "if my creed is well taught me, we ought not so to pray. We may, without offence, intimate in our prayers the end we wish to obtain; but it is not for us, poor mortals, to point out to an all-seeing Providence the precise manner in which our petitions are to be accomplished, or to wish the downfall of a country to end its commotions, as the death-stab terminates the agonies of the wounded stag. Whether I appeal to my heart or to my understanding, the dictate would be to petition Heaven for what is just and equal in the case; and if I should fear for thee, Sir Knight, in an encounter with James of Douglas, it is only because he upholds, as I conceive, the better side of the debate; and powers more earthly have presaged to him success."

"Do you tell me so, Sir Minstrel," said De Valence in a threatening tone, "knowing me and my office?"

"Your personal dignity and authority" said Bertram, "cannot change the right into wrong, or avert what Providence has decreed to take place. You know, I must presume, that the Douglas hath, by various devices, already contrived to make himself master of this Castle of Douglas three several

42

times, and that Sir John de Walton, the present governor, holds it with a garrison trebled in force, and under the assurance that if, without surprise, he should keep it from the Scottish power for a year and a day, he shall obtain the barony of Douglas, with its extensive appendages, in free property for his reward; while, on the other hand, if he shall suffer the fortress during this space to be taken, either by guile or by open force, as has happened successively to the holders of the Dangerous Castle, he will become liable to dishonour as a knight, and to attainder as a subject; and the chiefs who take share with him, and serve under him, will participate also in his guilt and his punishment?"

"All this I know well" said Sir Aymer; "and I only wonder that, having become public, the conditions have, nevertheless, been told with so much accuracy; but what has this to do with the issue of the combat, if the Douglas and I should chance to meet? I will not surely be disposed to fight with less animation because I wear my fortune upon my sword, or become coward because I fight for a portion of the Douglas's estate, as well as for fame and for fatherland? And after all"—

"Hear me," said the minstrel; "an ancient gleeman has said, that in a false quarrel there is no true valour, and the *los* or praise won therein, is, when balanced against honest fame, as valueless as a wreath formed out of copper, compared to a chaplet of pure gold; but I bid you not take me for thy warrant in this important question. Thou well knowest how James of Thirlwall, the last English commander before Sir John de Walton, was surprised, and the castle sacked with circumstances of great inhumanity."

"Truly," said Sir Aymer, "I think that Scotland and England both have heard of that onslaught, and of the disgusting proceedings of the Scottish chieftain, when he caused transport into the wild forest gold, silver, ammunition, and armour, and all things that could be easily removed, and destroyed a large quantity of provisions in a manner equally savage and unheard-of."

"Perhaps, Sir Knight," said Bertram, "you were yourself an eyewitness of that transaction, which has been spoken of far and wide, and is called the Douglas Larder?"

"I saw not the actual accomplishment of the deed," said De Valence; "that is, I witnessed it not a-doing, but I beheld enough of the sad relics to make the Douglas Larder never by me to be forgotten as a record of horror and abomination. I would speak it truly, by the hand of my father and by my honour as a knight! and I will leave it to thee to judge whether it was a deed calculated to secure the smiles of Heaven in favour of the actors. This is my edition of the story:—

"A large quantity of provisions had during two years or thereabouts been collected from different points, and the Castle of Douglas, newly repaired, and, as was thought, carefully guarded, was appointed as the place where the said provisions were to be put in store for the service of the King of England, or of the Lord Clifford, whichever should first enter the Western Marches with an English army, and stand in need of such a supply. This army was also to relieve our wants, I mean those of my uncle the Earl of Pembroke, who for some time before had lain with a considerable force in the town called Ayr, near the old Caledonian Forest, and where we had hot wars with the insurgent Scots. Well, sir, it happened, as in similar cases, that Thirlwall, though a bold and active soldier, was surprised in the Castle of Douglas, about Hallowmass, by this same worthy, young James Douglas. In no very good humour was he, as you may suppose; for his father, called William the Hardy, or William Longlegs, having refused, on any terms, to become Anglicized, was made a lawful prisoner, and died as such, closely confined in Berwick, or, as some say, in Newcastle. The news of his father's death had put young Douglas into no small rage, and tended, I think, to suggest what he did in his resentment. Embarrassed by the quantity of provisions which he found in the castle, which, the English being superior in the country, he had neither the means to remove, nor the leisure to stay and consume, the fiend, as I think, inspired him with a contrivance to render them unfit for human use. You shall judge yourself whether it was likely to be suggested by a good or an evil spirit.

"According to this device, the gold, silver, and other transportable commodities being carried to secret places of safety, Douglas caused the meat, the malt, and other corn or grain, to be brought down into the castle cellar, where he emptied the contents of the sacks into one loathsome heap, striking out the heads of the barrels and puncheons, so as to let the mingled drink run through the heap of meal, grain, and so forth. The bullocks provided for slaughter were in like manner knocked on the head, and their blood suffered to drain into the mass of edible substances; and lastly, the flesh of these oxen was buried in the same mass, in which was also included the dead bodies of those in the castle, who, receiving no quarter from the Douglas, paid dear enough for having kept no better watch. This base and unworthy abuse of provisions intended for the use of man, together with throwing into the well of the castle carcasses of men and horses, and other filth for polluting the same, has since that time been called the DOUGLAS LARDER."

"I pretend not, good Sir Aymer," said the minstrel, "to vindicate what you justly reprove, nor can I conceive any mode of rendering provisions arranged after the form of the Douglas Larder, proper for the use of any Christian; yet this young gentleman might perhaps act under the sting of

44

natural resentment, rendering his singular exploit more excusable than it may seem at first. Think, if your own noble father had just died in a lingering captivity, his inheritance seized upon, and occupied as a garrison by a foreign enemy, would not these things stir you to a mode of resentment, which in cold blood, and judging of it as the action of an enemy, your honour might hold in natural and laudable abhorrence?— Would you pay respect to dead and senseless objects, which no one could blame your appropriating to your own use, or even scruple the refusal of quarter to prisoners, which is so often practised even in wars which are otherwise termed fair and humane?"

"You press me close, minstrel," said Aymer de Valence. "I at least have no great interest to excuse the Douglas in this matter, since its consequences were, that I myself, and the rest of my uncle's host, laboured with Clifford and his army to rebuild this same Dangerous Castle; and feeling no stomach for the cheer that the Douglas had left us, we suffered hard commons, though I acknowledge we did not hesitate to adopt for our own use such sheep and oxen as the miserable Scots had still left around their farm-houses; and I jest not, Sir Minstrel, when I acknowledge in sad earnest, that we martial men ought to make our petitions with peculiar penitence to Heaven for mercy, when we reflect on the various miseries which the nature of our profession compels us to inflict on each other."

"It seems to me," answered the minstrel, "that those who feel the stings of their own conscience should be more lenient when they speak of the offences of others; nor do I greatly rely on a sort of prophecy which was delivered, as the men of this hill district say, to the young Douglas, by a man who in the course of nature should have been long since dead, promising him a course of success against the English for having sacrificed his own castle to prevent their making it a garrison."

"We have time enough for the story," said Sir Aymer, "and methinks it would suit a knight and a minstrel better than the grave converse we have hitherto held, which would have beseemed—so God save me—the mouths of two travelling friars."

"So be it," said the minstrel; "the rote or the viol easily changes its time and varies its note."

CHAPTER THE FIFTH.

A tale of sorrow, for your eyes may weep;
A tale of horror, for your flesh may tingle;
A tale of wonder, for the eyebrows arch,
And the flesh curdles if you read it rightly
                                    OLD PLAY.

"Your honour must be informed, gentle Sir Aymer de Valence, that I have heard this story told at a great distance from the land in which it happened, by a sworn minstrel, the ancient friend and servant of the house of Douglas, one of the best, it is said, who ever belonged to that noble family. This minstrel, Hugo Hugonet by name, attended his young master when on this fierce exploit, as was his wont.

"The castle was in total tumult; in one corner the war-men were busy breaking up and destroying provisions; in another, they were slaying men, horses, and cattle, and these actions were accompanied with appropriate sounds. The cattle, particularly, had become sensible of their impending fate, and with awkward resistance and piteous cries, testified that reluctance with which these poor creatures look instinctively on the shambles. The groans and screams of men, undergoing, or about to undergo, the stroke of death, and the screeches of the poor horses which were in mortal agony, formed a fearful chorus. Hugonet was desirous to remove himself from such unpleasant sights and sounds; but his master, the Douglas, had been a man of some reading, and his old servant was anxious to secure a book of poetry, to which he had been attached of old. This contained the Lays of an ancient Scottish Bard, who, if an ordinary human creature while he was in this life, cannot now perhaps be exactly termed such.

"He was, in short, that Thomas, distinguished by the name of the Rhymer, and whose intimacy, it is said, became so great with the gifted people, called the Faery folk, that he could, like them, foretell the future deed before it came to pass, and united in his own person the quality of bard and of soothsayer. But of late years he had vanished almost entirely from this mortal scene; and although the time and manner of his death were never publicly known, yet the general belief was, that he was not severed from the land of the living, but removed to the land of Faery, from whence he sometimes made excursions, and concerned himself only about matters which were to come hereafter. Hugonet was the more earnest to prevent the loss of the works of this ancient bard, as many of his poems and predictions were said to be preserved in the castle, and were supposed to contain much especially connected with the old house of Douglas, as well as other families of ancient descent, who had been subjects of this old man's prophecy; and accordingly he determined to save this volume from destruction in the general conflagration to which the building was about to be consigned by the heir of its ancient proprietors. With this view he hurried up into the little old vaulted room, called 'the Douglas's study,' in which there might be some dozen old books written by the ancient chaplains, in what the minstrels call *the letter black*. He immediately discovered the celebrated lay, called Sir Tristrem, which has been so often altered and abridged as to bear little resemblance to the original. Hugonet, who well knew the value in which this poem was held by the ancient lords of the castle, took the parchment volume from the shelves of the library, and laid it upon a small desk adjacent to the Baron's chair. Having made such preparation for putting it in safety, he fell into a brief reverie, in which the decay of light, and the preparations for the Douglas Larder, but especially the last sight of objects which had been familiar to his eyes, now on the eve of destruction, engaged him at that moment.

"The bard, therefore, was thinking within himself upon the uncommon mixture of the mystical scholar and warrior in his old master, when, as he bent his eyes upon the book of the ancient Rhymer, he was astonished to observe it slowly removed from the desk on which it lay by an invisible hand. The old man looked with horror at the spontaneous motion of the book, for the safety of which he was interested, and had the courage to approach a little nearer the table, in order to discover by what means it had been withdrawn.

"I have said the room was already becoming dark, so as to render it difficult to distinguish any person in the chair, though it now appeared, on closer examination, that a kind of shadowy outline of a human form was seated in it, but neither precise enough to convey its exact figure to the mind, nor so detailed as to intimate distinctly its mode of action. The Bard of Douglas, therefore, gazed upon the object of his fear, as if he had looked upon something not mortal; nevertheless, as he gazed more intently, he became more capable of discovering the object which offered itself to his eyes, and they grew by degrees more keen to penetrate what they witnessed. A tall thin form, attired in, or rather shaded with, a long flowing dusky robe, having a face and physiognomy so wild and overgrown with hair as to be hardly human, were the only marked outlines of the phantom; and, looking more attentively, Hugonet was still sensible of two other forms, the outlines, it seemed, of a hart and a hind, which appeared half to shelter themselves behind the person and under the robe of this supernatural figure."

"A probable tale," said the knight, "for you, Sir Minstrel, a man of sense as you seem to be, to recite so gravely! From what wise authority have you had this tale, which, though it might pass well enough amid clanging beakers, must be held quite apocryphal in the sober hours of the morning?"

"By my minstrel word, Sir Knight," answered Bertram, "I am no propagator of the fable, if it be one; Hugonet, the violer, when he had retired into a cloister near the Lake of Pembelmere in Wales, communicated the story to me as I now tell it. Therefore, as it was upon the authority of an eyewitness, I apologize not for relating it to you, since I could hardly discover a more direct source of knowledge."

"Be it so, Sir Minstrel," said the knight; "tell on thy tale, and may thy legend escape criticism from others as well as from me."

"Hugonet, Sir Knight," answered Bertram, "was a holy man, and maintained a fair character during his whole life, notwithstanding his trade may be esteemed a light one. The vision spoke to him in an antique language, like that formerly used in the kingdom of Strath-Clyde, being a species of Scots or Gaelic, which few would have comprehended.

"'You are a learned man,' said the apparition, 'and not unacquainted with the dialects used in your country formerly, although they are now out of date, and you are obliged to translate them into the vulgar Saxon of Deira or Northumberland; but highly must an ancient British bard prize one in this "remote term of time," who sets upon the poetry of his native country a value which invites him to think of its preservation at a moment of such terror as influences the present evening.'

"'It is, indeed,' said Hugonet, 'a night of terror, that calls even the dead from the grave, and makes them the ghastly and fearful companions of the living—Who or what art thou, in God's name, who breakest the bounds which divide them, and revisitest thus strangely the state thou hast so long bid adieu to?'

"'I am,' replied the vision, 'that celebrated Thomas the Rhymer, by some called Thomas of Erceldoun, or Thomas the True Speaker. Like other sages, I am permitted at times to revisit the scenes of my former life, nor am I incapable of removing the shadowy clouds and darkness which overhang futurity; and know, thou afflicted man, that what thou now seest in this woeful country, is not a general emblem of what shall therein befall hereafter, but in proportion as the Douglasses are now suffering the loss and destruction of their home for their loyalty to the rightful heir of the Scottish kingdom, so hath Heaven appointed for them a just reward; and as they have not spared to burn and destroy their own house and that of their fathers in the Bruce's cause, so is it the doom of Heaven, that as often as the walls of Douglas Castle shall be burnt to the ground, they shall be again rebuilt still more stately and more magnificent than before.'

"A cry was now heard like that of a multitude in the courtyard, joining in a fierce shout of exultation; at the same time a broad and ruddy glow seemed to burst from the beams and rafters, and sparks flew from them as from the smith's stithy, while the element caught to its fuel, and the conflagration broke its way through every aperture.

"'See ye that?' said the vision, casting his eye towards the windows and disappearing—'Begone! The fated hour of removing this book is not yet come, nor are thine the destined hands. But it will be safe where I have placed it, and the time of its removal shall come.' The voice was heard after the form had vanished, and the brain of Hugonet almost turned round at the wild scene which he beheld; his utmost exertion was scarcely sufficient to withdraw him from the terrible spot, and Douglas Castle that night sunk into ashes and smoke, to arise, in no great length of time, in a form stronger than ever." The minstrel stopt, and his hearer, the English knight, remained silent for some minutes ere at length he replied.

"It is true, minstrel," answered Sir Aymer, "that your tale is so far undeniable, that this castle—three times burned down by the heir of the house and of the barony—has hitherto been as often reared again by Henry Lord Clifford, and other generals of the English, who endeavoured on every occasion to build it up more artificially and more strongly than it had formerly existed, since it occupies a position too important to the safety of our Scottish border to permit our yielding it up. This I myself have partly witnessed. But I cannot think, that because the castle has been so destroyed, it is therefore decreed so to be repaired in future, considering that such cruelties, as surely cannot meet the approbation of Heaven, have attended the feats of the Douglasses. But I see thou art determined to keep thine own faith, nor can I blame thee, since the wonderful turns of fate which have attended this fortress, are sufficient to warrant any one to watch for what seem the peculiar indications of the will of Heaven; but thou mayst believe, good minstrel, that the fault shall not be mine, if the young Douglas shall have opportunity to exercise his cookery upon a second edition of his family larder, or to profit by the predictions of Thomas the Rhymer."

"I do not doubt due circumspection upon your own part and Sir John de Walton's," said Bertram; "but there is no crime in my saying that Heaven can accomplish its own purposes. I look upon Douglas Castle as in some degree a fated place, and I long to see what changes time may have made in it during the currency of twenty years. Above all, I desire to secure, if possible, the volume of this Thomas of Erceldoun, having in it such a fund of forgotten minstrelsy, and of prophecies respecting the future fates of the British kingdom, both northern and southern."

The knight made no answer, but rode a little space forward, keeping the

49

upper part of the ridge of the water, by which the road down the vale seemed to be rather sharply conducted. It at length attained the summit of an acclivity of considerable length. From this point, and behind a conspicuous rock, which appeared to have been pushed aside, as it were, like the scene of a theatre to admit a view of the under part of the valley, the travellers beheld the extensive vale, parts of which have been already shown in detail, but which, as the river became narrower, was now entirely laid bare in its height and depth as far as it extended, and displayed in its precincts, at a little distance from the course of the stream, the towering and lordly castle to which it gave the name. The mist which continued to encumber the valley with its fleecy clouds, showed imperfectly the rude fortifications which served to defend the small town of Douglas, which was strong enough to repel a desultory attack, but not to withstand what was called in those days a formal siege. The most striking feature was its church, an ancient Gothic pile raised on an eminence in the centre of the town, and even then extremely ruinous. To the left, and lying in the distance, might be seen other towers and battlements; and divided from the town by a piece of artificial water, which extended almost around it, arose the Dangerous Castle of Douglas.

Sternly was it fortified, after the fashion of the middle ages, with donjon and battlements; displaying, above others, the tall tower, which bore the name of Lord Henry's, or the Clifford's Tower.

"Yonder is the castle," said Aymer de Valence, extending his arm with a smile of triumph upon his brow; "thou mayst judge thyself, whether the defences added to it under the Clifford are likely to render its next capture a more easy deed than the last."

The minstrel barely shook his head, and quoted from the Psalmist—"*Nisi Dominus custodiet.*" Nor did he prosecute the discourse, though De Valence answered eagerly, "My own edition of the text is not very different from thine; but, methinks thou art more spiritually-minded than can always be predicated of a wandering minstrel."

"God knows," said Bertram, "that if I, or such as I, are forgetful of the finger of Providence in accomplishing its purposes in this lower world, we have heavier blame than that of other people, since we are perpetually called upon, in the exercise of our fanciful profession, to admire the turns of fate which bring good out of evil, and which render those who think only of their own passions and purposes the executors of the will of Heaven."

"I do submit to what you say, Sir Minstrel," answered the knight, "and it would be unlawful to express any doubt of the truths which you speak so solemnly, any more than of your own belief in them. Let me add, sir, that I think I have power enough in this garrison to bid you welcome, and Sir

John de Walton, I hope, will not refuse access to hall, castle, or knight's bower, to a person of your profession, and by whose conversation we shall, perhaps, profit somewhat. I cannot, however, lead you to expect such indulgence for your son, considering the present state of his health; but if I procure him the privilege to remain at the convent of Saint Bride, he will be there unmolested and in safety, until you have renewed your acquaintance with Douglas Dale and its history, and are disposed to set forward on your journey."

"I embrace your honour's proposal the more willingly," said the minstrel, "that I can recompense the Father Abbot."

"A main point with holy men or women," replied De Valence, "who, in time of warfare, subsist by affording the visitors of their shrine the means of maintenance in their cloisters for a passing season."

The party now approached the sentinels on guard at the castle, who were closely and thickly stationed, and who respectfully admitted Sir Aymer de Valence, as next in command under Sir John de Walton. Fabian—for so was the young squire named who attended on De Valence—mentioned it as his master's pleasure that the minstrel should also be admitted. An old archer, however, looked hard at the minstrel as he followed Sir Aymer. "It is not for us," said he, "or any of our degree, to oppose the pleasure of Sir Aymer do Valence, nephew to the Earl of Pembroke, in such a matter; and for us, Master Fabian, welcomes are you to make the gleeman your companion both at bed and board, as well as your visitant, a week or two at the Castle of Douglas; but your worship is well aware of the strict order of watch laid upon us, and if Solomon, King of Israel, were to come here as a travelling minstrel, by my faith I durst not give him entrance, unless I had positive authority from Sir John de Walton."

"Do you doubt, sirrah," said Aymer de Valence, who returned on hearing an altercation betwixt Fabian and the archer—"do you doubt that I have good authority to entertain a guest, or do you presume to contest it?"

"Heaven forbid!" said the old man, "that I should presume to place my own desire in opposition to your worship, who has so lately and so honourably acquired your spurs; but in this matter I must think what will be the wish of Sir John de Walton, who is your governor, Sir Knight, as well as mine; and so far I hold it worth while to detain your guest until Sir John return from a ride to the outposts of the castle; and this, I conceive, being my duty, will be no matter of offence to your worship."

"Methinks," said the knight, "it is saucy in thee to suppose that my commands can have any thing in them improper, or contradictory to those of Sir John de Walton; thou mayst trust to me at least that thou shalt come to no harm. Keep this man in the guard-room; let him not want good cheer, and when Sir John de Walton returns, report him as a person admitted by my invitation, and if any thing more be wanted to make out your excuse, I shall not be reluctant in stating it to the governor."

The archer made a signal of obedience with the pike which he held in his hand, and resumed the grave and solemn manner of a sentinel upon his post. He first, however, ushered in the minstrel, and furnished him with food and liquor, speaking at the same time to Fabian, who remained behind. The smart young stripling had become very proud of late, in consequence of obtaining the name of Sir Aymer's squire, and advancing a step in chivalry, as Sir Aymer himself had, somewhat earlier than the usual period, been advanced from squire to knight.

"I tell thee, Fabian," said the old archer, (whose gravity, sagacity, and skill in his vocation, while they gained him the confidence of all in the castle, subjected him, as he himself said, occasionally to the ridicule of the young coxcombs; and at the same time we may add, rendered him somewhat pragmatic and punctilious towards those who stood higher than himself in birth and rank;) "I tell thee, Fabian, thou wilt do thy master, Sir Aymer, good service, if thou wilt give him a hint to suffer an old archer, man-at-arms, or such like, to give him a fair and civil answer respecting that which he commands; for undoubtedly it is not in the first score of a man's years that he learns the various proper forms of military service; and Sir John de Walton, a most excellent commander no doubt, is one earnestly bent on pursuing the strict line of his duty, and will be rigorously severe, as well, believe me, with thy master as with a lesser person. Nay, he also possesses that zeal for his duty which induces him to throw blame, if there be the slightest ground for it, upon Aymer de Valence himself, although his uncle, the Earl of Pembroke, was John de Walton's steady patron, and laid the beginning of his good fortune; for all which, by training up his nephew in the true discipline of the French wars, Sir John has taken the best way of showing himself grateful to the eld Earl."

"Be it as you will, old Gilbert Greenleaf," answered Fabian, "thou knowest I never quarrel with thy sermonizing, and therefore give me credit for submitting to many a lecture from Sir John de Walton and thyself; but thou drivest this a little too far, if thou canst not let a day pass without giving me a flogging. Credit me, Sir John de Walton will not thank thee, if thou term him one too old to remember that he himself had once some green sap in his veins. Ay, thus it is, the old man will not forget that he has once been young, nor the young that he must some day be old; and so the one changes his manners into the lingering formality of advanced age, and the other remains like a midsummer torrent swoln with rain, every drop of water in it noise, froth, and overflow. There is a maxim for thee, Gilbert!—Heardest thou ever better? hang it up amidst thy axioms of wisdom, and see if it will not pass among them like fifteen to the dozen. It will serve to bring thee off, man, when the wine-pot (thine only fault, good Gilbert) hath brought thee on occasion into something of a scrape."

"Best keep it for thyself, good Sir Squire," said the old man; "methinks it is more like to stand thyself one day in good stead. Who ever heard of a knight, or of the wood of which a knight is made, and that is a squire, being punished corporally like a poor old archer or horseboy? Your worst fault will be mended by some of these witty sayings, and your best service will scarce be rewarded more thankfully than by giving thee the name of Fabian the Fabler, or some such witty title."

Having unloosed his repartee to this extent, old Greenleaf resumed a certain acidity of countenance, which may be said to characterise those whose preferment hath become frozen under the influence of the slowness of its progress, and who display a general spleen against such as have obtained the advancement for which all are struggling, earlier, and, as they suppose, with less merit than their own. From time to time the eye of the old sentinel stole from the top of his pike, and with an air of triumph rested upon the young man Fabian, as if to see how deeply the wound had galled him, while at the same time he held himself on the alert to perform whatever mechanical duty his post might require. Both Fabian and his master were at the happy period of life when such discontent as that of the grave archer affected them lightly, and, at the very worst, was considered as the jest of an old man and a good soldier; the more especially, as he was always willing to do the duty of his companions, and was much trusted by Sir John de Walton, who, though very much younger, had been bred up like Greenleaf in the wars of Edward the First, and was tenacious in upholding strict discipline, which, since the death of that great monarch, had been considerably neglected by the young and warm-blooded valour of England.

Meantime it occurred to Sir Aymer de Valence, that though in displaying the usual degree of hospitality shown, to such a man as Bertram, he had merely done what was becoming his own rank, as one possessed of the highest honours of chivalry—the self-styled minstrel might not in reality be a man of that worth which he assumed. There was certainly something in his conversation, at least more grave, if not more austere, than was common to those of his calling; and when he recollected many points of Sir John de Walton's minuteness, a doubt arose in his mind, that the governor might not approve of his having introduced into the castle a person of Bertram's character, who was capable of making observations from which the garrison might afterwards feel much danger and inconvenience. Secretly, therefore, he regretted that he had not fairly intimated to the wandering minstrel, that his reception, or that of any stranger, within the Dangerous Castle, was not at present permitted by the circumstances of the times. In this case, the express line of his duty would have been his vindication, and instead, perhaps of discountenance and blame, he would have had praise and honour from his superior.

With these thoughts passing through his mind, some tacit apprehension. arose of a rebuke on the part of his commanding-officer; for this officer, notwithstanding his strictness, Sir Aymer loved as well as feared. He went, therefore, towards the guard-room of the castle, under the pretence of seeing that the rites of hospitality had been duly observed towards his late travelling companion. The minstrel arose respectfully, and from the manner in which he paid his compliments, seemed, if he had not expected this call of enquiry, at least to be in no degree surprised at it. Sir Aymer, on the other hand, assumed an air something more distant than he had yet used towards Bertram, and in reverting to his former invitation, he now so far qualified it as to say, that the minstrel knew that he was only second in command, and that effectual permission to enter the castle ought to be sanctioned by Sir John de Walton.

There is a civil way of seeming to believe any apology which people are disposed to receive in payment, without alleging suspicion of its currency. The minstrel, therefore, tendered his thanks for the civility which had so far been shown to him. "It was a mere wish of passing curiosity," he said, "which, if not granted, could be attended with no consequences either inconvenient or disagreeable to him. Thomas of Erceldoun was, according to the Welsh triads, *one of the three bards of Britain*, who never stained a spear with blood, or was guilty either of taking or retaking castles and fortresses, and thus far not a person likely, after death, to be suspected of such warlike feats. But I can easily conceive why Sir John de Walton should have allowed the usual rites of hospitality to fall into disuse, and why a man of public character like myself ought not to desire food or lodging where it is accounted so dangerous; and it can surprise no one why the governor did not even invest his worthy young lieutenant with the power of dispensing with so strict and unusual a rule."

These words, very coolly spoken, had something of the effect of affronting the young knight, as insinuating, that he was not held sufficiently trustworthy by Sir John de Walton, with whom he had lived on terms of affection and familiarity, though the governor had attained his thirtieth year and upwards, and his lieutenant did not yet write himself one-and-twenty, the full age of chivalry having been in his case particularly dispensed with, owing to a feat of early manhood. Ere he had fully composed the angry thoughts which were chafing in his mind, the sound of

54

a hunting bugle was heard at the gate, and from the sort of general stir which it spread through the garrison, it was plain that the governor had returned from his ride. Every sentinel, seemingly animated by his presence, shouldered his pike more uprightly, gave the word of the post more sharply, and seemed more fully awake and conscious of his duty. Sir John de Walton having alighted from his horse, asked Greenleaf what had passed during his absence; the old archer thought it his duty to say that a minstrel, who seemed like a Scotchman, or wandering borderer, had been admitted into the castle, while his son, a lad sick of the pestilence so much talked of, had been left for a time at the Abbey of Saint Bride. This he said on Fabian's information. The archer added, that the father was a man of tale and song, who could keep the whole garrison amused, without giving them leave to attend to their own business.

"We want no such devices to pass the time," answered the governor; "and we would have been better satisfied if our lieutenant had been pleased to find us other guests, and fitter for a direct and frank communication, than one who, by his profession, is a detractor of God and a deceiver of man."

"Yet," said the old soldier, who could hardly listen even to his commander without indulging the humour of contradiction, "I have heard your honour intimate that the trade of a minstrel, when it is justly acted up to, is as worthy as even the degree of knighthood itself."

"Such it may have been in former days," answered the knight; "but in modern minstrelsy, the duty of rendering the art an incentive to virtue is forgotten, and it is well if the poetry which fired our fathers to noble deeds, does not now push on their children to such as are base and unworthy. But I will speak upon this to my friend Aymer, than whom I do not know a more excellent, or a more high-spirited young man."

While discoursing with the archer in this manner, Sir John de Walton, of a tall and handsome figure, advanced and stood within the ample arch of the guard-room chimney, and was listened to in reverential silence by trusty Gilbert, who filled up with nods and signs, as an attentive auditor, the pauses in the conversation. The conduct of another hearer of what passed was not equally respectful, but, from his position, he escaped observation.

This third person was no other than the squire Fabian, who was concealed from observation by his position behind the hob, or projecting portion of the old-fashioned fireplace, and hid himself yet more carefully when he heard the conversation between the governor and the archer turn to the prejudice, as he thought, of his master. The squire's employment at this time was the servile task of cleaning Sir Aymer's arms, which was conveniently performed by heating, upon the projection already specified, the pieces of steel armour for the usual thin coating of varnish. He could not, therefore, if he should be discovered, be considered as guilty of any thing insolent or disrespectful. He was better screened from view, as a thick smoke arose from a quantity of oak panelling, carved in many cases with the crest and achievements of the Douglas family, which being the fuel nearest at hand, lay smouldering in the chimney, and gathering to a blaze.

The governor, unconscious of this addition to his audience, pursued his conversation, with Gilbert Greenleaf: "I need not tell you," he said, "that I am interested in the speedy termination of this siege or blockade, with which Douglas continues to threaten us; my own honour and affections are engaged in keeping this Dangerous Castle safe in England's behalf, but I am troubled at the admission of this stranger; and young De Valence would have acted more strictly in the line of his duty, if he had refused to this wanderer any communication with this garrison without my permission."

"Pity it is," replied old Greenleaf, shaking his head, "that this good-natured and gallant young knight is somewhat drawn aside by the rash advices of his squire, the boy Fabian, who has bravery, but as little steadiness in him as a bottle of fermented small beer."

"Now hang thee," thought Fabian to himself, "for an old relic of the wars, stuffed full of conceit and warlike terms, like the soldier who, to keep himself from the cold, has lapped himself so close in a tattered ensign for a shelter, that his very outside may show nothing but rags and blazonry."

"I would not think twice of the matter, were the party less dear to me," said Sir John de Walton. "But I would fain be of use to this young man, even although I should purchase his improvement in military knowledge at the expense of giving him a little pain. Experience should, as it were, be burnt in upon the mind of a young man, and not merely impressed by marking the lines of his chart out for him with chalk; I will remember the hint you, Greenleaf, have given, and take an opportunity of severing these two young men; and though I most dearly love the one, and am far from wishing ill to the other, yet at present, as you well hint, the blind is leading the blind, and the young knight has for his assistant and counsellor too young a squire, and that must be amended."

"Marry! out upon thee, old palmer-worm!" said the page within himself; "have I found thee in the very fact of maligning myself and my master, as it is thy nature to do towards all the hopeful young buds of chivalry? If it were not to dirty the arms of an *eleve* of chivalry, by measuring them with one of thy rank, I might honour thee with a knightly invitation to the field, while the scandal which thou hast spoken is still foul upon thy tongue; as it is, thou shalt not carry one kind of language publicly in the castle, and another before the governor, upon the footing of having served with him under the banner of Longshanks. I will carry to my master this tale of thine evil intentions; and when we have concerted together, it shall appear whether the youthful spirits of the garrison or the grey beards are most likely to be the hope and protection, of this same Castle of Douglas."

It is enough to say that Fabian pursued his purpose, in carrying to his master, and in no very good humour, the report of what had passed between Sir John de Walton and the old soldier. He succeeded in representing the whole as a formal offence intended to Sir Aymer de Valence; while all that the governor did to remove the suspicions entertained by the young knight, could not in any respect bring him to take a kindly view of the feelings of his commander towards him. He retained the impression which he had formed from Fabian's recital of what he had heard, and did not think he was doing Sir John de Walton any injustice, in supposing him desirous to engross the greatest share of the fame acquired in the defence of the castle, and thrusting back his companions, who might reasonably pretend to a fair portion of it.

The mother of mischief, says a Scottish proverb, is no bigger than a midge's wing. [Footnote: i.e. Gnat's wing] In this matter of quarrel, neither the young man nor the older knight had afforded each other any just cause of offence. De Walton was a strict observer of military discipline, in which he had been educated from his extreme youth, and by which he was almost as completely ruled as by his natural disposition; and his present situation added force to his original education.

Common report had even exaggerated the military skill, the love of adventure, and the great variety of enterprise, ascribed to James, the young Lord of Douglas. He had, in the eyes of this Southern garrison, the faculties of a fiend, rather than those of a mere mortal; for if the English soldiers cursed the tedium of the perpetual watch and ward upon the Dangerous Castle, which admitted of no relaxation from the severity of extreme duty, they agreed that a tall form was sure to appear to them with a battle-axe in his hand, and entering into conversation in the most insinuating manner, never failed, with an ingenuity and eloquence equal to that of a fallen spirit, to recommend to the discontented sentinel some mode in which, by giving his assistance to betray the English, he might set himself at liberty. The variety of these devices, and the frequency of their recurrence, kept Sir John de Walton's anxiety so perpetually upon the stretch, that he at no time thought himself exactly out of the Black Douglas's reach, any more than the good Christian supposes himself out of reach of the wiles of the Devil; while every new temptation, instead of confirming his hope, seems to announce that the immediate retreat of the Evil One will be followed by some new attack yet more cunningly devised. Under this general state of anxiety and apprehension, the temper of the governor changed somewhat

57

for the worse, and they who loved him best, regretted most that he became addicted to complain of the want of diligence on the part of those, who, neither invested with responsibility like his, nor animated by the hope of such splendid rewards, did not entertain the same degree of watchful and incessant suspicion as himself. The soldiers muttered that the vigilance of their governor was marked with severity; the officers and men of rank, of whom there were several, as the castle was a renowned school of arms, and there was a certain merit attained even by serving within its walls, complained, at the same time, that Sir John de Walton no longer made parties for hunting, for hawking, or for any purpose which might soften the rigours of warfare, and suffered nothing to go forward but the precise discipline of the castle. On the other hand, it may be usually granted that the castle is well kept where the governor is a disciplinarian; and where feuds and personal quarrels are found in the garrison, the young men are usually more in fault than those whose greater experience has convinced them of the necessity of using the strictest precautions.

A generous mind—and such was Sir John de Walton's—is often in this way changed and corrupted by the habit of over-vigilance, and pushed beyond its natural limits of candour. Neither was Sir Aymer de Valence free from a similar change; suspicion, though from a different cause, seemed also to threaten to bias his open and noble disposition, in those qualities which had hitherto been proper to him. It was in vain that Sir John de Walton studiously sought opportunities to give his younger friend indulgences, which at times were as far extended as the duty of the garrison permitted. The blow was struck; the alarm had been given to a proud and fiery temper on both sides; and while De Valence entertained an opinion that he was unjustly suspected by a friend, who was in several respects bound to him, De Walton, on the other hand, was led to conceive that a young man, of whom he took a charge as affectionate as if he had been a son of his own, and who owed to his lessons what he knew of warfare, and what success he had obtained in life, had taken offence at trifles, and considered himself ill-treated on very inadequate grounds. The seeds of disagreement, thus sown between them, failed not, like the tares sown by the Enemy among the wheat, to pass from one class of the garrison to another; the soldiers, though without any better reason than merely to pass the time, took different sides between their governor and his young lieutenant; and so the ball of contention being once thrown up between them, never lacked some arm or other to keep it in motion.

CHAPTER THE SIXTH.

Alas! they had been friends in youth;
But whispering tongues can poison truth;
And constancy lives in realms above;
  And life is thorny, and youth is vain;
And to be wroth with one we love,
  Doth work like madness in' the brain.
* * * * * *

Each spoke words of high disdain,
And insult to his heart's dear brother,
But never either found another
To free the hollow heart from paining—
They stood aloof, the scars remaining,
  Like cliffs which had been rent asunder;
A dreary sea now flows between,
  But neither heat, nor frost, nor thunder,
Shall wholly do away, I ween,
The marks of that which once hath been.
                CHRISTABELLE OF COLERIDGE.

In prosecution of the intention which, when his blood was cool, seemed to him wisest, Sir John de Walton resolved that he would go to the verge of indulgence with his lieutenant and his young officers, furnish them with every species of amusement which the place rendered possible, and make them ashamed of their discontent, by overloading them with courtesy. The first time, therefore, that he saw Aymer de Valence after his return to the castle, he addressed him in high spirits, whether real or assumed.

"What thinkest thou, my young friend," said De Walton, "if we try some of the woodland sports proper, they say, to this country? There are still in our neighbourhood some herds of the Caledonian breed of wild cattle, which are nowhere to be found except among the moorlands—the black and rugged frontier of what was anciently called the Kingdom of Strath-Clyde. There are some hunters, too, who have been accustomed to the sport, and who vouch that these animals are by far the most bold and fierce subjects of chase in the island of Britain."

"You will do as you please," replied Sir Aymer, coldly; "but it is not I, Sir John, who would recommend, for the sake of a hunting-match, that you should involve the whole garrison in danger; you know best the responsibilities incurred by your office here, and no doubt must have heedfully attended to them before making a proposal of such a nature."

59

"I do indeed know my own duty," replied De Walton, offended in turn, "and might be allowed to think of yours also, without assuming more than my own share of responsibility; but it seems to me as if the commander of this Dangerous Castle, among other inabilities, were, as old people in this country say, subjected to a spell—and one which renders it impossible for him to guide his conduct so as to afford pleasure to those whom he is most desirous to oblige. Not a great many weeks since, whose eyes would have sparkled like those of Sir Aymer de Valence at the proposal of a general hunting-match after a new object of game; and now what is his bearing when such sport is proposed, merely, I think, to disappoint my purpose of obliging him?—a cold acquiescence drops half frozen from his lips, and he proposes to go to rouse the wild cattle with an air of gravity, as if he were undertaking a pilgrimage to the tomb of a martyr."

"Not so, Sir John," answered the young knight. "In our present situation we stand conjoined in more charges than one, and although the greater and controlling trust is no doubt laid upon you as the elder and abler knight, yet still I feel that I myself have my own share of a serious responsibility. I trust, therefore, you will indulgently hear my opinion, and bear with it, even though it should appear to have relation to that part of our common charge which is more especially intrusted to your keeping. The dignity of knighthood, which I have the honour to share with you, the *accolade* laid on my shoulder by the royal Plantagenet, entitles me, methinks, to so much grace."

"I cry you mercy," said the elder cavalier; "I forgot how important a person I had before me, dubbed by King Edward himself, who was moved no doubt by special reasons to confer such an early honour; and I certainly feel that I overstep my duty when I propose any thing that savours like idle sport to a person of such grave pretensions."

"Sir John de Walton," retorted De Valence, "we have had something too much of this—let it stop here. All that I mean to say is, that in this wardship of Douglas Castle, it will not be by my consent, if any amusement, which distinctly infers a relaxation of discipline, be unnecessarily engaged in, and especially such as compels us to summon to our assistance a number of the Scots, whose evil disposition towards us we well know; nor will I, though my years have rendered me liable to such suspicion, suffer any thing of this kind to be imputed to me; and if unfortunately—though I am sure I know not why—we are in future to lay aside those bonds of familiar friendship which formerly linked us to each other, yet I see no reason why we should not bear ourselves in our necessary communications like knights and gentlemen, and put the best construction on each other's motives, since there can be no reason for imputing the worst to any thing that comes from either of us."

"You may be right, Sir Aymer de Valence," said the governor, bending stiffly: "and since you say we are no longer bound to each other as friends, you may be certain, nevertheless, that I will never permit a hostile feeling, of which you are the object, to occupy my bosom. You have been long, and I hope not uselessly, my pupil in the duties of chivalry. You are the near relation of the Earl of Pembroke, my kind and constant patron; and if these circumstances are well weighed, they form a connexion which it would be difficult, at least for me, to break through. If you feel yourself, as you seem to intimate, less strictly tied by former obligations, you must take your own choice in fixing our relations towards each other."

"I can only say," replied De Valence, "that my conduct will naturally be regulated by your own; and you, Sir John, cannot hope more devoutly than I do that our military duties may be fairly discharged, without interfering with our friendly intercourse."

The knights here parted, after a conference which once or twice had very nearly terminated in a full and cordial explanation; but still there was wanting one kind heartfelt word from either to break, as it were, the ice which was fast freezing upon their intercourse, and neither chose to be the first in making the necessary advances with sufficient cordiality, though each would have gladly done so, had the other appeared desirous of meeting it with the same ardour; but their pride was too high, and prevented either from saying what might at once have put them upon an open and manly footing. They parted, therefore, without again returning to the subject of the proposed diversion; until it was afterwards resumed in a formal note, praying Sir Aymer de Valence to accompany the commandant of Douglas Castle upon a solemn hunting-match, which had for its object the wild cattle of the neighbouring dale.

The time of meeting was appointed at six in the morning, beyond the gate of the outer barricade; and the chase was declared to be ended in the afternoon, when the *recheat* should be blown beneath the great oak, known by the name of Sholto's Club, which stood a remarkable object, where Douglas Dale was bounded by several scattered trees, the outskirts of the forest and hill country. The usual warning was sent out to the common people, or vassals of the district, which they, notwithstanding their feeling of antipathy, received in general with delight, upon the great Epicurean principle of *carpe diem*, that is to say, in whatever circumstances it happens to present itself, be sure you lose no recreation which life affords. A hunting-match has still its attractions, even though an English knight take his pleasure in the woods of the Douglas.

It was no doubt afflicting to these faithful vassals, to acknowledge

61

another lord than the redoubted Douglas, and to wait by wood and river at the command of English officers, and in the company of their archers, whom they accounted their natural enemies. Still it was the only species of amusement which had been permitted them for a long time, and they were not disposed to omit the rare opportunity of joining in it. The chase of the wolf, the wild boar, or even the timid stag, required silvan arms; the wild cattle still more demanded this equipment of war-bows and shafts, boar-spears and sharp swords, and other tools of the chase similar to those used in actual war. Considering this, the Scottish inhabitants were seldom allowed to join in the chase, except under regulations as to number and arms, and especially in preserving a balance of force on the side of the English soldiers, which was very offensive to them. The greater part of the garrison was upon such occasions kept on foot, and several detachments, formed according to the governor's direction, were stationed in different positions in case any quarrel should suddenly break out.

CHAPTER THE SEVENTH.

The drivers thorough the wood went,
  For to raise the deer;
Bowmen bickered upon the bent,
  With their broad arrows clear.
The wylde thorough the woods went,
  On every side shear;
Grehounds thorough the groves glent,
  For to kill thir deer.

BALLAD OF CHEVY CHASE, *Old Edit.*

The appointed morning came in cold and raw, after the manner of the Scottish March weather. Dogs yelped, yawned, and shivered, and the huntsmen, though hardy and cheerful in expectation of the day's sport, twitched their mauds, or Lowland plaids, close to their throats, and looked with some dismay at the mists which floated about the horizon, now threatening to sink down on the peaks and ridges of prominent mountains, and now to shift their position under the influence of some of the uncertain gales, which rose and fell alternately, as they swept along the valley.

Nevertheless, the appearance of the whole formed, as is usual in almost all departments of the chase, a gay and a jovial spectacle. A brief truce seemed to have taken place between the nations, and the Scottish people appeared for the time rather as exhibiting the sports of their mountains in a friendly manner to the accomplished knights and bonny archers of Old England, than as performing a feudal service, neither easy nor dignified in itself, at the instigation of usurping neighbours. The figures of the cavaliers, now half seen, now exhibited fully, and at the height, of

62

strenuous exertion, according to the character of the dangerous and broken ground, particularly attracted the attention of the pedestrians, who, leading the dogs or beating the thickets, dislodged such objects of chase as they found in the dingles, and kept their eyes fixed upon their companions, rendered more remarkable from being mounted, and the speed at which they urged their horses; the disregard of all accidents being as perfect as Melton-Mowbray itself, or any other noted field of hunters of the present day, can exhibit.

The principles on which modern and ancient hunting were conducted, are, however, as different as possible. A fox, or even a hare is, in our own day, considered as a sufficient apology for a day's exercise to forty or fifty dogs, and nearly as many men and horses; but the ancient chase, even though not terminating, as it often did, in battle, carried with it objects more important, and an interest immeasurably more stirring. If indeed one species of exercise can be pointed out as more universally exhilarating and engrossing than others, it is certainly that of the chase. The poor over-laboured drudge, who has served out his day of life, and wearied all his energies in the service of his fellow-mortals—he who has been for many years the slave of agriculture, or (still worse) of manufactures, engaged in raising a single peck of corn from year to year, or in the monotonous labours of the desk—can hardly remain dead to the general happiness when the chase sweeps past him with hound and horn, and for a moment feels all the exultation of the proudest cavalier who partakes the amusement. Let any one who has witnessed the sight recall to his imagination the vigour and lively interest which he has seen inspired into a village, including the oldest and feeblest of its inhabitants. In the words of Wordsworth, it is, on such occasions,

"Up, Timothy, up with your staff and away,
Not a soul will remain in the village to-day;
The hare has just started from Hamilton's grounds,
And Skiddaw is glad with the cry of the hounds."

But compare those inspiring sounds to the burst of a whole feudal population enjoying the sport, whose lives, instead of being spent in the monotonous toil of modern avocations, have been agitated by the hazards of war, and of the chase, its near resemblance, and you must necessarily suppose that the excitation is extended, like a fire which catches to dry heath. To use the common expression, borrowed from another amusement, all is fish that comes in the net on such occasions. An ancient hunting-match (the nature of the carnage excepted) was almost equal to a modern battle, when the strife took place on the surface of a varied and unequal country. A whole district poured forth its inhabitants, who formed a ring of great extent, called technically, a tinchel, and, advancing and narrowing their circle by degrees, drove before them the alarmed animals of every kind; all and each of which, as they burst from the thicket or the moorland, were objects of the bow, the javelin, or whatever missile weapons the hunters possessed; while others were run down and worried by large greyhounds, or more frequently brought to bay, when the more important persons present claimed for themselves the pleasure of putting them to death with their chivalrous hands, incurring individually such danger as is inferred from a mortal contest even with the timid buck, when he is brought to the death-struggle, and has no choice but yielding his life or putting himself upon the defensive, by the aid of his splendid antlers, and with all the courage of despair.

The quantity of game found in Douglas Dale on this occasion was very considerable, for, as already noticed, it was a long time since a hunting upon a great scale had been attempted under the Douglasses themselves, whose misfortunes had commenced several years before, with those of their country. The English garrison, too, had not sooner judged themselves strong or numerous enough to exercise these valued feudal privileges. In the meantime, the game increased considerably. The deer, the wild cattle, and the wild boars, lay near the foot of the mountains, and made frequent irruptions into the lower part of the valley, which in Douglas Dale bears no small resemblance to an oasis, surrounded by tangled woods, and broken moors, occasionally rocky, and showing large tracts of that bleak dominion to which wild creatures gladly escape when pressed by the neighbourhood of man.

As the hunters traversed the spots which separated the field from the wood, there was always a stimulating uncertainty what sort of game was to be found, and the marksman, with his bow ready bent, or his javelin poised, and his good and well-bitted horse thrown upon its haunches, ready for a sudden start, observed watchfully what should rush from the covert, so that, were it deer, boar, wolf, wild cattle, or any other species of game, he might be in readiness.

The wolf, which, on account of its ravages, was the most obnoxious of the beasts of prey, did not, however, supply the degree of diversion which his name promised; he usually fled far—in some instances many miles—before he took courage to turn to bay, and though formidable at such moments, destroying both dogs and men by his terrible bite, yet at other times was rather despised for his cowardice. The boar, on the other hand, was a much more irascible and courageous animal.

The wild cattle, the most formidable of all the tenants of the ancient Caledonian forest, were, however, to the English cavaliers, by far the most interesting objects of pursuit. [Footnote: These Bulls are thus described by Hector Boetius, concerning whom he says—"In this wood (namely the Caledonian wood) were sometime white bulls, with crisp and curling manes, like fierce lions; and though they seemed meek and tame in the remanent figure of their bodies, they were more wild than any other beasts, and had such hatred against the society and company of men, that they never came in the woods nor lesuries where they found any foot or hand thereof, and many days after they eat not of the herbs that were touched or handled by man. These bulls were so wild, that they were never taken but by slight and crafty labour, and so impatient, that after they were taken they died from insupportable dolour. As soon as any man, invaded these bulls, they rushed with such, terrible press upon him that they struck him to the earth, taking no fear of hounds, sharp lances, or other most penetrative weapons."—*Boetius, Chron. Scot.* Vol. I. page xxxix.

The wild cattle of this breed, which are now only known in one manor in England, that of Chillingham Castle, in Northumberland, (the seat of the Earl of Tankerville,) were, in the memory of man, still preserved in three places in Scotland, namely, Drumlanrig, Cumbernauld, and the upper park at Hamilton Palace, at all of which places, except the last, I believe, they have now been destroyed, on account of their ferocity. But though those of modern days are remarkable for their white colour, with black muzzles, and exhibiting, in a small degree, the black mane, about three or four inches long, by which the bulls in particular are distinguished, they do not by any means come near the terrific description given us by the ancient authors, which has made some naturalists think that these animals should probably be referred to a different species, though possessing the same general habits, and included in the same genus. The bones, which are often discovered in Scottish mosses, belong certainly to a race of animals much larger than those of Chillingham, which seldom grow to above 80 stone (of 14 lbs.), the general weight varying from 60 to 80 stone. We should be accounted very negligent by one class of readers, did we not record that the beef furnished by those cattle is of excellent flavour, and finely marbled.

[The following is an extract from, a letter received by Sir Walter Scott, some time after the publication of the novel.—

"When it is wished to kill any of the cattle at Chillingham, the keeper goes into the herd on horseback, in which way they are quite accessible, and singling out his victim, takes aim with a large rifle-gun, and seldom fails in bringing him down. If the poor animal makes much bellowing in his agony, and especially if the ground be stained with his blood, his companions become very furious, and are themselves, I believe, accessory to his death. After which, they fly off to a distant part of the park, and he is drawn away on a sledge. Lord Tankerville is very tenacious of these singular animals; he will on no account part with a living one, and hardly allows of a sufficient number being killed, to leave pasturage for those that remain.

"It happened on one occasion, three or four years ago, that a party visiting at the castle, among whom were some men of war, who had hunted buffaloes in foreign parts, obtained permission to do the keeper's work, and shoot one of the wild cattle. They sallied out on horseback, and duly equipped for the enterprise, attacked their object. The poor animal received several wounds, but none of them proving fatal, he retired before his pursuers, roaring with pain and rage, till, planting himself against a wall or tree, he stood at bay, offering a front of defiance. In this position the youthful heir of the castle, Lord Ossulston, rode up to give him the fatal shot. Though warned of the danger of approaching near to the enraged animal, and especially of firing without first having turned his horse's head in a direction to be ready for flight, he discharged his piece; but ere he could turn his horse round to make his retreat, the raging beast had plunged his immense horns into its flank. The horse staggered and was near falling, but recovering by a violent effort, he extricated himself from his infuriated pursuer, making off with all the speed his wasting strength supplied, his entrails meanwhile dragging on the ground, till at length he fell, and died at the same moment. The animal was now close upon his rear, and the young Lord would unquestionably have shared the fate of his unhappy steed, had not the keeper, deeming it full time to conclude the day's diversion, fired at the instant. His shot brought the beast to the ground, and running in with his large knife, he put a period to his existence.

"This scene of gentlemanly pastime was viewed from a turret of the castle by Lady Tankerville and her female visitors. Such a situation for the mother of the young hero, was anything but enviable."]] Altogether, the ringing of bugles, the clattering of horses' hoofs, the lowing and bellowing of the enraged mountain cattle, the sobs of deer mingled by throttling dogs, the wild shouts of exultation of the men,—made a chorus which extended far through the scene in which it arose, and seemed to threaten the inhabitants of the valley even in its inmost recesses.

During the course of the hunting, when a stag or a boar was expected, one of the wild cattle often came rushing forward, bearing down the young trees, crashing the branches in its progress, and in general dispersing whatever opposition was presented to it by the hunters. Sir John de Walton was the only one of the chivalry of the party who individually succeeded in mastering one of these powerful animals. Like a Spanish tauridor, he bore down and killed with his lance a ferocious bull; two well-grown calves and three kine were also slain, being unable to carry off the quantity of arrows, javelins, and other missiles, directed against them by the archers and drivers; but many others, in spite of every endeavour to intercept them, escaped to their gloomy haunts in the remote skirts of the mountain called Cairntable, with their hides well feathered with those marks of human enmity.

A large portion of the morning was spent in this way, until a particular blast from the master of the hunt announced that he had not forgot the discreet custom of the repast, which, on such occasions, was provided for upon a scale proportioned to the multitude who had been convened to attend the sport.

The blast peculiar to the time, assembled the whole party in an open space in a wood, where their numbers had room and accommodation to sit down upon the green turf, the slain game affording a plentiful supply for roasting or broiling, an employment in which the lower class were all immediately engaged; while puncheons and pipes, placed in readiness, and scientifically opened, supplied Gascoigne wine, and mighty ale, at the pleasure of those who chose to appeal to them.

The knights, whose rank did not admit of interference, were seated by themselves, and ministered to by their squires and pages, to whom such menial services were not accounted disgraceful, but, on the contrary, a proper step of their education. The number of those distinguished persons seated upon the present occasion at the table of dais, as it was called, (in virtue of a canopy of green boughs with which it was overshadowed,) comprehended Sir John de Walton, Sir Aymer de Valance, and some reverend brethren dedicated to the service of Saint Bride, who, though Scottish ecclesiastics, were treated with becoming respect by the English soldiers. One or two Scottish retainers, or vavasours, maintaining, perhaps in prudence, a suitable deference to the English knights, sat at the bottom of the table, and as many English archers, peculiarly respected by their superiors, were invited, according to the modern phrase, to the honours of the sitting.

Sir John de Walton sat at the head of the table; his eye, though it seemed to have no certain object, yet never for a moment remained stationary, but glanced from one countenance to another of the ring formed by his guests, for such they all were, no doubt, though he himself could hardly have told upon what principle he had issued the invitations; and even apparently was at a loss to think what, in one or two cases, had procured him the honour of their presence.

One person in particular caught De Walton's eye, as having the air of a redoubted man-at-arms, although it seemed as if fortune had not of late smiled upon his enterprises. He was a tall raw-boned man, of an extremely rugged countenance, and his skin, which showed itself through many a loophole in his dress, exhibited a complexion which must have endured all the varieties of an outlawed life; and akin to one who had, according to the customary phrase, "ta'en the bent with Robin Bruce," in other words occupied the moors with him as an insurgent. Some such idea certainly crossed De Walton's mind. Yet the apparent coolness, and absence of alarm, with which the stranger sat at the board of an English officer, at the same time being wholly in his power, had much in it which was irreconcilable with any such suggestion. De Walton, and several of those about him, had in the course of the day observed that this tattered cavalier, the most remarkable parts of whose garb and equipments consisted of an old coat-of-mail and a rusted yet massive partisan about eight feet long, was possessed of superior skill in the art of hunting to any individual of their numerous party. The governor having looked at this suspicious figure until he had rendered the stranger aware of the special interest which he attracted, at length filled a goblet of choice wine, and requested him, as one of the best pupils of Sir Tristem who had attended upon the day's chase, to pledge him in a vintage superior to that supplied to the general company.

"I suppose, however, sir," said De Walton, "you will have no objections to put off my challenge of a brimmer, until you can answer my pledge in Gascoigne wine, which grew in the king's own demesne, was pressed for his own lip, and is therefore fittest to be emptied to his majesty's health and prosperity."

"One half of the island of Britain," said the woodsman, with great composure, "will be of your honour's opinion; but as I belong to the other half, even the choicest liquor in Gascony cannot render that health acceptable to me."

A murmur of disapprobation ran through the warriors present; the priests hung their heads, looked deadly grave, and muttered their paternosters.

"You see, stranger," said De Walton sternly, "that your speech discomposes the company."

"It may be so," replied the man, in the same blunt tone; "and it may happen that there is no harm in the speech notwithstanding."

"Do you consider that it is made in my presence?" answered De Walton.

"Yes, Sir Governor."

"And have you thought what must be the necessary inference?" continued

De Walton.

"I may form a round guess," answered the stranger, "what I might have to

68

fear, if your safe conduct and word of honour, when inviting me to this hunting, were less trustworthy than I know full well it really is. But I am your guest—your meat is even now passing my throat—your cup, filled with right good wine, I have just now quaffed off—and I would not fear the rankest Paynim infidel, if we stood in such relation together, much less an English knight. I tell you, besides, Sir Knight, you undervalue the wine we have quaffed. The high flavour and contents of your cup, grow where it will, give me spirit to tell you one or two circumstances, which cold cautious sobriety would, in a moment like this, have left unsaid. You wish, I doubt not, to know who I am? My Christian name is Michael—my surname is that of Turnbull, a redoubted clan, to whose honours, even in the field of hunting or of battle, I have added something. My abode is beneath the mountain of Rubieslaw, by the fair streams of Teviot. You are surprised that I know how to hunt the wild cattle,—I, who have made them my sport from infancy in the lonely forests of Jed and Southdean, and have killed more of them than you or any Englishman in your host ever saw, even if you include the doughty deeds of this day."

The bold borderer made this declaration with the same provoking degree of coolness which predominated in his whole demeanour, and was indeed his principal attribute. His effrontery did not fail to produce its effect upon Sir John De Walton, who instantly called out, "To arms! to arms!—Secure the spy and traitor! Ho! pages and yeomen—William, Anthony, Bend-the-bow, and Greenleaf—seize the traitor, and bind him with your bow-strings and dog-leashes—bind him, I say, until the blood start from beneath his nails!"

"Here is a goodly summons!" said Turnbull, with a sort of horselaugh. "Were I as sure of being answered by twenty men I could name, there would be small doubt of the upshot of this day."

The archers thickened around the hunter, yet laid no hold on him, none of them being willing to be the first who broke the peace proper to the occasion.

"Tell me," said De Walton, "thou traitor, for what waitest thou here?"

"Simply and solely," said the Jed forester, "that I may deliver up to the Douglas the castle of his ancestors, and that I may ensure thee, Sir Englishman, the payment of thy deserts, by cutting that very throat which thou makest such a brawling use of."

At the same time, perceiving that the yeomen were crowding behind him to carry their lord's commands into execution so soon as they should be reiterated, the huntsman turned himself short round upon those who appeared about to surprise him, and having, by the suddenness of the action, induced them to step back a pace, he proceeded—"Yes, John de

Walton, my purpose was ere now to have put thee to death, as one whom I find in possession of that castle and territory which belong to my master, a knight much more worthy than thyself; but I know not why I have paused—thou hast given me food when I have hungered for twenty-four hours, I have not therefore had the heart to pay thee at advantage as thou hast deserved. Begone from this place and country, and take the fair warning of a foe; thou hast constituted thyself the mortal enemy of this people, and there are those among them who have seldom been injured or defied with impunity. Take no care in searching after me, it will be in vain,—until I meet thee at a time which will come at my pleasure, not thine. Push not your inquisition into cruelty, to discover by what means I have deceived you, for it is impossible for you to learn; and with this friendly advice, look at me and take your leave, for although we shall one day meet, it may be long ere I see you again."

De Walton remained silent, hoping that his prisoner, (for he saw no chance of his escaping,) might, in his communicative humour, drop some more information, and was not desirous to precipitate a fray with which the scene was likely to conclude, unconscious at the same time of the advantage which he thereby gave the daring hunter.

As Turnbull concluded his sentence, he made a sudden spring backwards, which carried him out of the circle formed around him, and before they were aware of his intentions, at once disappeared among the underwood.

"Seize him—seize him!" repeated De Walton: "let us have him at least at our discretion, unless the earth has actually swallowed him."

This indeed appeared not unlikely, for near the place where Turnbull had made the spring, there yawned a steep ravine, into which he plunged, and descended by the assistance of branches, bushes, and copsewood, until he reached the bottom, where he found some road to the outskirts of the forest, through which he made his escape, leaving the most expert woodsmen among the pursuers totally at fault, and unable to trace his footsteps.

CHAPTER THE EIGHTH.

This interlude carried some confusion into the proceedings of the hunt, thus suddenly surprised by the apparition of Michael Turnbull, an armed and avowed follower of the House of Douglas, a sight so little to be expected in the territory where his master was held a rebel and a bandit, and where he himself must have been well known to most of the peasantry present. The circumstance made an obvious impression on the English chivalry. Sir John de Walton looked grave and thoughtful, ordered the hunters to be assembled on the spot, and directed his soldiers to commence a strict search among the persons who had attended the chase, so as to discover whether Turnbull had any companions among them; but it was too late to make that enquiry in the strict fashion which De Walton directed.

The Scottish attendants on the chase, when they beheld that the hunting, under pretence of which they were called together, was interrupted for the purpose of laying hands upon their persons, and subjecting them to examination, took care to suit their answers to the questions put to them; in a word, they kept their own secret, if they had any. Many of them, conscious of being the weaker party, became afraid of foul play, slipt away from the places to which they had been appointed, and left the hunting-match like men who conceived they had been invited with no friendly intent. Sir John de Walton became aware of the decreasing numbers of the Scottish—their gradual disappearance awakening in the English knight that degree of suspicion which had of late become his peculiar characteristic.

"Take, I pray thee," said he to Sir Aymer de Valence, "as many men-at-arms as thou canst get together in five minutes' space, and at least a hundred of the mounted archers, and ride as fast as thou canst, without permitting them to straggle from thy standard, to reinforce the garrison of Douglas; for I have my own thoughts what may have been attempted on the castle, when we observe with our own eyes such a nest of traitors here assembled."

"With reverence, Sir John," replied Aymer, "you shoot in this matter rather beyond the mark. That the Scottish peasants have had bad thoughts against us, I will be the last to deny; but, long debarred from any silvan sport, you cannot wonder at their crowding to any diversion by wood or river, and still less at their being easily alarmed as to the certainty of the safe footing on which they stand with us. The least rough usage is likely to strike them with fear, and with the desire of escape, and so"—

"And so," said Sir John de Walton, who had listened with a degree of impatience scarce consistent with the grave and formal politeness which one knight was accustomed to bestow upon another, "and so I would rather see Sir Aymer de Valence busy his horse's heels to execute my orders, than give his tongue the trouble of impugning them."

At this sharp reprimand, all present looked at each other with indications of marked displeasure. Sir Aymer was highly offended, but saw it was no time to indulge in reprisal. He bowed until the feather which was in his barret-cap mingled with his horse's mane, and without reply—for he did not even choose to trust his voice in reply at the moment—headed a considerable body of cavalry by the straightest road back to the Castle of Douglas.

When he came to one of those eminences from which he could observe the massive and complicated towers and walls of the old fortress, with the glitter of the broad lake which surrounded it on three sides, he felt much pleasure at the sight of the great banner of England, which streamed from the highest part of the building. "I knew it," he internally said; "I was certain that Sir John de Walton had become a very woman in the indulgence of his fears and suspicions. Alas! that a situation of responsibility should so much have altered a disposition which I have known so noble and so knightly! By this good day, I scarce know in what manner I should demean me when thus publicly rebuked before the garrison. Certainly he deserves that I should, at some time or other, let him understand, that however he may triumph in the exercise of his short-lived command, yet, when man is to meet with man, it will puzzle Sir John de Walton to show himself the superior of Aymer de Valence, or perhaps to establish himself as his equal. But if, on the contrary, his fears, however fantastic, are sincere at the moment he expresses them, it becomes me to obey punctually commands which, however absurd, are imposed in consequence of the governor's belief that they are rendered necessary by the times, and not inventions designed to vex and domineer over his officers in the indulgence of his official powers. I would I knew which is the true statement of the case, and whether the once famed De Walton is become afraid of his enemies more than fits a knight, or makes imaginary doubts the pretext of tyrannizing over his friend. I cannot say it would make much difference to me, but I would rather have it that the man I once loved had turned a petty tyrant than a weak-spirited coward; and I would be content that he should study to vex me, rather than be afraid of his own shadow."

With these ideas passing in his mind, the young knight crossed the causeway which traversed the piece of water that fed the moat, and, passing under the strongly fortified gateway, gave strict orders for letting down the portcullis, and elevating the drawbridge, even at the appearance of De Walton's own standard before it.

A slow and guarded movement from the hunting-ground to the Castle of Douglas, gave the governor ample time to recover his temper, and to forget that his young friend had shown less alacrity than usual in obeying his commands. He was even disposed to treat as a jest the length of time and extreme degree of ceremony with which every point of martial discipline was observed on his own re-admission to the castle, though the raw air of a wet spring evening whistled around his own unsheltered person, and those of his followers, as they waited before the castle gate for the exchange of pass-words, the delivery of keys, and all the slow minutiae attendant upon the movements of a garrison in a well-guarded fortress.

"Come," said he to an old knight, who was peevishly blaming the lieutenant-governor, "it was my own fault; I spoke but now to Aymer de Valence with more authoritative emphasis than his newly-dubbed dignity was pleased with, and this precise style of obedience is a piece of not unnatural and very pardonable revenge. Well, we will owe him a return, Sir Philip—shall we not? This is not a night to keep a man at the gate."

This dialogue, overheard by some of the squires and pages, was bandied about from one to another, until it entirely lost the tone of good-humour in which it was spoken, and the offence was one for which Sir John de Walton and old Sir Philip were to meditate revenge, and was said to have been represented by the governor as a piece of mortal and intentional offence on the part of his subordinate officer.

Thus an increasing feud went on from day to day between two warriors, who, with no just cause of quarrel, had at heart every reason to esteem and love each other. It became visible in the fortress even to those of the lower rank, who hoped to gain some consequence by intermingling in the species of emulation produced by the jealousy of the commanding officers—an emulation which may take place, indeed, in the present day, but can hardly have the same sense of wounded pride and jealous dignity attached to it, which existed in times when the personal honour of knighthood rendered those who possessed it jealous of every punctilio.

So many little debates took place between the two knights, that Sir Aymer de Valence thought himself under the necessity of writing to his uncle and namesake, the Earl of Pembroke, stating that his officer, Sir John de Walton, had unfortunately of late taken some degree of prejudice against him, and that after having borne with many provoking instances of his displeasure, he was now compelled to request that his place of service should be changed from the Castle of Douglas, to wherever honour could be acquired, and time might be given to put an end to his present cause of complaint against his commanding officer. Through the whole letter, young Sir Aymer was particularly cautious how he expressed his sense of Sir John de Walton's jealousy or severe usage: but such sentiments are not easily concealed, and in spite of him an air of displeasure glanced out from several passages, and indicated his discontent with his uncle's old friend and companion in arms, and with the sphere of military duty which his uncle had himself assigned him. An accidental movement among the English troops brought Sir Aymer an answer to his letter sooner than he could have hoped for at that time of day, in the ordinary course of correspondence, which was then extremely slow and interrupted.

Pembroke, a rigid old warrior, entertained the most partial opinion of Sir John de Walton, who was a work as it were of his own hands, and was indignant to find that his nephew, whom he considered as a mere boy, elated by having had the dignity of knighthood conferred upon him at an age unusually early, did not absolutely coincide with him in this opinion. He replied to him, accordingly, in a tone of high displeasure, and expressed himself as a person of rank would write to a young and dependent kinsman upon the duties of his profession; and, as he gathered his nephew's cause of complaint from his own letter, he conceived that he did him no injustice in making it slighter than it really was. He reminded the young man that the study of chivalry consisted in the faithful and patient discharge of military service, whether of high or low degree, according to the circumstances in which war placed the champion. That above all, the post of danger, which Douglas Castle had been termed by common consent, was also the post of honour; and that a young man should be cautious how he incurred the supposition of being desirous of quitting his present honourable command, because he was tired of the discipline of a military director so renowned as Sir John de Walton. Much also there was, as was natural in a letter of that time, concerning the duty of young men, whether in council or in arms, to be guided implicitly by their elders; and it was observed, with justice, that the commanding officer, who had put himself into the situation of being responsible with his honour, if not his life, for the event of the siege or blockade, might, justly, and in a degree more than common, claim the implicit direction of the whole defence. Lastly, Pembroke reminded his nephew that he was, in a great measure, dependent upon the report of Sir John de Walton for the character which he was to sustain in after life; and reminded him, that a few actions of headlong and inconsiderate valour would not so firmly found his military reputation, as months and years spent in regular, humble, and steady obedience to the commands which the governor of Douglas Castle might think necessary in so dangerous a conjuncture.

This missive arrived within so short a time after the despatch of the letter to which it was a reply, that Sir Aymer was almost tempted to suppose that his uncle had some mode of corresponding with De Walton, unknown to the young knight himself, and to the rest of the garrison. And as the earl alluded to some particular displeasure which had been exhibited by De Valence on a late trivial occasion, his uncle's knowledge of this, and other minutiae, seemed to confirm his idea that his own conduct was watched in a manner which he did not feel honourable to himself, or dignified on the part of his relative; in a word, he conceived himself exposed to that sort of surveillance of which, in all ages, the young have accused the old. It hardly needs to say that the admonition of the Earl of Pembroke greatly chafed the fiery spirit of his nephew; insomuch, that if the earl had wished to write a letter purposely to increase the prejudices which he desired to put an end

74

to, he could not have made use of terms better calculated for that effect.

The truth was, that the old archer, Gilbert Greenleaf, had, without the knowledge of the young knight, gone to Pembroke's camp, in Ayrshire, and was recommended by Sir John de Walton to the earl, as a person who could give such minute information respecting Aymer de Valence, as he might desire to receive. The old archer was, as we have seen, a formalist, and when pressed on some points of Sir Aymer de Valence's discipline, he did not hesitate to throw out hints, which connected with those in the knight's letter to his uncle, made the severe old earl adopt too implicitly the idea that his nephew was indulging a spirit of insubordination, and a sense of impatience under authority, most dangerous to the character of a young soldier. A little explanation might have produced a complete agreement in the sentiments of both; but for this, fate allowed neither time nor opportunity; and the old earl was unfortunately induced to become a party, instead of a negotiator, in the quarrel,

"And by decision more embroil'd the fray."

Sir John de Walton soon perceived, that the receipt of Pembroke's letter did not in any respect alter the cold ceremonious conduct of his lieutenant towards him, which limited their intercourse to what their situation rendered indispensable, and exhibited no advances to any more frank or intimate connexion. Thus, as may sometimes be the case between officers in their relative situations even at the present day, they remained in that cold stiff degree of official communication, in which their intercourse was limited to as few expressions as the respective duties of their situation absolutely demanded. Such a state of misunderstanding is, in fact, worse than a downright quarrel;—the latter may be explained or apologized for, or become the subject of mediation; but in such a case as the former, an *eclaircissement* is as unlikely to take place as a general engagement between two armies which have taken up strong defensive positions on both sides. Duty, however, obliged the two principal persons in the garrison of Douglas Castle to be often together, when they were so far from seeking an opportunity of making up matters, that they usually revived ancient subjects of debate.

It was upon such an occasion that De Walton, in a very formal manner, asked De Valence in what capacity, and for how long time, it was his pleasure that the minstrel, called Bertram, should remain at the castle.

"A week," said the governor, "is certainly long enough, in this time and place, to express the hospitality due to a minstrel."

"Certainly," replied the young man, "I have not interest enough in the subject to form a single wish upon it."

"In that case," resumed De Walton, "I shall request of this person to cut short his visit at the Castle of Douglas."

"I know no particular interest," replied Aymer de Valence, "which I can possibly have in this man's motions. He is here under pretence of making some researches after the writings of Thomas of Erceldoun, called the Rhymer, which he says are infinitely curious, and of which there is a volume in the old Baron's study, saved somehow from the flames at the last conflagration. This told, you know as much of his errand as I do; and if you hold the presence of a wandering old man, and the neighbourhood of a boy, dangerous to the castle under your charge, you will no doubt do well to dismiss them—it will cost but a word of your mouth."

"Pardon me," said De Walton; "the minstrel came here as one of your retinue, and I could not, in fitting courtesy, send him away without your leave."

"I am sorry, then," answered Sir Aymer, "in my turn, that you did not mention your purpose sooner. I never entertained a dependent, vassal or servant, whose residence in the castle I would wish to have prolonged a moment beyond your honourable pleasure."

"I am sorry," said Sir John de Walton, "that we two have of late grown so extremely courteous that it is difficult for us to understand each other. This minstrel and his son come from we know not where, and are bound we know not whither. There is a report among some of your escort, that this fellow Bertram upon the way had the audacity to impugn, even to your face, the King of England's right to the crown of Scotland, and that he debated the point with you, while your other attendants were desired by you to keep behind and out of hearing."

"Hah!" said Sir Aymer, "do you mean to found on that circumstance any charge against my loyalty? I pray you to observe, that such an averment would touch mine honour, which I am ready and willing to defend to the last gasp."

"No doubt of it, Sir Knight," answered the governor; "but it is the strolling minstrel, and not the high-born English knight, against whom the charge is brought. Well! the minstrel comes to this castle, and he intimates a wish that his son should be allowed to take up his quarters at the little old convent of Saint Bride, where two or three Scottish nuns and friars are still permitted to reside, most of them rather out of respect to their order, than for any good will which they are supposed to bear the English or their sovereign. It may also be noticed that his leave was purchased by a larger sum of money, if my information be correct, than is usually to be found in the purses of travelling minstrels, a class of wanderers alike remarkable for their poverty and for their genius. What do you think of all this?"

"I?"—replied De Valence; "I am happy that my situation, as a soldier,

76

under command, altogether dispenses with my thinking of it at all. My post, as lieutenant of your castle, is such, that if I can manage matters so as to call my honour and my soul my own, I must think that quite enough of free-will is left at my command; and I promise you shall not have again to reprove, or send a bad report of me to my uncle, on that account."

"This is beyond sufferance!" said Sir John de Walton half aside, and then proceeded aloud—"Do not, for Heaven's sake, do yourself and me the injustice of supposing that I am endeavouring to gain an advantage over you by these questions. Recollect, young knight, that when you evade giving your commanding officer your advice when required, you fail as much in point of duty, as if you declined affording him the assistance of your sword and lance."

"Such being the case," answered De Valence, "let me know plainly on what matter it is that you require my opinion? I will deliver it plainly, and stand by the result, even if I should have the misfortune (a crime unpardonable in so young a man, and so inferior an officer) to differ from that of Sir John de Walton."

"I would ask you then. Sir Knight of Valence," answered the governor, "what is your opinion with respect to this minstrel, Bertram, and whether the suspicions respecting him and his son are not such as to call upon me, in performance of my duty, to put them to a close examination, with the question ordinary and extraordinary, as is usual in such cases, and to expel them not only from the castle, but from the whole territory of Douglas Dale, under pain of scourging, if they be again found wandering in these parts?"

"You ask me my opinion," said De Valence, "and you shall have it, Sir Knight of Walton, and freely and fairly, as if matters stood betwixt us on a footing as friendly as they ever did. I agree with you, that most of those who in this day profess the science of minstrelsy, are altogether unqualified to support the higher pretensions of that noble order. Minstrels by right, are men who have dedicated themselves to the noble occupation of celebrating knightly deeds and generous principles; it is in their verse that the valiant knight is handed down to fame, and the poet has a right, nay is bound, to emulate the virtues which he praises. The looseness of the times has diminished the consequence, and impaired the morality of this class of wanderers; their satire and their praise are now too often distributed on no other principle than love of gain; yet let us hope that there are still among them some who know, and also willingly perform, their duty. My own opinion is that this Bertram holds himself as one who has not shared in the degradation of his brethren, nor bent the knee to the mammon of the times; it must remain with you, sir, to judge whether such a person, honourably and morally disposed, can cause any danger to the Castle of Douglas. But believing, from the sentiments he has manifested to me, that he is incapable of playing the part of a traitor, I must strongly remonstrate against his being punished as one, or subjected to the torture within the walls of an English garrison. I should blush for my country, if it required of us to inflict such wanton misery upon wanderers, whose sole fault is poverty; and your own knightly sentiments will suggest more than would become me to state to Sir John de Walton, unless in so far as is necessary to apologize for retaining my own opinion."

Sir John de Walton's dark brow was stricken with red when he heard an opinion delivered in opposition to his own, which plainly went to stigmatize his advice as ungenerous, unfeeling, and unknightly. He made an effort to preserve his temper while he thus replied with a degree of calmness. "You have given your opinion, Sir Aymer de Valence; and that you have given it openly and boldly, without regard to my own, I thank you. It is not quite so clear that I am obliged to defer my own sentiments to yours, in case the rules on which I hold my office—the commands of the king—and the observations which I may personally have made, shall recommend to me a different line of conduct from that which you think it right to suggest."

De Walton bowed, in conclusion, with great gravity; and the young knight returning the reverence with exactly the same degree of stiff formality, asked whether there were any particular orders respecting his duty in the castle; and having received an answer in the negative took his departure.

Sir John de Walton, after an expression of impatience, as if disappointed at finding that the advance which he had made towards an explanation with his young friend had proved unexpectedly abortive, composed his brow as if to deep thought, and walked several times to and fro in the apartment, considering what course he was to take in these circumstances. "It is hard to censure him severely," he said, "when I recollect that, on first entering upon life, my own thoughts and feelings would have been the same with those of this giddy and hot-headed, but generous boy. Now prudence teaches me to suspect mankind in a thousand instances where perhaps there is not sufficient ground. If I am disposed to venture my own honour and fortune, rather than an idle travelling minstrel should suffer a little pain, which at all events I might make up to him by money, still, have I a right to run the risk of a conspiracy against the king, and thus advance the treasonable surrender of the Castle of Douglas, for which I know so many schemes are formed; for which, too, none can be imagined so desperate but agents will be found bold enough to undertake the execution? A man who holds my situation, although the slave of conscience, ought to learn to set aside those false scruples which assume the appearance of flowing from our own moral feeling, whereas they are in fact instilled by the suggestion of affected delicacy. I will not, I swear by Heaven, be infected by the follies of a boy, such as Aymer; I will not, that I may defer to his caprices, lose all that love, honour, and ambition can propose, for the reward of twelve months' service, of a nature the most watchful and unpleasant. I—will go straight to my point, and use the ordinary precautions in Scotland which I should employ in Normandy or Gascoigny.—What ho! page! who waits there?"

One of his attendants replied to his summons—"Seek me out Gilbert Greenleaf the archer, and tell him I would speak with him touching the two bows and the sheaf of arrows, concerning which I gave him a commission to Ayr."

A few minutes intervened after the order was given, when the archer entered, holding in his hand two bow-staves, not yet fashioned, and a number of arrows secured together with a thong. He bore the mysterious looks of one whose apparent business is not of very great consequence, but is meant as a passport for other affairs which are in themselves of a secret nature. Accordingly, as the knight was silent, and afforded no other opening for Greenleaf, that judicious negotiator proceeded to enter upon such as was open to him.

"Here are the bow-staves, noble sir, which you desired me to obtain while I was at Ayr with the Earl of Pembroke's army. They are not so good as I could have wished, yet are perhaps of better quality than could have been procured by any other than a fair judge of the weapon. The Earl of Pembroke's whole camp are frantic mad in order to procure real Spanish staves from the Groyne, and other ports in Spain; but though two vessels laden with such came into the port of Ayr, said to be for the King's army, yet I believe never one half of them have come into English hands. These two grew in Sherwood, which having been seasoned since the time of Robin Hood, are not likely to fail either in strength or in aim, in so strong a hand, and with so just an eye, as those of the men who wait on your worship."

"And who has got the rest, since two ships' cargoes of new bow-staves are arrived at Ayr, and thou with difficulty hast only procured me two old ones?" said the governor.

"Faith, I pretend not skill enough to know," answered Greenleaf, shrugging his shoulders. "Talk there is of plots in that country as well as here. It is said that their Bruce, and the rest of his kinsmen, intend a new May-game, and that the outlawed king proposes to land near Turnberry, early in summer, with a number of stout kernes from Ireland; and no doubt the men of his mock earldom of Garrick are getting them ready with bow and spear for so hopeful an undertaking. I reckon that it will not cost us the expense of more than a few score of sheaves of arrows to put all that matter to rights."

"Do you talk then of conspiracies in this part of the country, Greenleaf?" said De Walton. "I know you are a sagacious fellow, well bred for many a day to the use of the bent stick and string, and will not allow such a practice to go on under thy nose, without taking notice of it."

"I am old enough, Heaven knows," said Greenleaf, "and have had good experience of these Scottish wars, and know well whether these native Scots are a people to be trusted to by knight or yeoman. Say they are a false generation, and say a good archer told you so, who, with a fair aim, seldom missed a handsbreadth of the white. Ah! sir, your honour knows how to deal with them—ride them strongly, and rein them hard,—you are not like those simple novices who imagine that all is to be done by gentleness, and wish to parade themselves as courteous and generous to those faithless mountaineers, who never, in the course of their lives, knew any tincture either of courteousness or generosity."

"Thou alludest to some one," said the governor, "and I charge thee, Gilbert, to be plain and sincere with me. Thou knowest, methinks, that in trusting me thou wilt come to no harm?"

"It is true, it is true, sir," said the old remnant of the wars, carrying his hand to his brow, "but it were imprudent to communicate all the remarks which float through an old man's brain in the idle moments of such a garrison as this. One stumbles unawares on fantasies, as well as realities, and thus one gets, not altogether undeservedly, the character of a tale-bearer and mischief-maker among his comrades, and methinks I would not willingly fall under that accusation."

"Speak frankly to me," answered De Walton, "and have no fear of being misconstrued, whosoever the conversation may concern."

"Nay, in plain truth," answered Gilbert, "I fear not the greatness of this young knight, being, as I am, the oldest soldier in the garrison, and having drawn a bow-string long and many a day ere he was weaned from his nurse's breast."

"It is, then." said De Walton, "my lieutenant and friend, Aymer de Valence, at whom your suspicions point?"

"At nothing," replied the archer, "touching the honour of the young knight himself, who is as brave as the sword he wears, and, his youth considered, stands high in the roll of English chivalry; but he is young, as your worship knows, and I own that in the choice of his company he disturbs and alarms me."

"Why, you know, Greenleaf," answered the governor, "that in the leisure of a garrison a knight cannot always confine his sports and pleasures among those of his own rank, who are not numerous, and may not be so gamesome or fond of frolic, as he would desire them to be."

"I know that well," answered the archer, "nor would I say a word concerning your honour's lieutenant for joining any honest fellows, however inferior their rank, in the wrestling ring, or at a bout of quarterstaff. But if Sir Aymer de Valence has a fondness for martial tales of former days, methinks he had better learn them from the ancient soldiers who have followed Edward the First, whom God assoilzie, and who have known before his time the Barons' wars and Other onslaughts, in which the knights and archers of merry England transmitted so many gallant actions to be recorded by fame; this truly, I say, were more beseeming the Earl of Pembroke's nephew, than to see him closet himself day after day with a strolling minstrel, who gains his livelihood by reciting nonsense and lies to such young men as are fond enough to believe him, of whom hardly any one knows whether he be English or Scottish in his opinions, and still less can any one pretend to say whether he is of English or Scottish birth, or with what purpose he lies lounging about this castle, and is left free to communicate every thing which passes within it to those old mutterers of matins at St. Bride's, who say with their tongues God save King Edward, but pray in their hearts God save King Robert the Bruce. Such a communication he can easily carry on by means of his son, who lies at Saint Bride's cell, as your worship knows, under pretence of illness."

"How do you say?" exclaimed the governor, "under pretence?—is he not then really indisposed?"

"Nay, he may be sick to the death for aught I know," said the archer; "but if so, were it not then more natural that the father should attend his son's sick-bed, than that he should be ranging about this castle, where one eternally meets him in the old Baron's study, or in some corner, where you least expect to find him?"

"If he has no lawful object," replied the knight, "it might be as you say; but he is said to be in quest of ancient poems or prophecies of Merlin, of the Rhymer, or some other old bard; and in truth it is natural for him to wish to enlarge his stock of knowledge and power of giving amusement, and where should he find the means save in a study filled with ancient books?"

"No doubt," replied the Archer, with a sort of dry civil sneer of incredulity; "I have seldom known an insurrection in Scotland but that it was prophesied by some old forgotten rhyme, conjured out of dust and cobwebs, for the sake of giving courage to these North Country rebels, who durst not otherwise have abidden the whistling of the grey-goose shaft; but curled heads are hasty, and, with license, even your own train, Sir Knight, retains too much of the fire of youth for such uncertain times as the present."

"Thou hast convinced me, Gilbert Greenleaf, and I will look into this man's business and occupation more closely than hitherto. This is no time to peril the safety of a royal castle for the sake of affecting generosity towards a man of whom we know so little, and to whom, till we receive a very full explanation, we may, without doing him injustice, attach grave suspicions. Is he now in the apartment called the Baron's study?"

"Your worship will be certain to find him there," replied Greenleaf.

"Then follow me, with two or three of thy comrades, and keep out of sight, but within hearing; it may be necessary to arrest this man."

"My assistance," said the old archer, "shall be at hand when you call, but"—

"But what?" said the knight; "I hope I am not to find doubts and disobedience on all hands?"

"Certainly not on mine," replied Greenleaf; "I would only remind your worship that what I have said was a sincere opinion expressed in answer to your worship's question; and that, as Sir Aymer de Valence has avowed himself the patron of this man, I would not willingly be left to the hazard of his revenge."

"Pshaw" answered De Walton, "is Aymer de Valence governor of this castle, or am I? or to whom do you imagine you are responsible for answering such questions as I may put to you?"

"Nay," replied the archer, secretly not displeased at seeing De Walton show some little jealousy of his own authority, "believe me, Sir Knight, that I know my own station and your worship's, and that I am not now to be told to whom I owe obedience."

"To the study, then, and let us find the man," said the governor.

"A fine matter, indeed," subjoined Greenleaf, following him, "that your worship should have to go in person to look after the arrest of so mean an individual. But your honour is right; these minstrels are often jugglers, and possess the power of making their escape by means which borrel [Footnote: Unlearned.] folk like myself are disposed to attribute to necromancy."

Without attending to these last words, Sir John de Walton set forth towards the study, walking at a quick pace, as if this conversation had augmented his desire to find himself in possession of the person of the suspected minstrel.

Traversing the ancient passages of the castle, the governor had no difficulty in reaching the study, which was strongly vaulted with stone, and furnished with a sort of iron cabinet, intended for the preservation of articles and papers of value, in case of fire. Here he found the minstrel seated at a small table, sustaining before him a manuscript, apparently of great antiquity, from which he seemed engaged in making extracts. The windows of the room were very small, and still showed some traces that they had originally been glazed with a painted history of Saint Bride—another mark of the devotion of the great family of Douglas to their tutelar saint.

The minstrel, who had seemed deeply wrapped in the contemplation of his task, on being disturbed by the unlooked-for entrance of Sir John de Walton, rose with every mark of respect and humility, and, remaining standing in the governor's presence, appeared to wait for his interrogations, as if he had anticipated that the visit concerned himself particularly.

"I am to suppose, Sir Minstrel," said Sir John de Walton, "that you have been successful in your search, and have found the roll of poetry or prophecies that you proposed to seek after amongst these broken shelves and tattered volumes?"

"More successful than I could have expected," replied the minstrel, "considering the effects of the conflagration. This, Sir Knight, is apparently the fatal volume for which I sought, and strange it is, considering the heavy chance of other books contained in this library, that I have been able to find a few though imperfect fragments of it."

"Since, therefore, you have been permitted to indulge your curiosity," said the governor, "I trust, minstrel, you will have no objection to satisfy mine?"

The minstrel replied with the same humility, "that if there was any thing within the poor compass of his skill which could gratify Sir John de Walton in any degree, he would but reach his lute, and presently obey his commands."

"You mistake, Sir," said Sir John, somewhat harshly. "I am none of those who have hours to spend in listening to tales or music of former days; my life has hardly given me time enough for learning the duties of my profession, far less has it allowed me leisure for such twangling follies. I care not who knows it, but my ear is so incapable judging of your art, which you doubtless think a noble one, that I can scarcely tell the modulation of one tune from another."

"In that case," replied the minstrel composedly, "I can hardly promise myself the pleasure of affording your worship the amusement which I might otherwise have done."

"Nor do I look for any from your hand," said the governor, advancing a step nearer to him, and speaking in a sterner tone. "I want information, sir, which I am assured you can give me, if you incline; and it is my duty to tell you, that if you show unwillingness to speak the truth, I know means by which it will become my painful duty to extort it in a more disagreeable manner than I would wish."

"If your questions, Sir Knight," answered Bertram, "be such as I can or ought to answer, there shall be no occasion to put them more than once. If they are such as I cannot, or ought not to reply to, believe me that no threats of violence will extort an answer from me."

"You speak boldly," said Sir John de Walton; "but take my word for it, that your courage will be put to the test. I am as little fond of proceeding to such extremities as you can be of undergoing them, but such will be the natural consequence of your own obstinacy. I therefore ask you, whether Bertram be your real name—whether you have any other profession than that of a travelling minstrel—and, lastly, whether you have any acquaintance or connexion with any Englishman or Scottishman beyond the walls of this Castle of Douglas?"

"To these questions," replied the minstrel, "I have already answered the worshipful knight, Sir Aymer de Valence, and having fully satisfied him, it is not, I conceive, necessary that I should undergo a second examination; nor is it consistent either with your worship's honour, or that of the lieutenant-governor, that such a re-examination should take place."

"You are very considerate," replied the governor, "of my honour and of that of Sir Aymer de Valence. Take my word for it, they are both in perfect safety in our own keeping, and may dispense with your attention. I ask you, will you answer the enquiries which it is my duty to make, or am I to enforce obedience by putting you under the penalties of the question? I have already, it is my duty to say, seen the answers you have returned to my lieutenant, and they do not satisfy me."

He at the same time clapped his hands, and two or three archers showed themselves stripped of their tunics, and only attired in their shirts and hose.

"I understand," said the minstrel, "that you intend to inflict upon me a punishment which is foreign to the genius of the English laws, in that no proof is adduced of my guilt. I have already told that I am by birth an Englishman, by profession a minstrel, and that I am totally unconnected with any person likely to nourish any design against this Castle of Douglas, Sir John de Walton, or his garrison. What answers you may extort from me by bodily agony, I cannot, to speak as a plain-dealing Christian, hold myself responsible for. I think that I can endure as much pain as any one; I am sure that I never yet felt a degree of agony, that I would not willingly prefer to breaking my plighted word, or becoming a false informer against innocent persons: but I own I do not know the extent to which the art of torture may be carried; and though I do not fear you, Sir John de Walton, yet I must acknowledge that I fear myself, since I know not to what extremity your cruelty may be capable of subjecting me, or how far I may be enabled to bear it. I, therefore, in the first place, protest, that I shall in no manner be liable for any words which I may utter in the course of any examination enforced from me by torture; and you must therefore, under such circumstances, proceed to the execution of an office, which, permit me to say, is hardly that which I expected to have found thus administered by an accomplished knight like yourself."

"Hark you, sir," replied the governor, "you and I are at issue, and in doing my duty, I ought instantly to proceed to the extremities I have threatened; but perhaps you yourself feel less reluctance to undergo the examination as proposed, than I shall do in commanding it; I will therefore consign you for the present to a place of confinement, suitable to one who is suspected of being a spy upon this fortress. Until you are pleased to remove such suspicions, your lodgings and nourishment are those of a prisoner. In the meantime, before subjecting you to the question, take notice, I will myself ride to the Abbey of Saint Bride, and satisfy myself whether the young person whom you would pass as your son, is possessed of the same determination as that which you yourself seem to assert. It may so happen that his examination and yours may throw such light upon each other as will decidedly prove either your guilt or innocence, without its being confirmed by the use of the extraordinary question. If it be otherwise, tremble for your son's sake, if not for your own.—Have I shaken you, sir?— or do you fear, for your boy's young sinews and joints, the engines which, in your case, you seem willing to defy?"

"Sir," answered the minstrel, recovering from the momentary emotion he had shown, "I leave it to yourself, as a man of honour and candour, whether you ought, in common fairness, to form a worse opinion of any man, because he is not unwilling to incur, in his own person, severities which he would not desire to be inflicted upon his child, a sickly youth, just recovering from a dangerous disease."

"It is my duty," answered De Walton, after a short pause, "to leave no stone unturned by which this business may be traced to the source; and if thou desirest mercy for thy son, thou wilt thyself most easily attain it, by setting him the example of honesty and plain-dealing."

The minstrel threw himself back on the seat, as if fully resolved to bear every extremity that could be inflicted, rather than make any farther answer than he had already offered. Sir John de Walton himself seemed in some degree uncertain what might now be his best course. He felt an invincible repugnance to proceed, without due consideration, in what most people would have deemed the direct line of his duty, by inflicting the torture both upon father and son; but deep as was his sense of devotion towards the King, and numerous as were the hopes and expectations he had formed upon the strict discharge of his present high trust, he could not resolve upon having recourse at once to this cruel method of cutting the knot. Bertram's appearance was venerable, and his power of words not unworthy of his aspect and bearing. The governor remembered that Aymer de Valence, whose judgment in general it was impossible to deny, had described him as one of those rare individuals, who vindicated the honour of a corrupted profession by their personal good behaviour; and he acknowledged to himself, that there was gross cruelty and injustice in refusing to admit the prisoner to the credit of being a true and honest man, until, by way of proving his rectitude, he had strained every sinew, and crushed every joint in his body, as well as those of his son. "I have no touchstone," he said internally, "which can distinguish truth from falsehood; the Bruce and his followers are on the alert,-he has certainly equipped the galleys which lay at Rachrin during winter. This story, too, of Greenleaf, about arms being procured for a new insurrection, tallies strangely with the appearance of that savage-looking forester at the hunt; and all tends to show, that something is upon the anvil which it is my duty to provide against. I will, therefore, pass over no circumstance by which I can affect the mind through hope or fear; but, please God to give me light from any other source, I will not think it lawful to torment these unfortunate, and, it may yet be, honest men." He accordingly took his departure from the library, whispering a word to Greenleaf respecting the prisoner.

He had reached the outward door of the study, and his satellites had already taken the minstrel into their grasp, when the voice of the old man was heard calling upon De Walton to return for a single moment.

"What hast thou to say, sir?" said the governor; "be speedy, for I have already lost more time in listening to thee than I am answerable for; and so I advise thee for thine own sake"—

"I advise thee," said the minstrel, "for thine own sake, Sir John de Walton, to beware how thou dost insist on thy present purpose, by which thou thyself alone, of all men living,—will most severely suffer. If thou harmest a hair of that young man's head—nay, if thou permittest him to undergo any privation which it is in thy power to prevent, thou wilt, in doing so, prepare for thine own suffering a degree of agony more acute than anything else in this mortal world could cause thee. I swear by the most blessed objects of our holy religion; I call to witness that holy sepulchre, of which I have been an unworthy visitor, that I speak nothing but the truth, and that thou wilt one day testify thy gratitude for the part I am now acting. It is my interest, as well as yours, to secure you in the safe possession of this castle, although assuredly I know some things respecting it, and respecting your worship, which I am not at liberty to tell without the consent of that youth. Bring me but a note under his hand, consenting to my taking you into our mystery, and believe me, you will soon see those clouds charmed away; since there was never a doleful uncertainty which more speedily changed to joy, or a thunder-cloud of adversity which more instantly gave way to sunshine, than would then the suspicions which appear now so formidable."

He spoke with so much earnestness as to make some impression upon Sir John de Walton, who was once more wholly at a loss to know what line his duty called upon him to pursue.

"I would most gladly," said the governor, "follow out my purpose by the gentlest means in my power; and I shall bring no further distress upon this poor lad, than thine own obstinacy and his shall appear to deserve. In the meantime, think, Sir Minstrel, that my duty has limits, and if I slack it for a day, it will become thee to exert every effort in thy power to meet my condescension. I will give thee leave to address thy son by a line under thy hand, and I will await his answer before I proceed farther in this matter, which seems to be very mysterious. Meantime, as thou hast a soul to be saved, I conjure thee to speak the truth, and tell me whether the secrets of which thou seemest to be a too faithful treasurer, have regard to the practices of Douglas, of Bruce, or of any in their names, against this Castle of Douglas?"

The prisoner thought a moment, and then replied—"I am aware, Sir Knight, of the severe charge under which this command is intrusted to your hands, and were it in my power to assist you, as a faithful minstrel and loyal subject, either with hand or tongue, I should feel myself called upon so to do; but so far am I from being the character your suspicions have apprehended, that I should have held it for certain that the Bruce and Douglas had assembled their followers, for the purpose of renouncing their rebellious attempts, and taking their departure for the Holy Land, but for the apparition of the forester, who, I hear, bearded you at the hunting, which impresses upon me the belief, that when so resolute a follower and henchman of the Douglas was sitting fearless among you, his master and comrades could be at no great distance—how far his intentions could be friendly to you, I must leave it to yourself to judge; only believe me thus far, that the rack, pulley, or pincers, would not have compelled me to act the informer, or adviser, in a quarrel wherein I have little or no share, if I had not been desirous of fixing the belief upon you, that you are dealing with a true man, and one who has your welfare at heart.—Meanwhile, permit me to have writing materials, or let my own be restored, for I possess, in some degree, the higher arts of my calling; nor do I fear but that I can procure for you an explanation of these marvels, without much more loss of time."

"God grant it prove so," said the governor; "though I see not well how I can hope for so favourable a termination, and I may sustain great harm by trusting too much on the present occasion. My duty, however, requires that, in the meantime, you be removed into strict confinement."

He handed to the prisoner, as he spoke, the writing materials, which had been seized upon by the archers on their first entrance, and then commanded those satellites to unhand the minstrel.

"I must, then," said Bertram, "remain subjected to all the severities of a strict captivity; but I deprecate no hardship whatever in my own person, so I may secure you from acting with a degree of rashness, of which you will all your life repent, without the means of atoning."

"No more words, minstrel," said the governor; "but since I have made my choice, perhaps a very dangerous one for myself, let us carry this spell into execution, which thou sayest is to serve me, as mariners say that oil spread upon the raging billows will assuage their fury."

CHAPTER THE NINTH.

Beware! beware! of the black Friar,
He still retains his sway,
For he is yet the Church's heir by right,
Whoever may be the lay.
Amundeville is lord by day,
But the monk is lord by night,
Nor wine nor wassel could raise a vassal
To question that friar's right.
Don Juan, CANTO XVII.

The minstrel made no vain boast of the skill which he possessed in the use of pen and ink. In fact, no priest of the time could have produced his little scroll more speedily, more neatly composed, or more fairly written, than were the lines addressed "To the youth called Augustine, son of Bertram the Minstrel."

"I have not folded this letter," said he, "nor tied it with silk, for it is not expressed so as to explain the mystery to you; nor, to speak frankly, do I think that it can convey to you any intelligence; but it may be satisfactory to show you what the letter does not contain, and that it is written from and to a person, who both mean kindly towards you and your garrison."

"That," said the governor, "is a deception which is easily practised; it tends, however, to show, though not with certainty, that you are disposed to act upon good faith; and until the contrary appear, I shall consider it a point of duty to treat you with as much gentleness as the matter admits of. Meantime, I will myself ride to the Abbey of Saint Bride, and in person examine the young prisoner; and as you say he has the power, so I pray to Heaven he may have the will, to read this riddle, which seems to throw us all into confusion." So saying, he ordered his horse, and while it was getting ready, he perused with great composure the minstrel's letter. Its contents ran thus:—

"DEAR AUGUSTINE,

"Sir John de Walton, the governor of this castle, has conceived those suspicions which I pointed out as likely to be the consequence of our coming to this country without an avowed errand. I at least am seized, and threatened with examination under torture, to force me to tell the purpose of our journey; but they shall tear the flesh from my bones, ere they force me to break the oath which I have taken. And the purport of this letter is to apprize you of the danger in which you stand of being placed in similar circumstances, unless you are disposed to authorize me to make the discovery to this knight; but on this subject you are only to express your own wishes, being assured they shall be in every respect attended to by your devoted

"BERTRAM."

This letter did not throw the smallest light upon the mystery of the writer. The governor read it more than once, and turned it repeatedly in his hand, as if he had hoped by that mechanical process to draw something from the missive, which at a first view the words did not express; but as no result of this sort appeared, De Walton retired to the hall, where he informed Sir Aymer de Valence, that he was going abroad as far as the Abbey of Saint Bride, and that he would be obliged by his taking upon him the duties of governor during his absence. Sir Aymer, of course, intimated his acquiescence in the charge; and the state of disunion in which they stood to each other, permitted no further explanation.

Upon the arrival of Sir John de Walton at the dilapidated shrine, the abbot, with trembling haste, made it his business immediately to attend the commander of the English garrison, upon whom for the present, their house depended for every indulgence they experienced, as well as for the subsistence and protection necessary to them in so perilous a period. Having interrogated this old man respecting the youth residing in the Abbey, De Walton was informed that he had been indisposed since left there by his father, Bertram, a minstrel. It appeared to the abbot, that his indisposition might be of that contagious kind which, at that period, ravaged the English Borders, and made some incursions into Scotland, where it afterwards worked a fearful progress. After some farther conversation, Sir John de Walton put into the abbot's hand the letter to the young person under his roof, on delivering which to Augustine, the reverend father was charged with a message to the English governor, so bold, that he was afraid to be the bearer of it. It signified, that the youth could not, and would not, at that moment, receive the English knight; but that, if he came back on the morrow after mass, it was probable he might learn something of what was requested.

"This is not an answer," said Sir John de Walton, "to be sent by a boy like this to a person in my charge; and me thinks, Father Abbot, you consult your own safety but slenderly in delivering such an insolent message."

The abbot trembled under the folds of his large coarse habit; and De Walton, imagining that his discomposure was the consequence of guilty fear, called upon him to remember the duties which he owed to England, the benefits which he had received from himself, and the probable consequence of taking part in a pert boy's insolent defiance of the power of the governor of the province.

The abbot vindicated himself from these charges with the utmost anxiety. He pledged his sacred word, that the inconsiderate character of the boy's message was owing to the waywardness arising from indisposition. He reminded the governor that, as a Christian and an Englishman, he had duties to observe towards the community of Saint Bride, which had never given the English government the least subject of complaint. As he spoke, the churchman seemed to gather courage from the immunities of his order. He said he could not permit a sick boy who had taken refuge within the sanctuary of the Church, to be seized or subjected to any species of force, unless he was accused of a specific crime, capable of being immediately proved. The Douglasses, a headstrong race, had, in former days, uniformly respected the sanctuary of Saint Bride, and it was not to be supposed that the king of England, the dutiful and obedient child of the Church of Rome, would act with less veneration for her rights, than the followers of a usurper, homicide, and excommunicated person like Robert Bruce.

Walton was considerably shaken with this remonstrance. He knew that, in the circumstances of the times, the Pope had great power in every controversy in which it was his pleasure to interfere. He knew that even in the dispute respecting the supremacy of Scotland, his Holiness had set up a claim to the kingdom which, in the temper of the times, might perhaps have been deemed superior both to that of Robert Bruce, and that of Edward of England, and he conceived his monarch would give him little thanks for any fresh embroilment which might take place with the Church. Moreover, It was easy to place a watch, so as to prevent Augustine from escaping during the night; and on the following morning he would be still as effectually in the power of the English governor as if he were seized on by open force at the present moment. Sir John de Walton, however, so far exerted his authority over the abbot, that he engaged, in consideration of the sanctuary being respected for this space of time, that, when it expired, he would be aiding and assisting with his spiritual authority to surrender the youth, should he not allege a sufficient reason to the contrary. This arrangement, which appeared still to flatter the governor with the prospect of an easy termination of this troublesome dispute, induced him to grant the delay which Augustine rather demanded than petitioned for.

"At your request, Father Abbot, whom I have hitherto found a true man, I will indulge this youth with the grace he asks, before taking him into custody, understanding that he shall not be permitted to leave this place; and thou art to be responsible to this effect, giving thee, as is reasonable, power to command our little, garrison at Hazelside, to which I will send a reinforcement on my return to the Castle, in case it should be necessary to use the strong hand, or circumstances impose upon me other measures."

"Worthy Sir Knight," replied the Abbot, "I have no idea that the frowardness of this youth will render any course necessary, saving that of persuasion; and I venture to say, that you yourself will in the highest degree approve of the method in which I shall acquit myself of my present trust."

The abbot went through the duties of hospitality, enumerating what simple cheer the cloister of the convent permitted him to offer to the English knight. Sir John de Walton declined the offer of refreshment, however—took a courteous leave of the churchman, and did not spare his horse until the noble animal had brought him again before the Castle of Douglas. Sir Aymer De Valence met him on the drawbridge, and reported the state of the garrison to be the same in winch he had left it, excepting that intimation had been received that twelve or fifteen men were expected on their way to the town of Lanark; and being on march from the neighbourhood of Ayr, would that night take up their quarters at the outpost of Hazelside.

"I am glad of it," replied the governor; "I was about to strengthen that detachment. This stripling, the son of Bertram the minstrel, or whoever he is, has engaged to deliver himself up for examination in the morning. As this party of soldiers are followers of your uncle, Lord Pembroke, may I request you will ride to meet them, and command them to remain at Hazelside until you make farther enquiries about this youth, who has still to clear up the mystery which hangs about him, and reply to a letter which I delivered with my own hand to the Abbot of Saint Bride. I have shown too much forbearance in this matter, and I trust to your looking to the security of this young man, and conveying him hither, with all due care and attention, as being a prisoner of some importance."

"Certainly, Sir John," answered Sir Aymer; "your orders shall be obeyed, since you have none of greater importance for one who hath the honour to be second only to yourself in this place."

"I crave your mercy, Sir Aymer," returned the governor, "if the commission be in any degree beneath your dignity; but it is our misfortune to misunderstand each other, when we endeavour to be most intelligible."

"But what am I to do," said Sir Aymer—"no way disputing your command, but only asking for information—what am I to do, if the Abbot of Saint Bride offers opposition?"

"How!" answered Sir John de Walton; "with the reinforcement from. my Lord of Pembroke, you will command at least twenty war-men, with bow and spear, against five or six timid old monks, with only gown and, hood."

"True," said Sir Aymer, "but ban and excommunication are sometimes; In the present day, too hard for the mail coat, and I would not willingly be thrown out of the pale of the Christian Church."

"Well, then, thou very suspicious and scrupulous young man," replied De Walton, "know that if this youth does not deliver himself up to thee of his own accord, the abbot has promised to put him into thy hands."

There was no farther answer to be made, and De Valence, though still thinking himself unnecessarily harassed with the charge of a petty commission, took the sort of half arms which were always used when the knights stirred, beyond the walls of the garrison, and proceeded to execute the commands of De Walton. A horseman or two, together with his squire Fabian, accompanied him.

The evening closed in with one of those Scottish mists which are commonly said to be equal to the showers of happier climates; the path became more and more dark, the hills more wreathed in vapours, and more difficult to traverse; and all the little petty inconveniences which rendered travelling through the district slow and uncertain, were augmented by the density of the fog which overhung every thing.

Sir Aymer, therefore, occasionally mended his pace, and often incurred the fate of one who is over-late, delaying himself by his efforts to make greater expedition. The knight bethought himself that he would get into a straight road by passing through the almost deserted town of Douglas—the inhabitants of which had been treated so severely by the English, in the course of those fierce troubles, that most of them who were capable of bearing arms had left it, and withdrawn themselves to different parts of the country. This almost deserted place was defended by a rude palisade, and a ruder drawbridge, which gave entrance into streets so narrow, as to admit with difficulty three horses abreast, and evincing with what strictness the ancient lords of the village adhered to their prejudice against fortifications, and their opinion in favour of keeping the field, so quaintly expressed in the well-known proverb of the family,—"It is better to hear the lark sing than the mouse cheep." The streets, or rather the lanes, were dark, but for a shifting gleam of moonlight, which, as that planet began to rise, was now and then visible upon some steep and narrow gable. No sound of domestic industry, or domestic festivity, was heard, and no ray of candle or firelight glanced from the windows of the houses; the ancient ordinance called the curfew, which the Conqueror had introduced into England, was at this time in full force in such parts of Scotland as were thought doubtful, and likely to rebel; under which description it need not be said the ancient possessions of the Douglas were most especially regarded. The Church, whose Gothic monuments were of a magnificent character, had been, as far as possible, destroyed by fire; but the ruins, held together by the weight of the massive stones of which they were composed, still sufficiently evinced the greatness of the family at whose cost it had been raised, and whose bones, from immemorial time, had been entombed in its crypts.

Paying little attention to these relics of departed splendour, Sir Aymer de Valence advanced with his small detachment, and had passed the scattered fragments of the cemetery of the Douglasses, when to his surprise, the noise of his horse's feet was seemingly replied to by sounds which rung like those of another knightly steed advancing heavily up the street, as if it were to meet him. Valence was unable to conjecture what might be the cause of these warlike sounds; the ring and the clang of armour was distinct, and the heavy tramp of a war-horse was not to be mistaken by the ear of a warrior. The difficulty of keeping soldiers from straying out of quarters by night, would have sufficiently accounted for the appearance of a straggling foot-soldier; but it was more difficult to account for a mounted horseman, in full armour; and such was the apparition which a peculiarly bright glimpse of moonlight now showed at the bottom of the causewayed hill. Perhaps the unknown warrior obtained at the same time a glance of Aymer de Valence and his armed followers—at least each of them shouted "Who goes there?"—the alarm of the times; and on the instant the deep answers of "St. George!" on the one side, and "The Douglas!" on the other, awakened the still echoes of the small and ruinous street, and the silent arches of the dilapidated church. Astonished at a war-cry with which so many recollections were connected, the English knight spurred his horse at full gallop down the steep and broken descent leading out at the south or south-east gate of the town; and it was the work of an instant to call out, "Ho! Saint George! upon the insolent villain all of you!—To the gate, Fabian, and cut him off from flight! —Saint George! I say, for England! Bows and bills!—bows and bills!" At the same time Aymer de Valence laid in rest his own long lance, which he snatched from the squire by whom it was carried. But the light was seen and gone in an instant, and though De Valence concluded that the hostile warrior had hardly room to avoid his career, yet he could take no aim for the encounter, unless by mere guess, and continued to plunge down the dark declivity, among shattered stones and other encumbrances, without groping out with his lance the object of his pursuit. He rode, in short, at a broken gallop, a descent of about fifty or sixty yards, without having any reason to suppose that he had met the figure which had appeared to him, although the narrowness of the street scarcely admitted his having passed him, unless both horse and horseman could have melted at the moment of encounter like an air-bubble. The riders of his suite, meanwhile, were struck with a feeling like supernatural terror, which a number of singular adventures, had caused most of them to attach to the name of Douglas; and when he reached the gate by which the broken street was terminated, there was none close behind him but Fabian, in whose head no suggestions of a timorous nature could outlive the sound of his dear master's voice.

Here there were a post of English, archers, who were turning out in considerable alarm, when De Valence and his page rode in amongst them. "Villains!" shouted De Valence, "why were you not upon your duty? Who was it passed through your post even now, with the traitorous cry of Douglas?"

"We know of no such," said the captain of the watch.

"That is to say, you besotted villains," answered the young knight, "you have been drinking, and have slept?"

The men protested the contrary, but in a confused manner, which was far from overcoming De Valence's suspicions. He called loudly to bring cressets, torches, and candles; and a few remaining inhabitants began to make their unwilling appearance, with such various means of giving light as they chanced to possess. They heard the story of the young English knight with wonder; nor, although it was confirmed by all his retinue, did they give credit to the recital, more than that the Englishmen wished somehow or other to pick a quarrel with the people of the palace, under the pretence of their having admitted a retainer of their ancient lord by night into the town. They protested, therefore, their innocence of the cause of tumult, and endeavoured to seem active in hastening from house to house, and corner to corner, with their torches, in order to discover the invisible cavalier. The English suspected them no less of treachery, than the Scottish imagined the whole matter a pretext for bringing an accusation, on the part of the young knight, against the citizens. The women, however, who now began to issue from the houses, had a key for the solution of the apparition, which at that time was believed of efficacy sufficient to solve any mystery. "The devil," they said, "must have appeared visibly amongst them," an explanation which had already occurred to the followers of the young knight; for that a living man and horse, both as it seemed, of a gigantic size, could be conjured in the twinkling of an eye, and appear in a street secured at one end by the best of the archers, and at the other by the horsemen under Valence himself, was altogether, it seemed, a thing impossible. The inhabitants did not venture to put their thoughts on the subject into language, for fear of giving offence, and only indicated by a passing word to each other the secret degree of pleasure which they felt in the confusion and embarrassment of the English garrison. Still, however, they continued to affect a great deal of interest in the alarm which De Valence had received, and the anxiety which he expressed to discover the cause.

At length a female voice spoke above the Babel of confused sounds, saying, "Where is the Southern Knight? I am sure that I can tell him where he can find the only person who can help him out of his present difficulty."

"And who is that, good woman?" said Aymer de Valence, who was growing every moment more impatient at the loss of time, which was flying fast, in an investigation which had something vexatious in it, and even ridiculous. At the same time, the sight of an armed partisan of the Douglasses, in their own native town, seemed to bode too serious consequences, if it should be suffered to pass without being probed to the bottom.

"Come hither to me," said the female voice, "and I will name to you the only person who can explain all matters of this kind that chance in this country." On this the knight snatched a torch from some of those who were present, and holding it up, descried the person who spoke, a tall woman, who evidently endeavoured to render herself remarkable. When he approached her, she communicated her intelligence in a grave and sententious tone of voice.

"We had once wise men, that could have answered any parables which might have been put to them for explanation in this country side. Whether you yourselves, gentlemen, have not had some hand in weeding them out, good troth, it is not for the like of me to say; at any rate, good counsel is not so easy come by as it was in this Douglas country, nor, may be, is it a safe thing to pretend to the power of giving it."

"Good woman," said De Valence, "if you will give me an explanation of this mystery, I will owe you a kirtle of the best raploch grey."

"It is not I," said the old woman, "that pretend to possess the knowledge which may assist you; but I would fain know that the man whom I shall name to you shall be skaithless and harmless. Upon your knighthood and your honour, will you promise to me so much?"

"Assuredly," said De Valence, "such a person shall even have thanks and reward, if he is a faithful informer; ay, and pardon, moreover, although he may have listened to any dangerous practices, or been concerned in any plots."

"Oh! not he," replied the female; "it is old Goodman Powheid, who has the charge of the muniments," (meaning probably monuments,) "that is, such part of them as you English have left standing; I mean the old sexton of the kirk of Douglas, who can tell more stories of these old folk, whom your honour is not very fond of hearing named, than would last us from this day to Yule."

"Does anybody," said the knight, "know whom it is that this old woman means?"

"I conjecture," replied Fabian, "that she speaks of an old dotard, who is, I think, the general referee concerning the history and antiquities of this old town, and of the savage family that lived here perhaps before the flood."

"And who, I dare say," said the knight, "knows as much about the matter as she herself does. But where is this man? a sexton is he? He may be acquainted with places of concealment, which are often fabricated in Gothic buildings, and known to those whose business calls them to frequent them. Come, my good old dame, bring this man to me; or, what may be better, I will go to him, for we have already spent too much time."

"Time!" replied the old woman,—"is time an object with your honour? I am sure I can hardly get so much for mine as will hold soul and body together. You are not far from the old man's house."

She led the way accordingly, blundering over heaps of rubbish, and encountering all the embarrassments of a ruinous street, in lighting the way to Sir Aymer, who, giving his horse to one of his attendants, and desiring Fabian to be ready at a call, scrambled after as well as the slowness of his guide would permit.

Both were soon involved in the remains of the old church, much dilapidated as it had been by wanton damage done to it by the soldiery, and so much impeded by rubbish, that the knight marvelled how the old woman could find the way. She kept talking all the while as she stumbled onward. Sometimes she called out in a screeching tone, "Powheid! Lazarus Powheid!"—and then muttered—"Ay, ay, the old man will be busy with some of his duties, as he calls them; I wonder he fashes wi' them in these times. But never mind, I warrant they will last for his day and for mine; and the times, Lord help us! for all that I can see, are well enough for those that are to live in them."

"Are you sure, good woman," replied the knight, "that there is any inhabitant in these ruins? For my part, I should rather suppose that you are taking me to the charnel-house of the dead."

"Maybe you are right," said the old woman, with a ghastly laugh; "carles and carlines agree weel with funeral vaults and charnel-houses, and when an auld bedral dwells near the dead, he is living, ye ken, among his customers—Halloo! Powheid! Lazarus Powheid! there is a gentleman would speak with you;" and she added, with some sort of emphasis, "an. English noble gentleman—-one of the honourable garrison."

An old man's step was now heard advancing, so slowly that the glimmering light which he held in his hand was visible on the ruined walls of the vault some time before it showed the person who bore it.

The shadow of the old man was also projected upon the illuminated wall ere his person came in view; his dress was in considerable confusion, owing to his having been roused from his bed; and since artificial light was forbidden by the regulations of the garrison, the natives of Douglas Dale spent in sleep the time that they could not very well get rid of by any other means. The sexton was a tall thin man, emaciated by years and by privations; his body was bent habitually by his occupation of grave-digging, and his eye naturally inclined downward to the scene of his labours. His hand sustained the cruise or little lamp, which he held so as to throw light upon his visitant; at the same time it displayed to the young knight the features of the person with whom he was now confronted, which, though neither handsome nor pleasing, were strongly marked, sagacious, and venerable, indicating, at the same time, a certain air of dignity, which age, even mere poverty, may be found occasionally to bestow, as conferring that last melancholy species of independence proper to those whose situation can hardly by any imaginable means, be rendered much worse than years and fortune have already made it. The habit of a lay brother added somewhat of religious importance to his appearance.

"What would you with me, young man?" said the sexton. "Your youthful features, and your gay dress, bespeak one who stands in need of my ministry neither for himself nor for others."

"I am indeed," replied the knight, "a living man, and therefore need not either shovel or pick-axe for my own behoof. I am not, as you see, attired in mourning, and therefore need not your offices in behalf of any friend; I would only ask you a few questions."

"What you would have done must needs be done, you being at present one of our rulers, and, as I think, a man of authority," replied the sexton;

"follow me this way into my poor habitation; I have had a better in my day; and yet, Heaven knows, it is good enough for me, when many men of much greater consequence must perforce content themselves with worse."

He opened a lowly door, which was fitted, though irregularly, to serve as the entrance of a vaulted apartment, where it appeared that the old man held, apart from the living world, his wretched and solitary dwelling. [Footnote: [This is a most graphic and accurate description of the present state of the ruin. Its being occupied by the sexton as a dwelling-place, and the whole scene of the old man's interview with De Valence, may be classed with our illustrious author's most felicitous imaginings.—*Note by the Rev. Mr. Stewart of Douglas.*]] The floor, composed of paving stones, laid together with some accuracy, and here and there inscribed with letters and hieroglyphics, as if they had once upon a time served to distinguish sepulchres, was indifferently well swept, and a fire at the upper end directed its smoke into a hole which served for a chimney. The spade and pick-axe, (with other tools,) which the chamberlain of mortality makes use of, lay scattered about the apartment, and, with a rude stool or two, and a table, where some inexperienced hand had unquestionably supplied the labours of the joiner, were nearly the only furniture, if we include the old man's bed of straw, lying in a corner, and discomposed, as if he had been just raised from it. At the lower end of the apartment, the wall was almost entirely covered by a large escutcheon, such as is usually hung over the graves of men of very high rank, having the appropriate quarters, to the number of sixteen, each properly blazoned and distinct, placed as ornaments around the principal armorial coat itself.

"Let us sit," said the old man; "the posture will better enable my failing ears to apprehend your meaning, and the asthma will deal with me more mercifully in permitting me to make you understand mine."

A peal of short asthmatic coughs attested the violence of the disorder which he had last named, and the young knight followed his host's example, in sitting down on one of the rickety stools by the side of the fire. The old man brought from one corner of the apartment an apron, which he occasionally wore, full of broken boards in irregular pieces, some of which were covered with black cloth, or driven full of nails, black, as it might happen, or gilded.

"You will find this fresh fuel necessary," said the old man, "to keep some degree of heat within this waste apartment; nor are the vapours of mortality, with which this vault is apt to be filled, if the fire is permitted to become extinct, indifferent to the lungs of the dainty and the healthy, like your worship, though to me they are become habitual. The wood will catch fire, although it is some time ere the damps of the grave are overcome by the drier air, and the warmth of the chimney."

Accordingly, the relics of mortality with which the old man had heaped his fireplace, began by degrees to send forth a thick unctuous vapour, which at length leaped to light, and blazing up the aperture, gave a degree of liveliness to the gloomy scene. The blazonry of the huge escutcheon met and returned the rays with as brilliant a reflection as that lugubrious object was capable of, and the whole apartment looked with a fantastic gaiety, strangely mingled with the gloomy ideas which its ornaments were calculated to impress upon the imagination.

"You are astonished," said the old man, "and perhaps, Sir Knight, you have never before seen these relics of the dead applied to the purpose of rendering the living, in some degree, more comfortable than their condition would otherwise admit of."

"Comfortable!" returned the Knight of Valence, shrugging his shoulders; "I should be sorry, old man, to know that I had a dog that was as indifferently quartered as thou art, whose grey hairs have certainly seen better days."

"It may be," answered the sexton, "and it may be otherwise; but it was not, I presume, concerning my own history that your worship seemed disposed to ask me some questions; and I would venture to enquire, therefore, to whom they have relation?"

"I will speak plainly to you," replied Sir Aymer, "and you will at once acknowledge the necessity of giving a short and distinct reply. I have even now met in the streets of this village a person only shown to me by a single flash of light, who had the audacity to display the armorial insignia and utter the war-cry of the Douglasses; nay, if I could trust a transient glance, this daring cavalier had the features and the dark complexion proper to the Douglas. I am referred to thee as to one who possesses means of explaining this extraordinary circumstance, which, as an English knight, and one holding a charge under King Edward, I am particularly called upon to make enquiry into."

"Let me make a distinction," said the old man. "The Douglasses of former generations are my near neighbours, and, according to my superstitious townsmen, my acquaintances and visitors; I can take it upon my conscience to be answerable for their good behaviour, and to become bound that none of the old barons, to whom the roots of that mighty tree may, it is said, be traced, will again disturb with their war-cry the towns or villages of their native country—not one will parade in moonshine the black armour which has long rusted upon their tombs.

'The knights are dust.
And their good swords are rust;

Their souls are with the saints, we trust.' [Footnote: [The author has somewhat altered part of a beautiful unpublished fragment of Coleridge:—

"Where is the grave of Sir Arthur Orellan,—
Where may the grave of that good knight be?
By the marge of a brook, on the slope of Helvellyn,
Under the boughs of a young birch tree.
The Oak that in summer was pleasant to hear,
That rustled in Autumn all withered and sear,
That whistled and groan'd thro' the Winter alone,
He hath gone, and a birch in his place is grown.
The knight's bones are dust,
His good sword is rust;
His spirit is with, the saints, we trust." *Edit.*]]

Look around, Sir Knight, you have above and around you the men of whom we speak. Beneath us, in a little aisle, (which hath not been opened since these thin grey locks were thick and brown,) there lies the first man whom I can name as memorable among those of this mighty line. It is he whom the Thane of Athol pointed out to the King of Scotland as Sholto Dhuglass, or the dark iron-coloured man, whose exertions had gained the battle for his native prince; and who, according to this legend, bequeathed his name to our dale and town, though others say that the race assumed the name of Douglass from the stream so called in unrecorded times, before they had their fastness on its banks. Others, his descendants, called Eachain, or Hector the first, and Orodh, or Hugh, William, the first of that name, and Gilmour, the theme of many a minstrel song, commemorating achievements done under the oriflamme of Charles the Great, Emperor of France, have all consigned themselves to their last sleep, nor has their memory been sufficiently preserved from the waste of time. Something we know concerning their great deeds, their great power, and, alas! their great crimes. Something we also know of a Lord of Douglas who sat in a parliament at Forfar, held by King Malcolm the First, and we are aware that from his attachment to hunting the wild hart, he built himself a tower called Blackhouse, in the forest of Ettrick, which perhaps still exists."

"I crave your forgiveness, old man," said the knight, "but I have no time at present to bestow upon the recitation of the pedigree of the House of Douglas. A less matter would hold a well-breathed minstrel in subject for recitation for a calendar month, Sundays and holidays included."

"What other information can you expect from me," said the sexton, "than that respecting those heroes, some of whom it has been my lot to consign to that eternal rest, which will for ever divide the dead from the duties of this world? I have told you where the race sleep, down to the reign of the royal Malcolm. I can tell you also of another vault, in which lie Sir John of Douglas-burn, with his son Lord Archibald, and a third William, known by an indenture with Lord Abernethy. Lastly, I can tell you of him to whom that escutcheon, with its appurtenances of splendour and dignity, justly belong. Do you envy that nobleman, whom, if death were in the sound, I would not hesitate to term my honourable patron? and have you any design of dishonouring his remains? It will be a poor victory! nor does it become a knight and nobleman to come in person to enjoy such a triumph over the dead, against whom, when he lived, there were few knights dared spur their horses. He fought in defence of his country, but he had not the good fortune of most of his ancestors, to die on the field of battle. Captivity, sickness, and regret for the misfortunes of his native land, brought his head to the grave in his prison-house, in the land of the stranger."

The old man's voice here became interrupted by emotion, and the English knight found it difficult to continue his examination in the stern fashion which his duty required.

"Old man," he said, "I do not require from thee this detail, which must be useless to me, as well as painful to thyself. Thou dost but thy duty in rendering justice to thy ancient lord; but thou hast not yet explained to me why I have met in this town, this very night, and not half an hour since, a person in the arms, and bearing the complexion, of one of the Black Douglasses, who cried his war-cry as if in contempt of his conquerors."

"Surely," replied the sexton, "it is not my business to explain such a fancy, otherwise than by supposing that the natural fears of the Southron will raise the spectre of a Douglas at any time, when he is within sight of their sepulchre. Methinks, in such a night as this, the fairest cavalier would wear the complexion of this swarthy race, nor can I hold it wonderful that the war-cry which was once in the throats of so many thousands in this country, should issue upon occasion from the mouth of a single champion."

"You are bold, old man," returned the English knight; "do you consider that your life is in my power, and that it may, in certain cases, be my duty to inflict death with that degree of pain at which humanity shudders?"

The old man rose up slowly in the light of the blazing fire, displaying his emaciated features, which resembled those ascribed by artists to Saint Anthony of the desert; and pointing to the feeble lamp, which he placed upon the coarse table, thus addressed his interrogator, with an appearance of perfect firmness, and something even resembling dignity:—

"Young knight of England, you see that utensil constructed for the purpose of dispensing light amid these fatal vaults,—it is as frail as any thing can well be, whose flame is supplied by living element, contained in a frame composed of iron. It is doubtless in your power entirely to end its service, by destroying the frame, or extinguishing the light. Threaten it with such annihilation, Sir Knight, and see whether your menace will impress any sense of fear either on the element or the iron. Know that you have no more power over the frail mortal whom you threaten with similar annihilation. You may tear from my body the skin in which it is now swathed, but although my nerves might glow with agony during the inhuman operation, it would produce no more impression on me than flaying on the stag which an arrow has previously pierced through the heart. My age sets me beyond your cruelty: if you think otherwise, call your agents, and commence your operations; neither threats nor inflictions will enable you to extort from me any thing that I am not ready to tell you of my own accord."

"You trifle with me, old man," said De Valence; "you talk as if you possessed some secret respecting the motions of these Douglasses, who are to you as gods, yet you communicate no intelligence to me whatever."

"You may soon know," replied the old man, "all that a poor sexton has to communicate; and it will not increase your knowledge respecting the living, though it may throw some light upon my proper domains, which are those of the dead. The spirits of the deceased Douglasses do not rest in their graves during the dishonour of their monuments, and the downfall of their house. That, upon death, the greater part of any line are consigned to the regions of eternal bliss, or of never-ending misery, religion will not suffer us to believe, and amidst a race who had so great a share of worldly triumph and prosperity, we must suppose there have existed many who have been justly subjected to the doom of an intermediate space of punishment. You have destroyed the temples—which were built by their posterity to propitiate Heaven for the welfare of their souls; you have silenced the prayers and stopt the choirs, by the mediation of which the piety of children had sought to appease the wrath of Heaven in behalf of their ancestors, subjected to expiatory fires. Can you wonder that the tormented spirits, thus deprived of the relief which had been proposed to them, should not, according to the common phrase, rest in their graves? Can you wonder they should show themselves like discontented loiterers near to the places which, but for the manner in which you have prosecuted your remorseless warfare, might have ere now afforded them rest? Or do you marvel that these fleshless warriors should interrupt your marches, and do what else their airy nature may permit to disturb your councils, and meet as far as they may the hostilities which you make it your boast to carry on, as well against those who are deceased, as against any who may yet survive your cruelty?"

"Old man," replied Aymer de Valence, "you cannot expect that I am to take for answer a story like this, being a fiction too gross to charm to sleep a schoolboy tormented with the toothache; nevertheless, I thank God that thy doom does not remain in my hands. My squire and two archers shall carry thee captive to the worshipful Sir John de Walton, Governor of the Castle and Valley, that he may deal with thee as seems meet; nor is he a person to believe in your apparitions and ghosts from purgatory.—What ho! Fabian! Come hither, and bring with thee two archers of the guard."

Fabian accordingly, who had waited at the entrance of the ruined building, now found his way, by the light of the old sexton's lamp, and the sound of his master's voice, into the singular apartment of the old man, the strange decorations of which struck the youth with great surprise, and some horror.

"Take the two archers with thee, Fabian," said the Knight of Valence, "and, with their assistance, convey this old man, on horseback, or in a litter, to the presence of the worshipful Sir John de Walton. Tell him what we have seen, which thou didst witness as well as I; and tell him that this old sexton, whom I send to be examined by his superior wisdom, seems to know more than he is willing to disclose respecting our ghostly cavalier, though he will give us no account of him, except intimating that he is a spirit of the old Douglasses from purgatory, to which Sir John de Walton will give what faith he pleases. You may say, that, for my part, my belief is, either that the sexton is crazed by age, want, and enthusiasm, or that he is connected with some plot which the country people are hatching. You may also say that I shall not use much ceremony with the youth under the care of the Abbot of St. Bride; there is something suspicious in all the occurrences that are now passing around us."

Fabian promised obedience; and the knight, pulling him aside, gave him an additional caution, to behave with attention in this business, seeing he must recollect that neither the judgment of himself, nor that of his master, were apparently held in very much esteem by the governor; and that it would ill become them to make any mistake in a matter where the safety of the Castle was perhaps concerned.

"Fear me not, worshipful sir," replied the youth; "I am returning to pure air in the first place, and a good fire in the second, both acceptable exchanges for this dungeon of suffocating vapours and execrable smells. You may trust to my making no delay; a very short time will carry me back to Castle Douglas, even moving with suitable attention to this old man's bones."

"Use him humanely," answered the knight. "And thou, old man, if thou art insensible to threats of personal danger in this matter, remember, that if thou art found paltering with us, thy punishment will perhaps be more severe than any we can inflict upon thy person."

"Can you administer the torture to the soul?" said the sexton.

"As to thee," answered the knight, "we have that power;—we will dissolve every monastery or religious establishment held for the souls of these Douglasses, and will only allow the religious people to hold their residence there upon condition of their praying for the soul of King Edward the First of glorious memory, the *malleus Scotorum*; and if the Douglasses are deprived of the ghostly benefit of the prayers and services of such shrines, they may term thy obstinacy the cause."

"Such a species of vengeance," answered the old man, in the same bold unsubdued tone which he had hitherto used, "were more worthy of the infernal fiends than of Christian men."

The squire raised his hand. The knight interposed: "Forbear him," he said, "Fabian, he is very old, and perhaps insane.—And you, sexton, remember that the vengeance threatened is lawfully directed towards a family which have been the obstinate supporters of the excommunicated rebel, who murdered the Red Comyn at the High Church in Dumfries."

So saying, Aymer strode out of the ruins, picking his way with much difficulty—took his horse, which he found at the entrance—repeated a caution to Fabian, to conduct himself with prudence—and, passing on to the south-western gate, gave the strongest injunctions concerning the necessity of keeping a vigilant watch, both by patrols and by sentinels, intimating, at the same time, that it must have been neglected during the preceding part of the evening. The men murmured an apology, the confusion of which seemed to express that there had existed some occasion for the reprimand.

Sir Aymer then proceeded on his journey to Hazelside, his train diminished by the absence of Fabian and his assistants. After a hasty, but not a short journey, the knight alighted at Thomas Dickson's, where he found the detachment from Ayr had arrived before him, and were snugly housed for the night. He sent one of the archers to announce his approach to the Abbot of Saint Bride and his young guest, intimating at the same time, that the archer must keep sight of the latter until he himself arrived at the chapel, which would be instantly.

CHAPTER THE TENTH.

When the nightengale singes, the wodes waxes grene,
Lef, and gras, and blosme, springeth in April I wene,
And love is to myne herte gone with one speare so kene.
Night and day my blood hyt drynkes, mine herte deth me fane.
MSS. Hail. Quoted by Warton.

Sir Aymer De Valance had no sooner followed his archer to the convent of Saint Bride, than he summoned the abbot to his presence, who came with the air of a man who loves his ease, and who is suddenly called from the couch where he has consigned himself to a comfortable repose, at the summons of one whom he does not think it safe to disobey, and to whom he would not disguise his sense of peevishness, if he durst.

"It is a late ride," he said, "which has brought your worthy honour hither from the castle. May I be informed of the cause, after the arrangement so recently gone into with the governor?"

"It is my hope," replied the knight, "that you, Father Abbot, are not already conscious of it; suspicions are afloat, and I myself have this night seen something to confirm them, that some of the obstinate rebels of this country are again setting afoot dangerous practices, to the peril of the garrison; and I come, father, to see whether, in requital of many favours received from the English monarch, you will not merit his bounty and protection, by contributing to the discovery of the designs of his enemies."

"Assuredly so," answered Father Jerome, in an agitated voice. "Most unquestionably my information should stand at your command; that is, if I knew any thing the communication of which could be of advantage to you."

"Father Abbot," replied the English knight, "although it is rash to make myself responsible for a North-country man in these times, yet I own I do consider you as one who has ever been faithfully subject to the King of England, and I willingly hope that you will still continue so."

"And a fine encouragement I have!" said the abbot; "to be called out of my bed at midnight, in this raw weather, to undergo the examination of a knight, who is the youngest, perhaps, of his own honourable rank, and who will not tell me the subject of the interrogatories, but detains me on this cold pavement, till, according to the opinion of Celsus, the podagra which lurks in my feet may be driven into my stomach, and then good-night to abbacy and examinations from henceforward."

"Good father," said the young man, "the spirit of the times must teach thee patience; recollect that I can feel no pleasure in this duty, and that if an insurrection should take place, the rebels, who are sufficiently displeased with thee for acknowledging the English monarch, would hang thee from thine own steeple to feed the crows; or that, if thou hast secured thy peace by some private compact with the insurgents, the English governor, who will sooner or later gain the advantage, will not fail to treat thee as a rebel to his sovereign."

"It may appear to you, my noble son," answered the abbot, obviously discomposed, "that I am hung up, in this case, on the horns of the dilemma which you have stated; nevertheless, I protest to you, that if any one accuses me of conspiring with the rebels against the King of England, I am ready, provided you give me time to swallow a potion recommended by Celsus in my perilous case, to answer with the most perfect sincerity every question which you can put to me upon that subject." So saying, he called upon a monk who had attended at his levee, and giving him a large key, whispered something in his ear. The cup which the monk brought was of such capacity as proved Celsus's draught required to be administered in considerable quantity, and a strong smell which it spread through the apartment, accredited the knight's suspicion that the medicine chiefly consisted of what were then termed distilled waters, a preparation known in the monasteries for some time before that comfortable secret had reached the laity in general. The abbot, neither overawed by the strength nor by the quantity of the potion, took it off with what he himself would have called a feeling of solace and pleasance, and his voice became much more composed; he signified himself as comforted extraordinarily by the medicine, and willing to proceed to answer any questions which could be put to him by his gallant young friend.

"At present," said the knight, "you are aware, father, that strangers travelling through this country, must be the first objects of our suspicions and enquiries. What is, for example, your own opinion of the youth termed Augustine, the son, or calling himself so, of a person called Bertram the minstrel, who has resided for some days in your convent?"

The abbot heard the question with eyes expressive of surprise at the quarter from which it came.

"Assuredly," said he, "I think of him as a youth who, from any thing I have seen, is of that excellent disposition, both with respect to loyalty and religion, which I should have expected, were I to judge from the estimable person who committed him to my care."

With this the abbot bowed to the knight, as if he had conceived that this repartee gave him a silencing advantage in any question which could follow upon that subject; and he was probably, therefore, surprised when Sir Aymer replied as follows:

"It is very true, Father Abbot, that I myself did recommend this stripling to you as a youth of a harmless disposition, and with respect to whom it would be unnecessary to exercise the strict vigilance extended to others in similar circumstances; but the evidence which seemed to me to vouch for this young man's innocence, has not appeared so satisfactory to my superior and commander; and it is by his orders that I now make farther enquiries of you. You must think they are of consequence, since we again trouble you, and at so unwonted an hour."

"I can only protest by my order, and by the veil of Saint Bride," replied the abbot, the spirit of Celsus appearing to fail his pupil, "that whatever evil may be in this matter, is totally unknown to me—nor could it be extorted from me by racks or implements of torture. Whatever signs of disloyalty may have been evinced by this young man, I have witnessed none of them, although I have been strictly attentive to his behaviour."

"In what respect?" said the knight—"and what is the result of your observation?"

"My answer," said the abbot of Saint Bride, "shall be sincere and downright. The youth condescended upon payment of a certain number of gold crowns, not by any means to repay the hospitality of the church of Saint Bride, but merely"—

"Nay, father," interrupted the knight, "you may cut that short, since the governor and I well understand the terms upon which the monks of Saint Bride exercise their hospitality. In what manner, it is more necessary to ask, was it received by this boy?"

"With the utmost gentleness and moderation, noble sir," answered the abbot; "indeed it appeared to me, at first, that he might be a troublesome guest, since the amount of his benevolence to the convent was such as to encourage, and, in some degree, to authorise, his demanding accommodation of a kind superior to what we had to bestow."

"In which case," said Sir Aymer, "you would have had the discomfort of returning some part of the money you have received?"

"That," replied the abbot, "would have been a mode of settlement contrary to our vows. What is paid to the treasury of Saint Bridget, cannot, agreeably to our rule, be on any account restored. But, noble knight, there was no occasion for this; a crust of white bread and a draught of milk were diet sufficient to nourish this poor youth for a day, and it was my own anxiety for his health that dictated the furnishing of his cell with a softer bed and coverlet than are quite consistent with the rules of our order."

"Now hearken to what I say, Sir Abbot, and answer me truly," said the Knight of Valence—"What communication has this youth held with the inmates of your convent, or with those beyond your house? Search your memory concerning this, and let me have a distinct answer, for your guest's safety and your own depend upon it."

"As I am a Christian man," said the abbot, "I have observed nothing which could give ground for your worship's suspicions. The boy Augustine, unlike those whom I have observed who have been educated in the world, showed a marked preference to the company of such sisters as the house of Saint Bride contains, rather than for that of the monks, my brethren, although there are among them pleasant and conversible men."

"Scandal," said the young knight, "might find a reason for that preference."

"Not in the case of the sisters of Saint Bridget," said the abbot, "most of whom have been either sorely misused by time, or their comeliness destroyed by some mishap previously to their being received into the seclusion of the house."

This observation the good father made with some internal movement of mirth, which was apparently excited at the idea of the sisterhood of Saint Bridget becoming attractive to any one by dint of their personal beauty, in which, as it happened, they were all notably, and almost ludicrously, deficient. The English knight, to whom the sisterhood were well known, felt also inclined to smile at this conversation.

"I acquit," he said, "the pious sisterhood of charming, otherwise than by their kind wishes, and attention to the wants of the suffering stranger."

"Sister Beatrice," continued the father, resuming his gravity, "is indeed blessed with a winning gift of making comfits and syllabubs; but, on minute enquiry, I do not find that the youth has tasted any of them. Neither is sister Ursula so hard-favoured by nature, as from the effects of an accident; but your honour knows that when a woman is ugly, the men do not trouble themselves about the cause of her hard favour. I will go, with your leave, and see in what state the youth now is, and summon him, before you."

"I request you to do so, father, for the affair is instant: and I earnestly advise you to watch, in the closest manner, this Augustine's behaviour: you cannot be too particular. I will wait your return, and either carry the boy to the castle, or leave him here, as circumstances may seem to require."

The abbot bowed, promised his utmost exertions, and hobbled out of the room to wait on the youth Augustine in his cell, anxious to favour, if possible, the wishes of De Valence, whom he looked upon as rendered by circumstances his military patron.

He remained long absent, and Sir Aymer began to be of opinion that the delay was suspicious, when the abbot returned with perplexity and discomposure in his countenance.

"I crave your pardon for keeping your worship waiting," said Jerome, with much anxiety; "but I have myself been detained and vexed by unnecessary formalities and scruples on the part of this peevish boy. In the first place, hearing my foot approaching his bedroom, my youth, instead of undoing the door, which would have been but proper respect to my place, on the contrary draws a strong bolt on the inside; and this fastening, forsooth, has been placed on his chamber by Ursula's command, that his slumbers might be suitably respected. I intimated to him as I best could, that he must attend you without delay, and prepare to accompany you to the Castle of Douglas; but he would not answer a single word, save recommending to me patience, to which I was fain to have recourse, as well as your archer, whom I found standing sentinel before the door of the cell, and contenting himself with the assurance of the sisters that there was no other passage by which Augustine could make his escape. At length the door opens, and my young master presents himself fully arrayed for his journey. The truth is, I think some fresh attack of his malady has affected the youth; he may perhaps be disturbed with some touch of hypochondria, or black choler, a species of dotage of the mind, which is sometimes found concomitant with and symptomatic of this disorder; but he is at present composed, and if your worship chooses to see him, he is at your command."

"Call him hither," said the knight. And a considerable space of time again elapsed ere the eloquence of the abbot, half chiding and half soothing, prevailed on the lady, in her adopted character, to approach, the parlour, in which at last she made her appearance, with a countenance on which the marks of tears might still be discovered, and a pettish sullenness, like that of a boy, or, with reverence, that of a girl, who is determined upon taking her own way in any matter, and equally resolved to give no reason for her doing so. Her hurried levee had not prevented her attending closely to all the mufflings and disguisings by which her pilgrim's dress was arranged, so as to alter her appearance, and effectually disguise her sex. But as civility prevented her wearing her large slouched hat, she necessarily exposed her countenance more than in the open air; and though the knight beheld a most lovely set of features, yet they were not such as were inconsistent with the character she had adopted, and which she had resolved upon maintaining to the last. She had, accordingly, mustered up a degree of courage which was not natural to her, and which she perhaps supported by hopes which her situation hardly admitted. So soon as she found herself in the same apartment with De Valence, she assumed a style of manners, bolder and more determined than she had hitherto displayed.

"Your worship," she said, addressing him even before he spoke, "is a knight of England, and possessed, doubtless, of the virtues which become that noble station. I am an unfortunate lad, obliged, by reasons which I am under the necessity of keeping secret, to travel in a dangerous country, where I am suspected, without any just cause, of becoming accessory to plots and conspiracies which are contrary to my own interest, and which my very soul abhors; and which I might safely abjure, by imprecating upon myself all the curses of our religion and renouncing all its promises, if I were accessory to such designs, in thought, word, or deed. Nevertheless, you, who will not believe my solemn protestations, are about to proceed against me as a guilty person, and in so doing I must warn you, Sir Knight, that you will commit a great and cruel injustice."

"I shall endeavour to avoid that," said the knight, "by referring the duty to Sir John de Walton, the governor, who will decide what is to be done; in this case, my only duty will be to place you in his hands at Douglas Castle."

"Must you do this?" said Augustine.

"Certainly," replied the knight, "or be answerable for neglecting my duty."

"But if I become bound to answer your loss with a large sum of money, a large tract of land"—

"No treasure, no land,—supposing such at your disposal," answered the knight, "can atone for disgrace; and, besides, boy, how should I trust to your warrant, were my avarice such as would induce me to listen to such proposals?"

"I must then prepare to attend you instantly to the Castle of Douglas and the presence of Sir John de Walton?" replied Augustine.

"Young man," answered De Valence, "there is no remedy, since if you delay me longer, I must carry you thither by force."

"What will be the consequence to my father?" said the youth.

"That," replied the knight, "will depend exactly on the nature of your confession and his; something you both have to say, as is evident from the terms of the letter Sir John de Walton conveyed to you; and I assure you, you were better to speak it out at once than to risk the consequences of more delay. I can admit of no more trifling; and, believe me, that your fate will be entirely ruled by your own frankness and candour."

"I must prepare, then, to travel at your command," said the youth. "But this cruel disease still hangs around me, and Abbot Jerome, whose leech-craft is famous, will himself assure you that I cannot travel without danger of my life; and that while I was residing in this convent, I declined every opportunity of exercise which was offered me by the kindness of the garrison at Hazelside, lest I might by mishap bring the contagion among your men."

"The youth says right," said the abbot; "the archers and men-at-arms have more than once sent to invite this lad to join in some of their military games, or to amuse them, perhaps, with some of his minstrelsy; but he has uniformly declined doing so; and, according to my belief, it is the effects of this disorder which have prevented his accepting an indulgence so natural to his age, and in so dull a place as the convent of Saint Bride must needs seem to a youth bred up in the world."

"Do you then hold, reverend father," said Sir Aymer, "that there is real danger in carrying this youth to the castle to-night, as I proposed?"

"I conceive such danger," replied the abbot, "to exist, not only as it may occasion the relapse of the poor youth himself, but as particularly likely, no preparations having been made, to introduce the infection among your honourable garrison; for it is in these relapses, more than in the first violence of the malady, that it has been found most contagious."

"Then," said the knight, "you must be content, my friend, to give a share of your room to an archer, by way of sentinel."

"I cannot object," said Augustine, "provided my unfortunate vicinity does not endanger the health of the poor soldier."

"He will be as ready to do his duty," said the abbot, "without the door of the apartment as within it; and if the youth should sleep soundly, which the presence of a guard in his chamber might prevent, he is the more likely to answer your purpose on the morrow."

"Let it be so," said Sir Aymer; "so you are sure that you do not minister any facility of escape."'

"The apartment," said the monk, "hath no other entrance than that which is guarded by the archer; but, to content you, I shall secure the door in your presence."

"So be it, then," said the Knight of Valence; "this done, I myself will lie down without doffing my mail-shirt, and snatch a sleep till the ruddy dawn calls me again to duty, when you, Augustine, will hold yourself ready to attend me to our Castle of Douglas."

The bells of the convent summoned the inhabitants and inmates of Saint Bride to morning prayers at the first peep of day. When this duty was over, the knight demanded his prisoner. The abbot marshalled him to the door of Augustine's chamber. The sentinel who was stationed there, armed with a brown-bill, or species of partisan, reported that he had heard no motion in the apartment during the whole night. The abbot tapped at the door, but received no answer. He knocked again louder, but the silence was unbroken from within.

"What means this?" said the reverend ruler of the convent of Saint Bride; "my young patient has certainly fallen into a syncope or swoon!"

"I wish, Father Abbot," said the knight, "that he may not have made his escape instead, an accident which both you and I may be required to answer, since, according to our strict duty, we ought to have kept sight of him, and detained him in close custody until daybreak."

"I trust your worship," said the abbot, "only anticipates a misfortune which I cannot think possible."

"We shall speedily see," said the knight; and raising his voice, he called aloud, so as to be heard within, "Bring crow-bars and levers, and burst me that door into splinters without an instant's delay."

The loudness of his voice, and the stern tone in which he spoke, soon brought around him the brethren of the house, and two or three soldiers of his own party, who were already busy in caparisoning their horses. The displeasure of the young knight was manifested by his flushed features, and the abrupt manner in which he again repeated his commands for breaking open the door. This was speedily performed, though it required the application of considerable strength, and as the shattered remains fell crashing into the apartment, De Valence sprung, and the abbot hobbled, into the cell of the prisoner, which, to the fulfilment of their worst suspicions, they found empty.

CHAPTER THE ELEVENTH.

Where is he? Has the deep earth swallow'd him?
Or hath he melted like some airy phantom
That shuns the approach of morn and the young sun?
Or hath he wrapt him in Cimmerian darkness,
And pass'd beyond the circuit of the sight
With things of the night's shadows?
ANONYMOUS.

The disappearance of the youth, whose disguise and whose fate have, we hope, inclined our readers to take some interest in him, will require some explanation ere we proceed with the other personages of the story, and we shall set about giving it accordingly.

When Augustine was consigned to his cell for the second time on the preceding evening, both the monk and the young Knight of Valence had seen the key turned upon him, and had heard him secure the door in the inside with the bolt which had been put on at his request by sister Ursula, in whose affections the youth of Augustine, his extreme handsomeness, and, above all, his indisposition of body and his melancholy of mind, had gained him considerable interest.

So soon, accordingly, as Augustine re-entered his apartment, he was greeted in a whisper by the sister, who, during the interval of his absence, had contrived to slip into the cell, and having tappiced herself behind the little bed, came out with great appearance of joy, to greet the return of the youth. The number of little attentions, the disposal of holly boughs, and such other evergreens as the season permitted, showed the anxiety of the holy sisters to decorate the chamber of their guest, and the greetings of sister Ursula expressed the same friendly interest, at the same time intimating that she was already in some degree in possession of the stranger's mystery.

As Augustine and the holy sister were busied in exchange of confidence, the extraordinary difference between, their countenances and their persons must have struck any one who might have been accidentally a witness of their interview. The dark pilgrim's robe of the disguised female was not a stronger contrast to the white woollen garment worn by the votaress of Saint Bride, than the visage of the nun, seamed with many a ghastly scar, and the light of one of her eyes extinguished for ever, causing it to roll a sightless luminary in her head, was to the beautiful countenance of Augustine, now bent with a confidential, and even affectionate look, upon the extraordinary features of her companion.

"You know," said the supposed Augustine, "the principal part of my story; can you, or will you, lend me your assistance? If not, my dearest sister, you must consent to witness my death, rather than my shame. Yes, sister Ursula, I will not be pointed at by the finger of scorn, as the thoughtless maiden who sacrificed so much for a young man, of whose attachment she was not so well assured as she ought to have been. I will not be dragged before De Walton, for the purpose of being compelled, by threats of torture, to declare myself the female in honour of whom he holds the Dangerous Castle. No doubt, he might be glad to give his hand in wedlock to a damsel whose dowry is so ample; but who can tell whether he will regard me with that respect which every woman would wish to command, or pardon that boldness of which I have been guilty, even though its consequences have been in his own favour?"

"Nay, my darling daughter," answered the nun, "comfort yourself; for in all I can aid you, be assured I will. My means are somewhat more than my present situation may express, and, be assured, they shall be tried to the uttermost. Methinks, I still hear that lay which you sung to the other sisters and myself, although I alone, touched by feelings kindred to yours, had the address to comprehend that it told your own tale."

"I am yet surprised," said Augustine, speaking beneath her breath, "how I had the boldness to sing in your ears the lay, which, in fact, was the history of my disgrace."

"Alas! that you will say so," returned the nun; "there was not a word but what resembled those tales of love and of high-spirited daring which the best minstrels love to celebrate, and the noblest knights and maidens weep at once and smile to hear. The Lady Augusta of Berkely, a great heiress, according to the world, both in land and movable goods, becomes the King's ward by the death of her parents; and thus is on the point of being given away in marriage to a minion of the King of England, whom in these Scottish valleys, we scruple not to call a peremptory tyrant."

"I must not say so, my sister," said the pilgrim; "and yet, true it is, that the cousin of the obscure parasite Gaviston, on whom the king wished to confer my poor hand, was neither by birth, merit, nor circumstance, worthy of such an alliance. Meantime, I heard of the fame of Sir John de Walton; and I heard of it not with the less interest that his feats of chivalry were said to adorn a knight, who, rich in everything else, was poor in worldly goods, and in the smiles of fortune. I saw this Sir John de Walton, and I acknowledge that a thought, which had already intruded itself on my imagination, became, after this interview, by frequent recurrence, more familiar, and more welcome to me. Methought that the daughter of a powerful English family, if she could give away with her hand such wealth as the world spoke of, would more justly and honourably bestow it in remedying the errors of fortune in regard to a gallant knight like De Walton, than in patching the revenues of a beggarly Frenchman, whose only merit was in being the kinsman of a man who was very generally detested by the whole kingdom of England, excepting the infatuated monarch himself."

"Nobly designed, my daughter," said the nun; "what more worthy of a noble heart, possessing riches, beauty, birth, and rank, than to confer them all upon indigent and chivalrous merit?"

"Such, dearest sister, was my intention," replied Augustine; "but I have, perhaps, scarce sufficiently explained the manner in which I meant to proceed. By the advice of a minstrel of our house, the same who is now prisoner at Douglas, I caused exhibit a large feast upon Christmas eve, and sent invitations abroad to the young knights of noble name who were known to spend their leisure in quest of arms and adventures. When the tables were drawn, and the feast concluded, Bertram, as had been before devised, was called upon to take his harp. He sung, receiving from all who were present the attention due to a minstrel of so much fame. The theme which he chose, was the frequent capture of this Douglas Castle, or, as the poet termed it, Castle Dangerous. 'Where are the champions of the renowned Edward the First,' said the minstrel, 'when the realm of England cannot furnish a man brave enough, or sufficiently expert in the wars, to defend a miserable hamlet of the North against the Scottish rebels, who have vowed to retake it over our soldiers' heads ere the year rolls to an end? Where are the noble ladies, whose smiles used to give countenance to the Knights of Saint George's Cross? Alas! the spirit of love and of chivalry is alike dead amongst us—our knights are limited to petty enterprises—and our noblest heiresses are given as prizes to strangers, as if their own country had no one to deserve them.'—Here stopt the harp; and I shame to say, that I myself, as if moved to enthusiasm by the song of the minstrel, arose, and taking from my neck the chain of gold which supported a crucifix of special sanctity, I made my vow, always under the King's permission, that I would give my hand, and the inheritance of my fathers, to the good knight, being of noble birth and lineage, who should keep the Castle of Douglas in the King of England's name, for a year and a day. I sat down, my dearest sister, deafened with the jubilee in which my guests expressed their applause of my supposed patriotism. Yet some degree of pause took place amidst the young knights, who might reasonably have been supposed ready to embrace this offer, although at the risk of being encumbered with Augusta of Berkely."

"Shame on the man," said sister Ursula, "who should think so! Put your beauty alone, my dearest, into consideration, and a true knight ought to have embraced the dangers of twenty Castles of Douglas, rather than let such an invaluable opportunity of gaining your favour be lost."

"It may be that some in reality thought so," said the pilgrim; "but it was supposed that the king's favour might be lost by those who seemed too anxious to thwart his royal purpose upon his ward's hand. At any rate, greatly to my joy, the only person who availed himself of the offer I had made was Sir John de Walton; and as his acceptance of it was guarded by a clause, saving and reserving the king's approbation, I hope he has not suffered any diminution of Edward's favour."

"Assure yourself, noble and high-spirited young lady," replied the nun, "that there is no fear of thy generous devotion hurting thy lover with the King of England. Something we hear concerning worldly passages, even in this remote nook of Saint Bride's cloister; and the report goes among the English soldiers that their king was indeed offended at your putting your will in opposition to his own; yet, on the other hand, this preferred lover, Sir John de Walton, was a man of such extensive fame, and your offer was so much in the character of better but not forgotten times, that even a king could not at the beginning of a long and stubborn war deprive an errant cavalier of his bride, if she should be duly won by his sword and lance."

"Ah! dearest sister Ursula!" sighed the disguised pilgrim, "but, on the other hand, how much time must pass by in the siege, by defeating which that suit must needs be advanced? While I sat in my lonely castle, tidings came to astound me with the numerous, or rather the constant dangers, with which my lover was surrounded, until at length, in a moment I think of madness, I resolved to set out in this masculine disguise; and having myself with my own eyes seen in what situation I had placed my knight, I determined to take such measures in respect to shortening the term of his trial, or otherwise, as a sight of Douglas Castle, and—why should I deny it?—of Sir John de Walton, might suggest. Perhaps you, my dearest sister, may not so well understand my being tempted into flinching from the resolution which I had laid down for my own honour, and that of my lover; but consider, that my resolution was the consequence of a moment of excitation, and that the course which I adopted was the conclusion of a long, wasting, sickening state of uncertainty, the effect of which was to weaken the nerves which were once highly strung with love of my country, as I thought; but in reality, alas! with fond and anxious feelings of a more selfish description."

"Alas!" said sister Ursula, evincing the strongest symptoms of interest and compassion, "am I the person, dearest child, whom you suspect of insensibility to the distresses which are the fruit of true love? Do you suppose that the air which is breathed within these walls has the property upon the female heart, of such marvellous fountains as they say change into stone the substances which are immersed into their waters? Hear my tale, and judge if it can be thus with one who possesses my causes of grief. And do not fear for loss of time; we must let our neighbours at Hazelside be settled for the evening, ere I furnish you with the means of escape; and you must have a trusty guide, for whose fidelity I will be responsible, to direct your path through these woods, and protect you in case of any danger, too likely to occur in these troublesome times. It will thus be nigh an hour ere you depart; and sure I am that in no manner can you spend the time better than in listening to distresses too similar to your own, and flowing from the source of disappointed affection which you must needs sympathize with."

The distresses of the Lady Augusta did not prevent her being in some degree affected, almost ludicrously, with the singular contrast between the hideous countenance of this victim of the tender passion, and the cause to which she imputed her sorrows; but it was not a moment for giving way to a sense of the ridiculous, which would have been in the highest degree offensive to the sister of Saint Bride, whose good-will she had so many reasons to conciliate. She readily, therefore, succeeded in preparing herself to listen to the votary—with an appearance of sympathy, which might reward that which she had herself experienced at the hands of sister Ursula; while the unfortunate recluse, with an agitation which made her ugliness still more conspicuous, narrated, nearly in a whisper, the following circumstances:—

"My misfortunes commenced long before I was called sister Ursula, or secluded as a votaress within these walls. My father was a noble Norman,

116

who, like many of his countrymen, sought and found fortune at the court of the King of Scotland. He was endowed with the sheriffdom of this county, and Maurice de Hattely, or Hautlieu, was numbered among the wealthy and powerful barons of Scotland. Wherefore should I deny it, that the daughter of this baron, then called Margaret de Hautlieu, was also distinguished among the great and fair of the land? It can be no censurable vanity which provokes me to speak the truth, and unless I tell it myself, you could hardly suspect what a resemblance I once bore even to the lovely Lady Augusta of Berkely. About this time broke out those unfortunate feuds of Bruce and Baliol, which have been so long the curse of this country. My father, determined in his choice of party by the arguments of his wealthy kinsmen at the court of Edward, embraced with passion the faction of the English interest, and became one of the keenest partisans, at first of John Baliol, and afterwards of the English monarch. None among the Anglocised-Scottish, as his party was called, were so zealous as he for the red cross, and no one was more detested by his countrymen who followed the national standard of Saint Andrew and the patriot Wallace. Among those soldiers of the soil, Malcolm Fleming of Biggar was one of the most distinguished by his noble birth, his high acquirements, and his fame in chivalry. I saw him; and the ghastly spectre who now addresses you must not be ashamed to say, that she loved, and was beloved by, one of the handsomest youths in Scotland. Our attachment was discovered to my father almost ere we had owned it to each other, and he was furious both against my lover and myself; he placed me under the charge of a religious woman of this rule, and I was immured within the house of Saint Bride, where my father shamed not to announce he would cause me to take the veil by force, unless I agreed to wed a youth bred at the English court, his nephew; and, as Heaven had granted him no son, the heir, as he had resolved, of the house of Hautlieu. I was not long in making my election. I protested that death should be my choice, rather than any other husband excepting Malcolm Fleming. Neither was my lover less faithful; he found means to communicate to me a particular night on which he proposed to attempt to storm the nunnery of Saint Bride, and carry me from hence to freedom and the greenwood, of which Wallace was generally called the king. In an evil hour—an hour I think of infatuation and witchery—I suffered the abbess to wheedle the secret out of me, which I might have been sensible would appear more horribly flagitious to her than to any other woman that breathed; but I had not taken the vows, and I thought Wallace and Fleming had the same charms for every body as for me, and the artful woman gave me reason to believe that her loyalty to Bruce was without a flaw of suspicion, and she took part in a plot of which my freedom was the object.

The abbess engaged to have the English guards removed to a distance, and in appearance the troops were withdrawn. Accordingly, in the middle of the night appointed, the window of my cell, which was two stories from the ground, was opened without noise; and never were my eyes more gladdened than, as ready disguised and arrayed for flight, even in a horseman's dress, like yourself, fairest. Lady Augusta, I saw Malcolm Fleming spring into the apartment. He rushed towards me; but at the same time my father with ten of his strongest men filled the room, and cried their war-cry of Baliol. Blows were instantly dealt on every side. A form like a giant, however, appeared in the midst of the tumult, and distinguished himself, even to my half-giddy eye, by the ease with which he bore down and dispersed those who fought against our freedom. My father alone offered an opposition which threatened to prove fatal to him; for Wallace, it was said, could foil any two martial champions that ever drew sword. Brushing from him the armed men, as a lady would drive away with her fan a swarm of troublesome flies, he secured me in one arm, used his other for our mutual protection, and I found myself in the act of being borne in safety down the ladder by which my deliverers had ascended from without, —but an evil fate awaited this attempt.

"My father, whom the Champion of Scotland had spared for my sake, or rather for Fleming's, gained by his victor's compassion and lenity a fearful advantage, and made a remorseless use of it. Having only his left hand to oppose to the maniac attempts of my father, even the strength of Wallace could not prevent the assailant, with all the energy of desperation, from throwing down the ladder, on which his daughter was perched like a dove in the grasp of an eagle. The champion saw our danger, and exerting his inimitable strength and agility, cleared himself and me from the ladder, and leaped free of the moat of the convent, into which we must otherwise have been precipitated. The Champion of Scotland was saved in the desperate attempt, but I who fell among a heap of stones and rubbish, I the disobedient daughter, wellnigh the apostate vestal, waked only from a long bed of sickness, to find myself the disfigured wretch, which you now see me. I then learned that Malcolm had escaped from the fray, and shortly after I heard, with feelings less keen perhaps than they ought to have been, that my father was slain in one of the endless battles which took place between the contending factions. If he had lived, I might have submitted to the completion of my fate; but since he was no more, I felt that it would be a preferable lot to be a beggar in the streets of a Scottish village, than, an abbess in this miserable house of Saint Bride; nor was even that poor object of ambition, on which my father used to expatiate when desirous of persuading me to enter the monastic state by milder means than throwing me off the battlements, long open to me. The old abbess died of a cold caught the evening of the fray; and the place, which might have been kept open until I was capable of filling it, was disposed of otherwise, when the English thought fit to reform, as they termed it, the discipline of the house; and instead of electing a new abbess, sent hither two or three friendly monks, who have now the absolute government of the community, and wield it entirely according to the pleasure of the English. But I, for one, who have had the honour to be supported by the arms of the Champion of my country, will not remain here to be commanded by this Abbot Jerome. I will go forth, nor do I fear to find relations and friends, who will provide a more fitting place of refuge for Margaret de Hautlieu than the convent of Saint Bride; you, too, dearest lady, shall obtain your freedom, and it will be well to leave such information as will make Sir John de Walton aware of the devotion with which his happy fate has inspired you."

"It is not, then, your own intention," said the Lady Augusta, "to return into the world again, and you are about to renounce the lover, in a union with whom you and he once saw your joint happiness?"

"It is a question, my dearest child," said sister Ursula, "which I dare not ask myself, and to which I am absolutely uncertain what answer I should return. I have not taken the final and irrevocable vows; I have done nothing to alter my situation with regard to Malcolm Fleming. He also, by the vows plighted in the Chancery of Heaven, is my affianced bridegroom, nor am I conscious that I less deserve his faith, in any respect now, than at the moment when it was pledged to me; but, I confess, dearest lady, that rumours have reached me, which sting me to the quick; the reports of my wounds and scars are said to have estranged the knight of my choice. I am now, indeed, poor," she added, with a sigh, "and I am no longer possessed of those personal charms, which they say attract the love, and fix the fidelity, of the other sex. I teach myself, therefore, to think, in my moments of settled resolution, that all betwixt me and Malcolm Fleming is at an end, saving good wishes on the part of both towards the other; and yet there is a sensation in my bosom which whispers, in spite of my reason, that if I absolutely believed that which I now say, there would be no object on earth worthy my living for in order to attain it. This insinuating prepossession whispers, to my secret soul, and in very opposition to my reason and understanding, that Malcolm Fleming, who could pledge his all upon the service of his country, is incapable of nourishing the versatile affection of an ordinary, a coarse, or a venal character. Methinks, were the difference upon his part instead of mine, he would not lose his interest in my eyes, because he was seamed with honourable scars, obtained in asserting the freedom of his choice, but that such wounds would, in my opinion, add to his merit, whatever they took away from his personal comeliness. Ideas rise on my soul, as if Malcolm and Margaret might yet be to each other all that their affections once anticipated with so much security, and that a change, which took nothing from the honour and virtue of the beloved person, must rather add to, than diminish, the charms of the union. Look at me, dearest Lady Augusta!—look me—if you have courage—full in the face, and tell me whether I do not rave when my fancy is thus converting mere possibilities into that which is natural and probable."

The Lady of Berkely, conscious of the necessity, raised her eyes on the unfortunate nun, afraid of losing her own chance of deliverance by the mode in which she should conduct herself in this crisis; yet not willing at the same time to flatter the unfortunate Ursula, with suggesting ideas for which her own sense told her she could hardly find any rational grounds. But her imagination, stored with the minstrelsy of the time, brought back to her recollection the Loathly Lady in "The marriage of Sir Gawain," and she conducted her reply in the following manner:—

"You ask me, my dear Lady Margaret, a trying question, which it would be unfriendly to answer otherwise than sincerely, and most cruel to answer with too much rashness. It is true, that what is called beauty, is the first quality on which we of the weaker sex learn to set a value; we are flattered by the imputation of personal charms, whether we actually possess them or not; and no doubt we learn to place upon them a great deal more consequence than in reality is found to belong to them. Women, however, even, such as are held by their own sex, and perhaps in secret by themselves, as devoid of all pretensions to beauty, have been known to become, from their understanding, their talents, or their accomplishments, the undoubted objects of the warmest attachment. Wherefore then should you, in the mere rashness of your apprehension, deem it impossible that your Malcolm Fleming should be made of that porcelain clay of the earth, which despises the passing captivations of outward form in comparison to the charms of true affection, and the excellence of talents and virtue?"

The nun pressed her companion's hand to her bosom, and answered her with a deep sigh.

"I fear," she said, "you flatter me; and yet in a crisis like this, it does one good to be flattered, even as cordials, otherwise dangerous to the constitution, are wisely given to support a patient through a paroxysm of agony, and enable him to endure at least what they cannot cure. Answer only one question, and it will be time to drop this conversation. Could you, sweet lady—you upon whom fortune has bestowed so many charms—could any argument make you patient under the irretrievable loss of your personal advantages, with the concomitant loss, as in my case is most probable, of that lover for whom you have already done so much?"

The English lady cast her eyes again on her friend, and could not help shuddering a little at the thought of her own beautiful countenance being exchanged for the seamed and scarred features of the Lady of Hautlieu, irregularly lighted by the beams of a single eye.

"Believe me," she said, looking solemnly upwards, "that even in the case which you suppose, I would not sorrow so much for myself, as I would for the poor-spirited thoughts of the lover who could leave me because those transitory charms (which must in any case erelong take their departure) had fled ere yet the bridal day. It is, however, concealed by the decrees of Providence, in what manner, or to what extent, other persons, with whose disposition we are not fully acquainted, may be affected by such changes. I can only assure you that my hopes go with yours, and that there is no difficulty which shall remain in your path in future, if it is in my power to remove it.—Hark!"—

"It is the signal of our freedom," replied Ursula, giving attention to something resembling the whoop of the night-owl. "We must prepare to leave the convent in a few minutes. Have you anything to take with you?"

"Nothing," answered the Lady of Berkely, "except the few valuables, which I scarce know why I brought with me on my flight hither. This scroll, which I shall leave behind, gives my faithful minstrel permission to save himself, by confessing to Sir John de Walton who the person really is whom he has had within his reach."

"It is strange," said the novice of Saint Bride, "through what extraordinary labyrinths this Love, this Will-of-the-Wisp, guides his votaries, Take heed as you descend; this trap-door, carefully concealed, curiously jointed and oiled, leads to a secret postern, where I conceive the horses already wait, which will enable us speedily to bid adieu to Saint Bride's—Heaven's blessing on her, and on her convent! We can have no advantage from any light, until we are in the open air."

During this time, sister Ursula, to give her for the last time her conventual name, exchanged her stole, or loose upper garment, for the more succinct cloak and hood of a horseman. She led the way through divers passages, studiously complicated, until the Lady of Berkely, with throbbing heart, stood in the pale and doubtful moonlight, which was shining with grey uncertainty upon the walls of the ancient building. The imitation of an owlet's cry directed them to a neighbouring large elm, and on approaching it, they were aware of three horses, held by one, concerning whom they could only see that he was tall, strong, and accoutred in the dress of a man-at-arms.

"The sooner," he said, "we are gone from this place, Lady Margaret, it is so much the better. You have only to direct the course which we shall hold."

Lady Margaret's answer was given beneath her breath; and replied to with a caution from the guide to ride slowly and silently for the first quarter of an hour, by which time inhabited places would be left at a distance.

CHAPTER THE TWELFTH.

Great was the astonishment of the young Knight of Valence and the reverend Father Jerome, when, upon breaking into the cell, they discovered the youthful pilgrim's absence; and, from the garments which were left, saw every reason to think that the one-eyed novice, sister Ursula, had accompanied him in his escape from custody. A thousand thoughts thronged upon Sir Aymer, how shamefully he had suffered himself to be outwitted by the artifices of a boy and of a novice. His reverend companion in error felt no less contrition for having recommended to the knight a mild exercise of his authority. Father Jerome had obtained his preferment as abbot upon the faith of his zeal for the cause of the English monarch, with the affected interest in which he was at a loss to reconcile his proceedings of the last night. A hurried enquiry took place, from which little could be learned, save that the young pilgrim had most certainly gone off with the Lady Margaret de Hautlieu, an incident at which the females of the convent expressed surprise, mingled with a great deal of horror; while that of the males, whom the news soon reached, was qualified with a degree of wonder, which seemed to be founded upon the very different personal appearance of the two fugitives.

"Sacred Virgin," said a nun, "who could have conceived the hopeful votaress, sister Ursula, so lately drowned in tears for her father's untimely fate, capable of eloping with a boy scarce fourteen years old!"

"And, holy Saint Bride!" said the Abbot Jerome, "what could have made so handsome a young man lend his arm to assist such a nightmare as sister Ursula, in the commission of so great an enormity? Certainly he can neither plead temptation nor seduction, but must have gone, as the worldly phrase is,—to the devil with a dish-clout."

"I must disperse the soldiers to pursue the fugitives," said De Valence, "unless this letter, which the pilgrim must have left behind him, shall contain some explanations respecting our mysterious prisoner."

After viewing the contents with some surprise, he read aloud,—"The undersigned, late residing in the house of Saint Bride, do you, father Jerome, the abbot of said house, to know, that finding you were disposed to treat me as a prisoner and a spy, in the sanctuary to which you had received me as a distressed person, I have resolved to use my natural

122

liberty, with which you have no right to interfere, and therefore have withdrawn myself from your abbacy. Moreover, finding that the novice called in your convent sister Ursula (who hath, by monastic rule and discipline, a fair title to return to the world unless she is pleased, after a year's novitiate, to profess herself sister of your order) is determined to use such privilege, I joyfully take the opportunity of her company in this her lawful resolution, as being what is in conformity to the law of God, and the precepts of Saint Bride, which gave you no authority to detain any person in your convent by force, who hath not taken upon her irrevocably the vows of the order.

"To you, Sir John de Walton, and Sir Aymer de Valence, knights of England, commanding the garrison of Douglas Dale, I have only to say, that you have acted and are acting against me under a mystery, the solution of which is comprehended in a secret known only to my faithful minstrel, Bertram of the many Lays, as whose son I have found it convenient to pass myself. But as I cannot at this time prevail upon myself personally to discover a secret which cannot well be unfolded without feelings of shame, I not only give permission to the said Bertram the minstrel, but I charge and command him that he tell to you the purpose with which I came originally to the Castle of Douglas. When this is discovered, it will only remain to express my feelings towards the two knights, in return for the pain and agony of mind which their violence and threats of further severities have occasioned me.

"And first respecting Sir Aymer de Valence, I freely and willingly forgive him for having been involved in a mistake to which I myself led the way, and I shall at all times be happy to meet with him as an acquaintance, and never to think farther of his part in these few days' history, saving as matter of mirth and ridicule.

"But respecting Sir John de Walton, I must request of him to consider whether his conduct towards me, standing as we at present do towards each, other, is such as he himself ought to forget or I ought to forgive; and I trust he will understand me when I tell him, that all former connexions must henceforth be at an end between him and the supposed "AUGUSTINE."

"This is madness," said the abbot, when he had read the letter,—"very midsummer madness; not unfrequently an accompaniment of this pestilential disease, and I should do well in requiring of those soldiers who shall first apprehend this youth Augustine, that they reduce his victuals immediately to water and bread, taking care that the diet do not exceed in measure what is necessary to sustain nature; nay, I should be warranted by the learned, did I recommend a sufficient intermixture of flagellation with belts, stirrup-leathers, or surcingles, and failing those, with riding-whips, switches, and the like."

"Hush! my reverend father," said De Valence, "a light begins to break in upon me. John de Walton, if my suspicions be true, would sooner expose his own flesh to be hewn from his bones, than have this Augustine's finger stung by a gnat. Instead of treating this youth as a madman, I for my own part, will be contented to avow that I myself have been bewitched and fascinated; and by my honour, if I send out my attendants in quest of the fugitives, it shall be with the strict charge, that, when apprehended, they treat them with all respect, and protect them, if they object to return to this house, to any honourable place of refuge which they may desire."

"I hope," said the abbot, looking strangely confused, "I shall be first heard in behalf of the Church concerning this affair of an abducted nun? You see yourself, Sir Knight, that this scapegrace of a minstrel avouches neither repentance nor contrition at his share in a matter so flagitious."

"You shall be secured an opportunity of being fully heard," replied the knight, "if you shall find at last that you really desire one. Meantime, I must back, without a moment's delay, to inform Sir John de Walton of the turn which affairs have taken. Farewell, reverend father. By my honour we may wish each other joy that we have escaped from a troublesome charge, which brought as much terror with it as the phantoms of a fearful dream, and is yet found capable of being dispelled by a cure as simple as that of awakening the sleeper. But, by Saint Bride! both churchmen and laymen are bound to sympathise with the unfortunate Sir John de Walton. I tell thee, father, that if this letter"—touching the missive with his finger—"is to be construed literally, as far as respects him, he is the man most to be pitied betwixt the brink of Solway and the place where we now stand. Suspend thy curiosity, most worthy churchman, lest there should be more in this matter than I myself see; so that, while thinking that I have lighted on the true explanation, I may not have to acknowledge that I have been again leading you into error. Sound to horse there! Ho?" he called out from the window of the apartment; "and let the party I brought hither prepare to scour the woods on their return."

"By my faith!" said Father Jerome, "I am right glad that this young nut-cracker is going to leave me to my own meditation. I hate when a young person pretends to understand whatever passes, while his betters are obliged to confess that it is all a mystery to them. Such an assumption is like that of the conceited fool, sister Ursula, who pretended to read with a single eye a manuscript which I myself could not find intelligible with the assistance of my spectacles."

This might not have quite pleased the young knight, nor was it one of those truths which the abbot would have chosen to deliver in his hearing. But the knight had shaken him by the hand, said adieu, and was already at Hazelside, issuing particular orders to little troops of the archers and others, and occasionally chiding Thomas Dickson, who, with a degree of curiosity which the English knight was not very willing to excuse, had been endeavouring to get some account of the occurrences of the night.

"Peace, fellow!" he said, "and mind thine own business, being well assured that the hour will come in which it will require all the attention thou canst give, leaving others to take care of their own affairs."

"If I am suspected of any thing," answered Dickson, in a tone rather dogged and surly than otherwise, "methinks it were but fair to let me know what accusation is brought against me. I need not tell you that chivalry prescribes that a knight should not attack an enemy undefied."

"When you are a knight," answered Sir Aymer de Valence, "it will be time enough for me to reckon with you upon the points of form due to you by the laws of chivalry. Meanwhile, you had best let me know what share you have had in playing off the martial phantom which sounded the rebellious slogan of Douglas in the town of that name?"

"I know nothing of what you speak," answered the goodman of Hazelside.

"See then," said the knight, "that you do not engage yourself in the affairs of other people, even if your conscience warrants that you are in no danger from your own."

So saying, he rode off, not waiting any answer. The ideas which filled his head were to the following purpose.

"I know not how it is, but one mist seems no sooner to clear away than. we find ourselves engaged in another. I take it for granted that the disguised damsel is no other than the goddess of Walton's private idolatry, who has cost him and me so much trouble, and some certain, degree of misunderstanding during these last weeks. By my honour! this fair lady is right lavish in the pardon which she has so frankly bestowed upon me, and if she is willing to be less complaisant to Sir John de Walton, why then—And what then?—It surely does not infer that she would receive me into that place in her affections, from which she has just expelled De Walton? Nor, if she did, could I avail myself of a change in favour of myself, at the expense of my friend and companion in arms. It were a folly even to dream of a thing so improbable. But with respect to the other business, it is worth serious consideration. Yon sexton seems to have kept company with dead bodies, until he is unfit for the society of the living; and as to that Dickson of Hazelside, as they call him, there is no attempt against the English during these endless wars, in which that man has not been concerned; had my life depended upon it, I could not have prevented myself from intimating my suspicions of him, let him take it as he lists." So saying, the knight spurred his horse, and arriving at Douglas Castle without farther adventure, demanded in a tone of greater cordiality than he had of late used, whether he could be admitted to Sir John de Walton, having something of consequence to report to him. He was immediately ushered into an apartment, in which the governor was seated at his solitary breakfast. Considering the terms upon which they had lately stood, the governor of Douglas Dale was somewhat surprised at the easy familiarity with which De Valence now approached him.

"Some uncommon news," said Sir John, rather gravely, "have brought me the honour of Sir Aymer de Valence's company."

"It is," answered Sir Aymer, "what seems of high importance to your interest, Sir John de Walton, and therefore I were to blame if I lost a moment in communicating it."

"I shall be proud to profit by your intelligence," said Sir John de Walton.

"And I too," said the young knight, "am both to lose the credit of having penetrated a mystery which blinded Sir John de Walton. At the same time, I do not wish to be thought capable of jesting with you, which might be the case were I, from misapprehension, to give a false key to this matter. With your permission, then, we will proceed thus: We go together to the place of Bertram the minstrel's confinement. I have in my possession a scroll from the young person who was intrusted to the care of the Abbot Jerome; it is written in a delicate female hand, and gives authority to the minstrel to declare the purpose which brought them to this vale of Douglas."

"It must be as you say," said Sir John de Walton, "although can scarce see occasion for adding so much form to a mystery which can be expressed in such small compass."

Accordingly the two knights, the warder leading the way, proceeded to the dungeon to which the minstrel had been removed.

CHAPTER THE THIRTEENTH.

The doors of the stronghold being undone, displayed a dungeon such as in those days held victims hopeless of escape, but in which the ingenious knave of modern times would scarcely have deigned to remain many hours. The huge rings by which the fetters were soldered together, and attached to the human body, were, when examined minutely, found to be clenched together by riveting so very thin, that when rubbed with corrosive acid, or patiently ground with a bit of sandstone, the hold of the fetters upon each other might easily be forced asunder, and the purpose of them entirely frustrated. The locks also, large, and apparently very strong, were so coarsely made, that an artist of small ingenuity could easily contrive to get

126

the better of their fastenings upon the same principle. The daylight found its way to the subterranean dungeon only at noon, and through a passage which was purposely made tortuous, so as to exclude the rays of the sun, while it presented no obstacle to wind or rain. The doctrine that a prisoner was to be esteemed innocent until he should be found guilty by his peers, was not understood in those days of brute force, and he was only accommodated with a lamp or other alleviation of his misery, if his demeanour was quiet, and he appeared disposed to give his jailor no trouble by attempting to make his escape. Such a cell of confinement was that of Bertram, whose moderation of temper and patience had nevertheless procured for him such mitigations of his fate as the warder could grant. He was permitted to carry into his cell the old book, in the perusal of which he found an amusement of his solitude, together with writing materials, and such other helps towards spending his time as were consistent with his abode in the bosom of the rock, and the degree of information with which his minstrel craft had possessed him. He raised his head from the table as the knights entered, while the governor observed to the young knight:—

"As you seem to think yourself possessed of the secret of this prisoner, I leave it to you, Sir Aymer de Valence, to bring it to light in the manner which you shall judge most expedient. If the man or his son have suffered unnecessary hardship, it shall be my duty to make amends—which, I suppose, can be no very important matter."

Bertram looked up, and fixed his eyes full upon the governor, but read nothing in his looks which indicated his being better acquainted than before with the secret of his imprisonment. Yet, upon turning his eye towards Sir Aymer, his countenance evidently lighted up, and the glance which passed between them was one of intelligence.

"You have my secret, then," said he, "and you know who it is that passes under the name of Augustine?"

Sir Aymer exchanged with him a look of acquiescence; while the eyes of the governor glancing wildly from the prisoner to the knight of Valence, exclaimed,—

"Sir Aymer de Valence, as you are belted knight and Christian man, as you have honour to preserve on earth, and a soul to rescue after death, I charge you to tell me the meaning of this mystery! It may be that you conceive, with truth, that you have subject of complaint against me;—If so, I will satisfy you as a knight may."

The minstrel spoke at the same moment.

"I charge this knight," he said, "by his vow of chivalry, that he do not divulge any secret belonging to a person of honour and of character, unless he has positive assurance that it is done entirely by that person's own consent."

"Let this note remove your scruples," said Sir Aymer, putting the scroll into the hands of the minstrel; "and for you, Sir John de Walton, far from retaining the least feeling of any misunderstanding which may have existed between us, I am disposed entirely to bury it in forgetfulness, as having arisen out of a series of mistakes which no mortal could have comprehended. And do not be offended, my dear Sir John, when I protest, on my knightly faith, that I pity the pain which I think this scroll is likely to give you, and that if my utmost efforts can be of the least service to you in unravelling this tangled skein, I will contribute them with as much earnestness as ever I did aught in my life. This faithful minstrel will now see that he can have no difficulty in yielding up a secret, which I doubt not, but for the writing I have just put into his hands, he would have continued to keep with unshaken fidelity."

Sir Aymer now placed in De Walton's hand a note, in which he had, ere he left Saint Bride's convent, signified his own interpretation, of the mystery; and the governor had scarcely read the name it contained, before the same name was pronounced aloud by Bertram, who, at the same moment, handed to the governor the scroll which he had received from the Knight of Valence.

The white plume which floated over the knight's cap of maintenance, which was worn as a headpiece within doors, was not more pale in complexion than was the knight himself at the unexpected and surprising information, that the lady who was, in chivalrous phrase, empress of hia thoughts, and commander of his actions, and to whom, even in less fantastic times, he must have owed the deepest gratitude for the generous election which she had made in his favour, was the same person whom he had threatened with personal violence, and subjected to hardships and affronts which he would not willingly have bestowed even upon the meanest of her sex.

Yet Sir John de Walton seemed at first scarcely to comprehend the numerous ill consequences which might probably follow this unhappy complication of mistakes. He took the paper from the minstrel's hand, and while his eye, assisted by the lamp, wandered over the characters without apparently their conveying any distinct impression to his understanding, De Valence even became alarmed that he was about to lose his faculties.

"For Heaven's sake, sir," he said, "be a man, and support with manly steadiness these unexpected occurrences—I would fain think they will reach to nothing else—which the wit of man could not have prevented. This fair lady, I would fain hope, cannot be much hurt or deeply offended by a train of circumstances, the natural consequence of your anxiety to discharge perfectly a duty upon which must depend the accomplishment of all the hopes she had permitted you to entertain. In God's name, rouse up, sir; let it not be said, that an apprehended frown of a fair lady hath damped to such a degree the courage of the boldest knight in England; be what men have called you, 'Walton the Unwavering;' in Heaven's name, let us at least see that the lady is indeed offended, before we conclude that she is irreconcilably so. To whose fault are we to ascribe the source of all these errors? Surely, with all due respect, to the caprice of the lady herself, which has engendered such a nest of mistakes. Think of it as a man, and as a soldier. Suppose that you yourself, or I, desirous of proving the fidelity of our sentinels, or for any other reason, good or bad, attempted to enter this Dangerous Castle of Douglas without giving the password to the warders, would we be entitled to blame those upon duty, if, not knowing our persons, they manfully refused us entrance, made us prisoners, and mishandled us while resisting our attempt, in terms of the orders which we ourselves had imposed upon them? What is there that makes a difference between such a sentinel and yourself, John de Walton, in this curious affair, which, by Heaven! would rather form a gay subject for the minstrelsy of this excellent bard, than the theme of a tragic lay? Come! look not thus, Sir John de Walton; be angry, if you will, with the lady who has committed such a piece of folly, or with me who have rode up and down nearly all night on a fool's errand, and spoiled my best horse, in absolute uncertainty how I shall get another till my uncle of Pembroke and I shall be reconciled; or, lastly, if you desire to be totally absurd in your wrath, direct it against this worthy minstrel on account of his rare fidelity, and punish him for that for which he better deserves a chain of gold. Let passion out, if you will; but chase this desponding gloom from the brow of a man and a belted knight."

Sir John de Walton made an effort to speak, and succeeded with some difficulty.

"Aymer de Valence," he said, "in irritating a madman you do but sport with your own life;" and then remained silent.

"I am glad you can say so much," replied his friend; "for I was not jesting when I said I would rather that you were at variance with me, than that you laid the whole blame on yourself. It would be courteous, I think, to set this minstrel instantly at liberty. Meantime, for his lady's sake, I will entreat him, in all honour, to be our guest till the Lady Augusta de Berkely shall do us the same honour, and to assist us in our search after her place of retirement.—Good minstrel," he continued, "you hear what I say, and you will not, I suppose, be surprised, that in all honour and kind usage, you find yourself detained for a short space in this Castle of Douglas?"

"You seem, Sir Knight," replied the minstrel, "not so much to keep your eye upon the right of doing what you should, as to possess the might of doing what you would. I must necessarily be guided by your advice, since you have the power to make it a command."

"And I trust," continued De Valence, "that when your mistress and you again meet, we shall have the benefit of your intercession for any thing which we may have done to displeasure her, considering that the purpose of our action was exactly the reverse."

"Let me," said Sir John de Walton, "say a single word. I will offer thee a chain of gold, heavy enough to bear down the weight of these shackles, as a sign of regret for having condemned thee to suffer so many indignities."

"Enough said, Sir John," said De Valence; "let us promise no more till this good minstrel shall see some sign of performance. Follow me this way, and I will tell thee in private of other tidings, which it is important that you should know."

So saying, he withdrew De Walton from the dungeon, and sending for the old knight, Sir Philip de Montenay, already mentioned, who acted as seneschal of the castle, he commanded that the minstrel should be enlarged from the dungeon, well looked to in other respects, yet prohibited, though with every mark of civility, from leaving the castle without a trusty attendant.

"And now, Sir John de Walton," he said, "methinks you are a little churlish in not ordering me some breakfast, after I have been all night engaged in your affairs; and a cup of muscadel would, I think, be no bad induction to a full consideration of this perplexed matter."

"Thou knowest," answered De Walton, "that thou mayest call for what thou wilt, provided always thou tellest me, without loss of time, what else thou knowest respecting the will of the lady, against whom we have all sinned so grievously—and I, alas, beyond hope of forgiveness!"

"Trust me, I hope," said the Knight of Valence, "the good lady bears me no malice, as indeed she has expressly renounced any ill-will against me. The words, you see, are as plain as you yourself may read—'The lady pardons poor Aymer de Valence, and willingly, for having been involved in a mistake, to which she herself led the way; she herself will at all times be happy to meet with him as an acquaintance, and never to think farther of these few days' history, except as matter of mirth and ridicule.' So it is expressly written and set down."

"Yes," replied Sir John de Walton, "but see you not that her offending lover is expressly excluded from the amnesty granted to the lesser offender? Mark you not the concluding paragraph?" He took the scroll with a trembling hand, and read with a discomposed voice its closing words. "It

130

is even so: 'All former connexion must henceforth be at an end between him and the supposed Augustine.' Explain to me how the reading of these words is reconcilable to anything but their plain sense of condemnation and forfeiture of contract, implying destruction of the hopes of Sir John de Walton?"

"You are somewhat an older man than I, Sir Knight," answered De Valence, "and I will grant, by far the wiser and more experienced; yet I will uphold that there is no adopting the interpretation which you seem to have affixed in your mind to this letter, without supposing the preliminary, that the fair writer was distracted in her understanding, —nay, never start, look wildly, or lay your hand on your sword, I do not affirm this is the case. I say again, that no woman in her senses would have pardoned a common acquaintance for his behaving to her with unintentional disrespect and unkindness, during the currency of a certain masquerade, and, at the same time, sternly and irrevocably broke off with the lover to whom her troth was plighted, although his error in joining in the offence was neither grosser nor more protracted than that of the person indifferent to her love."

"Do not blaspheme," said Sir John do Walton; "and forgive me, if, in justice to truth and to the angel whom I fear I have forfeited for ever, I point out to you the difference which a maiden of dignity and of feeling must make between an offence towards her, committed by an ordinary acquaintance, and one of precisely the same kind offered by a person who is bound by the most undeserved preference, by the most generous benefits, and by every thing which can bind human feeling, to think and reflect ere he becomes an actor in any case in which it is possible for her to be concerned."

"Now, by mine honour," said Aymer de Valence, "I am glad to hear thee make some attempt at reason, although it is but an unreasonable kind of reason too, since its object is to destroy thine own hopes, and argue away thine own chance of happiness; but if I have, in the progress of this affair, borne me sometimes towards thee, as to give not only the governor, but even the friend, some cause of displeasure, I will make it up to thee now, John de Walton, by trying to convince thee in spite of thine own perverse logic. But here comes the muscadel and the breakfast; wilt thou take some refreshment;—or shall we go on without the spirit of muscadel?"

"For Heaven's sake," replied De Walton, "do as thou wilt, so thou make me clear of thy well-intended babble."

"Nay, thou shalt not brawl me out of my powers of argument," said De Valence, laughing, and helping himself to a brimming cup of wine; "if thou acknowledgest thyself conquered, I am contented to give the victory to the

131

inspiring strength of the jovial liquor."

"Do as thou listest," said De Walton, "but make an end of an argument which thou canst not comprehend."

"I deny the charge," answered the younger knight, wiping his lips, after having finished his draught; "and listen, Walton the Warlike, to a chapter in the history of woman, in which thou art more unskilled than I would wish thee to be. Thou canst not deny that, be it right or wrong, the lady Augusta hath ventured more forward with you than is usual upon the sea of affection; she boldly made thee her choice, while thou wert as yet known to her only as a flower of English chivalry,—faith, and I respect her for her frankness—but it was a choice, which the more cold of her own sex might perhaps claim occasion to term rash and precipitate.—Nay, be not, I pray thee, offended—I am far from thinking or saying so; on the contrary, I will uphold with my lance, her selection of John de Walton against the minions of a court, to be a wise and generous choice, and her own behaviour as alike candid and noble. But she herself is not unlikely to dread unjust misconstruction; a fear of which may not improbably induce her, upon any occasion, to seize some opportunity of showing an unwonted and unusual rigour towards her lover, in order to balance her having extended towards him, in the beginning of their intercourse, somewhat of an unusual degree of frank encouragement. Nay, it might be easy for her lover so far to take part against himself, by arguing as thou dost, when out of thy senses, as to make it difficult for her to withdraw from an argument which he himself was foolish enough to strengthen; and thus, like a maiden too soon taken at her first nay-say, she shall perhaps be allowed no opportunity of bearing herself according to her real feelings, or retracting a sentence issued with consent of the party whose hopes it destroys."

"I have heard thee, De Valence," answered the governor of Douglas Dale; "nor is it difficult for me to admit, that these thy lessons may serve as a chart to many a female heart, but not to that of Augusta de Berkely. By my life, I say I would much sooner be deprived of the merit of those few deeds of chivalry which thou sayest have procured for me such enviable distinction, than I would act upon them with the insolence, as if I said that my place in the lady's bosom was too firmly fixed to be shaken even by the success of a worthier man, or by my own gross failure in respect to the object of my attachment. No, herself alone shall have power to persuade me that even goodness equal to that of an interceding saint will restore me to the place in her affections which I have most unworthily forfeited, by a stupidity only to be compared to that of brutes."

"If you are so minded," said Aymer De Valence, "I have only one word more—forgive me if I speak it peremptorily—the lady, as you say, and say truly, must be the final arbitress in this question. My arguments do not extend to insisting that you should claim her hand, whether she herself will or no; but, to learn her determination, it is necessary that you should find out where she is, of which I am unfortunately not able to inform you."

"How! what mean you!" exclaimed the governor, who now only began to comprehend the extent of his misfortune; "whither hath she fled? or with whom?"

"She is fled, for what I know," said De Valence, "in search of a more enterprising lover than one who is so willing to interpret every air of frost as a killing blight to his hopes; perhaps she seeks the Black Douglas, or some such hero of the Thistle, to reward with her lands, her lordships, and beauty, those virtues of enterprise and courage, of which John de Walton was at one time thought possessed. But, seriously, events are passing around us of strange import. I saw enough last night, on my way to Saint Bride's, to make me suspicious of every one. I sent to you as a prisoner the old sexton of the church of Douglas. I found him contumacious as to some enquiries which I thought it proper to prosecute; but of this more at another time. The escape of this lady adds greatly to the difficulties which encircle this devoted castle."

"Aymer de Valence," replied De Walton, in a solemn and animated tone, "Douglas Castle shall be defended, as we have hitherto been able, with the aid of heaven, to spread from its battlements the broad banner of St. George. Come of me what lists during my life, I will die the faithful lover of Augusta de Berkely, even although I no longer live as her chosen knight. There are cloisters and hermitages"—

"Ay, marry are there," replied Sir Aymer; "and girdles of hemp, moreover, and beads of oak; but all these we omit in our reckonings, till we discover where the Lady Augusta is, and what she purposes to do in this matter."

"You say well," replied De Walton; "let us hold counsel together by what means we shall, if possible, discover the lady's too hasty retreat, by which she has done me great wrong; I mean, if she supposed her commands would not have been fully obeyed, had she honoured with them the governor of Douglas Dale, or any who are under his command."

"Now," replied De Valence, "you again speak like a true son of chivalry. With your permission I would summon this minstrel to our presence. His fidelity to his mistress has been remarkable; and, as matters stand now, we must take instant measures for tracing the place of her retreat."

CHAPTER THE FOURTEENTH.

The way is long, my children, long and rough
The moors are dreary, and the woods are dark;
But he that creeps from cradle on to grave,
Unskill'd save in the velvet course of fortune,
Hath miss'd the discipline of noble hearts.

OLD PLAY.

It was yet early in the day, when, after the Governor and De Valence had again summoned Bertram to their councils, the garrison of Douglas was mustered, and a number of small parties, in addition to those already despatched by De Valence from Hazelside, were sent out to scour the woods in pursuit of the fugitives, with strict injunctions to treat them, if overtaken, with the utmost respect, and to obey their commands, keeping an eye, however, on the place where they might take refuge. To facilitate this result, some who were men of discretion were intrusted with the secret who the supposed pilgrim and the fugitive nun really were. The whole ground, whether forest or moorland, within many miles of Douglas Castle, was covered and traversed by parties, whose anxiety to detect the fugitives was equal to the reward for their safe recovery, liberally offered by De Walton and De Valence. They spared not, meantime, to make such enquiries in all directions as might bring to light any machinations of the Scottish insurgents which might be on foot in those wild districts, of which, as we have said before, De Valence, in particular, entertained strong suspicions. Their instructions were, in case of finding such, to proceed against the persons engaged, by arrest and otherwise, in the most rigorous manner, such as had been commanded by De Walton himself at the time when the Black Douglas and his accomplices had been the principal objects of his wakeful suspicions. These various detachments had greatly reduced the strength of the garrison; yet, although numerous, alert, and despatched in every direction, they had not the fortune either to fall on the trace of the Lady of Berkely, or to encounter any party whatever of the insurgent Scottish.

Meanwhile, our fugitives had, as we have seen, set out from the convent of St. Bride under the guidance of a cavalier, of whom the Lady Augusta knew nothing, save that he was to guide their steps in a direction where they would not be exposed to the risk of being overtaken. At length Margaret de Hautlieu herself spoke upon the subject.

"You have made no enquiry," she said, "Lady Augusta, whither you are travelling, or under whose charge, although methinks it should much concern you to know."

"Is it not enough for me to be aware," answered Lady Augusta, "that I am

134

travelling, kind sister, under the protection of one to whom you yourself trust as to a friend; and why need I be anxious for any farther assurance of my safety?"

"Simply," said Margaret, de Hautlieu, "because the persons with whom, from national as well as personal circumstances, I stand connected, are perhaps not exactly the protectors to whom you, lady, can with such perfect safety intrust yourself."

"In what sense," said the Lady Augusta, "do you use these words?"

"Because," replied Margaret de Hautlieu, "the Bruce, the Douglas, Malcolm Fleming, and others of that party, although they are incapable of abusing such an advantage to any dishonourable purpose, might nevertheless, under a strong temptation, consider you as an hostage thrown into their hands by Providence, through whom they might meditate the possibility of gaining some benefit to their dispersed and dispirited party."

"They might make me," answered the Lady Augusta, "the subject of such a treaty, when I was dead, but, believe me, never while I drew vital breath. Believe me also that, with whatever pain, shame, or agony, I would again deliver myself up to the power of De Walton, yes, I would rather put myself in his hands—what do I say? his!—I would rather surrender myself to the meanest archer of my native country, than combine with its foes to work mischief to merry England—-my own England—that country which is the envy of every other country, and the pride of all who can term themselves her natives!"

"I thought that your choice might prove so," said Lady Margaret; "and since you have honoured me with your confidence, gladly would I provide for your liberty by placing you as nearly in the situation which you yourself desire, as my poor means have the power of accomplishing. In half an hour we shall be in danger of being taken by the English parties, which will be instantly dispersed in every direction in quest of us. Now, take notice, lady, I know a place in which I can take refuge with my friends and countrymen, those gallant Scots, who have never even in this dishonoured age bent the knee to Baal. For their honour, their nicety of honour, I could in other days have answered with my own; but of late, I am bound to tell you, they have been put to those trials by which the most generous affections may be soured, and driven to a species of frenzy, the more wild that it is founded originally on the noblest feelings. A person who feels himself deprived of his natural birthright, denounced, exposed to confiscation and death, because he avouches the rights of his king, the cause of his country, ceases on his part to be nice or precise in estimating the degree of retaliation which it is lawful for him to exercise in the requital of such injuries; and,

135

believe me, bitterly should I lament having guided you into a situation which you might consider afflicting or degrading."

"In a word then," said the English lady, "what is it you apprehend I am like to suffer at the hands of your friends, whom I must be excused for terming rebels?"

"If," said the sister Ursula, "*your* friends, whom I should term oppressors and tyrants, take our land and our lives, seize our castles, and confiscate our property, you must confess, that the rough laws of war indulge *mine* with the privilege of retaliation. There can be no fear, that such men, under any circumstances, would ever exercise cruelty or insult upon a lady of your rank; but it is another thing to calculate that they will abstain from such means of extorting advantage from your captivity as are common in warfare. You would not, I think, wish to be delivered up to the English, on consideration of Sir John de Walton surrendering the Castle of Douglas to its natural lord; yet, were you in the hands of the Bruce or Douglas, although I can answer for your being treated with all the respect which they have the means of showing, yet I own, their putting you at such a ransom might be by no means unlikely."

"I would sooner die," said the Lady Berkely, "than have my name mixed up in a treaty so disgraceful; and De Walton's reply to it would, I am certain, be to strike the head from the messenger, and throw it from the highest tower of Douglas Castle."

"Where, then, lady, would you now go," said sister Ursula, "were the choice in your power?"

"To my own castle," answered Lady Augusta, "where, if necessary, I could be defended even against the king himself, until I could place at least my person under the protection of the Church."

"In that case," replied Margaret de Hautlieu, "my power of rendering you assistance is only precarious, yet it comprehends a choice which I will willingly submit to your decision, notwithstanding I thereby subject the secrets of my friends to some risk of being discovered and frustrated. But the confidence which you have placed in me, imposes on me the necessity of committing to you a like trust. It rests with you, whether you will proceed with me to the secret rendezvous of the Douglas and his friends, which I may be blamed for making known, and there take your chance of the reception which you may encounter, since I cannot warrant you of any thing save honourable treatment, so far as your person is concerned; or if you should think this too hazardous, make the best of your way at once for the Border; in which last case I will proceed as far as I can with you towards the English line, and then leave you to pursue your journey, and to obtain a guard and a conductor among your own countrymen. Meantime, it will be well for me if I escape being taken, since the abbot would not shrink at inflicting upon me the death due to an apostate nun."

"Such cruelty, my sister, could hardly be inflicted upon one who had never taken the religious vows, and who still, according to the laws of the Church, had a right to make a choice between the world and the veil."

"Such choice as they gave their gallant victims," said Lady Margaret, "who have fallen into English hands during these merciless wars,—such choice as they gave to Wallace, the Champion of Scotland,—such as they gave to Hay, the gentle and the free,—to Sommerville, the flower of chivalry,—and to Athol, the blood relation of King Edward himself—all of whom were as much traitors, under which name they were executed, as Margaret de Hautlieu is an apostate nun, and subject to the rule of the cloister."

She spoke with some eagerness, for she felt as if the English lady imputed to her more coldness than she was, in such doubtful circumstances, conscious of manifesting.

"And after all," she proceeded, "you, Lady Augusta de Berkely, what do you venture, if you run the risk of falling into the hands of your lover? What dreadful risk do you incur? You need not, methinks, fear being immured between four walls, with a basket of bread and a cruise of water, which, were I seized, would be the only support allowed to me for the short space that my life would be prolonged. Nay, even were you to be betrayed to the rebel Scots, as you call them, a captivity among the hills, sweetened by the hope of deliverance, and rendered tolerable by all the alleviations which the circumstances of your captors allowed them the means of supplying, were not, I think, a lot so very hard to endure."

"Nevertheless," answered the Lady of Berkely, "frightful enough it must have appeared to me, since, to fly from such, I threw myself upon your guidance."

"And, whatever you think or suspect," answered the novice, "I am as true to you as ever was one maiden to another; and as sure as ever sister Ursula was true to her vows, although they were never completed, so will I be faithful to your secret, even at the risk of betraying my own."

"Hearken, lady!" she said, suddenly pausing, "do you hear that?"

The sound to which she alluded was the same imitation of the cry of an owlet, which the lady had before heard under the walls of the convent.

"These sounds," said Margaret de Hautlieu, "announce that one is near, more able than I am to direct us in this matter. I must go forward and speak with him; and this man, our guide, will remain by you for a little space; nor, when he quits your bridle, need you wait for any other signal, but ride forward on the woodland path, and obey the advice and directions which will be given you."

"Stay! stay! sister Ursula!" cried the Lady de Berkely—"abandon me not in this moment of uncertainty and distress!"

"It must be, for the sake of both," returned Margaret de Hautlieu. "I also am in uncertainty—I also am in distress—and patience and obedience are the only virtues which can save us both."

So saying, she struck her horse with the riding rod, and moving briskly forward, disappeared among the tangled boughs of a thicket. The Lady of Berkely would have followed her companion, but the cavalier who attended them laid a strong hand upon the bridle of her palfrey, with a look which implied that he would not permit her to proceed in that direction. Terrified, therefore, though she could not exactly state a reason why, the Lady of Berkely remained with her eyes fixed upon the thicket, instinctively, as it were, expecting to see a band of English archers, or rugged Scottish insurgents, issue from its tangled skirts, and doubtful which she should have most considered as the objects of her terror. In the distress of her uncertainty, she again attempted to move forward, but the stern check which her attendant again bestowed upon her bridle, proved sufficiently that in restraining her wishes, the stranger was not likely to spare the strength which he certainly possessed. At length, after some ten minutes had elapsed, the cavalier withdrew his hand from her bridle, and pointing with his lance towards the thicket, through which there winded a narrow, scarce visible path, seemed to intimate to the lady that her road lay in that direction, and that he would no longer prevent her following it.

"Do you not go with me?" said the lady, who, having been accustomed to this man's company since they left the convent, had by degrees come to look upon him as a sort of protector. He, however, gravely shook his head, as if to excuse complying with a request, which it was not in his power to grant; and turning his steed in a different direction, retired at a pace which soon carried him from her sight. She had then no alternative but to take the path of the thicket, which had been followed by Margaret de Hautlieu, nor did she pursue it long before coming in sight of a singular spectacle. The trees grew wider as the lady advanced, and when she entered the thicket, she perceived that, though hedged in as it were by an enclosure of copsewood, it was in the interior altogether occupied by a few of the magnificent trees, such as seemed to have been the ancestors of the forest, and which, though few in number, were sufficient to overshade all the unoccupied ground, by the great extent of their complicated branches. Beneath one of these lay stretched something of a grey colour, which, as it drew itself together, exhibited the figure of a man sheathed in armour, but strangely accoutred, and in a manner so bizarre, as to indicate some of the wild fancies peculiar to the knights of that period. His armour was ingeniously painted, so as to represent a skeleton; the ribs being constituted by the corselet and its back-piece. The shield represented an owl with its wings spread, a device which was repeated upon the helmet, which appeared to be completely covered by an image of the same bird of ill omen. But that which was particularly calculated to excite surprise in the spectator, was the great height and thinness of the figure, which, as it arose from the ground, and placed itself in an erect posture, seemed rather to resemble an apparition in the act of extricating itself from the grave, than that of an ordinary man rising upon his feet. The horse, too, upon which the lady rode, started back and snorted, either at the sudden change of posture of this ghastly specimen of chivalry, or disagreeably affected by some odour which accompanied his presence. The lady herself manifested some alarm, for although she did not utterly believe she was in the presence of a super natural being, yet, among all the strange half-frantic disguises of chivalry this was assuredly the most uncouth which she had ever seen; and, considering how often the knights of the period pushed their dreamy fancies to the borders of insanity, it seemed at best no very safe adventure to meet? one accoutred in the emblems of the King of Terrors himself, alone, and in the midst of a wild forest. Be the knight's character and purposes what they might, she resolved, however, to accost him in the language and manner observed in romances upon such occasions, in the hope even that if he were a madman he might prove a peaceable one, and accessible to civility.

"Sir Knight," she said, in as firm a tone as she could assume, "right sorry am I, if, by my hasty approach, I have disturbed your solitary meditations. My horse, sensible I think of the presence of yours, brought me hither, without my being aware whom or what I was to encounter."

"I am one," answered the stranger, in a solemn tone, "whom few men seek to meet, till the time comes that they can avoid me no longer."

"You speak, Sir Knight," replied the Lady de Berkely, "according to the dismal character of which it has pleased you to assume the distinction. May I appeal to one whose exterior is so formidable, for the purpose of requesting some directions to guide me through this wild wood; as, for instance, what is the name of the nearest castle, town, or hostelry, and by what course I am best likely to reach such?"

"It is a singular audacity," answered the Knight of the Tomb, "that would enter into conversation with him who is termed the Inexorable, the Unsparing, and the Pitiless, whom even the most miserable forbears to call to his assistance, lest his prayers should be too soon answered."

"Sir Knight," replied the Lady Augusta, "the character which you have assumed, unquestionably for good reasons, dictates to you a peculiar course of speech; but although your part is a sad one, it does not, I should suppose, render it necessary for you to refuse those acts of civility to which you must have bound yourself in taking the high vows of chivalry."

"If you will trust to my guidance," replied the ghastly figure, "there is only one condition upon which I can grant you the information which you require; and that is, that you follow my footsteps without any questions asked as to the tendency of our journey."

"I suppose I must submit to your conditions," she answered, "if you are indeed pleased to take upon yourself the task of being my guide. In my heart I conceive you to be one of the unhappy gentlemen of Scotland, who are now in arms, as they say, for the defence of their liberties. A rash undertaking has brought me within the sphere of your influence, and now the only favour I have to request of you, against whom I never did, nor planned any evil, is the guidance which your knowledge of the country permits you easily to afford me in my way to the frontiers of England. Believe that what I may see of your haunts or of your practices, shall be to me things invisible, as if they were actually concealed by the sepulchre itself, of the king of which it has pleased you to assume the attributes; and if a sum of money, enough to be the ransom of a wealthy earl, will purchase such a favour at need, such a ransom will be frankly paid, and with as much fidelity as ever it was rendered by a prisoner to the knight by whom he was taken. Do not reject me, princely Bruce—noble Douglas—if indeed it is to either of these that I address myself in this my last extremity—men speak of both as fearful enemies, but generous knights and faithful friends. Let me entreat you to remember how much you would wish your own friends and connexions to meet with compassion under similar circumstances, at the hands of the knights of England."

"And have they done so?" replied the Knight, in a voice more gloomy than before, "or do you act wisely, while imploring the protection of one whom you believe to be a true Scottish knight, for no other reason than the extreme and extravagant misery of his appearance?—is it, I say, well or wise to remind him of the mode in which the lords of England have treated the lovely maidens and the high-born dames of Scotland? Have not their prison cages been suspended from the battlements of castles, that their captivity might be kept in view of every base burgher, who should desire to look upon the miseries of the noblest peeresses, yea, even the Queen of Scotland? [Footnote: The Queen of Robert the Bruce, and the Countess of Buchan, by whom, as one of Macduff's descent, he was crowned at Scone, were secured in the manner described.] Is this a recollection which can inspire a Scottish knight with compassion towards an English lady? or is it a

140

thought which can do aught but swell the deeply sworn hatred of Edward Plantagenet, the author of these evils, that boils in every drop of Scottish blood which still feels the throb of life? No;—it is all you can expect, if, cold and pitiless as the sepulchre I represent, I leave you unassisted in the helpless condition in which you describe yourself to be."

"You will not be so inhuman," replied the lady; "in doing so you must surrender every right to honest fame, which you have won either by sword or lance. You must surrender every pretence to that justice which affects the merit of supporting the weak against the strong. You must make it your principle to avenge the wrongs and tyranny of Edward Plantagenet upon the dames and damosels of England, who have neither access to his councils, nor perhaps give him their approbation in his wars against Scotland."

"It would not then," said the Knight of the Sepulchre, "induce you to depart from your request, should I tell you the evils to which you would subject yourself should we fall into the hands of the English troops, and should they find you under such ill-omened protection as my own?"

"Be assured," said the lady, "the consideration of such an event does not in the least shake my resolution, or desire of confiding in your protection. You may probably know who I am, and may judge how far even, Edward would hold himself entitled to extend punishment towards me."

"How am I to know you," replied the ghastly cavalier, "or your circumstances? They must be extraordinary indeed, if they could form a check, either of justice or humanity, upon the revengeful feelings of Edward. All who know him are well assured that it is no ordinary motive that will induce him to depart from the indulgence of his evil temper. But be it as it may, you, lady, if a lady you be, throw yourself as a burden upon me, and I must discharge myself of my trust as I best may; for this purpose you must be guided implicitly by my directions, which will be given after the fashion of those of the spiritual world, being intimations, rather than detailed instructions for your conduct, and expressed rather by commands, than, by any reason or argument. In this way it is possible that I may be of service to you; in any other case, it is most likely that I may fail you at need, and melt from your side like a phantom which dreads the approach of day."

"You cannot be so cruel!" answered the lady. "A gentleman, a knight, and a nobleman—and I persuade myself I speak to all—hath duties which he cannot abandon."

"He has, I grant it, and they are most sacred to me," answered the Spectral Knight; "but I have also duties whose obligations are doubly binding, and to which I must sacrifice those which would otherwise lead me to devote myself to your rescue. The only question is whether you feel inclined to accept my protection on the limited terms on which alone I can extend it, or whether you deem it better that each go their own way, and limit themselves to their own resources, and trust the rest to Providence?" "Alas!" replied the lady, "beset and hard pressed as I am, to ask me to form a resolution for myself, is like calling on the wretch in the act of falling from a precipice, to form a calm judgment by what twig he may best gain the chance of breaking his fall. His answer must necessarily be, that he will cling to that which he can easiest lay hold of, and trust the rest to Providence. I accept therefore your offer of protection in the modified way you are pleased to limit it, and I put my faith in Heaven and in you. To aid me effectually, however, you must know my name and my circumstances."

"All these," answered the Knight of the Sepulchre, "have already been told me by your late companion; for deem not, young lady, that either beauty, rank, extended domains, unlimited wealth, or the highest accomplishments, can weigh any thing in the consideration of him who wears the trappings of the tomb, and whose affections and desires are long buried in the charnel-house."

"May your faith," said the Lady Augusta de Berkely, "be as steady as your words appear severe, and I submit to your guidance, without the least doubt or fear that it will prove otherwise than as I venture to hope."

CHAPTER THE FIFTEENTH.

Like the dog following its master, when engaged in training him to the sport in which he desires he should excel, the Lady Augusta felt herself occasionally treated with a severity, calculated to impress upon her the most implicit obedience and attention to the Knight of the Tomb, in whom she had speedily persuaded herself she saw a principal man among the retainers of Douglas, if not James of Douglas himself. Still, however, the ideas which the lady had formed of the redoubted Douglas, were those of a knight highly accomplished in the duties of chivalry, devoted in particular to the service of the fair sex, and altogether unlike the personage with whom she found herself so strangely united, or rather for the present enthralled to. Nevertheless, when, as if to abridge farther communication, he turned short into one of the mazes of the wood, and seemed to adopt a pace, which, from the nature of the ground, the horse on which the Lady Augusta was mounted had difficulty to keep up with, she followed him with the alarm and speed of the young spaniel, which from fear rather than fondness, endeavours to keep up with the track of its severe master. The simile, it is true, is not a very polite one, nor entirely becoming an age, when women were worshipped with a certain degree of devotion; but such circumstances as the present were also rare, and the Lady Augusta de Berkely could not but persuade herself that the terrible champion, whose

142

name had been so long the theme of her anxiety, and the terror indeed of the whole country, might be able, some way or other, to accomplish her deliverance. She, therefore, exerted herself to the utmost, so as to keep pace with the phantom-like apparition, and followed the knight, as the evening shadow keeps watch upon the belated rustic.

As the lady obviously suffered under the degree of exertion necessary to keep her palfrey from stumbling in these steep and broken paths, the Knight of the Tomb slackened his pace, looked anxiously around him, and muttered apparently to himself, though probably intended for his companion's ear, "There is no occasion for so much haste."

He proceeded at a slower rate, until they seemed to be on the brink of a ravine, being one of many irregularities on the surface of the ground, effected by the sudden torrents peculiar to that country, and which, winding among the trees and copse-wood, formed, as it were, a net of places of concealment, opening into each other, so that there was perhaps no place in the world so fit for the purpose of ambuscade. The spot where the borderer Turnbull had made his escape at the hunting match, was one specimen of this broken country, and perhaps connected itself with the various thickets and passes through which the knight and pilgrim occasionally seemed to take their way, though that ravine was at a considerable distance from their present route.

Meanwhile the knight led the way, as if rather with the purpose of bewildering the Lady Augusta amidst these interminable woods, than following any exact or fixed path. Here they ascended, and anon appeared to descend in the same direction, finding only boundless wildernesses, and varied combinations of tangled woodland scenery. Such part of the country as seemed arable, the knight appeared carefully to avoid; yet he could not direct his course with so much certainty but that he occasionally crossed the path of inhabitants and cultivators, who showed a consciousness of so singular a presence, but never as the lady observed evinced any symptoms of recognition. The inference was obvious, that the spectre knight was known in the country, and that he possessed adherents or accomplices there, who were at least so far his friends, as to avoid giving any alarm, which might be the means of his discovery. The well-imitated cry of the night-owl, too frequent a guest in the wilderness that its call should be a subject of surprise, seemed to be a signal generally understood among them; for it was heard in different parts of the wood, and the Lady Augusta, experienced in such journeys by her former travels under the guidance of the minstrel Bertram, was led to observe, that on hearing such wild notes, her guide changed the direction of his course, and betook himself to paths which led through deeper wilds, and more impenetrable thickets. This happened so often, that a new alarm came upon the unfortunate pilgrim, which suggested other motives of terror. Was she not the confidant, and almost the tool of some artful design, laid with a view to an extensive operation, which was destined to terminate, as the efforts of Douglas had before done, in the surprise of his hereditary castle, the massacre of the English garrison—and finally in the dishonour and death of that Sir John de Walton, upon whose fate she had long believed, or taught herself to believe, that her own was dependent?

It no sooner flashed across the mind of the Lady Augusta that she was engaged in some such conspiracy with a Scottish insurgent, than she shuddered at the consequences of the dark transactions in which she had now become involved, and which appeared to have a tendency so very different from what she had at first apprehended.

The hours of the morning of this remarkable day, being that of Palm Sunday, were thus drawn out in wandering from place to place; while the Lady de Berkely occasionally interposed by petitions for liberty, which she endeavoured to express in the most moving and pathetic manner, and by offers of wealth and treasures, to which no answer whatever was returned by her strange guide.

At length, as if worn out by his captive's importunity, the knight, coming close up to the bridle-rein of the Lady Augusta, said in a solemn tone—

"I am, as you may well believe, none of those knights who roam through wood and wild, seeking adventures, by which I may obtain grace in the eyes of a fair lady: Yet will I to a certain degree grant the request which thou dost solicit so anxiously, and the arbitration of thy fate shall depend upon the pleasure of him to whose will thou hast expressed thyself ready to submit thine own. I will, on our arrival at the place of our destination, which is now at hand, write to Sir John de Walton, and send my letter, together with thy fair self, by a special messenger. He will, no doubt, speedily attend our summons, and thou shalt thyself be satisfied, that even he who has as yet appeared deaf to entreaty, and insensible to earthly affections, has still some sympathy for beauty and for virtue. I will put the choice of safety, and thy future happiness, into thine own hands, and those of the man whom thou hast chosen; and thou mayst select which thou wilt betwixt those and misery."

While he thus spoke, one of those ravines or clefts in the earth seemed to yawn before them, and entering it at the upper end, the spectre knight, with an attention which he had not yet shown, guided the lady's courser by the rein down the broken and steep path by which alone the bottom of the tangled dingle was accessible.

When placed on firm ground after the dangers of a descent, in which her palfrey seemed to be sustained by the personal strength and address of the singular being who had hold of the bridle, the lady looked with some astonishment at a place so well adapted for concealment as that which she had now reached. It appeared evident that it was used for this purpose, for more than one stifled answer was given to a very low bugle-note emitted by the Knight of the Tomb; and when the same note was repeated, about half a score of armed men, some wearing the dress of soldiers, others those of shepherds and agriculturists, showed themselves imperfectly, as if acknowledging the summons.

CHAPTER THE SIXTEENTH.

"Hail to you, my gallant friends!" said the Knight of the Tomb to his companions, who seemed to welcome him with the eagerness of men engaged in the same perilous undertaking. "The winter has passed over, the festival of Palm Sunday is come, and as surely as the ice and snow of this season shall not remain to chill the earth through the ensuing summer, so surely we, in a few hours, keep our word to those southern braggarts, who think their language of boasting and malice has as much force over our Scottish bosoms, as the blast possesses over the autumn fruits; but it is not so. While we choose to remain concealed, they may as vainly seek to descry us, as a housewife would search for the needle she has dropped among the withered foliage of yon gigantic oak. Yet a few hours, and the lost needle shall become the exterminating sword of the Genius of Scotland, avenging ten thousand injuries, and especially the life of the gallant Lord Douglas, cruelly done to death as an exile from his native country."

An exclamation between a yell and a groan burst from the assembled retainers of Douglas, upon being reminded of the recent death of their chieftain; while they seemed at the same time sensible of the necessity of making little noise, lest they should give the alarm to some of the numerous English parties which were then traversing different parts of the forest. The acclamation, so cautiously uttered, had scarce died away in silence, when the Knight of the Tomb, or, to call him by his proper name, Sir James Douglas, again addressed his handful of faithful followers.

"One effort, my friends, may yet be made to end our strife with the Southron without bloodshed. Fate has within a few hours thrown into my power the young heiress of Berkely, for whose sake it is said Sir John de Walton keeps with such obstinacy the castle which is mine by inheritance. Is there one among you who dare go, as the honourable escort of Augusta de Berkely, bearing a letter, explaining the terms on which I am willing to restore her to her lover, to freedom, and to her English lordships?"

"If there is none other," said a tall man, dressed in the tattered attire of a woodsman, and being, in fact, no other than the very Michael Turnbull,

145

who had already given so extraordinary a proof of his undaunted manhood, "I will gladly be the person who will be the lady's henchman on this expedition."

"Thou art never wanting," said the Douglas, "where a manly deed is to be done; but remember, this lady must pledge to us her word and oath that she will hold herself our faithful prisoner, rescue or no rescue; that she will consider herself as pledged for the life, freedom, and fair usage of Michael Turnbull; and that if Sir John de Walton refuse my terms, she must hold herself obliged to return with Turnbull to our presence, in order to be disposed of at our pleasure."

There was much in these conditions, which struck the Lady Augusta with natural doubt and horror; nevertheless, strange as it may seem, the declaration of the Douglas gave a species of decision to her situation, which might have otherwise been unattainable; and from the high opinion which she entertained of the Douglas's chivalry, she could not bring herself to think, that any part which he might play in the approaching drama would be other than that which a perfect good knight would, under all circumstances, maintain towards his enemy. Even with respect to De Walton, she felt herself relieved of a painful difficulty. The idea of her being discovered by the knight himself, in a male disguise, had preyed upon her spirits; and she felt as if guilty of a departure from the laws of womanhood, in having extended her favour towards him beyond maidenly limits; a step, too, which might tend to lessen her in the eyes of the lover for whom she had hazarded so much.

"The heart, she said, is lightly prized,
   That is but lightly won;
And Long shall mourn the heartless man,
   That leaves his love too soon."

On the other hand, to be brought before him as a prisoner, was indeed a circumstance equally perplexing as unpleasing, but it was one which was beyond her control, and the Douglas, into whose hands she had fallen, appeared to her to represent the deity in the play, whose entrance was almost sufficient to bring its perplexities to a conclusion; she therefore not unwillingly submitted to take what oaths and promises were required by the party in whose hands she found herself, and accordingly engaged to be a true prisoner, whatever might occur. Meantime she strictly obeyed the directions of those who had her motions at command, devoutly praying that circumstances, in themselves so adverse, might nevertheless work together for the safety of her lover and her own freedom.

A pause ensued, during which a slight repast was placed before the Lady Augusta, who was well-nigh exhausted with the fatigues of her journey.

146

Douglas and his partisans, meanwhile, whispered together, as if unwilling she should hear their conference; while, to purchase their good-will, if possible, she studiously avoided every appearance of listening.

After some conversation, Turnbull, who appeared to consider the lady as peculiarly his charge, said to her in a harsh voice, "Do not fear, lady; no wrong shall be done you; nevertheless, you must be content for a space to be blindfolded."

She submitted to this in silent terror; and the trooper, wrapping part of a mantle round her head, did not assist her to remount her palfrey, but lent her his arm to support her in this blinded state.

CHAPTER THE SEVENTEENTH.

The ground which they traversed was, as Lady Augusta could feel, very broken and uneven, and sometimes, as she thought, encumbered with ruins, which were difficult to surmount. The strength of her comrade assisted her forward on such occasions; but his help was so roughly administered, that the lady once or twice, in fear or suffering, was compelled to groan or sigh heavily, whatever was her desire to suppress such evidence of the apprehension which she underwent, or the pain which she endured. Presently, upon an occasion of this kind, she was distinctly sensible that the rough woodsman was removed from her side, and another of the party substituted in his stead, whose voice, more gentle than that of his companions, she thought she had lately heard.

"Noble lady," were the words, "fear not the slightest injury at our hands, and accept of my ministry instead of that of my henchman, who has gone forward with our letter; do not think me presuming on my situation if I bear you in my arms through ruins where you could not easily move alone and blindfold."

At the same time the Lady Augusta Berkely felt herself raised from the earth in the strong arms of a man, and borne onward with the utmost gentleness, without the necessity of making those painful exertions which had been formerly required. She was ashamed of her situation; but, however delicate, it was no time to give vent to complaints, which might have given offence to persons whom it was her interest to conciliate. She, therefore, submitted to necessity, and heard the following words whispered in her ear.

"Fear nothing; there is no evil intended you; nor shall Sir John de Walton, if he loves you as you deserve at his hand, receive any harm on our part. We call on him but to do justice to ourselves and to you; and be assured you will best accomplish your own happiness by aiding our views, which are equally in favour of your wishes and your freedom."

The Lady Augusta would have made some answer to this, but her breath, betwixt fear and the speed with which she was transported, refused to permit her to use intelligible accents. Meantime she began to be sensible that she was enclosed within some building, and probably a ruinous one—for although the mode of her transportation no longer permitted her to ascertain the nature of her path in any respect distinctly, yet the absence of the external air—which was, however, sometimes excluded, and sometimes admitted in furious gusts—intimated that she was conducted through buildings partly entire, and in other places admitting the wind through wide rents and gaps. In one place it seemed to the lady as if she passed through a considerable body of people, all of whom observed silence, although there was sometimes heard among them a murmur, to which every one present in some degree contributed, although the general sound did not exceed a whisper. Her situation made her attend to every circumstance, and she did not fail to observe that these persons made way for him who bore her, until at length she became sensible that he descended by the regular steps of a stair, and that she was now alone excepting his company. Arrived, as it appeared to the lady, on more level ground, they proceeded on their singular road by a course which appeared neither direct nor easy, and through an atmosphere which was close to a smothering degree, and felt at the same time damp and disagreeable, as if from the vapours of a new-made grave. Her guide again spoke.

"Bear up, Lady Augusta, for a little longer, and continue to endure that atmosphere which must be one day common to us all. By the necessity of my situation, I must resign my present office to your original guide, and can only give you my assurance, that neither he, nor any one else, shall offer you the least incivility or insult—and on this you may rely, on the faith of a man of honour."

He placed her, as he said these words, upon the soft turf, and, to her infinite refreshment, made her sensible that she was once more in the open air, and free from the smothering atmosphere which had before oppressed her like that of a charnel-house. At the same time, she breathed in a whisper an anxious wish that she might be permitted to disencumber herself from the folds of the mantle which excluded almost the power of breathing, though intended only to prevent her seeing by what road she travelled. She immediately found it unfolded, agreeably to her request, and hastened, with uncovered eyes, to take note of the scene around her.

It was overshadowed by thick oak trees, among which stood some remnants of buildings, or what might have seemed such, being perhaps the same in which she had been lately wandering. A clear fountain of living water bubbled forth from under the twisted roots of one of those trees, and offered the lady the opportunity of a draught of the pure element, and in which she also bathed her face, which had received more than one scratch in the course of her journey, in spite of the care, and almost the tenderness, with which she had latterly been borne along. The cool water speedily stopt the bleeding of those trifling injuries, and the application served at the same time to recall the scattered senses of the damsel herself. Her first idea was, whether an attempt to escape, if such should appear possible, was not advisable. A moment's reflection, however, satisfied her that such a scheme was not to be thought of; and such second thoughts were confirmed by the approach of the gigantic form of the huntsman Turnbull, the rough tones of whose voice were heard before his figure was obvious to her eye.

"Were you impatient for my return, fair lady? Such as I," he continued in an ironical tone of voice, "who are foremost in the chase of wild stags and silvan cattle, are not in use to lag behind, when fair ladies, like you, are the objects of pursuit; and if I am not so constant in my attendance as you might expect, believe me, it is because I was engaged in another matter, to which I must sacrifice for a little even the duty of attending on you."

"I offer no resistance," said the lady; "forbear, however, in discharging thy duty, to augment my uneasiness by thy conversation, for thy master hath pledged me his word that he will not suffer me to be alarmed or ill treated."

"Nay, fair one," replied the huntsman, "I ever thought it was fit to make interest by soft words with fair ladies; but if you like it not, I have no such pleasure in hunting for fine holyday terms, but that I can with equal ease hold myself silent. Come, then, since we must wait upon this lover of yours ere morning closes, and learn his last resolution touching a matter which is become so strangely complicated, I will hold no more intercourse with you as a female, but talk to you as a person of sense, although an Englishwoman."

"You will," replied the lady, "best fulfil the intentions of those by whose orders you act, by holding no society with me whatever, otherwise than is necessary in the character of guide."

The man lowered his brows, yet seemed to assent to what the Lady of Berkely proposed, and remained silent as they for some time pursued their course, each pondering over their own share of meditation, which probably turned upon matters essentially different. At length the loud blast of a bugle was heard at no great distance from the unsocial fellow-travellers.

"That is the person we seek," said Turnbull; "I know his blast from any other who frequents this forest, and my orders are to bring you to speech of him."

The blood darted rapidly through the lady's veins at the thought of being thus unceremoniously presented to the knight, in whose favour she had confessed a rash preference more agreeable to the manners of those times, when exaggerated sentiments often inspired actions of extravagant generosity, than in our days, when every thing is accounted absurd which does not turn upon a motive connected with the immediate selfish interests of the actor himself. When Turnbull, therefore, winded his horn, as if in answer to the blast which they had heard, the lady was disposed to fly at the first impulse of shame and of fear. Turnbull perceived her intention, and caught hold of her with no very gentle grasp, saying—"Nay, lady, it is to be understood that you play your own part in the drama, which, unless you continue on the stage, will conclude unsatisfactorily to us all, in a combat at outrance between your lover and me, when it will appear which of us is most worthy of your favour."

"I will be patient," said the lady, bethinking her that even this strange man's presence, and the compulsion which he appeared to use towards her, was a sort of excuse to her female scruples, for coming into the presence of her lover, at least at her first appearance before him, in a disguise which her feelings confessed was not extremely decorous, or reconcilable to the dignity of her sex.

The moment after these thoughts had passed through her mind, the tramp of a horse was heard approaching; and Sir John de Walton, pressing through the trees, became aware of the presence of his lady, captive, as it seemed, in the grasp of a Scottish outlaw, who was only known to him by his former audacity at the hunting-match.

His surprise and joy only supplied the knight with those hasty expressions—"Caitiff, let go thy hold! or die in thy profane attempt to control the motions of one whom the very sun in heaven should be proud to obey." At the same time, apprehensive that the huntsman might hurry the lady from his sight by means of some entangled path—such as upon a former occasion had served him for escape Sir John de Walton dropt his cumbrous lance, of which the trees did not permit him the perfect use, and springing from his horse, approached Turnbull with his drawn sword.

The Scotchman, keeping his left hand still upon the lady's mantle, uplifted with his right his battle-axe, or Jedwood staff, for the purpose of parrying and returning the blow of his antagonist, but the lady spoke.

"Sir John de Walton," she said, "for heaven's sake, forbear all violence, till you hear upon what pacific object I am brought hither, and by what peaceful means these wars may be put an end to. This man, though an enemy of yours, has been to me a civil and respectful guardian; and I entreat you to forbear him while he speaks the purpose for which he has brought me hither."

"To speak of compulsion and the Lady de Berkely in the same breath, would itself be cause enough for instant death," said the Governor of Douglas Castle; "but you command, lady, and I spare his insignificant life, although I have causes of complaint against him, the least of which were good warrant, had he a thousand lives, for the forfeiture of them all."

"John de Walton," replied Turnbull, "this lady well knows that no fear of thee operates in my mind to render this a peaceful meeting; and were I not withheld by other circumstances of great consideration to the Douglas as well as thyself, I should have no more fear in facing the utmost thou couldst do, than I have now in levelling that sapling to the earth it grows upon."

So saying, Michael Turnbull raised his battle-axe, and struck from a neighbouring oak-tree a branch, wellnigh as thick as a man's arm, which (with all its twigs and leaves) rushed to the ground between De Walton and the Scotchman, giving a singular instance of the keenness of his weapon, and the strength and dexterity with which he used it.

"Let there be truce, then, between us, good fellow," said Sir John de Walton, "since it is the lady's pleasure that such should be the case, and let me know what thou hast to say to me respecting her?"

"On that subject," said Turnbull, "my words are few, but mark them, Sir Englishman. The Lady Augusta Berkely, wandering in this country, has become a prisoner of the noble Lord Douglas, the rightful inheritor of the Castle and lordship, and he finds himself obliged to attach to the liberty of this lady the following conditions, being in all respects such as good and lawful warfare entitles a knight to exact. That is to say, in all honour and safety the Lady Augusta shall be delivered to Sir John de Walton, or those whom he shall name, for the purpose of receiving her. On the other hand, the Castle of Douglas itself, together with all out-posts or garrisons thereunto belonging, shall be made over and surrendered by Sir John de Walton, in the same situation, and containing the same provisions and artillery, as are now within their walls; and the space of a month of truce shall be permitted to Sir James Douglas and Sir John de Walton farther to regulate the terms of surrender on both parts, having first plighted their knightly word and oath, that in the exchange of the honourable lady for the foresaid castle, lies the full import of the present agreement, and that every other subject of dispute shall, at the pleasure of the noble knights foresaid, be honourably compounded and agreed betwixt them; or at their pleasure, settled knightly by single combat according to usage, and in a fair field, before any honourable person, that may possess power enough to preside."

It is not easy to conceive the astonishment of Sir John de Walton at hearing the contents of this extraordinary cartel; he looked towards the Lady of Berkely with that aspect of despair with which a criminal may be supposed to see his guardian angel prepare for departure. Through her mind also similar ideas flowed, as if they contained a concession of what she had considered as the summit of her wishes, but under conditions disgraceful to her lover, like the cherub's fiery sword of yore, which was a barrier between our first parents and the blessings of Paradise. Sir John de Walton, after a moment's hesitation, broke silence in these words:—

"Noble lady, you may be surprised if a condition be imposed upon me, having for its object your freedom; and if Sir John de Walton, already standing under those obligations to you, which he is proud of acknowledging, should yet hesitate on accepting, with the utmost eagerness, what must ensure your restoration to freedom and independence; but so it is, that the words now spoken have thrilled in mine ear without reaching to my understanding, and I must pray the Lady of Berkely for pardon if I take time to reconsider them for a short space."

"And I," replied Turnbull, "have only power to allow you half an hour for the consideration of an offer, in accepting which, methinks, you should jump shoulder-height instead of asking any time for reflection. What does this cartel exact, save what your duty as a knight implicitly obliges you to? You have engaged yourself to become the agent of the tyrant Edward, in holding Douglas Castle, as his commander, to the prejudice of the Scottish nation, and of the Knight of Douglas Dale, who never, as a community or as an individual, were guilty of the least injury towards you; you are therefore prosecuting a false path, unworthy of a good knight. On the other hand, the freedom and safety of your lady is now proposed to be pledged to you, with a full assurance of her liberty and honour, on consideration of your withdrawing from the unjust line of conduct, in which you have suffered yourself to be imprudently engaged. If you persevere in it, you place your own honour, and the lady's happiness, in the hands of men whom you have done everything in your power to render desperate, and whom, thus irritated, it is most probable you may find such."

"It is not from thee at least," said the knight, "that I shall learn to estimate the manner in which Douglas will explain the laws of war, or De Walton receive them at his dictating."

"I am not, then," said Turnbull, "received as a friendly messenger? Farewell, and think of this lady as being in any hands but those which are safe, while you make up at leisure your mind upon the message I have brought you. Come, madam, we must be gone."

So saying, he seized upon the lady's hand, and pulled her, as if to force her to withdraw. The lady had stood motionless, and almost senseless, while these speeches were exchanged between the warriors; but when she felt the grasp of Michael Turnbull, she exclaimed, like one almost beside herself with fear—"Help me, De Walton!"

The knight, stung to instant rage, assaulted the forester with the utmost fury, and dealt him with his long sword, almost at unawares, two or three heavy blows, by which he was so wounded that he sunk backwards in the thicket, and. De Walton was about to despatch him, when he was prevented by the anxious cry of the lady—"Alas! De Walton, what have you done? This man was only an ambassador, and should have passed free from injury, while he confined himself to the delivery of what he was charged with; and if thou hast slain him, who knows how frightful may prove the vengeance exacted!"

The voice of the lady seemed to recover the huntsman from the effects of the blows he had received: he sprung on his feet, saying—"Never mind me, nor think of my becoming the means of making mischief. The knight, in his haste, spoke without giving me warning and defiance, which gave him an advantage which, I think, he would otherwise have scorned to have taken, in such a case, I will renew the combat on fairer terms, or call another champion, as the knight pleases." With these words he disappeared.

"Fear not, empress of De Walton's thoughts," answered the knight, "but believe, that if we regain together the shelter of Douglas Castle, and the safeguard of Saint George's Cross, thou may'st laugh at all. And if you can but pardon, what I shall never be able to forgive myself, the mole-like blindness which did not recognise the sun while under a temporary eclipse, the task cannot be named too hard for mortal valour to achieve which I shall not willingly undertake, to wipe out the memory of my grievous fault."

"Mention it no more," said the lady; "it is not at such a time as—this, when our lives are for the moment at stake, that quarrels upon slighter topics are to be recurred to. I can tell you, if you do not yet know, that the Scots are in arms in this vicinity, and that even the earth has yawned to conceal them from the sight of your garrison."

"Let it yawn, then," said Sir John de Walton, "and suffer every fiend in the infernal abyss to escape from his prison-house and reinforce our enemies—still, fairest, having received in thee a pearl of matchless price, my spurs shall be hacked from my heels by the basest scullion, if I turn my horse's head to the rear before the utmost force these ruffians can assemble, either upon earth or from underneath it. In thy name I defy them all to instant combat."

As Sir John de Walton pronounced these last words, in something of an exalted tone, a tall cavalier, arrayed in black armour of the simplest form, stepped forth from that part of the thicket where Turnbull had disappeared. "I am," he said, "James of Douglas, and your challenge is accepted. I, the challenged, name the arms our knightly weapons as we now wear them, and our place of combat this field or dingle, called the Bloody Sykes, the time being instant, and the combatants, like true knights, foregoing each advantage on either side." [Footnote: The ominous name of Bloodmire-sink or Syke, marks a narrow hollow to the north-west of Douglas Castle, from which it is distant about the third of a mile. Mr. Haddow states, that according to local tradition, the name was given in consequence of Sir James Douglas having at this spot intercepted and slain part of the garrison of the castle, while De Walton was in command.]

"So be it, in God's name," said the English knight, who, though surprised at being called upon to so sudden an encounter with so formidable a warrior as young Douglas, was too proud to dream of avoiding the combat. Making a sign to the lady to retire behind him, that he might not lose the advantage which he had gained by setting her at liberty from the forester, he drew his sword, and with a deliberate and prepared attitude of offence, moved slowly to the encounter. It was a dreadful one, for the courage and skill both of the native Lord of Douglas Dale, and of De Walton, among the most renowned of the times, and perhaps the world of chivalry could hardly have produced two knights more famous. Their blows fell as if urged by some mighty engine, where they were met and parried with equal strength and dexterity; nor seemed it likely, in the course of ten minutes' encounter, that an advantage would be gained by either combatant over the other. An instant they stopped by mutually implied assent, as it seemed, for the purpose of taking breath, during which Douglas said, "I beg that this noble lady may understand, that her own freedom is no way concerned in the present contest, which entirely regards the injustice done by this Sir John de Walton, and by his nation of England, to the memory of my father, and to my own natural rights."

"You are generous, Sir Knight," replied the lady; "but in what circumstances do you place me, if you deprive me of my protector by death or captivity, and leave me alone in a foreign land?"

"If such should be the event of the combat," replied Sir James, "the Douglas himself, lady, will safely restore thee to thy native land; for never did his sword do an injury for which he was not willing to make amends with the same weapon; and if Sir John de Walton will make the slightest admission that he renounces maintaining the present strife, were it only by yielding up a feather from the plume of his helmet, Douglas will renounce every purpose on his part which can touch the lady's honour or safety, and the combat may be suspended until the national quarrel again brings us together."

Sir John de Walton pondered a moment, and the lady, although she did not speak, looked at him with eyes which plainly expressed how much she wished that he would choose the less hazardous alternative. But the knight's own scruples prevented his bringing the case to so favourable an arbitrement.

"Never shall it be said of Sir John de Walton," he replied, "that he compromised, in the slightest degree, his own honour, or that of his country. This battle may end in my defeat, or rather death, and in that case my earthly prospects are closed, and I resign to Douglas, with my last breath, the charge of the Lady Augusta, trusting that he will defend her with his life, and find the means of replacing her with safety in the halls of her fathers. But while I survive, she may have a better, but will not need another protector than he who is honoured by being her own choice; nor will I yield up, were it a plume from my helmet, implying that I have maintained an unjust quarrel, either in the cause of England, or of the fairest of her daughters. Thus far alone I will concede to Douglas—an instant truce, provided the lady shall not be interrupted in her retreat to England, and the combat be fought out upon another day. The castle and territory of Douglas is the property of Edward of England, the governor in his name is the rightful governor, and on this point I will fight while my eyelids are unclosed."

"Time flies," said Douglas, "without waiting for our resolves; nor is there any part of his motions of such value as that which is passing with every breath of vital air which we presently draw. Why should we adjourn till to-morrow that which can be as well finished today? Will our swords be sharper, or our arms stronger to wield them, than they are at this moment? Douglas will do all which knight can do to succour a lady in distress; but he will not grant to her knight the slightest mark of deference, which Sir John de Walton vainly supposes himself able to extort by force of arms."

With these words, the knights engaged once more in mortal combat, and the lady felt uncertain whether she should attempt her escape through the devious paths of the wood, or abide the issue of this obstinate fight. It was rather her desire to see the fate of Sir John de Walton, than any other consideration, which induced her to remain, as if fascinated, upon the spot, where one of the fiercest quarrels ever fought—was disputed by two of the bravest champions that ever drew sword. At last the lady attempted to put a stop to the combat, by appealing to the bells which began to ring for the service of the day, which was Palm Sunday.

"For Heaven's sake," she said—"for your own sakes, and for that of lady's love, and the duties of chivalry, hold your hands only for an hour, and take chance, that where strength is so equal, means will be found of converting the truce into a solid peace. Think this is Palm Sunday, and will you defile with blood such a peculiar festival of Christianity! Intermit your feud at least so far as to pass to the nearest church, bearing with you branches, not in the ostentatious mode of earthly conquerors, but as rendering due homage to the rules of the blessed Church, and the institutions of our holy religion."

"I was on my road, fair lady, for that purpose, to the holy church of Douglas," said the Englishman, "when I was so fortunate as to meet you at this place; nor do I object to proceed thither even, now, holding truce for an hour, and I fear not to find there friends to whom I can commit you with assurance of safety, in case I am unfortunate in the combat which is now broken off, to be resumed after the service of the day."

"I also assent," said the Douglas, "to a truce for such short space; nor do I fear that there may be good Christians enough at the church, who will not see their master overpowered by odds. Let us go thither, and each take the chance of what Heaven shall please to send us."

From these words Sir John de Walton little doubted that Douglas had assured himself of a party among those who should there assemble; but he doubted not of so many of the garrison being present as would bridle every attempt at rising; and the risk, he thought, was worth incurring, since ha should thereby secure an opportunity to place Lady Augusta de Berkely in safety, at least so far as to make her liberty depend on the event of a general conflict, instead of the precarious issue of a combat between himself and Douglas.

Both these distinguished knights were inwardly of opinion, that the proposal of the lady, though it relieved them from their present conflict, by no means bound them to abstain from the consequences which an accession of force might add to their general strength, and each relied upon his superiority, in some degree provided for by their previous proceedings. Sir John de Walton made almost certain of meeting with several of his bands of soldiers, who were scouring the country and traversing the woods by his direction; and Douglas, it may be supposed, had not ventured himself in person, where a price was set upon his head, without being attended by a sufficient number of approved adherents, placed in more or less connexion with each other, and stationed for mutual support. Each, therefore, entertained well-grounded hopes, that by adopting the truce proposed, he would ensure himself an advantage over his antagonist, although neither exactly knew in what manner or to what extent this success was to be obtained.

CHAPTER THE EIGHTEENTH.

His talk was of another world—his bodiments
Strange, doubtful, and mysterious; those who heard him
Listen'd as to a man in feverish dreams,
Who speaks of other objects than the present,
And mutters like to him who sees a vision.

OLD PLAY.

On the same Palm Sunday when De Walton and Douglas measured together their mighty swords, the minstrel Bertram was busied with the ancient Book of Prophecies, which we have already mentioned as the supposed composition of Thomas the Rhymer, but not without many anxieties as to the fate of his lady, and the events which were passing around him. As a minstrel he was desirous of an auditor to enter into the discoveries which he should make in that mystic volume, as well as to assist in passing away the time; Sir John de Walton had furnished him, in Gilbert Greenleaf the archer, with one who was well contented to play the listener "from morn to dewy eve," provided a flask of Gascon wine, or a stoup of good English ale, remained on the board. It may be remembered that De Walton, when he dismissed the minstrel from the dungeon, was sensible that he owed him some compensation for the causeless suspicion which had dictated his imprisonment, more particularly as he was a valued servant, and had shown himself the faithful confidant of the Lady Augusta de Berkely, and the person who was moreover likely to know all the motives and circumstances of her Scottish journey. To secure his good wishes was, therefore, politic; and De Walton had intimated to his faithful archer that he was to lay aside all suspicion of Bertram, but at the same time keep him in sight, and, if possible, in good humour with the governor of the castle, and his adherents. Greenleaf accordingly had no doubt in his own mind, that the only way to please a minstrel was to listen with patience and commendation to the lays which he liked best to sing, or the tales which he most loved to tell; and in order to ensure the execution of his master's commands, he judged it necessary to demand of the butler such store of good liquor, as could not fail to enhance the pleasure of his society.

Having thus fortified himself with the means of bearing a long interview with the minstrel, Gilbert Greenleaf proposed to confer upon him the bounty of an early breakfast, which, if it pleased him, they might wash down with a cup of sack, and, having his master's commands to show the minstrel any thing about the castle which he might wish to see, refresh their overwearied spirits by attending a part of the garrison of Douglas to the service of the day, which, as we have already seen, was of peculiar sanctity. Against such a proposal the minstrel, a good Christian by profession, and, by his connexion with the joyous science, a good fellow, having no objections to offer, the two comrades, who had formerly little good-will towards each other, commenced their morning's repast on that fated Palm Sunday, with all manner of cordiality and good fellowship.

"Do not believe, worthy minstrel," said the archer, "that my master in any respect disparages your worth or rank in referring you for company or conversation to so poor a man as myself. It is true I am no officer of this garrison; yet for an old archer, who, for these thirty years, has lived by bow and bowstring, I do not (Our Lady make me thankful!) hold less share in the grace of Sir John de Walton, the Earl of Pembroke, and other approved good soldiers, than many of those giddy young men on whom commissions are conferred, and to whom confidences are intrusted, not on account of what they have done, but what their ancestors have done before them. I pray you to notice among them one youth placed at our head in De Walton's absence, and who bears the honoured name of Aymer de Valence, being the same with that of the Earl of Pembroke, of whom I have spoken; this knight has also a brisk young page, whom men call Fabian Harbothel."

"Is it to these gentlemen that your censure applies?" answered the minstrel; "I should have judged differently, having never, in the course of my experience, seen a young man more courteous and amiable than the young knight you named."

"I nothing dispute that it may be so," said the archer, hastening to amend the false step which he had made; "but in order that it should be so, it will be necessary that he conform to the usages of his uncle, taking the advice of experienced old soldiers in the emergencies which may present themselves; and not believing, that the knowledge which it takes many years of observation to acquire, can be at once conferred by the slap of the flat of a sword, and the magic words, 'Rise up, Sir Arthur'—or however the case may be."

"Doubt not, Sir Archer," replied Bertram, "that I am fully aware of the advantage to be derived from conversing with men of experience like you: it benefiteth men of every persuasion, and I myself am oft reduced to lament my want of sufficient knowledge of armorial bearings, signs, and cognizances, and would right fain have thy assistance, where I am a stranger alike to the names of places, of persons, and description of banners and emblems by which great families are distinguished from each other, so absolutely necessary to the accomplishment of my present task."

"Pennons and banners," answered the archer, "I have seen right many, and can assign, as is a soldier's wont, the name of the leader to the emblem under which he musters his followers; nevertheless, worthy minstrel, I cannot presume to understand what you call prophecies, with or under warranted authority of old painted books, expositions of dreams, oracles, revelations, invocations of damned spirits, judicials, astrologicals, and other gross and palpable offences, whereby men, pretending to have the assistance of the devil, do impose upon the common people, in spite of the warnings of the Privy Council; not however, that I suspect you, worthy minstrel, of busying yourself with these attempts to explain futurity, which are dangerous attempts, and may be truly said to be penal, and part of treason."

"There is something in what you say," replied the minstrel; "yet it applieth not to books and manuscripts such as I have been consulting; part, of which things therein written having already come to pass, authorize us surely to expect the completion of the rest; nor would I have much difficulty in showing you from this volume, that enough has been already proved true, to entitle us to look with certainty to the accomplishment of that which remains."

"I should be glad to hear that," answered the archer, who entertained little more than a soldier's belief respecting prophecies and auguries, but yet cared not bluntly to contradict the minstrel upon such subjects, as he had been instructed by Sir John de Walton to comply with his humour. Accordingly the minstrel began to recite verses, which, in our time, the ablest interpreter could not make sense out of.

"When the cook crows, keep well his comb,
For the fox and the fulmart they are false both.
When the raven and the rook have rounded together,
And the kid in his cliff shall accord to the same.
Then shall they be bold, and soon to battle thereafter.
Then the birds of the raven rugs and reives,
And the leal men of Lothian, are louping on their horse;
Then shall the poor people be spoiled full near,
And the Abbeys be burnt truly that stand upon Tweed
They shall burn and slay, and great reif make:
There shall no poor man who say whose man he is:
Then shall the land be lawless, for love there is none.
Then falset shall have foot fully five years;
Then truth surely shall be tint, and none shall lippen to other;
The one cousing shall not trust the other,
Not the son the father, nor the father the son:
For to have his goods he would have him hanged."
&c. &c. &c.

The archer listened to these mystic prognostications, which were not the less wearisome that they were, in a considerable degree, unintelligible; at the same time subduing his Hotspur-like disposition to tire of the recitation, yet at brief intervals comforting himself with an application to the wine flagon, and enduring as he might what he neither understood nor took interest in. Meanwhile the minstrel proceeded with his explanation of the dubious and imperfect vaticinations of which we have given a sufficient specimen.

"Could you wish," said he to Greenleaf, "a more exact description of the miseries which have passed over Scotland in these latter days? Have not these the raven and rook, the fox and the fulmart, explained; either because the nature of the birds or beasts bear an individual resemblance to those of the knights who display them on their banners, or otherwise are bodied forth by actual blazonry on their shields, and come openly into the field to ravage and destroy? Is not the total disunion of the land plainly indicated by these words, that connexions of blood shall be broken asunder, that kinsmen shall not trust each other, and that the father and son, instead, of putting faith in their natural connexion, shall seek each other's life, in order to enjoy his inheritance? The *leal men* of Lothian are distinctly mentioned as taking arms, and there is plainly allusion to the other events of these late Scottish troubles. The death of this last William is obscurely intimated under the type of a hound, which was that good lord's occasional cognizance.

'The hound that was harm'd then muzzled shall be,
Who loved him worst shall weep for his wreck;
Yet shall a whelp rise of the same race,
That rudely shall roar, and rule the whole north,
And quit the whole quarrel of old deeds done,
Though he from his hold be kept back awhile.
True Thomas told me this in a troublesome time,
In a harvest morning at Eldoun hills.'"

"This hath a meaning, Sir Archer," continued the minstrel, "and which flies as directly to its mark as one of your own arrows, although there may be some want of wisdom in making the direct explication. Being, however, upon assurance with you, I do not hesitate to tell you, that in my opinion this lion's whelp that awaits its time, means this same celebrated Scottish prince, Robert the Bruce, who, though repeatedly defeated, has still, while hunted with bloodhounds, and surrounded by enemies of every sort, maintained his pretensions to the crown of Scotland, in despite of King Edward, now reigning."

"Minstrel," answered the soldier, "you are my guest, and we have sat down together as friends to this simple meal in good comradeship. I must tell thee, however, though I am loath to disturb our harmony, that thou art

160

the first who hast adventured to speak a word before Gilbert Greenleaf in favour of that outlawed traitor, Robert Bruce, who has by his seditions so long disturbed the peace of this realm. Take my advice, and be silent on this topic; for, believe me, the sword of a true English archer will spring from its scabbard without consent of its master, should it hear aught said to the disparagement of bonny St. George and his ruddy cross; nor shall the authority of Thomas the Rhymer, or any other prophet in Scotland, England, or Wales, be considered as an apology for such unbecoming predictions."

"I were loth to give offence at any time," said the minstrel, "much more to provoke you to anger, when I am in the very act of experiencing your hospitality. I trust, however, you will remember that I do not come your uninvited guest, and that if I speak to you of future events, I do so without having the least intention to add my endeavour to bring them to pass; for, God knows, it is many years since my sincere prayer has been for peace and happiness to all men, and particularly honour and happiness to the land of Bowmen, in which I was born, and which I am bound to remember in my prayers beyond all other nations in the world."

"It is well that you do so," said the archer; "for so you shall best maintain your bounden duty to the fair land of your birth, which is the richest that the sun shines upon. Something, however, I would know, if it suits with your pleasure to tell me, and that is, whether you find anything in these rude rhymes appearing to affect the safety of the Castle of Douglas, where we now are?—for, mark me, Sir Minstrel, I have observed that these mouldering parchments, when or by whomsoever composed, have so far a certain coincidence with the truth, that when such predictions which they contain are spread abroad in the country, and create rumours of plots, conspiracies, and bloody wars, they are very apt to cause the very mischances which they would be thought only to predict."

"It were not very cautious in me," said the minstrel, "to choose a prophecy for my theme, which had reference to any attack on this garrison; for in such case I should, according to your ideas, lay myself under suspicion of endeavouring to forward what no person could more heartily regret than myself."

"Take my word for it, good friend," said the archer, "that it shall not be thus with thee; for I neither will myself conceive ill of thee, nor report thee to Sir John de Walton as meditating harm against him or his garrison—nor, to speak truth, would Sir John de Walton be willing to believe anyone who did. He thinks highly, and no doubt deservedly, of thy good faith towards thy lady, and would conceive it unjust to suspect the fidelity of one who has given evidence of his willingness to meet death rather than betray the least secret of his mistress."

"In preserving her secret," said Bertram, "I only discharged the duty of a faithful servant, leaving it to her to judge how long such a secret ought to be preserved; for a faithful servant ought to think as little of the issue towards himself of the commission which he bears, as the band of flock silk concerns itself with the secret of the letter which it secures. And, touching your question—I have no objections, although merely to satisfy your curiosity, to unfold to you that these old prophecies do contain some intimations of wars befalling in Douglas Dale, between an haggard, or wild hawk, which I take to be the cognizance of Sir John de Walton, and the three stars, or martlets, which is the cognizance of the Douglas; and more particulars I could tell of these onslaughts, did I know whereabouts is a place in these woods termed Bloody Sykes, the scene also, as I comprehend, of slaughter and death, between the followers of the three stars and those who hold the part of the Saxon, or King of England."

"Such a place," replied Gilbert Greenleaf, "I have heard often mentioned by that name among the natives of these parts; nevertheless it is vain to seek to discover the precise spot, as these wily Scots conceal from us with care every thing respecting the geography of their country, as it is called by learned men; but we may here mention the Bloody Sykes, Bottomless Myre, and other places, as portentous names, to which their traditions attach some signification of war and slaughter. If it suits your wish, however, we can, on our way to the church, try to find this place called Bloody Sykes, which I doubt not we shall trace out long before the traitors who meditate an attack upon us will find a power sufficient for the attempt."

Accordingly the minstrel and archer, the latter of whom was by this time reasonably well refreshed with wine, marched out of the castle of Douglas, without waiting for others of the garrison, resolving to seek the dingle bearing the ominous name of Bloody Sykes, concerning which the archer only knew that by mere accident he had heard of a place bearing such a name, at the hunting match made under the auspices of Sir John de Walton, and knew that it lay in the woods somewhere near the town of Douglas and in the vicinage of the castle.

CHAPTER THE NINETEENTH.

Hotspur. I cannot choose; sometimes he angers me
With telling me of the moldwarp and the ant,
Of the dreamer Merlin, and his prophecies;
And of a dragon and a finless fish,
A clipt-wing'd griffin and a moulten raven,
A couching lion, and a ramping cat.
And such a deal of skimble-skamble stuff,

162

As puts me from my faith.
                    KING HENRY IV.

The conversation between the minstrel and the ancient archer naturally pursued a train somewhat resembling that of Hotspur and Glendower, in which Gilbert Greenleaf by degrees took a larger share than was apparently consistent with his habits and education: but the truth was that as he exerted himself to recall the recognisances of military chieftains, their war-cries, emblems, and other types by which they distinguished themselves in battle, and might undoubtedly be indicated in prophetic rhymes, he began to experience the pleasure which most men entertain when they find themselves unexpectedly possessed of a faculty which the moment calls upon them to employ, and renders them important in the possession of. The minstrel's sound good sense was certainly somewhat surprised at the inconsistencies sometimes displayed by his companion, as he was carried off by the willingness to make show of his newly-discovered faculty on the one hand, and, on the other, to call to mind the prejudices which he had nourished during his whole life against minstrels, who, with the train of legends and fables, were the more likely to be false, as being generally derived from the "North Countrie."

As they strolled from one glade of the forest to another, the minstrel began to be surprised at the number of Scottish votaries whom they met, and who seemed to be hastening to the church, and, as it appeared by the boughs which they carried, to assist in the ceremony of the day. To each of these the archer put a question respecting the existence of a place called Bloody Sykes, and where it was to be found—but all seemed either to be ignorant on the subject, or desirous of evading it, for which they found some pretext in the jolly archer's manner of interrogation, which savoured a good deal of the genial breakfast. The general answer was, that they knew no such place, or had other matters to attend to upon the morn of a holy-tide than answering frivolous questions. At last, when, in one or two; instances, the answer of the Scottish almost approached to sullenness, the minstrel remarked it, observing that there was ever some mischief on foot when the people of this country could not find a civil answer to their betters, which is usually so ready among them, and that they appeared to be making a strong muster for the service of Palm Sunday.

"You will doubtless, Sir Archer," continued the minstrel, "make your report to your knight accordingly; for I promise you, that if you do not, I myself, whose lady's freedom is also concerned, will feel it my duty to place before Sir John de Walton the circumstances which make me entertain suspicion of this extraordinary confluence of Scottish men, and the surliness which has replaced their wonted courtesy of manners."

163

"Tush, Sir Minstrel," replied the archer, displeased at Bertram's interference, "believe me, that armies have ere now depended on my report to the general, which has always been perspicuous and clear, according to the duties of war. Your walk, my worthy friend, has been in a separate department, such as affairs of peace, old songs, prophecies, and the like, in which it is far from my thoughts to contend with you; but credit me, it will be most for the reputation, of both, that we do not attempt to interfere with what concerns each other."

"It is far from my wish to do so," replied the minstrel; "but I would. wish that a speedy return should be made to the castle, in order to ask Sir John de Walton's opinion of that which we have but just seen."

"To this," replied Greenleaf, "there can be no objection; but, would you seek the governor at the hour which now is, you will find him most readily by going to the church of Douglas, to which he regularly wends on occasions such as the present, with the principal part of his officers, to ensure, by his presence, that no tumult arise (of which there is no little dread) between the English and the Scottish. Let us therefore hold to our original intention of attending the service of the day, and we shall rid ourselves of these entangled woods, and gain the shortest road to the church of Douglas."

"Let us go, then, with all despatch," said the minstrel; "and with the greater haste, that it appears to me that something has passed on this very spot this morning, which argues that the Christian peace due to the day has not been inviolably observed. What mean these drops of blood?" alluding to those which had flowed from the wounds of Turnbull—"Wherefore is the earth impressed with these deep tints, the footsteps of armed men advancing and retreating, doubtless, according to the chances of a fierce and heady conflict?"

"By Our Lady," returned Greenleaf, "I must own that thou seest clear. What were my eyes made of when they permitted thee to be the first discoverer of these signs of conflict? Here are feathers of a blue plume, which I ought to remember, seeing my knight assumed it, or at least permitted me to place it in his helmet, this morning, in sign of returning hope, from the liveliness of its colour. But here it lies, shorn from his head, and, if I may guess, by no friendly hand. Come, friend, to the church—to the church—and thou shalt have my example of the manner in which De Walton ought to be supported when in danger."

He led the way through the town of Douglas, entering at the southern gate, and up the very street in which Sir Aymer de Valence had charged the Phantom Knight.

We can now say more fully, that the church of Douglas had originally been a stately Gothic building, whose towers, arising high above the walls of the town, bore witness to the grandeur of its original construction. It was now partly ruinous, and the small portion of open space which was retained for public worship was fitted up in the family aisle where its deceased lords rested from worldly labours and the strife of war. From the open ground in the front of the building, their eye could pursue a considerable part of the course of the river Douglas, which approached the town from the south-west, bordered by a line of hills fantastically diversified in their appearance, and in many places covered with copsewood, which descended towards the valley, and formed a part of the tangled and intricate woodland by which the town was surrounded. The river itself, sweeping round the west side of the town, and from thence northward, supplied that large inundation or artificial piece of water which we have already mentioned. Several of the Scottish people, bearing willow branches, or those of yew, to represent the palms which were the symbol of the day, seemed wandering in the churchyard as if to attend the approach of some person of peculiar sanctity, or procession, of monks and friars, come to render the homage due to the solemnity. At the moment almost that Bertram and his companion entered the churchyard, the Lady of Berkely, who was in the act of following Sir John de Walton into the church, after having witnessed his conflict with the young Knight of Douglas, caught a glimpse of her faithful minstrel, and instantly determined to regain the company of that old servant of her house and confidant of her fortunes, and trust to the chance afterwards of being rejoined by Sir John de Walton, with a sufficient party to provide for her safety, which she in no respect doubted it would be his care to collect. She darted away accordingly from the path in which she was advancing, and reached the place where Bertram, with his new acquaintance Greenleaf, were making some enquiries of the soldiers of the English garrison, whom the service of the day had brought there.

Lady Augusta Berkely, in the meantime, had an opportunity to say privately to her faithful attendant and guide, "Take no notice of me, friend Bertram, but take heed, if possible, that we be not again separated from each other." Having given him this hint, she observed that it was adopted by the minstrel, and that he presently afterwards looked round and set his eye upon her, as, muffled in her pilgrim's cloak, she slowly withdrew to another part of the cemetery, and seemed to halt, until, detaching himself from Greenleaf, he should find an opportunity of joining her.

Nothing, in truth, could have more sensibly affected the faithful minstrel than the singular mode of communication which acquainted him that his mistress was safe, and at liberty to choose her own motions, and, as he might hope, disposed to extricate herself from the dangers which surrounded her in Scotland, by an immediate retreat to her own country and domain. He would gladly have approached and joined her, but she took an opportunity by a sign to caution him against doing so, while at the same time he remained somewhat apprehensive of the consequences of bringing her under the notice of his new friend, Greenleaf, who might perhaps think it proper to busy himself so as to gain some favour with the knight who was at the head of the garrison. Meantime the old archer continued his conversation with Bertram, while the minstrel, like many other men similarly situated, heartily wished that his well-meaning companion had been a hundred fathoms under ground, so his evanishment had given him license to join his mistress; but all he had in his power was to approach her as near as he could, without creating any suspicion.

"I would pray you, worthy minstrel," said Greenleaf, after looking carefully round, "that we may prosecute together the theme which we were agitating before we came hither; is it not your opinion, that the Scottish natives have fixed this very morning for some of those dangerous attempts which they have repeatedly made, and which are so carefully guarded against by the governors placed in this district of Douglas by our good King Edward, our rightful sovereign?"

"I cannot see," replied the minstrel, "on what grounds you found such an apprehension, or what you see here in the churchyard different from that you talked of as we approached it, when you held me rather in scorn, for giving way to some suspicions of the same kind."

"Do you not see," added the archer, "the numbers of men, with strange faces, and in various disguisements, who are thronging about these ancient ruins, which are usually so solitary? Yonder, for example, sits a boy who seems to shun observation, and whose dress, I will be sworn, has never been shaped in Scotland."

"And if he is an English pilgrim," replied the minstrel, observing that the archer pointed towards the Lady of Berkely, "he surely affords less matter of suspicion."

"I know not that," said old Greenleaf, "but I think it will bo my duty to inform Sir John de Walton, if I can reach him, that there are many persons here, who in outward appearance neither belong to the garrison, nor to this part of the country.'"

"Consider," said Bertram, "before you harass with accusation a poor young man, and subject him to the consequences which must necessarily attend upon suspicions of this nature, how many circumstances call forth men peculiarly to devotion at this period. Not only is this the time of the triumphal entrance of the founder of the Christian religion into Jerusalem, but the day itself is called Dominica Confitentium, or the Sunday of Confessors, and the palm-tree, or the box and yew, which are used as its substitutes, and which are distributed to the priests, are burnt solemnly to ashes, and those ashes distributed among the pious, by the priests, upon the Ash-Wednesday of the succeeding year, all which rites and ceremonies in our country, are observed, by order of the Christian Church; nor ought you, gentle archer, nor can you without a crime, persecute those as guilty of designs upon your garrison, who can ascribe their presence here to their desire to discharge the duties of the day; and look ye at yon numerous procession approaching with banner and cross, and, as it appears, consisting of some churchman of rank, and his attendants; let us first enquire who he is, and it is probable we shall find in his name and rank sufficient security for the peaceable and orderly behaviour of those whom piety has this day assembled at the church of Douglas."

Greenleaf accordingly made the investigation recommended by his companion, and received information that the holy man who headed the procession, was no other than the diocesan of the district, the Bishop of Glasgow, who had come to give his countenance to the rites with which the day was to be sanctified.

The prelate accordingly entered the walls of the dilapidated churchyard, preceded by his cross-bearers, and attended by numbers, with boughs of yew and other evergreens, used on the festivity instead of palms. Among them the holy father showered his blessing, accompanied by signs of the cross, which were met with devout exclamations by such of the worshippers as crowded around him:—"To thee, reverend father, we apply for pardon for our offences, which we humbly desire to confess to thee, in order that we may obtain pardon from Heaven."

In this manner the congregation and the dignified clergyman met together, exchanging pious greeting, and seemingly intent upon nothing but the rites of the day. The acclamations of the congregation, mingled with the deep voice of the officiating priest, dispensing the sacred ritual; the whole forming a scene which, conducted with the Catholic skill and ceremonial, was at once imposing and affecting.

The archer, on seeing the zeal with which the people in the churchyard, as well as a number who issued from the church, hastened proudly to salute the bishop of the diocese, was rather ashamed of the suspicions which he had entertained of the sincerity of the good man's purpose in coming hither. Taking advantage of a fit of devotion, not perhaps very common with old Greenleaf, who at this moment thrust himself forward to share in those spiritual advantages which the prelate was dispensing, Bertram. slipped clear of his English friend, and, gliding to the side of the Lady

167

Augusta, exchanged, by the pressure of the hand, a mutual congratulation upon having rejoined company. On a sign by the minstrel, they withdrew to the inside of the church, so as to remain unobserved amidst the crowd, in which they were favoured by the dark shadows of some parts of the building.

The body of the church, broken as it was, and hung round with the armorial trophies of the last Lords of Douglas, furnished rather the appearance of a sacrilegiously desecrated ruin, than the inside of a holy place; yet some care appeared to have been taken to prepare it for the service of the day. At the lower end hung the great escutcheon of William Lord of Douglas, who had lately died a prisoner in England; around that escutcheon were placed the smaller shields of his sixteen ancestors, and a deep black shadow was diffused by the whole mass, unless where relieved by the glance of the coronets, or the glimmer of bearings particularly gay in emblazonry. I need not say that in other respects the interior of the church was much dismantled, it being the very same place in which Sir Aymer de Valence held an interview with the old sexton; and who now, drawing into a separate corner some of the straggling parties whom he had collected and brought to the church, kept on the alert, and appeared ready for an attack as well at mid-day as at the witching hour of midnight. This was the more necessary, as the eye of Sir John de Walton seemed busied in searching from one place to another, as if unable to find the object he was in quest of, which the reader will easily understand to be the Lady Augusta de Berkely, of whom he had lost sight in the pressure of the multitude. At the eastern part of the church was fitted up a temporary altar, by the side of which, arrayed in his robes, the Bishop of Glasgow had taken his place, with such priests and attendants as composed his episcopal retinue. His suite was neither numerous nor richly attired, nor did his own appearance present a splendid specimen of the wealth and dignity of the episcopal order. When he laid down, however, his golden cross, at the stern command of the King of England, that of simple wood, which he assumed instead thereof, did not possess less authority, nor command less awe among the clergy and people of the diocese.

The various persons, natives of Scotland, now gathered around, seemed to watch his motions, as those of a descended saint, and the English waited in mute astonishment, apprehensive that at some unexpected signal an attack would be made upon them, either by the powers of earth or heaven, or perhaps by both in combination. The truth is, that so great was the devotion of the Scottish clergy of the higher ranks to the interests of the party of Bruce, that the English had become jealous of permitting them to interfere even with those ceremonies of the Church which were placed

168

under their proper management, and thence the presence of the Bishop of Glasgow, officiating at a high festival in the church of Douglas, was a circumstance of rare occurrence, and not unattended both with wonder and suspicion. A council of the Church, however, had lately called the distinguished prelates of Scotland to the discharge of their duty on the festivity of Palm Sunday, and neither English nor Scottish saw the ceremony with indifference. An unwonted silence which prevailed in the church, filled, as it appeared, with persons of different views, hopes, wishes, and expectations, resembled one of those solemn pauses which often take place before a strife of the elements, and are well understood to be the forerunners of some dreadful concussion of nature. All animals, according to their various nature, express their sense of the approaching tempest; the cattle, the deer, and other inhabitants of the walks of the forest, withdraw to the inmost recesses of their pastures; the sheep crowd into their fold; and the dull stupor of universal nature, whether animate or inanimate, presages its speedily awakening into general convulsion and disturbance, when the lurid lightning shall hiss at command of the diapason of the thunder.

It was thus that, in deep suspense, those who had come to the church in arms, at the summons, of Douglas, awaited and expected every moment a signal to attack, while the soldiers of the English garrison, aware of the evil disposition of the natives towards them, were reckoning every moment when the well-known shouts of "Bows and bills!" should give signal for a general conflict, and both parties, gazing fiercely upon each other, seemed to expect the fatal onset.

Notwithstanding the tempest, which appeared every moment ready to burst, the Bishop of Glasgow proceeded with the utmost solemnity to perform the ceremonies proper to the day; he paused from time to time to survey the throng, as if to calculate whether the turbulent passions of those around him would be so long kept under as to admit of his duties being brought to a close in a manner becoming the time and place.

The prelate had just concluded the service, when a person advanced towards him with a solemn and mournful aspect, and asked if the reverend father could devote a few moments to administer comfort to a dying man, who was lying wounded close by.

The churchman signified a ready acquiescence, amidst a stillness which, when he surveyed the lowering brows of one party at least of those who were in the church, boded no peaceful termination to this fated day. The father motioned to the messenger to show him the way, and proceeded on his mission, attended by some of those who were understood to be followers of the Douglas.

169

There was something peculiarly striking, if not suspicious, in the interview which followed. In a subterranean vault was deposited the person of a large tall man, whose blood flowed copiously through two or three ghastly wounds, and streamed amongst the trusses of straw on which he lay; while his features exhibited a mixture of sternness and ferocity, which seemed prompt to kindle into a still more savage expression.

The reader will probably conjecture that the person in question was no other than Michael Turnbull, who, wounded in the rencounter of the morning, had been left by some of his friends upon the straw, which was arranged for him by way of couch, to live or die as he best could. The prelate, on entering the vault, lost no time in calling the attention of the wounded man to the state of his spiritual affairs, and assisting him to such comfort as the doctrine of the Church directed should be administered to departing sinners. The words exchanged between them were of that grave and severe character which passes between the ghostly father and his pupil, when one world is rolling away from the view of the sinner, and another is displaying itself in all its terrors, and thundering in the ear of the penitent that retribution which the deeds done in the flesh must needs prepare him to expect. This is one of the most solemn meetings which can take place between earthly beings; and the courageous character of the Jedwood forester, as well as the benevolent and pious expression of the old churchman, considerably enhanced the pathos of the scene.

"Turnbull," said the churchman, "I trust you will believe me when I say that it grieves my heart to see thee brought to this situation by wounds which it is my duty to tell you, you must consider mortal."

"Is the chase ended, then?" said the Jedwood man with a sigh. "I care not, good father, for I think I have borne me as becomes a gallant quarry, and that the old forest has lost no credit by me, whether in pursuit, or in bringing to bay; and even in this last matter, methinks this gay English knight would not have come off with such advantage had the ground on which we stood been alike indifferent to both, or had I been aware of his onset; but it will be seen, by any one who takes the trouble to examine, that poor Michael Turnbull's foot slipped twice in the *melee*, otherwise it had not been his fate to be lying here in the dead-thraw; [Footnote: Or death agony.] while yonder southron would probably have died like a dog, upon this bloody straw, in his place."

The bishop replied, advising his penitent to turn from vindictive thoughts respecting the death of others, and endeavour to fix his attention upon his own departure from existence, which seemed shortly about to take place.

"Nay," replied the wounded man, "you, father, undoubtedly know best what is fit for me to do; yet methinks it would not be very well with me if I had prolonged to this time of day the task of revising my life, and I am not the man to deny that mine has been a bloody and a desperate one. But you will grant me I never bore malice to a brave enemy for having done me an injury, and show me the man, being a Scotchman born, and having a natural love for his own country, who hath not, in these times, rather preferred a steel cap to a hat and feather, or who hath not been more conversant with drawn blades than with prayer-book; and you yourself know, father, whether, in our proceedings against the English interest, we have not uniformly had the countenance of the sincere fathers of the Scottish Church, and whether we have not been exhorted to take arms and make use of them, for the honour of the King of Scotland, and the defence of our own rights."

"Undoubtedly," said the prelate, "such have been our exhortations towards our oppressed countrymen, nor do I now teach you a different doctrine; nevertheless, having now blood around me, and a dying man before me, I have need to pray that I have not been misled from the true path, and thus become the means of misdirecting others. May Heaven forgive me if I have done so, since I have only to plead my sincere and honest intention in excuse for the erroneous counsel which I may have given to you and others touching these wars. I am conscious that encouraging you so to stain your swords in blood, I have departed in some degree from the character of my profession, which enjoins that we neither shed blood, nor are the occasion of its being shed. May Heaven enable us to obey our duties, and to repent of our errors, especially such as have occasioned the death or distress of our fellow-creatures. And, above all, may this dying Christian become aware of his errors, and repent with sincerity of having done to others that which he would not willingly have suffered at their hand!"

"For that matter," answered Turnbull, "the time has never been when I would not exchange a blow with the best man who ever lived; and if I was not in constant practice of the sword, it was because I have been brought up to the use of the Jedwood-axe, which the English call a partisan, and which makes little difference, I understand, from the sword and poniard."

"The distinction is not great," said the bishop; "but I fear, my friend, that life taken with what you call a Jedwood-axe, gives you no privilege over him who commits the same deed, and inflicts the same injury, with any other weapon."

"Nay, worthy father," said the penitent, "I must own that the effect of the weapons is the same, as far as concerns the man who suffers; but I would pray of you information, why a Jedwood man ought not to use, as is the custom of his country, a Jedwood-axe, being, as is implied in the name, the offensive weapon proper to his country?"

"The crime of murder," said the bishop, "consists not in the weapon with which the crime is inflicted, but in the pain which the murderer inflicts upon his fellow-creature, and the breach of good order which he introduces into heaven's lovely and peaceable creation; and it is by turning your repentance upon this crime that you may fairly expect to propitiate Heaven for your offences, and at the same time to escape the consequences which are denounced in Holy Writ against those by whom man's blood shall be shed."

"But, good father," said the wounded man, "you know as well as any one, that in this company, and in this very church, there are upon the watch scores of both Scotchmen and Englishmen, who come here not so much to discharge the religious duties of the day, as literally to bereave each other of their lives, and give a new example of the horror of those feuds which the two extremities of Britain nourish against each other. What conduct, then, is a poor man like me to hold? Am I not to raise this hand against the English, which methinks I still can make a tolerably efficient one—or am I, for the first time in my life, to hear the war-cry when it is raised, and hold back my sword from the slaughter? Methinks it will be difficult, perhaps altogether impossible, for me to do so; but if such is the pleasure of Heaven, and your advice, most reverend father, unquestionably I must do my best to be governed by your directions, as of one who has a right and title to direct us in every dilemma, or case, as they term it, of troubled conscience."

"Unquestionably," said the bishop, "it is my duty, as I have already said, to give no occasion this day for the shedding of blood, or the breach of peace; and I must charge you, as my penitent, that upon your soul's safety, you do not minister any occasion to affray or bloodshed, either by maintaining such in your own person, or inciting others to the same; for by following a different course of advice, I am certain that you, as well as myself, would act sinfully and out of character."

"So I will endeavour to think, reverend father," answered the huntsman; "nevertheless, I hope it will be remembered in my favour that I am the first person bearing the surname of Turnbull, together with the proper name of the Prince of Archangels himself, who has at any time been able to sustain the affront occasioned by the presence of a southron with a drawn sword, and was not thereby provoked to pluck forth his own weapon, and to lay about him."

"Take care, my son," returned the Prelate of Glasgow, "and observe, that even now thou art departing from those resolutions which, but a few minutes since, thou didst adopt upon serious and just consideration; wherefore do not be, O my son! like the sow that has wallowed in the mire,

172

and, having been washed, repeats its act of pollution, and becomes again yet fouler than it was before."

"Well, reverend father," replied the wounded man, "although it seems almost unnatural for Scottishmen and English to meet and part without a buffet, yet I will endeavour most faithfully not to minister any occasion of strife, nor, if possible, to snatch at any such occasion as shall be ministered to me."

"In doing so," returned the bishop, "thou wilt best atone for the injury which thou hast done to the law of Heaven upon former occasions, and thou shalt prevent the causes for strife betwixt thee and thy brethren of the southern land, and shalt eschew the temptation towards that blood-guiltiness which is so rife in this our day and generation. And do not think that I am imposing upon thee, by these admonitions, a duty more difficult than it is in thy covenant to bear, as a man and as a Christian. I myself am a man and a Scotchman, and, as such, I feel offended at the unjust conduct of the English towards our country and sovereign; and thinking as you do yourself, I know what you must suffer when you are obliged to submit to national insults, unretaliated and unrevenged. But let us not conceive ourselves the agents of that retributive vengeance which Heaven has, in a peculiar degree, declared to be its own attribute. Let us, while we see and feel the injuries inflicted on our own country, not forget that our own raids, ambuscades, and surprisals, have been at least equally fatal to the English as their attacks and forays have been to us; and, in short, let the mutual injuries of the crosses of Saint Andrew and of Saint George be no longer considered as hostile to the inhabitants of the opposite district, at least during the festivals of religion; but as they are mutually signs of redemption, let them be, in like manner, intimations of forbearance and peace on both sides."

"I am contented," answered Turnbull, "to abstain from all offences towards others, and shall even endeavour to keep myself from resenting those of others towards me, in the hope of bringing to pass such a quiet and godly state of things as your words, reverend father, induce me to expect." Turning his face to the wall, the Borderer lay in stern expectation of approaching death, which the bishop left him to contemplate. The peaceful disposition which the prelate had inspired into Michael Turnbull, had in some degree diffused itself among those present, who heard with awe the spiritual admonition to suspend the national antipathy, and remain in truce and amity with each other. Heaven had, however, decreed that the national quarrel, in which so much blood had been sacrificed, should that day again be the occasion of deadly strife.

A loud flourish of trumpets, seeming to proceed from beneath the earth, now rung through the church, and roused the attention of the soldiers and worshippers then assembled. Most of those who heard these warlike sounds betook themselves to their weapons, as if they considered it useless to wait any longer for the signal of conflict. Hoarse voices, rude exclamations, the rattle of swords against their sheaths, or their clashing against other pieces of armour, gave an awful presage of an onset, which, however, was for a time averted by the exhortations of the bishop. A second flourish of trumpets having taken place, the voice of a herald made proclamation to the following purpose:—

"That whereas there were many noble pursuivants of chivalry presently assembled in the Kirk of Douglas, and whereas there existed among them the usual causes of quarrel and points of debate for their advancement in chivalry, therefore the Scottish knights were ready to fight any number of the English who might be agreed, either upon the superior beauty of their ladies, or upon the national quarrel in any of its branches, or upon whatever point might be at issue between them, which should be deemed satisfactory ground of quarrel by both; and the knights who should chance to be worsted in such dispute should renounce the prosecution thereof, or the bearing arms therein thereafter, with such other conditions to ensue upon their defeat as might be agreed upon by a council of the knights present at the Kirk of Douglas aforesaid. But foremost of all, any number of Scottish knights, from one to twenty, will defend the quarrel which has already drawn blood, touching the freedom of Lady Augusta de Berkely, and the rendition of Douglas Castle to the owner here present. Wherefore it is required that the English knights do intimate their consent that such trial of valour take place, which, according to the rules of chivalry, they cannot refuse, without losing utterly the reputation of valour, and incurring the diminution of such other degree of estimation as a courageous pursuivant of arms would willingly be held in, both by the good knights of his own country, and those of others."

This unexpected gage of battle realized the worst fears of those who had looked with suspicion on the extraordinary assemblage this day of the dependents of the House of Douglas. After a short pause, the trumpets again flourished lustily, when the reply of the English knights was made in the following terms:—

"That God forbid the rights and privileges of England's knights, and the beauty of her damsels, should not be asserted by her children, or that such English knights as were here assembled, should show the least backwardness to accept the combat offered, whether grounded upon the superior beauty of their ladies, or whether upon the causes of dispute between the countries, for either or all of which the knights of England

174

here present were willing to do battle in the terms of the indenture aforesaid, while sword and lance shall endure. Saving and excepting the surrender of the Castle of Douglas, which can be rendered to no one but England's king, or those acting under his orders."

CHAPTER THE TWENTIETH.

Cry the wild war-note, let the champions pass,
Do bravely each, and God defend the right;
Upon Saint Andrew thrice can they thus cry,
And thrice they shout on height,
And then marked them on the Englishmen,
As I have told you right.
Saint George the bright, our ladies' knight,
To name they were full fain;
Our Englishmen they cried on height,
And thrice they shout again.

OLD BALLAD.

The extraordinary crisis mentioned in the preceding chapter, was the cause, as may be supposed, of the leaders on both sides now throwing aside all concealment, and displaying their utmost strength, by marshalling their respective adherents; the renowned Knight of Douglas, with Sir Malcolm Fleming and other distinguished cavaliers, were seen in close consultation.

Sir John de Walton, startled by the first flourish of trumpets, while anxiously endeavouring to secure a retreat for the Lady Augusta, was in a moment seen collecting his followers, in which he was assisted by the active friendship of the Knight of Valence.

The Lady of Berkely showed no craven spirit at these warlike preparations; she advanced, closely followed by the faithful Bertram, and a female in a riding-hood, whose face, though carefully concealed, was no other than that of the unfortunate Margaret de Hautlieu, whose worst fears had been realized as to the faithlessness of her betrothed knight.

A pause ensued, which for some time no one present thought himself of authority sufficient to break.

At last the Knight of Douglas stepped forward and said, loudly, "I wait to know whether Sir John de Walton requests leave of James of Douglas to evacuate his castle without further wasting that daylight which might show us to judge a fair field, and whether he craves Douglas's protection in doing so?"

The Knight of Walton drew his sword. "I hold the Castle of Douglas," he said, "in spite of all deadly,—and never will I ask the protection from any one which my own sword is competent to afford me."

"I stand by you, Sir John," said Aymer de Valence, "as your true comrade,

175

against whatever odds may oppose themselves to us."

"Courage, noble English," said the voice of Greenleaf; "take your weapons in God's name. Bows and bills! bows and bills!—A messenger brings us notice that Pembroke is in full march hither from the borders of Ayrshire, and will be with us in half an hour. Fight on, gallant English! Valence to the rescue! and long life to the gallant Earl of Pembroke!"

Those English within and around the church no longer delayed to take arms, and De Walton, crying out at the height of his voice, "I implore the Douglas to look nearly to the safety of the ladies," fought his way to the church door; the Scottish finding themselves unable to resist the impression of terror which affected them at the sight of this renowned knight, seconded by his brother-in-arms, both of whom had been so long the terror of the district. In the meantime, it is possible that De Walton might altogether have forced his way out of the church, had he not been met boldly by the young son of Thomas Dickson of Hazelside, while his father was receiving from Douglas the charge of preserving the stranger ladies from all harm from the fight, which, so long suspended, was now on the point of taking place.

De Walton cast his eye upon the Lady Augusta, with a desire of rushing to the rescue; but was forced to conclude, that he provided best for her safety by leaving her under the protection of Douglas's honour.

Young Dickson, in the meantime, heaped blow on blow, seconding with all his juvenile courage every effort he could make, in order to attain the prize due to the conqueror of the renowned De Walton.

"Silly boy," at length said Sir John, who had for some time forborne the stripling, "take, then, thy death from a noble hand, since thou preferrest that to peace and length of days."

"I care not," said the Scottish youth, with his dying breath; "I have lived long enough, since I have kept you so long in the place where you now stand."

And the youth said truly, for as he fell never again to rise, the Douglas stood in his place, and without a word spoken, again engaged with De Walton in the same formidable single combat, by which they had already been distinguished, but with even additional fury. Aymer de Valence drew up to his friend De Walton's left hand, and seemed but to desire the apology of one of Douglas's people attempting to second him, to join in the fray; but as he saw no person who seemed disposed to give him such opportunity, he repressed the inclination, and remained an unwilling spectator. At length it seemed as if Fleming, who stood foremost among the Scottish knights, was desirous to measure his sword with De Valence. Aymer himself, burning with the desire of combat, at last called out, "Faithless Knight of Boghall!

step forth and defend yourself against the imputation of having deserted your lady-love, and of being a man-sworn disgrace to the rolls of chivalry!"

"My answer," said Fleming, "even to a less gross taunt, hangs by my side." In an instant his sword was in his hand, and even the practised warriors who looked on felt difficulty in discovering the progress of the strife, which rather resembled a thunder storm in a mountainous country than the stroke and parry of two swords, offending on the one side, and keeping the defensive on the other.

Their blows were exchanged with surprising rapidity; and although the two combatants did not equal Douglas and De Walton in maintaining a certain degree of reserve, founded upon a respect which these knights mutually entertained for each other, yet the want of art was supplied by a degree of fury, which gave chance at least an equal share in the issue.

Seeing their superiors thus desperately engaged, the partisans, as they were accustomed, stood still on either side, and looked on with the reverence which they instinctively paid to their commanders and leaders in arms. One or two of the women were in the meanwhile attracted, according to the nature of the sex, by compassion for those who had already experienced the casualties of war. Young Dickson, breathing his last among the feet of the combatants, [Footnote: [The fall of this, brave stripling by the hand of the English governor, and the stern heroism of the father in turning from the spot where he lay, "a model of beauty and strength," that he might not be withdrawn from the duty which Douglas had assigned him of protecting the Lady of Berkely, excites an interest for both, with which it is almost to be regretted that history interferes. It was the old man, Thomas Dickson, not his son, who fell. The *slogan*, "a Douglas, a Douglas," having been prematurely raised, Dickson, who was within the church, thinking that his young Lord with his armed band was at hand, drew his sword, and with only one, man to assist him, opposed the English, who now rushed to the door. Cut across the middle by an English sword, he still continued his opposition, till he fell lifeless at the threshold. Such is tradition, and it is supported by a memorial of some authority—a tombstone, still to be seen in the church-yard of Douglas, on winch is sculptured a figure of Dickson, supporting with his left arm his protruding entrails, and raising his sword with the other in the attitude of combat.]—*Note by the Rev, Mr. Stewart of Douglas.*] was in some sort rescued from the tumult by the Lady of Berkely, in whom the action seemed less strange, owing to the pilgrim's dress which she still retained, and who in vain endeavoured to solicit the attention of the boy's father to the task in which she was engaged.

"Cumber yourself not, lady, about that which is bootless," said old Dickson, "and distract not your own attention and mine from preserving you, whom it is the Douglas's wish to rescue, and whom, so please God and St. Bride, I consider as placed by my Chieftain under my charge. Believe me, this youth's death is in no way forgotten, though this be not the time to remember it. A time will come for recollection, and an hour for revenge."

So said the stern old man, reverting his eyes from the bloody corpse which lay at his feet, a model of beauty and strength. Having taken one more anxious look, he turned round, and placed himself where he could best protect the Lady of Berkely, not again turning his eyes on his son's body.

In the interim the combat continued, without the least cessation on either side, and without a decided advantage. At length, however, fate seemed disposed to interfere; the Knight of Fleming, pushing fiercely forward, and brought by chance almost close to the person of the Lady Margaret de Hautlieu, missed his blow, and his foot sliding in the blood of the young victim, Dickson, he fell before his antagonist, and was in imminent danger of being at his mercy, when Margaret de Hautlieu, who inherited the soul of a warrior, and, besides, was a very strong, as well as an undaunted person, seeing a mace of no great weight lying on the floor, where it had been dropped by the fallen Dickson, it, at the same instant, caught her eye, armed her hand, and intercepted, or struck down the sword of Sir Aymer de Valence, who would otherwise have remained the master of the day at that interesting moment. Fleming had more to do to avail himself of an unexpected chance of recovery, than to make a commentary upon the manner in which it had been so singularly brought about; he instantly recovered the advantage he had lost, and was able in the ensuing close to trip up the feet of his antagonist, who fell on the pavement, while the voice of his conqueror, if he could properly be termed such, resounded through the church with the fatal words, "Yield thee, Aymer de Valence—rescue or no rescue—yield thee! —yield ye!" he added, as he placed his sword to the throat of the fallen knight, "not to me, but to this noble lady—rescue or no rescue."

With a heavy heart the English knight perceived that he had lost so favourable an opportunity of acquiring fame, and was obliged to submit to his destiny, or be slain upon the spot. There was only one consolation, that no battle was ever more honourably sustained, being gained as much by accident as by valour.

The fate of the protracted and desperate combat between Douglas and De Walton did not much longer remain in suspense; indeed, the number of conquests in single combat achieved by the Douglas in these wars, was so great, as to make it doubtful whether he was not, in personal strength and skill, even a superior knight to Bruce himself, and he was at least acknowledged nearly his equal in the art of war.

So however it was, that when three quarters of an hour had passed in hard contest, Douglas and De Walton, whose nerves were not actually of iron, began to show some signs that their human bodies were feeling the effect of the dreadful exertion. Their blows began to be drawn more slowly, and were parried with less celerity. Douglas, seeing that the combat must soon come to an end, generously made a signal, intimating to his antagonist to hold his hand for an instant.

"Brave De Walton," he said, "there is no mortal quarrel between us, and you must be sensible that in this passage of arms, Douglas, though he is only worth his sword and his cloak, has abstained from taking a decisive advantage when the chance of arms has more than once offered it. My father's house, the broad domains around it, the dwelling, and the graves of my ancestors, form a reasonable reward for a knight to fight for, and call upon me in an imperative voice the prosecute to strife which has such an object, while you are as welcome to the noble lady, in all honour and safety, as if you had received her from the hands of King Edward himself; and I give you my word, that the utmost honours which can attend a prisoner, and a careful absence of every thing like injury or insult, shall attend De Walton when he yields up the castle, as well as his sword to James of Douglas."

"It is the fate to which I am perhaps doomed," replied Sir John de Walton; "but never will I voluntarily embrace it, and never shall it be said that my own tongue, saving in the last extremity, pronounced upon me the fatal sentence to sink the point of my own sword. Pembroke is upon the march with his whole army, to rescue the garrison of Douglas. I hear the tramp of his horse's feet even now; and I will maintain my ground while I am within reach of support; nor do I fear that the breath which now begins to fail will not last long enough to uphold the struggle till the arrival of the expected succour. Come on, then, and treat me not as a child, but as one who, whether I stand or fall, fears not to encounter the utmost force of my knightly antagonist."

"So be it then," said Douglas, a darksome hue, like the lurid colour of the thunder-cloud, changing his brow as he spoke, intimating that he meditated a speedy end to the contest, when, just as the noise of horses' feet drew nigh, a Welsh knight, known as such by the diminutive size of his steed, his naked limbs, and his bloody spear, called out loudly to the combatants to hold their hands.

"Is Pembroke near?" said De Walton.

"No nearer than Loudon Hill," said the Prestantin; "but I bring his commands to John de Walton."

"I stand ready to obey them through every danger," answered the knight.

"Woe is me," said the Welshman, "that my mouth should bring to the ears of so brave a man tidings so unwelcome! The Earl of Pembroke yesterday received information that the castle of Douglas was attacked by the son of the deceased Earl, and the whole inhabitants of the district. Pembroke, on hearing this, resolved to march to your support, noble knight, with all the forces he had at his disposal. He did so, and accordingly entertained every assurance of relieving the castle, when unexpectedly he met, on Loudon Hill, a body of men of no very inferior force to his own, and having at their head that famous Bruce whom the Scottish rebels acknowledge as their king. He marched instantly to the attack, swearing he would not even draw a comb through his grey beard until he had rid England of his recurring plague. But the fate of war was against us."

He stopt here for lack of breath.

"I thought so!" exclaimed Douglas. "Robert Bruce will now sleep at night, since he has paid home Pembroke for the slaughter of his friends and the dispersion of his army at Methuen Wood. His men are, indeed, accustomed to meet with dangers, and to conquer them: those who follow him have been trained under Wallace, besides being partakers of the perils of Bruce himself. It was thought that the waves had swallowed them when they shipped themselves from the west; but know, that the Bruce was determined with the present reviving spring to awaken his pretensions, and that he retires not from Scotland again while he lives, and while a single lord remains to set his foot by his sovereign, in spite of all the power which has been so feloniously employed against him."

"It is even too true," said the Welshman Meredith, "although it is said by a proud Scotchman.—The Earl of Pembroke, completely defeated, is unable to stir from Ayr, towards which he has retreated with great loss: and he sends his instructions to Sir John de Walton, to make the best terms he can for the surrender of the Castle of Douglas, and trust nothing to his support."

The Scottish, who heard this unexpected news, joined in a shout so loud and energetic, that the ruins of the ancient church seemed actually to rock and threaten to fall on the heads of those who were crowded within it.

The brow of De Walton was overclouded at the news of Pembroke's defeat, although in some respects it placed him at liberty to take measures for the safety of the Lady of Berkely. He could not, however, claim the same honourable terms which had been offered to him by Douglas before the news of the battle of Loudon Hill had arrived.

"Noble knight," he said, "it is entirely at your pleasure to dictate the terms of surrender of your paternal castle; nor have I a right to claim from you those conditions which, a little while since, your generosity put in my offer. But I submit to my fate; and upon whatever terms you think fit to grant me, I must be content to offer to surrender to you the weapon, of which I now put the point in the earth, in evidence that I will never more direct it against you until a fair ransom shall place it once more at my own disposal."

"God forbid," answered the noble James of Douglas, "that I should take such advantage of the bravest knight out of not a few who have found me work in battle! I will take example from the Knight of Fleming, who has gallantly bestowed his captive in guerdon upon a noble damsel here present; and in like manner I transfer my claim upon the person of the redoubted Knight of Walton, to the high and noble Lady Augusta Berkely, who, I hope, will not scorn to accept from the Douglas a gift which the chance of war has thrown into his hands."

Sir John de Walton, on hearing this unexpected decision, looked up like the traveller who discovers the beams of the sun breaking through and dispersing the tempest which has accompanied him for a whole morning. The Lady of Berkely recollected what became her rank, and showed her sense of the Douglas's chivalry. Hastily wiping off the tears which had unwillingly flowed to her eyes, while her lover's safety and her own were resting on the precarious issue of a desperate combat, she assumed the look proper to a heroine of that age, who did not feel averse to accept the importance which was conceded to her by the general voice of the chivalry of the period. Stepping forward, bearing her person gracefully, yet modestly, in the attitude of a lady accustomed to be looked to in difficulties like the present, she addressed the audience in a tone which might not have misbecome the Goddess of Battle dispersing her influence at the close of a field covered with the dead and the dying.

"The noble Douglas," she said, "shall not pass without a prize from the field which he has so nobly won. This rich string of brilliants, which my ancestor won from the Sultan of Trebisond, itself a prize of battle, will be honoured by sustaining, under the Douglas's armour, a lock of hair of the fortunate lady whom the victorious lord has adopted for his guide in. chivalry; and if the Douglas, till he shall adorn it with that lock, will permit the honoured lock of hair which it now bears to retain its station, she on whose head it grew will hold it as a signal that poor Augusta de Berkely is pardoned for having gaged any mortal man in strife with the Knight of Douglas."

"Woman's love," replied the Douglas, "shall not divorce this locket from my bosom, which I will keep till the last day of my life, as emblematic of female worth and female virtue. And, not to encroach upon the valued and honoured province of Sir John de Walton, be it known to all men, that whoever shall say that the Lady Augusta of Berkely has, in this entangled matter, acted otherwise than becomes the noblest of her sex, he will do well to be ready to maintain such a proposition with his lance, against James of Douglas, in a fair field."

This speech was heard with approbation on all sides; and the news brought by Meredith of the defeat of the Earl of Pembroke, and his subsequent retreat, reconciled the fiercest of the English soldiers to the surrender of Douglas Castle. The necessary conditions were speedily agreed on, which put the Scottish in possession of this stronghold, together with the stores, both of arms and ammunition, of every kind which it contained. The garrison had it to boast, that they obtained a free passage, with their horses and arms, to return by the shortest and safest route to the marches of England, without either suffering or inflicting damage.

Margaret of Hautlieu was not behind in acting a generous part; the gallant Knight of Valence was allowed to accompany his friend De Walton and the Lady Augusta to England, and without ransom.

The venerable prelate of Glasgow, seeing what appeared at one time likely to end in a general conflict, terminate so auspiciously for his country, contented himself with bestowing his blessing on the assembled multitude, and retiring with those who came to assist in the service of the day.

This surrender of Douglas Castle upon the Palm Sunday of 19th March, 1306-7, was the beginning of a career of conquest which was uninterrupted, in which the greater part of the strengths and fortresses of Scotland were yielded to those who asserted the liberty of their country, until the crowning mercy was gained in the celebrated field of Bannockburn, where the English sustained a defeat more disastrous than is mentioned upon any other occasion in their annals.

Little need be said of the fate of the persons of this story. King Edward was greatly enraged at Sir John de Walton for having surrendered the Castle of Douglas, securing at the same time his own object, the envied hand of the heiress of Berkely. The knights to whom he referred the matter as a subject of enquiry, gave it nevertheless as their opinion that De Walton was void of all censure, having discharged his duty in its fullest extent, till the commands of his superior officer obliged him to surrender tho Dangerous Castle.

A singular renewal of intercourse took place, many months afterwards, between Margaret of Hautlieu and her lover, Sir Malcolm Fleming. The use which the lady made of her freedom, and of the doom of the Scottish Parliament, which put her in possession of her father's inheritance, was to follow her adventurous spirit through dangers not usually encountered by those of her sex; and the Lady of Hautlieu was not only a daring follower of the chase, but it was said that she was even not daunted in the battlefield. She remained faithful to the political principles which she had adopted at an early period; and it seemed as if she had formed the gallant resolution of shaking the god Cupid from her horse's mane, if not treading him beneath her horse's feet.

The Fleming, although he had vanished from the neighbourhood of the counties of Lanark and Ayr, made an attempt to state his apology to the Lady de Hautlieu herself, who returned his letter unopened, and remained to all appearance resolved never again to enter upon the topic of their original engagement. It chanced, however, at a later period of the war with England, while Fleming was one night travelling upon the Border, after the ordinary fashion of one who sought adventures, a waiting-maid, equipped in a fantastic habit, asked the protection of his arm in the name of her lady, who, late in the evening, had been made captive, she said, by certain ill-disposed caitiffs, who were carrying her by force through the forest. The Fleming's lance was, of course, in its rest, and woe betide the faitour whose lot it was to encounter its thrust; the first fell, incapable of further combat, and another of the felons encountered the same fate with little more resistance. The lady, released from the discourteous cord which restrained her liberty, did not hesitate to join company with the brave knight by whom she had been rescued; and although the darkness did not permit her to recognise her old lover in her liberator, yet she could not but lend a willing ear to the conversation with which he entertained her, as they proceeded on the way. He spoke of the fallen caitiffs as being Englishmen, who found a pleasure in exercising oppression and barbarities upon the wandering damsels of Scotland, and whose cause, therefore, the champions of that country were bound to avenge while the blood throbbed in their veins. He spoke of the injustice of the national quarrel which had afforded a pretence for such deliberate oppression; and the lady, who herself had suffered so much by the interference of the English in the affairs of Scotland, readily acquiesced in the sentiments which he expressed on a subject which she had so much reason for regarding as an afflicting one. Her answer was given in the spirit of a person who would not hesitate, if the times should call for such an example, to defend even with her hand the rights which she asserted with her tongue.

Pleased with the sentiments which she expressed, and recognising in her voice that secret charm, which, once impressed upon the human heart, is rarely wrought out of the remembrance by a long train of subsequent events, he almost persuaded himself that the tones were familiar to him, and had at one time formed the key to his innermost affections. In proceeding on their journey, the knight's troubled state of mind was augmented instead of being diminished. The scenes of his earliest youth were recalled by circumstances so slight, as would in ordinary cases have produced no effect whatever; the sentiments appeared similar to those which his life had been devoted to enforce, and he half persuaded himself that the dawn of day was to be to him the beginning of a fortune equally singular and extraordinary.

In the midst of this anxiety, Sir Malcolm Fleming had no anticipation that the lady whom he had heretofore rejected was again thrown into his path, after years of absence; still less, when daylight gave him a partial view of his fair companion's countenance, was he prepared to believe that he was once again to term himself the champion of Margaret de Hautlieu, but it was so. The lady, on that direful morning when she retired from the church of Douglas, had not resolved (indeed what lady ever did?) to renounce, without some struggle, the beauties which she had once possessed. A long process of time, employed under skilful hands, had succeeded in obliterating the scars which remained as the marks of her fall. These were now considerably effaced, and the lost organ of sight no longer appeared so great a blemish, concealed, as it was, by a black ribbon, and the arts of the tirewoman, who made it her business to shadow it over by a lock of hair. In a word, he saw the same Margaret de Hautlieu, with no very different style of expression from that which her face, partaking of the high and passionate character of her soul, had always presented. It seemed to both, therefore, that their fate, by bringing them together after a separation which appeared so decisive, had intimated its *fiat* that their fortunes were inseparable from each other. By the time that the summer sun had climbed high in the heavens, the two travellers rode apart from their retinue, conversing together with an eagerness which marked the important matters of discussion between them; and in a short time it was made generally known through Scotland, that Sir Malcolm Fleming and the Lady Margaret de Hautlieu were to be united at the court of the good King Robert, and the husband invested with the honours of Biggar and Cumbernauld, an earldom so long known in the family of Fleming.

The gentle reader is acquainted, that these are, in all probability, the last tales which it will be the lot of the Author to submit to the public. He is now on the eve of visiting foreign parts; a ship of war is commissioned by its Royal Master to carry the Author of Waverley to climates in which he may possibly obtain such a restoration of health as may serve him to spin his thread to an end in his own country. Had he continued to prosecute his usual literary labours, it seems indeed probable, that at the term of years he has already attained, the bowl, to use the pathetic language of Scripture,

184

would have been broken at the fountain; and little can one, who has enjoyed on the whole an uncommon share of the most inestimable of worldly blessings, be entitled to complain, that life, advancing to its period, should be attended with its usual proportions of shadows and storms. They have affected him at least in no more painful manner than is inseparable from the discharge of this part of the debt of humanity. Of those whose relation to him in the ranks of life might have ensured him their sympathy under indisposition, many are now no more; and those who may yet follow in his wake, are entitled to expect, in bearing inevitable evils, an example of firmness and patience, more especially on the part of one who has enjoyed no small good fortune during the course of his pilgrimage.

The public have claims on his gratitude, for which the Author of Waverley has no adequate means of expression; but he may be permitted to hope, that the powers of his mind, such as they are, may not have a different date from those of his body; and that he may again meet his patronising friends, if not exactly in his old fashion of literature, at least in some branch, which may not call forth the remark, that—

"Superfluous lags the veteran on the stage."

ABBOTSFORD, *September*, 1831.

END OF CASTLE DANGEROUS.

MY AUNT MARGARET'S MIRROR

INTRODUCTION.—(1831.)

The species of publication—which has come to be generally known by the title of *Annual*, being a miscellany of prose and verse, equipped with numerous engravings, and put forth every year about Christmas, had flourished for a long while in Germany, before it was imitated in this country by an enterprising bookseller, a German by birth, Mr. Ackermann. The rapid success of his work, as is the custom of the time, gave birth to a host of rivals, and, among others, to an Annual styled The Keepsake, the first volume of which appeared in 1828, and attracted much notice, chiefly in consequence of the very uncommon splendour of its illustrative accompaniments. The expenditure which the spirited proprietors lavished on this magnificent volume, is understood to have been not less than from ten to twelve thousand pounds sterling!

Various gentlemen, of such literary reputation that any one might think it an honour to be associated with them, had been announced as contributors to this Annual, before application was made to me to assist in it; and I accordingly placed with much pleasure at the Editor's disposal a few fragments, originally designed to have been worked into the Chronicles of the Canongate, besides a MS. Drama, the long-neglected performance of my youthful days,—the House of Aspen.

185

The Keepsake for 1828 included, however, only three of these little prose tales—of which the first in order was that entitled "My Aunt Margaret's Mirror." By way of *introduction* to this, when now included in a general collection of my lucubrations, I have only to say that it is a mere transcript, or at least with very little embellishment, of a story that I remembered being struck with in my childhood, when told at the fireside by a lady of eminent virtues, and no inconsiderable share of talent, one of the ancient and honourable house of Swinton. She was a kind relation of my own, and met her death in a manner so shocking, being killed in a fit of insanity by a female attendant who had been attached to her person for half a lifetime, that I cannot now recall her memory, child as I was when the catastrophe occurred, without a painful reawakening of perhaps the first images of horror that the scenes of real life stamped on my mind.

This good spinster had in her composition a strong vein of the superstitious, and was pleased, among other fancies, to read alone in her chamber by a taper fixed in a candlestick which she had formed out of a human skull. One night, this strange piece of furniture acquired suddenly the power of locomotion, and, after performing some odd circles on her chimneypiece, fairly leaped on the floor, and continued to roll about the apartment. Mrs. Swinton calmly proceeded to the adjoining room for another light, and had the satisfaction to penetrate the mystery on the spot. Rats abounded in the ancient building she inhabited, and one of these had managed to ensconce itself within her favourite *memento mori*. Though thus endowed with a more than feminine share of nerve, she entertained largely that belief in supernaturals, which in those times was not considered as sitting ungracefully on the grave and aged of her condition; and the story of the Magic Mirror was one for which she vouched with particular confidence, alleging indeed that one of her own family had been an eye-witness of the incidents recorded in it.

"I tell the tale as it was told to me."

Stories enow of much the same cast will present themselves to the recollection of such of my readers as have ever dabbled in a species of lore to which I certainly gave more hours, at one period of my life, than I should gain any credit by confessing.

August, 1831.

MY AUNT MARGARET'S MIRROR.

"There are times
When Fancy plays her gambols, in despite
Even of our watchful senses, when in sooth
Substance seems shadow, shadow substance seems
When the broad, palpabale, and mark'd partition

'Twixt that which is and is not, seems dissolved
As if the mental eye gain'd power to gaze
Beyond the limits of the existing world.
Such hours of shadowy dreams I better love
Than all the gross realities of life."

ANONYMOUS.

My Aunt Margaret was one of that respected sisterhood, upon whom devolve all the trouble and solicitude incidental to the possession of children, excepting only that which attends their entrance into the world. We were a large family, of very different dispositions and constitutions. Some were dull and peevish—they were sent to Aunt Margaret to be amused; some were rude, romping, and boisterous—they were sent to Aunt Margaret to be kept quiet, or rather that their noise might be removed out of hearing: those who were indisposed were sent with the prospect of being nursed—those who were stubborn, with the hope of their being subdued by the kindness of Aunt Margaret's discipline; in short, she had all the various duties of a mother, without the credit and dignity of the maternal character. The busy scene of her various cares is now over—of the invalids and the robust, the kind and the rough, the peevish and pleased children, who thronged her little parlour from morning to night, not one now remains alive but myself; who, afflicted by early infirmity, was one of the most delicate of her nurslings, yet nevertheless, have outlived them all.

It is still my custom, and shall be so while I have the use of my limbs, to visit my respected relation at least three times a-week. Her abode is about half a mile from the suburbs of the town in which I reside; and is accessible, not only by the high-road, from which it stands at some distance, but by means of a greensward footpath, leading through some pretty meadows. I have so little left to torment me in life, that it is one of my greatest vexations to know that several of these sequestered fields have been devoted as sites for building. In that which is nearest the town, wheelbarrows have been at work for several weeks in such numbers, that, I verily believe, its whole surface, to the depth of at least eighteen inches, was mounted in these monotrochs at the same moment, and in the act of being transported from one place to another. Huge triangular piles of planks are also reared in different parts of the devoted messuage; and a little group of trees, that still grace the eastern end, which rises in a gentle ascent, have just received warning to quit, expressed by a daub of white paint, and are to give place to a curious grove of chimneys.

It would, perhaps, hurt others in my situation to reflect that this little range of pasturage once belonged to my father, (whose family was of some consideration in the world,) and was sold by patches to remedy distresses

187

in which he involved himself in an attempt by commercial adventure to redeem, his diminished fortune. While the building scheme was in full operation, this circumstance was often pointed out to me by the class of friends who are anxious that no part of your misfortunes should escape your observation. "Such pasture-ground!—lying at the very town's end—in turnips and potatoes, the parks would bring 20_l_. per acre, and if leased for building—Oh, it was a gold mine!—And all sold for an old song out of the ancient possessor's hands!" My comforters cannot bring me to repine much on this subject. If I could be allowed to look back on the past without interruption, I could willingly give up the enjoyment of present income, and the hope of future profit, to those who have purchased what my father sold. I regret the alteration of the ground only because it destroys associations, and I would more willingly (I think) see the Earl's Closes in the hands of strangers, retaining their silvan appearance, than know them for my own, if torn up by agriculture, or covered with buildings. Mine are the sensations of poor Logan:

"The horrid plough has rased the green
Where yet a child I stray'd;
The axe has fell'd the hawthorn screen,
The schoolboy's summer shade."

I hope, however, the threatened devastation will not be consummated in my day. Although the adventurous spirit of times short while since passed gave rise to the undertaking, I have been encouraged to think, that the subsequent changes have so far damped the spirit of speculation, that the rest of the woodland footpath leading to Aunt Margaret's retreat will be left undisturbed for her time and mine. I am interested in this, for every step of the way, after I have passed through the green already mentioned, has for me something of early remembrance :—There is the stile at which I can recollect a cross child's-maid upbraiding me with my infirmity, as she lifted me coarsely and carelessly over the flinty steps, which my brothers traversed with shout and bound. I remember the suppressed bitterness of the mo-ment, and, conscious of my own inferiority, the feeling of envy with which I regarded the easy movements and elastic steps of my more happily formed brethren. Alas! these goodly barks have all perished on life's wide ocean, and only that which seemed so little seaworthy, as the naval phrase goes, has reached the port when the tempest is over. Then there is the pool, where, manoeuvring our little navy, constructed out of the broad water flags, my elder brother fell in, and was scarce saved from the watery element to die under Nelson's banner. There is the hazel copse also, in which my brother Henry used to gather nuts, thinking little that he was to die in an Indian jungle in quest of rupees.

188

There is so much more of remembrance about the little walk, that—as I stop, rest on my crutch-headed cane, and look round with that species of comparison between the thing I was and that which I now am—it almost induces me to doubt my own identity; until I find myself in face of the honeysuckle porch of Aunt Margaret's dwelling, with its irregularity of front, and its odd projecting latticed windows; where the workmen seem to have made a study that no one of them should resemble another, in form, size, or in the old-fashioned stone entablature and labels which adorn them. This tenement, once the manor-house of Earl's Closes, we still retain a slight hold upon; for, in some family arrangements, it had been settled upon Aunt Margaret during the term of her life. Upon this frail tenure depends, in a great measure, the last shadow of the family of Bothwell of Earl's Closes, and their last slight connection with their paternal inheritance. The only representative will then be an infirm old man, moving not unwillingly to the grave, which has devoured all that were dear to his aifections.

When I have indulged such thoughts for a minute or two, I enter the mansion, which is said to have been the gatehouse only of the original building, and find one being on whom time seems to have made little impression; for the Aunt Margaret of to-day bears the same proportional ago to the Aunt Margaret of my early youth, that the boy of ten years old does to the man of (by'r Lady!) some fifty-six years. The old lady's invariable costume has doubtless some share in confirming one in the opinion, that time has stood still with Aunt Margaret.

The brown or chocolate-coloured silk gown, with ruffles of the same stuff at the elbow, within which are others of Mechlin lace—the black silk gloves, or mitts, the white hair combed back upon a roll, and the cap of spotless cambric, which closes around the venerable countenance, as they were not the costume of 1780, so neither were they that of 1826; they are altogether a style peculiar to the individual Aunt Margaret. There she still sits, as she sat thirty years since, with her wheel or the stocking, which she works by the fire in winter, and by the window in summer; or, perhaps, venturing as far as the porch in an unusually fine summer evening. Her frame, like some well-constructed piece of mechanics, still performs the operations for which it had seemed destined; going its round with an activity which is gradually diminished, yet indicating no probability that it will soon come to a period.

The solicitude and affection which had made Aunt Margaret the willing slave to the inflictions of a whole nursery, have now for their object the health and comfort of one old and infirm man, the last remaining relative of her family, and the only one who can still find interest in the traditional

189

stores which she hoards as some miser hides the gold which he desires that no one should enjoy after his death.

My conversation with Aunt Margaret generally relates little either to the present or to the future: for the passing day we possess as much as we require, and we neither of us wish for more; and for that which is to follow we have on this side of the grave neither hopes, nor fears, nor anxiety. We therefore naturally look back to the past; and forget the present fallen fortunes and declined importance of our family, in recalling the hours when it was wealthy and prosperous.

With this slight introduction, the reader will know as much of Aunt Margaret and her nephew as is necessary to comprehend the following conversation and narrative.

Last week, when, late in a summer evening, I went to call on the old lady to whom my reader is now introduced, I was received by her with all her usual affection and benignity; while, at the same time, she seemed abstracted and disposed to silence. I asked her the reason. "They have been clearing out the old chapel," she said; "John Clayhudgeons having, it seems, discovered that the stuff within—being, I suppose, the remains of our ancestors—was excellent for top-dressing the meadows."

Here I started up with more alacrity than I have displayed for some years; but sat down while my aunt added, laying her hand upon my sleeve, "The chapel has been long considered as common ground, my dear, and used for a penfold, and what objection can we have to the man for employing what is his own, to his own profit? Besides, I did speak to him, and he very readily and civilly promised, that, if he found bones or monuments, they should be carefully respected and reinstated; and what more could I ask? So, the first stone they found bore the name of Margaret Bothwell, 1585, and I have caused it to be laid carefully aside, as I think it betokens death; and having served my namesake two hundred years, it has just been cast up in time to do me the same good turn. My house has been long put in order, as far as the small earthly concerns require it, but who shall say that their account with Heaven is sufficiently revised?"

"After what you have said, aunt," I replied, "perhaps I ought to take my hat and go away, and so I should, but that there is on this occasion a little alloy mingled with our devotion. To think of death at all times is a duty—to suppose it nearer, from the finding of an old gravestone, is superstition; and you, with your strong useful common sense, which was so long the prop of a fallen family, are the last person whom I should have suspected of such weakness."

"Neither would I have deserved your suspicions, kinsman" answered Aunt Margaret, "if we were speaking of any incident occurring in the actual

190

business of human life. But for all this I have a sense of superstition about me, which I do not wish to part with. It is a feeling which separates me from this age, and links me with that to which I am hastening; and even when it seems, as now, to lead me to the brink of the grave, and bids me gaze on it, I do not love that it should be dispelled. It soothes my imagination, without influencing my reason or conduct."

"I profess, my good lady," replied I, "that had any one but you made such a declaration, I should have thought it as capricious as that of the clergyman, who, without vindicating his false reading, preferred, from habit's sake, his old Mumpsimus to the modern Sumpsimus."

"Well," answered my aunt, "I must explain my inconsistency in this particular, by comparing it to another. I am, as you know, a piece of that old-fashioned thing called a Jacobite; but I am so in sentiment and feeling only; for a more loyal subject never joined in prayers, for the health and wealth of George the Fourth, whom God long preserve! But I dare say that kind-hearted sovereign would not deem that an old woman did him, much injury if she leaned back in her arm-chair, just in such a twilight as this, and thought of the high-mettled men, whose sense of duty called them to arms against his grandfather; and how, in a cause which they deemed that of their rightful prince and country,

'They fought till their hands to the broadsword were glued,

They fought against fortune with hearts unsubdued.'

do not come at such a moment, when my head is full of plaids, pibrochs, and claymores, and ask my reason to admit what, I am afraid, it cannot deny—I mean, that the public advantage peremptorily demanded that these things should cease to exist. I cannot, indeed, refuse to allow the justice of your reasoning; but yet, being convinced against my will, you will gain little by your motion. You might as well read to an infatuated lover the catalogue of his mistress's imperfections; for, when he has been compelled to listen to the summary, you will only get for answer, that, 'he lo'es her a' the better.'"

I was not sorry to have changed the gloomy train of Aunt Margaret's thoughts, and replied in the same tone, "Well, I can't help being persuaded that our good king is the more sure of Mrs. Bothwell's loyal affection, that he has the Stuart right of birth, as well as the Act of Succession in his favour."

"Perhaps my attachment, were its source of consequence, might be foumd warmer for the union of the rights you mention," said Aunt Margaret? "but, upon my word, it would be as sincere if the king's right were founded only on the will of the nation, as declared at the Revolution. I am none of your *jure divino* folk."

"And a Jacobite notwithstanding."

"And a Jacobite notwithstanding; or rather, I will give you leave to call me one of the party which, in Queen Anne's time, were called *Whimsicals*; because they were sometimes operated upon by feelings, sometimes by principle. After all, it is very hard that you will not allow an old woman to be as inconsistent in her political sentiments, as mankind in general show themselves in all the various courses of life; since you cannot point out one of them, in which the passions and prejudices of those who pursue it are not perpetually carrying us away from the path which our reason points out."

"True, aunt; but you are a wilful wanderer, who should be forced back into the right path."

"Spare me, I entreat you," replied Aunt Margaret. "You remember the Gaelic song, though I dare say I mispronounce the words—

'Hatil mohatil, na dowski mi.'

'I am asleep, do not waken me.'

I tell you, kinsman, that the sort of waking dreams which my imagination spins out, in what your favourite Wordsworth calls 'moods of my own mind,' are worth all the rest of my more active days. Then, instead of looking forwards as I did in youth, and forming for myself fairy palaces, upon the verge of the grave, I turn my eyes backward upon the days and manners of my better time; and the sad, yet soothing recollections come so close and interesting, that I almost think it sacrilege to be wiser, or more rational, or less prejudiced, than those to whom I looked up in my younger years."

"I think I now understand what you mean," I answered, "and can comprehend why you should occasionally prefer the twilight of illusion to the steady light of reason."

"Where there is no task," she rejoined, "to be performed, we may sit in the dark if we like it—if we go to work, we must ring for candles."

"And amidst such shadowy and doubtful light," continued I, "imagination frames her enchanted and enchanting visions, and sometimes passes them upon the senses for reality."

"Yes," said Aunt Margaret, who is a well-read woman, "to those who resemble the translator of Tasso,

'Prevailing poet, whose undoubting mind
Believed the magic wonders which he sung.'

It is not required for this purpose, that you should be sensible of the painful horrors which an actual belief in such prodigies inflicts—such a belief, now-a-days, belongs only to fools and children. It is not necessary that your ears should tingle, and your complexion change, like that of Theodore, at the approach of the spectral huntsman. All that is

192

indispensable for the enjoyment of the milder feeling of supernatural awe is, that you should be susceptible of the slight shuddering which creeps over you when you hear a tale of terror—that well-vouched tale which the narrator, having first expressed his general disbelief of all such legendary lore, selects and produces, as having something in it which he has been always obliged to give up as inexplicable. Another symptom is, a momentary hesitation to look round you, when the interest of the narrative is at the highest; and the third, a desire to avoid looking into a mirror, when you are alone, in your chamber, for the evening. I mean such are signs which indicate the crisis, when a female imagination is in due temperature to enjoy a ghost story. I do not pretend to describe those which express the same disposition in a gentleman."

"This last symptom, dear aunt, of shunning the mirror, seems likely to be a rare occurrence amongst the fair sex."

"You are a novice in toilet fashions, my dear kinsman. All women consult the looking-glass with anxiety before they go into company; but when they return home, the mirror has not the same charm. The die has been cast-the party has been successful or unsuccessful, in the impression which she desired to make. But, without going deeper into the mysteries of the dressing-table, I will tell you that I myself, like many other honest folk, do not like to see the blank black front of a large mirror in a room dimly lighted, and where the reflection of the candle seems rather to lose itself in the deep obscurity of the glass, than to be reflected back again into the apartment. That space of inky darkness seems to be a field for Fancy to play her revels in. She may call up other features to meet us, instead of the reflection of our own; or, as in the spells of Hallowe'en, which we learned in childhood some unknown form may be seen peeping over our shoulder. In short, when I am in a ghost-seeing humour, I make my handmaiden draw the green curtains over the mirror, before I go into the room, so that she may have the first shock of the apparition, if there be any to be seen. But, to tell you the truth, this dislike to look into a mirror in particular times and places, has, I believe, its original foundation in a story which came to me by tradition from my grandmother, who was a party concerned in the scene of which I will now tell you."

THE MIRROR.
CHAPTER THE FIRST.

You are fond (said my aunt) of sketches of the society which has passed away. I wish I could describe to you Sir Philip Forester, the "chartered libertine" of Scottish good company, about the end of the last century. I never saw him indeed; but my mother's traditions were full of his wit, gallantry and dissipation. This gay knight flourished about the end of the

17th and beginning of the 18th century. He was the Sir Charles Easy and the Lovelace of his day and country; renowned for the number of duels he had fought, and the successful intrigues which he had carried on. The supremacy which he had attained in the fashionable world was absolute; and when we combine with it one or two anecdotes, for which, "if laws were made for every degree," he ought certainly to have been hanged, the popularity of such a person really serves to show, either that the present times are much more decent, if not more virtuous, than they formerly were; or, that high breeding then was of more difficult attainment than that which is now so called; and, consequently, entitled the successful professor to a proportionable degree of plenary indulgences and privileges. No beau of this day could have borne out so ugly a story as that of Pretty Peggy Grindstone, the miller's daughter at Sillermills—it had well-nigh made work for the Lord Advocate. But it hurt Sir Philip Forester no more than the hail hurts the hearth-stone. He was as well received in society as ever, and dined with the Duke of A—— the day the poor girl was buried. She died of heart-break. But that has nothing to do with my story.

Now, you must listen to a single word upon kith, kin, and ally; I promise you I will not be prolix. But it is necessary to the authenticity of my legend, that you should know that Sir Philip Forester, with his handsome person, elegant accomplishments, and fashionable manners, married the younger Miss Falconer of King's Copland. The elder sister of this lady had previously become the wife of my grandfather, Sir Geoffrey Bothwell, and brought into our family a good fortune. Miss Jemima, or Miss Jemmie Falconer, as she was usually called, had also about ten thousand pounds sterling—then thought a very handsome portion indeed.

The two sisters were extremely different, though each had their admirers while they remained single. Lady Bothwell had some touch of the old King's Copland blood about her. She was bold, though not to the degree of audacity; ambitious, and desirous to raise her house and family; and was, as has been said, a considerable spur to my grandfather, who was otherwise an indolent man; but whom, unless he has been slandered, his lady's influence involved in some political matters which had been more wisely let alone. She was a woman of high principle, however, and masculine good sense, as some of her letters testify, which are still in my wainscot cabinet.

Jemmie Falconer was the reverse of her sister in every respect. Her understanding did not reach above the ordinary pitch, if, indeed, she could be said to have attained it. Her beauty, while it lasted, consisted, in a great measure, of delicacy of complexion and regularity of features, without any peculiar force of expression. Even these charms faded under the sufferings attendant on an ill-sorted match. She was passionately attached to her husband, by whom she was treated with a callous, yet polite indifference, which, to one whose heart was as tender as her judgment was weak, was more painful perhaps than absolute ill-usage. Sir Philip was a voluptuary, that is, a completely selfish egotist, whose disposition and character resembled the rapier he wore, polished, keen, and brilliant, but inflexible and unpitying. As he observed carefully all the usual forms towards his lady, he had the art to deprive her even of the compassion of the world; and useless and unavailing as that may be while actually possessed by the sufferer, it is, to a mind like Lady Forester's, most painful to know she has it not.

The tattle of society did its best to place the peccant husband above the suffering wife. Some called her a poor spiritless thing, and declared, that, with a little of her sister's spirit, she might have brought to reason any Sir Philip whatsoever, were it the termagant Falconbridge himself. But the greater part of their acquaintance affected candour, and saw faults on both sides; though, in fact, there only existed the oppressor and the oppressed. The tone of such critics was—"To be sure, no one will justify Sir Philip Forester, but then we all know Sir Philip, and Jemmie Falconer might have known what she had to expect from the beginning.—What made her set her cap at Sir Philip?—He would never have looked at her if she had not thrown herself at his head, with her poor ten thousand pounds. I am sure, if it is money he wanted, she spoiled his market. I know where Sir Philip could have done much better.—And then, if she *would* have the man, could not she try to make him more comfortable at home, and have his friends oftener, and not plague him with the squalling children, and take care all was handsome and in good style about the house? I declare I think Sir Philip would have made a very domestic man, with a woman who knew how to manage him."

Now these fair critics, in raising their profound edifice of domestic felicity, did not recollect that the corner-stone was wanting; and that to receive good company with good cheer, the means of the banquet ought to have been furnished by Sir Philip; whose income (dilapidated as it was) was not equal to the display of hospitality required, and, at the same time, to the supply of the good knight's *menus plaisirs*. So, in spite of all that was so sagely suggested by female friends, Sir Philip carried his good-humour every where abroad, and left at home a solitary mansion and a pining spouse.

At length, inconvenienced in his money affairs, and tired even of the short time which he spent in his own dull house, Sir Philip Forester determined to take a trip to the Continent, in the capacity of a volunteer. It was then common for men of fashion to do so; and our knight perhaps was of opinion that a touch of the military character, just enough to exalt, but not render pedantic, his qualities as a *beau garcon*, was necessary to maintain possession of the elevated situation which he held in the ranks of fashion.

Sir Philip's resolution threw his wife into agonies of terror, by which the worthy baronet was so much annoyed, that, contrary to his wont, he took some trouble to soothe her apprehensions; and once more brought her to shed tears, in which sorrow was not altogether unmingled with pleasure. Lady Bothwell asked, as a favour, Sir Philip's permission to receive her sister and her family into her own house during his absence on the Continent. Sir Philip readily assented to a proposition which saved expense, silenced the foolish people who might have talked of a deserted wife and family, and gratified Lady Bothwell, for whom he felt some respect, as for one who often spoke to him, always with freedom, and sometimes with severity, without being deterred either by his raillery, or the *prestige* of his reputation.

A day or two before Sir Philip's departure, Lady Bothwell took the liberty of asking him, in her sister's presence, the direct question, which his timid wife had often desired, but never ventured, to put to him.

"Pray, Sir Philip, what route do you take when you reach the Continent?"

"I go from Leith to Helvoet by a packet with advices."

"That I comprehend perfectly," said Lady Bothwell dryly; "but you do not mean to remain long at Helvoet, I presume, and I should like to know what is your next object?"

"You ask me, my dear lady," answered Sir Philip, "a question which I have not dared to ask myself. The answer depends on the fate of war. I shall, of course, go to headquarters, wherever they may happen to be for the time; deliver my letters of introduction; learn as much of the noble art of war as may suffice a poor interloping amateur; and then take a glance at the sort of thing of which we read so much in the Gazette."

"And I trust, Sir Philip," said Lady Bothwell, "that you will remember that you are a husband and a father; and that though you think fit to indulge this military fancy, you will not let it hurry you into dangers which it is certainly unnecessary for any save professional persons to encounter?"

"Lady Bothwell does me too much honour," replied the adventurous knight, "in regarding such a circumstance with the slightest interest. But to soothe your flattering anxiety, I trust your ladyship will recollect, that I cannot expose to hazard the venerable and paternal character which you so obligingly recommend to my protection, without putting in some peril an honest fellow, called Philip Forester, with whom I have kept company for thirty years, and with whom, though some folk consider him a coxcomb, I have not the least desire to part."

"Well, Sir Philip, you are the best judge of your own affairs; I have little right to interfere—you are not my husband."

"God forbid!"—said Sir Philip hastily; instantly adding, however, "God forbid that I should deprive my friend Sir Geoffrey of so inestimable a treasure."

"But you are my sister's husband," replied the lady; "and I suppose you are aware of her present distress of mind—"

"If hearing of nothing else from morning to night can make me aware of it," said Sir Philip, "I should know something of the matter."

"I do not pretend to reply to your wit, Sir Philip," answered Lady Bothwell, "but you must be sensible that all this distress is on account of apprehensions for your personal safety."

"In that case, I am surprised that Lady Bothwell, at least, should give herself so much trouble upon so insignificant a subject."

"My sister's interest may account for my being anxious to learn something of Sir Philip Forester's motions; about which otherwise, I know, he would not wish me to concern myself. I have a brother's safety, too, to be anxious for."

"You mean Major Falconer, your brother by the mother's side:—What can he possibly have to do with our present agreeable conversation?"

"You have had words together, Sir Philip," said Lady Bothwell.

"Naturally; we are connections," replied Sir Philip, "and as such have always had the usual intercourse."

"That is an evasion of the subject," answered the lady. "By words, I mean angry words, on the subject of your usage of your wife."

"If," replied Sir Philip Forester, "you suppose Major Falconer simple enough to intrude his advice upon me, Lady Bothwell, in my domestic matters, you are indeed warranted in believing that I might possibly be so far displeased with the interference, as to request him to reserve his advice till it was asked."

"And, being on these terms, you are going to join the very army in which my brother Falconer is now serving?"

"No man knows the path of honour better than Major Falconer," said Sir Philip. "An aspirant after fame, like me, cannot choose a better guide than his footsteps."

Lady Bothwell rose and went to the window, the tears gushing from her eyes.

"And this heartless raillery," she said, "is all the consideration that is to be given to our apprehensions of a quarrel which may bring on the most terrible consequences? Good God! of what can men's hearts be made, who can thus dally with the agony of others?"

Sir Philip Forester was moved; he laid aside the mocking tone in which he had hitherto spoken.

"Dear Lady Bothwell," he said, taking her reluctant hand, "we are both wrong:—you are too deeply serious; I, perhaps, too little. The dispute I had with Major Falconer was of no earthly consequence. Had any thing occurred betwixt us that ought to have been settled *par voie du fait*, as we say in France, neither of us are persons that are likely to postpone such a meeting. Permit me to say, that were it generally known that you or my Lady Forester are apprehensive of such a catastrophe, it might be the very means of bringing about what would not otherwise be likely to happen. I know your good sense, Lady Bothwell, and that you will understand me when I say, that really my affairs require my absence for some months;— this Jemima cannot understand; it is a perpetual recurrence of questions, why can you not do this, or that, or the third thing; and, when you have proved to her that her expedients are totally ineffectual, you have just to begin the whole round again. Now, do you tell her, dear Lady Bothwell, that *you* are satisfied. She is, you must confess, one of those persons with whom authority goes farther than reasoning. Do but repose a little confidence in me, and you shall see how amply I will repay it."

Lady Bothwell shook her head, as one but half satisfied. "How difficult it is to extend confidence, when the basis on which it ought to rest has been so much shaken! But I will do my best to make Jemima easy; and farther, I can only say, that for keeping your present purpose, I hold you responsible both to God and man."

"Do not fear that I will deceive you," said Sir Philip; "the safest conveyance to me will be through the general post-office, Helvoetsluys, where I will take care to leave orders for forwarding my letters. As for Falconer, our only encounter will be over a bottle of Burgundy! so make yourself perfectly easy on his score."

Lady Bothwell could not make herself easy; yet she was sensible that her sister hurt her own cause by *taking on*, as the maid-servants call it, too vehemently; and by showing before every stranger, by manner, and sometimes by words also, a dissatisfaction with her husband's journey, that was sure to come to his ears, and equally certain to displease him. But there was no help for this domestic dissension, which ended only with the day of separation.

I am sorry I cannot tell, with precision, the year in which Sir Philip Forester went over to Flanders; but it was one of those in which the campaign opened with extraordinary fury; and many bloody, though indecisive, skirmishes were fought between the French on the one side, and the Allies on the other. In all our modern improvements, there are none, perhaps, greater than in the accuracy and speed with which intelligence is transmitted from any scene of action to those in this country whom it may concern. During Marlborough's campaigns, the sufferings of the many who had relations in, or along with, the army, were greatly augmented by the suspense in which they were detained for weeks, after they had heard of bloody battles in which, in all probability, those for whom their bosoms throbbed with anxiety had been personally engaged. Amongst those who were most agonized by this state of uncertainty, was the—I had almost said deserted—-wife of the gay Sir Philip Forester. A single letter had informed her of his arrival on the Continent—no others were received. One notice occurred in the newspapers, in which Volunteer Sir Philip Forester was mentioned as having been entrusted with a dangerous reconnoissance, which he had executed with the greatest courage, dexterity, and intelligence, and received the thanks of the commanding officer. The sense of his having acquired distinction brought a momentary glow into the lady's pale cheek; but it—was instantly lost in ashen whiteness at the recollection of his danger. After this, they had no news whatever, neither from Sir Philip, nor even from their brother Falconer. The case of Lady Forester was not indeed different from that of hundreds in the same situation; but a feeble mind is necessarily an irritable one, and the suspense which some bear with constitutional indifference or philosophical resignation, and some with a disposition to believe and hope the best, was intolerable to Lady Forester, at once solitary and sensitive, low-spirited, and devoid of strength of mind, whether natural or acquired.

CHAPTER THE SECOND.

As she received no farther news of Sir Philip, whether directly or indirectly, his unfortunate lady began now to feel a sort of consolation, even in those careless habits which had so often given her pain. "He is so thoughtless," she repeated a hundred times a day to her sister, "he never writes when things are going on smoothly; it is his way: had any thing happened he would have informed us."

Lady Bothwell listened to her sister without attempting to console her. Probably she might be of opinion, that even the worst intelligence which could be received from Flanders might not be without some touch of consolation; and that the Dowager Lady Forester, if so she was doomed to be called, might have a source of happiness unknown to the wife of the gayest and finest gentleman in Scotland. This conviction became stronger as they learned from inquiries made at headquarters, that Sir Philip was no longer with the army; though whether he had been taken or slain in some of those skirmishes which were perpetually occurring, and in which he loved to distinguish himself, or whether he had, for some unknown reason or capricious change of mind, voluntarily left the service, none of his countrymen in the camp of the Allies could form even a conjecture. Meantime his creditors at home became clamorous, entered into possession of big property, and threatened his person, should he be rash enough to return to Scotland. These additional disadvantages aggravated Lady Bothwell's displeasure against the fugitive husband; while her sister saw nothing in any of them, save what tended to increase her grief for the absence of him whom her imagination now represented,—as it had before marriage,—gallant, gay, and affectionate.

About this period there appeared in Edinburgh a man of singular appearance and pretensions. He was commonly called the Paduan Doctor, from having received his education at that famous university. He was supposed to possess some rare receipts in medicine, with which, it was affirmed, he had wrought remarkable cures. But though, on the one hand, the physicians of Edinburgh termed him an empiric, there were many persons, and among them some of the clergy, who, while they admitted the truth of the cures and the force of his remedies, alleged that Doctor Baptisti Damiotti made use of charms and unlawful arts in order to obtain success in his practice. The resorting to him was even solemnly preached against, as a seeking of health from idols, and a trusting to the help which was to come from Egypt. But the protection which the Paduan Doctor received from some friends of interest and consequence, enabled him to set these imputations at defiance, and to assume, even in the city of Edinburgh, famed as it was for abhorrence of witches and necromancers, the dangerous character of an expounder of futurity. It was at length rumoured, that for a certain gratification, which, of course, was not an inconsiderable one, Doctor Baptisti Damiotti could tell the fate of the absent, and even show his visitors the personal form of their absent friends, and the action in which they were engaged at the moment. This rumour came to the ears of Lady Forester, who had reached that pitch of mental agony in which the sufferer will do any thing, or endure any thing, that suspense may be converted into certainty.

Gentle and timid in most cases, her state of mind made her equally obstinate and reckless, and it was with no small surprise and alarm that her sister, Lady Bothwell, heard her express a resolution to visit this man of art, and learn from him the fate of her husband. Lady Bothwell remonstrated on the improbability that such pretensions as those of this foreigner could be founded on any thing but imposture.

"I care not," said the deserted wife, "what degree of ridicule I may incur; if there be any one chance out of a hundred that I may obtain some certainty of my husband's fate, I would not miss that chance for whatever else the world can offer me."

Lady Bothwell next urged the unlawfulness of resorting to such sources of forbidden knowledge.

"Sister," replied the sufferer, "he who is dying of thirst cannot refrain from drinking poisoned water. She who suffers under suspense must seek information, even were the powers which offer it unhallowed and infernal. I go to learn my fate alone; and this very evening will I know it: the sun that rises to-morrow shall find me, if not more happy, at least more resigned."

"Sister," said Lady Bothwell, "if you are determined upon this wild step, you shall not go alone. If this man be an impostor, you may be too much agitated by your feelings to detect his villany. If, which I cannot believe, there be any truth in what he pretends, you shall not be exposed alone to a communication of so extraordinary a nature. I will go with you, if indeed you determine to go. But yet reconsider your project, and renounce inquiries which cannot be prosecuted without guilt, and perhaps without danger."

Lady Forester threw herself into her sister's arms, and, clasping her to her bosom, thanked her a hundred times for the offer of her company; while she declined with a melancholy gesture the friendly advice with which it was accompanied.

When the hour of twilight arrived,—which was the period when the Paduan Doctor was understood to receive the visits of those who came to consult with him,—the two ladies left their apartments in the Canongate of Edinburgh, having their dress arranged like that of women of an inferior description, and their plaids disposed around their faces as they were worn by the same class; for, in those days of aristocracy, the quality of the wearer was generally indicated by the manner in which her plaid was disposed, as well as by the fineness of its texture. It was Lady Bothwell who had suggested this species of disguise, partly to avoid observation as they should go to the conjuror's house, and partly in order to make trial of his penetration, by appearing before him in a feigned character. Lady Forester's servant, of tried fidelity, had been employed by her to propitiate the Doctor by a suitable fee, and a story intimating that a soldier's wife desired to know the fate of her husband; a subject upon which, in all probability, the sage was very frequently consulted.

To the last moment, when the palace clock struck eight, Lady Bothwell earnestly watched her sister, in hopes that she might retreat from, her rash undertaking; but as mildness, and even timidity, is capable at times of vehement and fixed purposes, she found Lady Forester resolutely unmoved and determined when the moment of departure arrived. Ill satisfied with

201

the expedition, but determined not to leave her sister at such a crisis, Lady Bothwell accompanied Lady Forester through more than one obscure street and lane, the servant walking before, and acting as their guide. At length he suddenly turned into a narrow court, and knocked at an arched door, which seemed to belong to a building of some antiquity. It opened, though no one appeared to act as porter; and the servant, stepping aside from the entrance, motioned the ladies to enter. They had no sooner done so, than it shut, and excluded their guide. The two ladies found themselves in a small vestibule, illuminated by a dim lamp, and having, when the door was closed, no communication with the external light or air. The door of an inner apartment, partly open, was at the farther side of the vestibule.

"We must not hesitate now, Jemima," said Lady Bothwell, and walked forwards into the inner room, where, surrounded by books, maps, philosophical utensils, and other implements of peculiar shape and appearance, they found the man of art.

There was nothing very peculiar in the Italian's appearance. He had the dark complexion and marked features of his country, seemed about fifty years old, and was handsomely, but plainly, dressed in a full suit of black clothes, which was then the universal costume of the medical profession. Large wax-lights, in silver sconces, illuminated the apartment, which was reasonably furnished. He rose as the ladies entered; and, not-withstanding the inferiority of their dress, received them with the marked respect due to their quality, and which foreigners are usually punctilious in rendering to those to whom such honours are due.

Lady Bothwell endeavoured to maintain her proposed incognito; and, as the Doctor ushered them to the upper end of the room, made a motion declining his courtesy, as unfitted for their condition. "We are poor people, sir," she said; "only my sister's distress has brought us to consult your worship whether—"

He smiled as he interrupted her—"I am aware, madam, of your sister's distress, and its cause; I am aware, also, that I am honoured with a visit from two ladies of the highest consideration—Lady Bothwell and Lady Forester. If I could not distinguish them from the class of society which their present dress would indicate, there would be small possibility of my being able to gratify them by giving the information which they come to seek."

"I can easily understand," said Lady Bothwell——

"Pardon my boldness to interrupt you, milady," cried the Italian; "your ladyship was about to say, that you could easily understand that I had got possession of your names by means of your domestic. But in thinking so, you do injustice to the fidelity of your servant, and, I may add, to the skill of one who is also not less your humble servant—Baptisti Damiotti."

"I have no intention to do either, sir," said Lady Bothwell, maintaining a tone of composure, though somewhat surprised, "but the situation is something new to me. If you know who we are, you also know, sir, what brought us here."

"Curiosity to know the fate of a Scottish gentleman of rank, now, or lately upon the Continent," answered the seer; "his name is Il Cavaliero Philippo Forester; a gentleman who has the honour to be husband to this lady, and, with your ladyship's permission for using plain language, the misfortune not to value as it deserves that inestimable advantage."

Lady Forester sighed deeply, and Lady Bothwell replied—

"Since you know our object without our telling it, the only question that remains is, whether you have the power to relieve my sister's anxiety?"

"I have, madam," answered the Paduan scholar; "but there is still a previous inquiry. Have you the courage to behold with your own eyes what the Cavaliero Philippo Forester is now doing? or will you take it on my report?"

"That question my sister must answer for herself," said Lady Bothwell.

"With my own eyes will I endure to see whatever you have power to show me," said Lady Forester, with the same determined spirit which had stimulated her since her resolution was taken upon this subject.

"There may be danger in it."

"If gold can compensate the risk," said Lady Forester, taking out her purse.

"I do not such things for the purpose of gain," answered the foreigner. "I dare not turn my art to such a purpose. If I take the gold of the wealthy, it is but to bestow it on the poor; nor do I ever accept more than the sum I have already received from your servant. Put up your purse, madam; an adept needs not your gold."

Lady Bothwell considering this rejection of her sister's offer as a mere trick of an empiric, to induce her to press a larger sum upon him, and willing that the scene should be commenced and ended, offered some gold in turn, observing that it was only to enlarge the sphere of his charity.

"Let Lady Bothwell enlarge the sphere of her own charity," said the Paduan, "not merely in giving of alms, in which I know she is not deficient, but in judging the character of others; and let her oblige Baptisti Damiotti by believing him honest, till she shall discover him to be a knave. Do not be surprised, madam, if I speak in answer to your thoughts rather than your expressions, and tell me once more whether you have courage to look on what I am prepared to show?"

"I own, sir," said Lady Bothwell. "that your words strike me with some

203

sense of fear; but whatever my sister desires to witness, I will not shrink from witnessing along with her."

"Nay, the danger only consists in the risk of your resolution failing you. The sight can only last for the space of seven minutes; and should you interrupt the vision by speaking a single word, not only would the charm be broken, but some danger might result to the spectators. But if you can remain steadily silent for the seven minutes, your curiosity will be gratified without the slightest risk; and for this I will engage my honour."

Internally Lady Bothwell thought the security was but an indifferent one; but she suppressed the suspicion, as if she had believed that the adept, whose dark features wore a half-formed smile, could in reality read even her most secret reflections. A solemn pause then ensued, until Lady Forester gathered courage enough to reply to the physician, as he termed himself, that she would abide with firmness and silence the sight which he had promised to exhibit to them. Upon this, he made them a low obeisance, and saying he went to prepare matters to meet their wish, left the apartment. The two sisters, hand in hand, as if seeking by that close union to divert any danger which might threaten them, sat down on two seats in immediate contact with each other: Jemima seeking support in the manly and habitual courage of Lady Bothwell; and she, on the other hand, more agitated than she had expected, endeavouring to fortify herself by the desperate resolution which circumstances had forced her sister to assume. The one perhaps said to herself, that her sister never feared anything; and the other might reflect, that what so feeble a minded woman as Jemima did not fear, could not properly be a subject of apprehension to a person of firmness and resolution like herself.

In a few moments the thoughts of both were diverted from their own situation, by a strain of music so singularly sweet and solemn, that, while it seemed calculated to avert or dispel any feeling unconnected with its harmony, increased, at the same time, the solemn excitation which the preceding interview was calculated to produce. The music was that of some instrument with which they were unacquainted; but circumstances afterwards led my ancestress to believe that it was, that of the harmonica, which she heard at a much later period in life.

When these heaven-born sounds had ceased, a door opened in the upper end of the apartment, and they saw Damiotti, standing at the head of two or three steps, sign to them to advance. His dress was so different from that which he had worn a few minutes before, that they could hardly recognize him; and the deadly paleness of his countenance, and a certain rigidity of muscles, like that of one whose mind is made up to some strange and daring action, had totally changed the somewhat sarcastic expression with which he had previously regarded them both, and particularly Lady Bothwell. He was barefooted, excepting a species of sandals in the antique fashion; his legs were naked beneath the knees; above them he wore hose, and a doublet of dark crimson silk close to his body; and over that a flowing loose robe, something resembling a surplice, of snow-white linen; his throat and neck were uncovered, and his long, straight, black hair was carefully combed down at full length.

As the ladies approached at his bidding, he showed no gesture of that ceremonious courtesy of which he had been formerly lavish. On the contrary, he made the signal of advance with an air of command; and when, arm in arm, and with insecure steps, the sisters approached the spot where he stood, it was with a warning frown that he pressed his finger to his lips, as if reiterating his condition of absolute silence, while, stalking before them, he led the way into the next apartment.

This was a large room, hung with black, as if for a funeral. At the upper end was a table, or rather a species of altar, covered with the same lugubrious colour, on which lay divers objects resembling the usual implements of sorcery. These objects were not indeed visible as they advanced into the apartment; for the light which displayed them, being only that of two expiring lamps, was extremely faint. The master —to use the Italian phrase for persons of this description—approached the upper end of the room with a genuflexion like that of a Catholic to the crucifix, and at the same time crossed himself. The ladies followed in silence, and arm in arm. Two or three low broad steps led to a platform in front of the altar, or what resembled such. Here the sage took his stand, and placed the ladies beside him, once more earnestly repeating by signs his injunctions of silence. The Italian then, extending his bare arm from under his linen vestment, pointed with his forefinger to five large flambeaux, or torches, placed on each side of the altar. They took fire successively at the approach of his hand, or rather of his finger, and spread a strong light through the room. By this the visitors could discern that, on the seeming altar, were disposed two naked swords laid crosswise; a large open book, which they conceived to be a copy of the Holy Scriptures, but in a language to them unknown; and beside this mysterious volume was placed a human skull. But what struck the sisters most was a very tall and broad mirror, which occupied all the space behind the altar, and, illuminated by the lighted torches, reflected the mysterious articles which were laid upon it.

The master then placed himself between the two ladies, and, pointing to the mirror, took each by the hand, but without speaking a syllable. They gazed intently on the polished and sable space to which he had directed their attention. Suddenly the surface assumed a new and singular appearance. It no longer simply reflected the objects placed before it, but, as if it had self-contained scenery of its own, objects began to appear within it, at first in a disorderly, indistinct, and miscellaneous manner, like form arranging itself out of chaos; at length, in distinct and defined shape and symmetry. It was thus that, after some shifting of light and darkness over the face of the wonderful glass, a long perspective of arches and columns began to arrange itself on its sides, and a vaulted roof on the upper part of it; till, after many oscillations, the whole vision gained a fixed and stationary appearance, representing the interior of a foreign church. The pillars were stately, and hung with scutcheons; the arches were lofty and magnificent; the floor was lettered with funeral inscriptions. But there were no separate shrines, no images, no display of chalice or crucifix on the altar. It was, therefore, a Protestant church upon the Continent. A clergyman, dressed in the Geneva gown and band, stood by the communion-table, and, with the Bible opened before him, and his clerk awaiting in the background, seemed prepared to perform some service of the church to which he belonged.

At length there entered the middle aisle of the building a numerous party, which appeared to be a bridal one, as a lady and gentleman walked first, hand in hand, followed by a large concourse of persons of both sexes, gaily, nay richly, attired. The bride, whose features they could distinctly see, seemed not more than sixteen years old, and extremely beautiful. The bridegroom, for some seconds, moved rather with his shoulder towards them, and his face averted; but his elegance of form and step struck the sisters at once with the same apprehension. As he turned his face suddenly, he was frightfully realized, and they saw, in the gay bridegroom before them, Sir Philip Forester. His wife uttered an imperfect exclamation, at the sound of which the whole scene stirred and seemed to separate.

"I could compare it to nothing," said Lady Bothwell, while recounting the wonderful tale, "but to the dispersion of the reflection offered by a deep and calm pool, when a stone is suddenly cast into it, and the shadows become dissipated and broken." The master pressed both the ladies' hands severely, as if to remind them of their promise, and of the danger which they incurred. The exclamation died away on Lady Forester's tongue without attaining perfect utterance, and the scene in the glass, after the fluctuation of a minute, again resumed to the eye its former appearance of a real scene, existing within the mirror, as if represented in a picture, save that the figures were moveable instead of being stationary.

The representation of Sir Philip Forester, now distinctly visible in form and feature, was seen to lead on towards the clergyman that beautiful girl, who advanced at once with diffidence, and with a species of affectionate pride. In the meantime, and just as the clergyman had arranged the bridal company before him, and seemed about to commence the service, another group of persons, of whom two or three were officers, entered the church. They moved, at first, forward, as though they came to witness the bridal ceremony, but suddenly one of the officers, whose back was towards the spectators, detached himself from his companions, and rushed hastily towards the marriage party, when the whole of them, turned towards him, as if attracted by some exclamation which had accompanied his advance Suddenly the intruder drew his sword; the bridegroom unsheathed his own, and made towards him; swords were also drawn by other individuals, both of the marriage party, and of those who had last entered. They fell into a sort of confusion, the clergyman, and some elder and graver persons, labouring apparently to keep the peace, while the hotter spirits on both sides brandished their weapons. But now the period of brief space during which the soothsayer, as he pretended, was permitted to exhibit his art, was arrived. The fumes again mixed together, and dissolved gradually from observation; the vaults and columns of the church rolled asunder, and disappeared; and the front of the mirror reflected nothing save the blazing torches, and the melancholy apparatus placed on the altar or table before it.

The doctor led the ladies, who greatly required his support, into the apartment from whence they came; where wine, essences, and other means of restoring suspended animation, had been provided during his absence. He motioned them to chairs, which they occupied in silence; Lady Forester, in particular, wringing her hands, and casting her eyes up to heaven, but without speaking a word, as if the spell had been still before her eyes.

"And what we have seen is even now acting?" said Lady Bothwell, collecting herself with difficulty.

"That," answered Baptisti Damiotti, "I cannot justly, or with certainty, say. But it is either now acting, or has been acted, during a short space before this. It is the last remarkable transaction in which the Cavalier Forester has been engaged."

Lady Bothwell then expressed anxiety concerning her sister, whose altered countenance and apparent unconsciousness of what passed around her, excited her apprehensions how it might be possible to convey her home.

"I have prepared for that," answered the adept; "I have directed the servant to bring your equipage as near to this place as the narrowness of the street will permit. Fear not for your sister; but give her, when you return home, this composing draught, and she will be better to-morrow morning. Few," he added, in a melancholy tone, "leave this house as well in health as they entered it. Such being the consequence of seeking knowledge by mysterious means, I leave you to judge the condition of those who have the power of gratifying such irregular curiosity. Farewell, and forget not the potion."

"I will give her nothing that comes from you," said Lady Bothwell; "I have seen enough of your art already. Perhaps you would poison us both to conceal your own necromancy. But we are persons who want neither the means of making our wrongs known, nor the assistance of friends to right them."

"You have had no wrongs from me, madam," said the adept. "You sought one who is little grateful for such honour. He seeks no one, and only gives responses to those who invite and call upon him. After all, you have but learned a little sooner the evil which you must still be doomed to endure. I hear your servant's step at the door, and will detain your ladyship and Lady Forester no longer. The next packet from the continent will explain what you have partly witnessed. Let it not, if I may advise, pass too suddenly into your sister's hands."

So saying, he bid Lady Bothwell good-night. She went, lighted by the adept, to the vestibule, where he hastily threw a black cloak over his singular dress, and opening the door intrusted his visitors to the care of the servant. It was with difficulty that Lady Bothwell sustained her sister to the carriage, though it was only twenty steps distant. When they arrived at home, Lady Forester required medical assistance. The physician of the family attended, and shook his head on feeling her pulse.

"Here has been," he said, "a violent and sudden shock on the nerves. I must know how it has happened."

Lady Bothwell admitted they had visited the conjuror, and that Lady Forester had received some bad news respecting her husband, Sir Philip.

"That rascally quack would make my fortune were he to stay in Edinburgh," said the graduate; "this is the seventh nervous case I have heard of his making for me, and all by effect of terror." He next examined the composing draught which Lady Bothwell had unconsciously brought in her hand, tasted it, and pronounced it very germain to the matter, and what would save an application to the apothecary. He then paused, and looking at Lady Bothwell very significantly, at length added, "I suppose I must not ask your ladyship anything about this Italian warlock's proceedings?"

"Indeed, Doctor," answered Lady Bothwell, "I consider what passed as confidential; and though the man may be a rogue, yet, as we were fools enough to consult him, we should, I think, be honest enough to keep his counsel."

"*May* be a knave—come," said the Doctor, "I am glad to hear your ladyship allows such a possibility in any thing that comes from Italy."

"What comes from Italy may be as good as what conies from Hanover, Doctor. But you and I will remain good friends, and that it may be so, we will say nothing of Whig and Tory."

"Not I," said the Doctor, receiving his fee, and taking his hat; "a Carolus serves my purpose as well as a Willielmus. But I should like to know why old Lady Saint Ringan's, and all that set, go about wasting their decayed lungs in puffing this foreign fellow."

"Ay—you had best set him down a Jesuit, as Scrub says." On these terms they parted.

The poor patient—whose nerves, from an extraordinary state of tension, had at length become relaxed in as extraordinary a degree—continued to struggle with a sort of imbecility, the growth of superstitious terror, when the shocking tidings were brought from Holland, which fulfilled even her worst expectations.

They were sent by the celebrated Earl of Stair, and contained the melancholy event of a duel betwixt Sir Philip Forester, and his wife's half-brother, Captain Falconer, of the Scotch-Dutch, as they were then called, in which the latter had been killed. The cause of quarrel rendered the incident still more shocking. It seemed that Sir Philip had left the army suddenly, in consequence of being unable to pay a very considerable sum, which he had lost to another volunteer at play. He had changed his name, and taken up his residence at Rotterdam, where he had insinuated himself into the good graces of an ancient and rich burgomaster, and, by his handsome person and graceful manners, captivated the affections of his only child, a very young person, of great beauty, and the heiress of much wealth. Delighted with the specious attractions of his proposed son-in-law, the wealthy merchant—whose idea of the British character was too high to admit of his taking any precaution to acquire evidence of his condition and circumstances—gave his consent to the marriage. It was about to be celebrated in the principal church of the city, when it was interrupted by a singular occurrence.

Captain Falconer having been detached to Rotterdam to bring up a part of the brigade of Scottish auxiliaries, who were in quarters there, a person of consideration in the town, to whom he had been formerly known, proposed to him for amusement to go to the high church, to see a countryman of his own married to the daughter of a wealthy burgomaster. Captain Falconer went accordingly, accompanied by his Dutch acquaintance with a party of his friends, and two or three officers of the Scotch brigade. His astonishment may be conceived when he saw his own brother-in-law, a married man, on the point of leading to the altar the innocent and beautiful creature, upon whom he was about to practise a base and unmanly deceit. He proclaimed his villany on the spot, and the marriage was interrupted of course. But against the opinion of more thinking men, who considered Sir Philip Forester as having thrown himself out of the rank of men of honour, Captain Falconer admitted him to the privilege of such, accepted a challenge from him, and in the rencounter received a mortal wound. Such are the ways of Heaven, mysterious in our eyes. Lady Forester never recovered the shock of this dismal intelligence.

* * * * *

"And did this tragedy," said I, "take place exactly at the time when the scene in the mirror was exhibited?"

"It is hard to be obliged to maim one's story," answered my aunt; "but, to speak the truth, it happened some days sooner than the apparition was exhibited."

"And so there remained a possibility," said I, "that by some secret and speedy communication the artist might have received early intelligence of that incident."

"The incredulous pretended so," replied my aunt.

"What became of the adept?" demanded I.

"Why, a warrant came down shortly afterwards to arrest him for high-treason, as an agent of the Chevalier St. George; and Lady Bothwell, recollecting the hints which had escaped the Doctor, an ardent friend of the Protestant succession, did then call to remembrance, that this man was chiefly *prone* among the ancient matrons of her own political persuasion. It certainly seemed probable that intelligence from the continent, which could easily have been transmitted by an active and powerful agent, might have enabled him to prepare such a scene of phantasmagoria as she had herself witnessed. Yet there were so many difficulties in assigning a natural explanation, that, to the day of her death, she remained in great doubt on the subject, and much disposed to cut the Gordian knot, by admitting the existence of supernatural agency."

"But, my dear aunt," said I, "what became of the man of skill?"

"Oh, he was too good a fortune-teller not to be able to foresee that his own destiny would be tragical if he waited the arrival of the man with the silver greyhound upon his sleeve. He made, as we say, a moonlight flitting, and was nowhere to be seen or heard of. Some noise there was about papers or letters found in the house, but it died away, and Doctor Baptisti Damiotti was soon as little talked of as Galen or Hippocrates."

"And Sir Philip Forester," said I, "did he too vanish for ever from the public scene?"

"No," replied my kind informer. "He was heard of once more, and it was upon a remarkable occasion. It is said that we Scots, when there was such a nation in existence, have, among our full peck of virtues, one or two little barleycorns of vice. In particular, it is alleged that we rarely forgive, and never forget, any injuries received; that we used to make an idol of our resentment, as poor Lady Constance did of her grief; and are addicted, as Burns says, to 'nursing our wrath to keep it warm.' Lady Bothwell was not without this feeling; and, I believe, nothing whatever, scarce the restoration of the Stuart line, could have happened so delicious to her feelings as an opportunity of being revenged on Sir Philip Forester, for the deep and double injury which had deprived her of a sister and of a brother. But nothing of him was heard or known till many a year had passed away."

At length—it was on a Fastern's E'en (Shrovetide) assembly, at which the whole fashion of Edinburgh attended, full and frequent, and when Lady Bothwell had a seat amongst the lady patronesses, that one of the attendants on the company whispered into her ear, that a gentleman wished to speak with her in private.

"In private? and in an assembly-room?—he must be mad—Tell him to call upon me to-morrow morning."

"I said, so, my lady," answered the man; "but he desired me to give you this paper."

She undid the billet, which was curiously folded and sealed. It only bore the words, "*On business of life and death*," written in a hand which she had never seen before. Suddenly it occurred to her, that it might concern the safety of some of her political friends; she therefore followed the messenger to a small apartment where the refreshments were prepared, and from which the general company was excluded. She found an old man, who, at her approach, rose up and bowed profoundly. His appearance indicated a broken constitution; and his dress, though sedulously rendered conforming to the etiquette of a ball-room, was worn and tarnished, and hung in folds about his emaciated person. Lady Bothwell was about to feel for her purse, expecting to get rid of the supplicant at the expense of a little money, but some fear of a mistake arrested her purpose. She therefore gave the man leisure to explain himself.

"I have the honour to speak with the Lady Bothwell?"

"I am Lady Bothwell; allow me to say, that this is no time or place for long explanations.—What are your commands with me?"

"Your ladyship," said the old man, "had once a sister."

"True; whom I loved as my own soul."

"And a brother."

"The bravest, the kindest, the most affectionate!" said Lady Bothwell.

211

"Both these beloved relatives you lost by the fault of an unfortunate man," continued the stranger.

"By the crime of an unnatural, bloody-minded murderer," said the lady.

"I am answered," replied the old man, bowing, as if to withdraw.

"Stop, sir, I command you," said Lady Bothwell.—"Who are you, that, at such a place and time, come to recall these horrible recollections? I insist upon knowing."

"I am one who intends Lady Bothwell no injury; but, on the contrary, to offer her the means of doing a deed of Christian charity, which the world would wonder at, and which Heaven would reward; but I find her in no temper for such a sacrifice as I was prepared to ask."

"Speak out, sir; what is your meaning?" said Lady Bothwell.

"The wretch that has wronged you so deeply," rejoined the stranger, "is now on his death-bed. His days have been days of misery, his nights have been sleepless hours of anguish—yet he cannot die without your forgiveness. His life has been an unremitting penance—yet he dares not part from his burden while your curses load his soul."

"Tell him," said Lady Bothwell, sternly, "to ask pardon of that Being whom he has so greatly offended; not of an erring mortal like himself. What could my forgiveness avail him?"

"Much," answered the old man. "It will be an earnest of that which he may then venture to ask from his Creator, lady, and from yours. Remember, Lady Bothwell, you too have a death-bed to look forward to; your soul may, all human souls must, feel the awe of facing the judgment seat, with the wounds of an untented conscience, raw, and rankling—what thought would it be then that should whisper, 'I have given no mercy, how then shall I ask it?'"

"Man, whosoever thou mayst be," replied Lady Bothwell, "urge me not so cruelly. It would be but blasphemous hypocrisy lo utter with my lips the words which every throb of my heart protests against. They would open the earth and give to light the wasted form of my sister—the bloody form of my murdered brother—forgive him?—Never, never!"

"Great God!" cried the old man, holding up his hands, "is it thus the worms which thou hast called out of dust obey the commands of their Maker? Farewell, proud and unforgiving woman. Exult that thou hast added to a death in want and pain the agonies of religious despair; but never again mock Heaven by petitioning for the pardon which thou host refused to grant."

He was turning from her.

"Stop," she exclaimed; "I will try; yes, I will try to pardon him."

"Gracious lady," said the old man, "you will relieve the over-burdened soul, which dare not sever itself from its sinful companion of earth without being at peace with you. What do I know—your forgiveness may perhaps preserve for penitence the dregs of a wretched life."

"Ha!" said the lady, as a sudden light broke on her, "it is the villain himself!" And grasping Sir Philip Forester—for it was he, and no other—by the collar, she raised a cry of "Murder, murder! Seize the murderer!"

At an exclamation so singular, in such a place, the company thronged into the apartment, but Sir Philip Forester was no longer there. He had forcibly extricated himself from Lady Bothwell's hold, and had run out of the apartment which opened on the landing-place of the stair. There seemed no escape in that direction, for there were several persons coming up the steps, and others descending. But the unfortunate man was desperate. He threw himself over the balustrade, and alighted safely in the lobby, though a leap of fifteen feet at least, then dashed into the street and was lost in darkness. Some of the Bothwell family made pursuit, and, had they come up with the fugitive, they might have perhaps slain him; for in those days men's blood ran warm in their veins. But the police did not interfere; the matter most criminal having happened long since, and in a foreign land. Indeed, it was always thought, that this extraordinary scene originated in a hypocritical experiment, by which Sir Philip desired to ascertain whether he might return to his native country in safety from the resentment of a family which he had injured so deeply. As the result fell out so contrary to his wishes, he is believed to have returned to the Continent, and there died in exile.

So closed the tale of the MYSTERIOUS MIRROR.

THE TAPESTRIED CHAMBER;
OR,
THE LADY IN THE SACQUE.

THIS is another little story, from the Keepsake of 1828. It was told to me many years ago, by the late Miss Anna Seward, who, among other accomplishments that rendered her an amusing inmate in a country house, had that of recounting narratives of this sort with very considerable effect; much greater, indeed, than any one would be apt to guess from the style of her written performances. There are hours and moods when most people are not displeased to listen to such things; and I have heard some of the greatest and wisest of my contemporaries take their share in telling them.

August, 1831.

THE following narrative is given from the pen, so far as memory permits, in the same character in which it was presented to the author's ear; nor has he claim to farther praise, or to be more deeply censured, than in proportion to the good or bad judgment which he has employed in selecting his materials, as he has studiously avoided any attempt at ornament, which might interfere with the simplicity of the tale.

At the same time, it must be admitted, that the particular class of stories which turns on the marvellous, possesses a stronger influence when told than when committed to print. The volume taken up at noonday, though rehearsing the same incidents, conveys a much more feeble impression than, is achieved by the voice of the speaker on a circle of fireside auditors, who hang upon the narrative as the narrator details the minute incidents which serve to give it authenticity, and lowers his voice with an affectation of mystery while he approaches the fearful and wonderful part. It was with such advantages that the present writer heard the following events related, more than twenty years since, by the celebrated Miss Seward, of Litchfield, who, to her numerous accomplishments, added, in a remarkable degree, the power of narrative in private conversation. In its present form, the tale must necessarily lose all the interest which was attached to it, by the flexible voice and intelligent features of the gifted narrator. Yet still, read aloud, to an undoubting audience by the doubtful light of the closing evening, or in silence, by a decaying taper, and amidst the solitude of a half-lighted apartment, it may redeem its character as a good ghost story. Miss Seward always affirmed that she had derived her information from an authentic source, although she suppressed the names of the two persons chiefly concerned. I will not avail myself of any particulars I may have since received concerning the localities of the detail, but suffer them to rest under the same general description in which they were first related to me; and, for the same reason, I will not add to, or diminish the narrative, by any circumstances, whether more or less material, but simply rehearse, as I heard it, a story of supernatural terror.

About the end of the American war, when the officers of Lord Cornwallis's army, which surrendered at York-town, and others, who had been made prisoners during the impolitic and ill-fated controversy, were returning to their own country, to relate their adventures, and repose themselves after their fatigues; there was amongst them a general officer, to whom Miss S. gave the name of Browne, but merely, as I understood, to save the inconvenience of introducing a nameless agent in the narrative. He was an officer of merit, as well as a gentleman of high consideration for family and attainments.

Some business had carried General Browne upon a tour through the western counties, when, in the conclusion of a morning stage, he found himself in the vicinity of a small country town, which presented a scene of uncommon beauty, and of a character peculiarly English.

The little town, with its stately church, whose tower bore testimony to the devotion of ages long past, lay amidst pasture and corn-fields of small extent, but bounded and divided with hedge-row timber of great age and size. There were few marks of modern improvement. The environs of the place intimated neither the solitude of decay, nor the bustle of novelty; the houses were old, but in good repair; and the beautiful little river murmured freely on its way to the left of the town, neither restrained by a dam, nor bordered by a towing-path.

Upon a gentle eminence, nearly a mile to the southward of the town, were seen, amongst many venerable oaks and tangled thickets, the turrets of a castle, as old as the wars of York and Lancaster, but which seemed to have received important alterations during the age of Elizabeth and her successors. It had not been a place of great size; but whatever accommodation it formerly afforded, was, it must be supposed, still to be obtained within its walls; at least, such was the inference which General Browne drew from observing the smoke arise merrily from several of the ancient wreathed and carved chimney-stalks. The wall of the park ran alongside of the highway for two or three hundred yards; and through the different points by which the eye found glimpses into the woodland scenery, it seemed to be well stocked. Other points of view opened in succession; now a full one, of the front of the old castle, and now a side glimpse at its particular towers; the former rich in all the bizarrerie of the Elizabethan school, while the simple arid solid strength of other parts of the building seemed to show that they had been raised more for defence than ostentation. Delighted with the partial glimpses which he obtained of the castle through the woods and glades by which this ancient feudal fortress was surrounded, our military traveller was determined to inquire whether it might not deserve a nearer view, and whether it contained family pictures or other objects of curiosity worthy of a stranger's visit; when, leaving the vicinity of the park, he rolled through a clean and well-paved street, and stopped at the door of a well-frequented inn.

Before ordering horses to proceed on his journey, General Browne made inquiries concerning the proprietor of the chateau which had so attracted his admiration, and was equally surprised and pleased at hearing in reply a nobleman named whom we shall call Lord Woodville. How fortunate! Much of Browne's early recollections, both at school and at college, had been connected with young Woodville, whom, by a few questions, he now ascertained to be the same with the owner of this fair domain. He had been raised to the peerage by the decease of his father a few months before, and, as the General learned from the landlord, the term of mourning being ended, was now taking possession of his paternal estate, in the jovial season of merry autumn, accompanied by a select party of friends to enjoy the sports of a country famous for game.

This was delightful news to our traveller. Frank Woodville had been Richard Browne's fag at Eton, and his chosen intimate at Christ Church; their pleasures and their tasks had been the same; and the honest soldier's heart warmed to find his early friend in possession of so delightful a residence, and of an estate, as the landlord assured him with a nod and a wink, fully adequate to maintain and add to his dignity. Nothing was more natural than that the traveller should suspend a journey, which there was nothing to render hurried, to pay a visit to an old friend under such agreeable circumstances.

The fresh horses, therefore, had only the brief task of conveying the General's travelling carriage to Woodville Castle. A porter admitted them at a modern Gothic Lodge, built in that style to correspond with the Castle itself, and at the same time rang a bell to give warning of the approach of visitors. Apparently the sound of the bell had suspended the separation of the company, bent on the various amusements of the morning; for, on entering the court of the chateau, several young men were lounging about in their sporting dresses, looking at, and criticising, the dogs which the keepers held in readiness to attend their pastime. As General Browne alighted, the young lord came to the gate of the hall, and for an instant gazed, as at a stranger, upon the countenance of his friend, on which war, with its fatigues and its wounds, had made a great alteration. But the uncertainty lasted no longer than till the visitor had spoken, and the hearty greeting which followed was such as can only be exchanged betwixt those who have passed together the merry days of careless boyhood or early youth.

"If I could have formed a wish, my dear Browne," said Lord Woodville, "it would have been to have you here, of all men, upon this occasion, which my friends are good enough to hold as a sort of holyday. Do not think you have been unwatched during the years you have been absent from us. I have traced you through your dangers, your triumphs, your misfortunes, and was delighted to see that, whether in victory or defeat, the name of my old friend was always distinguished with applause."

The General made a suitable reply, and congratulated his friend on his new dignities, and the possession of a place and domain so beautiful.

"Nay, you have seen nothing of it as yet," said Lord Woodville, "and I trust you do not mean to leave us till you are better acquainted with it. It is true, I confess, that my present party is pretty large, and the old house, like other places of the kind, does not possess so much accommodation as the extent of the outward walls appears to promise. But we can give you a comfortable old-fashioned room; and I venture to suppose that your campaigns have taught you to be glad of worse quarters."

The General shrugged his shoulders, and laughed. "I presume," he said, "the worst apartment in your chateau is considerably superior to the old tobacco-cask, in which I was fain to take up my night's lodging when I was in the Bush, as the Virginians call it, with the light corps. There I lay, like Diogenes himself, so delighted with my covering from the elements, that I made a vain attempt to have it rolled on to my next quarters; but my commander for the time would give way to no such luxurious provision, and I took farewell of my beloved cask with tears in my eyes."

"Well, then, since you do not fear your quarters," said Lord Woodville, "you will stay with me a week at least. Of guns, dogs, fishing-rods, flies, and means of sport by sea and land, we have enough and to spare: you cannot pitch on an amusement, but we will pitch on the means of pursuing it. But if you prefer the gun and pointers, I will go with you myself, and see whether you have mended your shooting since you have been amongst the Indians of the back settlements."

The General gladly accepted his friendly host's proposal in all its points. After a morning of manly exercise, the company met at dinner, where it was the delight of Lord Woodville to conduce to the display of the high properties of his recovered friend, so as to recommend him to his guests, most of whom were persons of distinction. He led General Browne to speak of the scenes he had witnessed; and as every word marked alike the brave officer and the sensible man, who retained possession of his cool judgment under the most imminent dangers, the company looked upon the soldier with general respect, as no one who had proved himself possessed of an uncommon portion of personal courage—that attribute, of all others, of which every body desires to be thought possessed.

The day at Woodville Castle ended as usual in such mansions. The hospitality stopped within the limits of good order; music, in which the young lord was a proficient, succeeded to the circulation of the bottle: cards and billiards, for those who preferred such amusements, were in readiness: but the exercise of the morning required early hours, and not long after eleven o'clock the guests began to retire to their several apartments.

The young lord himself conducted his friend, General Browne, to the chamber destined for him, which answered the description he had given of it, being comfortable, but old-fashioned. The bed was of the massive form used in the end of the seventeenth century, and the curtains of faded silk, heavily trimmed with tarnished gold. But then the sheets, pillows, and blankets looked delightful to the campaigner, when he thought of his mansion, the cask. There was an air of gloom in the tapestry hangings, which, with their worn-out graces, curtained the walls of the little chamber, and gently undulated as the autumnal breeze found its way through the ancient lattice-window, which pattered and whistled as the air gained entrance. The toilet too, with its mirror, turbaned, after the manner of the beginning of the century, with a coiffure of murrey-coloured silk, and its hundred strange-shaped boxes, providing for arrangements which had been obsolete for more than fifty years, had an antique, and in so far a melancholy, aspect. But nothing could blaze more brightly and cheerfully than the two large wax candles; or if aught could rival them, it was the flaming bickering fagots in the chimney, that sent at once their gleam and their warmth through the snug apartment; which, notwithstanding the general antiquity of its appearance, was not wanting in the least convenience that modern habits rendered either necessary or desirable.

"This is an old-fashioned sleeping apartment, General," said the young lord; "but I hope you will find nothing that makes you envy your old tobacco-cask."

"I am not particular respecting my lodgings," replied the General; "yet were I to make any choice, I would prefer this chamber by many degrees, to the gayer and more modern rooms of your family mansion. Believe me, that when I unite its modern air of comfort with its venerable antiquity, and recollect that it is your lordship's property, I shall feel in better quarters here, than if I were in the best hotel London could afford."

"I trust—I have no doubt—that you will find yourself as comfortable as I wish you, my dear General," said the young nobleman; and once more bidding his guest good-night, he shook him by the hand, and withdrew.

The General again looked round him, and internally congratulating himself on his return to peaceful life, the comforts of which were endeared by the recollection of the hardships and dangers he had lately sustained, undressed himself, and prepared himself for a luxurious night's rest.

Here, contrary to the custom of this species of tale, we leave the General in possession of his apartment until the next morning.

The company assembled for breakfast at an early hour, but without the appearance of General Browne, who seemed the guest that Lord Woodville was desirous of honouring above all whom his hospitality had assembled around him. He more than once expressed surprise at the General's absence, and at length sent a servant to make inquiry after him. The man brought back information that General Browne had been walking abroad since an early hour of the morning, in defiance of the weather, which was misty and ungenial.

"The custom of a soldier,"—said the young nobleman to his friends; "many of them acquire habitual vigilance, and cannot sleep after the early hour at which their duty usually commands them to be alert."

Yet the explanation which Lord Woodville thus offered to the company seemed hardly satisfactory to his own mind, and it was in a fit of silence and abstraction that he awaited the return of the General. It took place near an hour after the breakfast bell had rung. He looked fatigued and feverish. His hair, the powdering and arrangement of which was at this time one of the most important occupations of a man's whole day, and marked his fashion as much as, in the present time, the tying of a cravat, or the want of one, was dishevelled, uncurled, void of powder, and dank with dew. His clothes were huddled on with a careless negligence, remarkable in a military man, whose real or supposed duties are usually held to include some attention to the toilet; and his looks were haggard and ghastly in a peculiar degree.

"So you have stolen a march upon us this morning, my dear General," said Lord Woodville; "or you have not found your bed so much to your mind as I had hoped and you seemed to expect. How did you rest last night?"

"Oh, excellently well! remarkably well! never better in my life"—said General Browne rapidly, and yet with an air of embarrassment which was obvious to his friend. He then hastily swallowed a cup of tea, and neglecting or refusing whatever else was offered, seemed to fall into a fit of abstraction.

"You will take the gun to-day, General;" said his friend and host, but had to repeat the question twice ere he received the abrupt answer, "No, my lord; I am sorry I cannot have the honour of spending another day with your lordship; my post horses are ordered, and will be here directly."

All who were present showed surprise, and Lord Woodville immediately replied, "Post horses, my good friend! what can you possibly want with them, when you promised to stay with me quietly for at least a week?"

"I believe," said the General, obviously much embarrassed, "that I might, in the pleasure of my first meeting with your lordship, have said something about stopping here a few days; but I have since found it altogether impossible."

"That is very extraordinary," answered the young nobleman. "You seemed quite disengaged yesterday, and you cannot have had a summons to-day; for our post has not come up from the town, and therefore you cannot have received any letters."

General Browne, without giving any farther explanation, muttered something of indispensable business, and insisted on the absolute necessity of his departure in a manner which silenced all opposition on the part of his host, who saw that his resolution was taken, and forbore farther importunity.

"At least, however," he said, "permit me, my dear Browne, since go you will or must, to show you the view from the terrace, which the mist, that is now rising, will soon display."

He threw open a sash window, and stepped down upon the terrace as he spoke. The General followed him mechanically, but seemed little to attend to what his host was saying, as, looking across an extended and rich prospect, he pointed out the different objects worthy of observation. Thus they moved on till Lord Woodville had attained his purpose of drawing his guest entirely apart from the rest of the company, when, turning round upon him with an air of great solemnity, he addressed him thus:

"Richard Browne, my old and very dear friend, we are now alone. Let me conjure you to answer me upon the word of a friend, and the honour of a soldier. How did you in reality rest during last night?"

"Most wretchedly indeed, my lord," answered the General, in the same tone of solemnity;—"so miserably, that I would not run the risk of such a second night, not only for all the lands belonging to this castle, but for all the country which I see from this elevated point of view."

"This is most extraordinary," said the young lord, as if speaking to himself; "then there must be something in the reports concerning that apartment." Again turning to the General, he said, "For God's sake, my dear friend, be candid with me, and let me know the disagreeable particulars, which have befallen you under a roof, where, with consent of the owner, you should have met nothing save comfort."

The General seemed distressed by this appeal, and paused a moment before he replied. "My dear lord," he at length said, "what happened to me last night is of a nature so peculiar and so unpleasant, that I could hardly bring myself to detail it even to your lordship, were it not that, independent of my wish to gratify any request of yours, I think that sincerity on my part may lead to some explanation about a circumstance equally painful and mysterious. To others, the communication I am about to make, might place me in the light of a weak-minded, superstitious fool who suffered his own imagination to delude and bewilder him; but you have known me in childhood and youth, and will not suspect me of having adopted in manhood the feelings and frailties from which my early years were free." Here he paused, and his friend replied:

"Do not doubt my perfect confidence in the truth of your communication, however strange it may be," replied Lord Woodville; "I know your firmness of disposition too well, to suspect you could be made the object of imposition, and am aware that your honour and your friendship will equally deter you from exaggerating whatever you may have witnessed."

"Well then," said the General, "I will proceed with my story as well as I can, relying upon your candour; and yet distinctly feeling that I would rather face a battery than recall to my mind the odious recollection's of last night."

He paused a second time, and then perceiving that Lord Woodville remained silent and in an attitude of attention, he commenced, though not without obvious reluctance, the history of his night's adventures in the Tapestried Chamber.

"I undressed and went to bed, so soon as your lordship left me yesterday evening; but the wood in the chimney, which nearly fronted my bed, blazed brightly and cheerfully, and, aided by a hundred exciting recollections of my childhood and youth, which had been recalled by the unexpected pleasure of meeting your lordship, prevented me from falling immediately asleep. I ought, however, to say, that these reflections were all of a pleasant and agreeable kind, grounded on a sense of having for a time exchanged the labour, fatigues, and dangers of my profession, for the enjoyments of a peaceful life, and the reunion of those friendly and affectionate ties, which I had torn asunder at the rude summons of war.

"While such pleasing reflections were stealing over my mind, and gradually lulling me to slumber, I was suddenly aroused by a sound like that of the rustling of a silken gown, and the tapping of a pair of high-heeled shoes, as if a woman were walking in the apartment. Ere I could draw the curtain to see what the matter was, the figure of a little woman passed between the bed and the fire. The back of this form was turned to me, and I could observe, from the shoulders and neck, it was that of an old woman, whose dress was an old-fashioned gown, which, I think, ladies call a sacque; that is, a sort of robe, completely loose in the body, but gathered into broad plaits upon the neck and shoulders, which fall down to the ground, and terminate in a species of train.

"I thought the intrusion singular enough, but never harboured for a moment the idea that what I saw was any thing more than the mortal form of some old woman about the establishment, who had a fancy to dress like her grandmother, and who, having perhaps (as your lordship mentioned that you were rather straitened for room) been dislodged from her chamber for my accommodation, had forgotten the circumstance, and returned by twelve to her old haunt. Under this persuasion I moved myself in bed and coughed a little, to make the intruder sensible of my being in possession of the premises.—She turned slowly round, but gracious heaven! my lord, what a countenance did she display to me! There was no longer any question what she was, or any thought of her being a living being. Upon a face which wore the fixed features of a corpse, were imprinted the traces of the vilest and most hideous passions which had animated her while she lived. The body of some atrocious criminal seemed to have been given up from the grave, and the soul restored from the penal fire, in order to form, for a space, a union with the ancient accomplice of its guilt. I started up in bed, and sat upright, supporting myself on my palms, as I gazed on this horrible spectre. The hag made, as it seemed, a single and swift stride to the bed where I lay, and squatted herself down upon it, in precisely the same attitude which I had assumed in the extremity of horror, advancing her diabolical countenance within half a yard of mine, with a grin which seemed to intimate the malice and the derision of an incarnate fiend."

Here General Browne stopped, and wiped from his brow the cold perspiration with which the recollection of his horrible vision had covered it.

"My lord," he said, "I am no coward. I have been in all the mortal dangers incidental to my profession, and I may truly boast, that no man ever knew Richard Browne dishonour the sword he wears; but in these horrible circumstances, under the eyes, and as it seemed, almost in the grasp of an incarnation of an evil spirit, all firmness forsook me, all manhood melted from me like wax in the furnace, and I felt my hair individually bristle. The current of my life-blood ceased to flow, and I sank back in a swoon, as very a victim to panic terror as ever was a village girl, or a child of ten years old. How long I lay in this condition I cannot pretend to guess.

"But I was roused by the castle clock striking one, so loud that it seemed as if it were in the very room. It was some time before I dared open my eyes, lest they should again encounter the horrible spectacle. When, however, I summoned courage to look up, she was no longer visible. My first idea was to pull my bell, wake the servants, and remove to a garret or a hay-loft, to be ensured against a second visitation. Nay, I will confess the truth, that my resolution was altered, not by the shame of exposing myself, but by the fear that, as the bell-cord hung by the chimney, I might, in making my way to it, be again crossed by the fiendish hag, who, I figured to myself, might be still lurking about some corner of the apartment.

"I will not pretend to describe what hot and cold fever-fits tormented me for the rest of the night, through broken sleep, weary vigils, and that dubious state which forms the neutral ground between them. A hundred terrible objects appeared to haunt me; but there was the great difference betwixt the vision which I have described, and those which followed, that I knew the last to be deceptions of my own fancy and over-excited nerves.

"Day at last appeared, and I rose from my bed ill in health, and humiliated in mind. I was ashamed of myself as a man and a soldier, and still more so, at feeling my own extreme desire to escape from the haunted apartment, which, however, conquered all other considerations; so that, huddling on my clothes with the most careless haste, I made my escape from your lordship's mansion, to seek in the open air some relief to my nervous system, shaken as it was by this horrible encounter with a visitant, for such I must believe her, from the other world. Your lordship has now heard the cause of my discomposure, and of my sudden desire to leave your hospitable castle. In other places I trust we may often meet; but God protect me from ever spending a second night under that roof!"

Strange as the General's tale was, he spoke with such a deep air of conviction, that it cut short all the usual commentaries which are made on such stories. Lord Woodville never once asked him if he was sure he did not dream of the apparition, or suggested any of the possibilities by which it is fashionable to explain supernatural appearances, as wild vagaries of the fancy, or deceptions of the optic nerves. On the contrary, he seemed deeply impressed with the truth and reality of what he had heard; and, after a considerable pause, regretted, with much appearance of sincerity, that his early friend should in his house have suffered so severely.

"I am the more sorry for your pain, my dear Browne," he continued, "that it is the unhappy, though most unexpected, result of an experiment of my own! You must know, that for my father and grandfather's time, at least, the apartment which was assigned to you last night, had been shut on account of reports that it was disturbed by supernatural sights and noises. When I came, a few weeks since, into possession of the estate, I thought the accommodation, which the castle afforded for my friends, was not extensive enough to permit the inhabitants of the invisible world to retain possession of a comfortable sleeping apartment. I therefore caused the Tapestried Chamber, as we call it, to be opened; and without destroying its air of antiquity, I had such new articles of furniture placed in it as became the modern times. Yet as the opinion that the room was haunted very strongly prevailed among the domestics, and was also known in the neighbourhood and to many of my friends, I feared some prejudice might be entertained by the first occupant of the Tapestried Chamber, which might tend to revive the evil report which it had laboured under, and so disappoint my purpose of rendering it a useful part of the house. I must confess, my dear Browne, that your arrival yesterday, agreeable to me for a thousand reasons besides, seemed the most favourable opportunity of removing the unpleasant rumours which attached to the room, since your courage was indubitable and your mind free of any pre-occupation on the subject. I could not, therefore, have chosen a more fitting subject for my experiment."

"Upon my life," said General Browne, somewhat hastily, "I am infinitely obliged to your lordship—very particularly indebted indeed. I am likely to remember for some time the consequences of the experiment, as your lordship is pleased to call it."

"Nay, now you are unjust, my dear friend," said Lord Woodville. "You have only to reflect for a single moment, in order to be convinced that I could not augur the possibility of the pain to which you have been so unhappily exposed. I was yesterday morning a complete sceptic on the subject of supernatural appearances. Nay, I am sure that had I told you what was said about that room, those very reports would have induced you, by your own choice, to select it for your accommodation. It was my misfortune, perhaps my error, but really cannot be termed my fault, that you have been afflicted so strangely."

"Strangely indeed!" said the General, resuming his good temper; "and I acknowledge that I have no right to be offended with your lordship for treating me like what I used to think myself—a man of some firmness and courage.—But I see my post horses are arrived, and I must not detain your lordship from your amusement."

"Nay, my old friend," said Lord Woodville, "since you cannot stay with us another day, which, indeed, I can no longer urge, give me at least half an hour more. You used to love pictures, and I have a gallery of portraits, some of them by Vandyke, representing ancestry to whom this property and castle formerly belonged. I think that several of them will strike you as possessing merit."

General Browne accepted the invitation, though somewhat unwillingly. It was evident he was not to breathe freely or at ease till he left Woodville Castle far behind him. He could not refuse his friend's invitation, however; and the less so, that he was a little ashamed of the peevishness which he had displayed towards his well-meaning entertainer.

The General, therefore, followed Lord Woodville through several rooms, into a long gallery hung with pictures, which the latter pointed out to his guest, telling the names, and giving some account of the personages whose portraits presented themselves in progression. General Browne was but little interested in the details which these accounts conveyed to him. They were, indeed, of the kind which are usually found in an old family gallery. Here was a cavalier who had ruined the estate in the royal cause; there a fine lady who had reinstated it by contracting a match with a wealthy Roundhead. There hung a gallant who had been in danger for corresponding with the exiled Court at St. Germain's; here one who had taken arms for William at the Revolution; and there a third that had thrown his weight alternately into the scale of whig and tory.

While Lord Woodville was cramming these words into his guest's ear, "against the stomach of his sense," they gained the middle of the gallery, when he beheld General Browne suddenly start, and assume an attitude of the utmost surprise, not unmixed with fear, as his eyes were caught and suddenly riveted by a portrait of an old lady in a sacque, the fashionable dress of the end of the seventeenth century.

"There she is!" he exclaimed; "there she is, in form and features, though inferior in demoniac expression, to the accursed hag who visited me last night."

"If that be the case," said the young nobleman, "there can remain no longer any doubt of the horrible reality of your apparition. That is the picture of a wretched ancestress of mine, of whose crimes a black and fearful catalogue is recorded in a family history in my charter-chest. The recital of them would be too horrible; it is enough to say, that in yon fatal apartment incest and unnatural murder were committed. I will restore it to the solitude, to which the better judgment of those who preceded me had consigned it; and never shall any one, so long as I can prevent it, be exposed to a repetition of the supernatural horrors which could shake such courage as yours."

Thus the friends, who had met with such glee, parted in a very different mood; Lord Woodville to command the Tapestried Chamber to be unmantled, and the door built up; and General Browne to seek in some less beautiful country, and with some less dignified friend, forgetfulness of the painful night which he had passed in Woodville Castle.

DEATH OF THE LAIRD'S JOCK.

[The manner in which this trifle was introduced at the time to Mr. F.M. Reynolds, editor of the Keepsake of 1828, leaves no occasion for a preface.]
August, 1831.

TO THE EDITOR OF THE KEEPSAKE.

You have asked me, sir, to point out a subject for the pencil, and I feel the difficulty of complying with your request; although I am not certainly unaccustomed to literary composition, or a total stranger to the stores of history and tradition, which afford the best copies for the painter's art. But although *sicut pictura poesis* is an ancient and undisputed axiom—although poetry and painting both address themselves to the same object of exciting the human imagination, by presenting to it pleasing or sublime images of ideal scenes; yet the one conveying itself through the ears to the understanding, and the other applying itself only to the eyes, the subjects which are best suited to the bard or tale-teller are often totally unfit for painting, where the artist must present in a single glance all that his art has power to tell us. The artist can neither recapitulate the past nor intimate the future. The single *now* is all which he can present; and hence, unquestionably, many subjects which delight us in poetry, or in narrative, whether real or fictitious, cannot with advantage be transferred to the canvass.

Being in some degree aware of these difficulties, though doubtless unacquainted both with their extent, and the means by which they may be modified or surmounted, I have, nevertheless, ventured to draw up the following traditional narrative as a story in which, when the general details are known, the interest is so much concentrated in one strong moment of agonizing passion, that it can be understood, and sympathized with, at a single glance. I therefore presume that it may be acceptable as a hint to some one among the numerous artists, who have of late years distinguished themselves as rearing up and supporting the British school.

Enough has been said and sung about
> The well-contested ground,
> The warlike border-land—

to render the habits of the tribes who inhabited them before the union of England and Scotland familiar to most of your readers. The rougher and sterner features of their character were softened by their attachment to the fine arts, from which has arisen the saying that, on the frontiers every dale had its battle, and every river its song. A rude species of chivalry was in constant use, and single combats were practised as the amusement of the few intervals of truce which suspended the exercise of war. The inveteracy of this custom may be inferred from the following incident:—

Bernard Gilpin, the apostle of the north, the first who undertook to preach the Protestant doctrines to the Border dalesmen, was surprised, on entering one of their churches, to see a gauntlet, or mail-glove, hanging above the altar. Upon inquiring the meaning of a symbol so indecorous being displayed in that sacred place, he was informed by the clerk, that the glove was that of a famous swordsman who hung it there as an emblem of a general challenge and gage of battle, to any who should dare to take the fatal token down. "Reach it to me," said the reverend churchman. The clerk and sexton equally declined the perilous office: and the good Bernard Gilpin was obliged to remove the glove with his own hands, desiring those who were present to inform the champion, that he, and no other, had possessed himself of the gage of defiance. But the champion was as much ashamed to face Bernard Gilpin as the officials of the church had been to displace his pledge of combat.

The date of the following story is about the latter years of Queen Elizabeth's reign; and the events took place in Liddesdale, a hilly and pastoral district of Roxburghshire, which, on a part of its boundary, is divided from England only by a small river;

During the good old times of *rugging and riving*, (that is, tugging and tearing,) under which term the disorderly doings of the warlike age are affectionately remembered, this valley was principally cultivated by the sept or clan of the Armstrongs. The chief of this warlike race was the Laird of Mangertown. At the period of which I speak, the estate of Mangertown, with the power and dignity of chief, was possessed by John Armstrong, a man of great size, strength and courage. While his father was alive, he was distinguished from others of his clan who bore the same name by the epithet of the *Laird's Jock*, that is to say, the Laird's son Jock, or Jack. This name he distinguished by so many bold and desperate achievements, that he retained it even after his father's death, and is mentioned under it both in authentic records and in tradition. Some of his feats are recorded in the Minstrelsy of the Scottish Border, and others mentioned in contemporary chronicles.

At the species of singular combat which we have described, the Laird's Jock was unrivalled; and no champion of Cumberland, Westmoreland, or Northumberland, could endure the sway of the huge two-handed sword which he wielded, and which few others could even lift. This "awful sword," as the common people term it, was as dear to him as Durindana or Fushberta to their respective masters, and was nearly as formidable to his enemies as those renowned falchions proved to the foes of Christendom. The weapon had been bequeathed to him by a celebrated English outlaw named Hobbie Noble, who, having committed some deed for which he was in danger from justice, fled to Liddesdale, and became a follower, or rather a brother-in-arms, to the renowned Laird's Jock; till, venturing into England with a small escort, a faithless guide, and with a light single-handed sword instead of his ponderous brand, Hobbie Noble, attacked by superior numbers, was made prisoner and executed.

With this weapon, and by means of his own strength and address, the Laird's Jock maintained the reputation of the best swordsman on the Border side, and defeated or slew many who ventured to dispute with him the formidable title.

But years pass on with the strong and the brave as with the feeble and the timid. In process of time, the Laird's Jock grew incapable of wielding his weapon, and finally of all active exertion, even of the most ordinary kind. The disabled champion became at length totally bed-ridden, and entirely dependent for his comfort on the pious duties of an only daughter, his perpetual attendant and companion.

Besides this dutiful child, the Laird's Jock had an only son, upon whom devolved the perilous task of leading the clan to battle, and maintaining the warlike renown of his native country, which was now disputed by the

English upon many occasions. The young Armstrong was active, brave, and strong, and brought home from dangerous adventures many tokens of decided success. Still the ancient chief conceived, as it would seem, that his son was scarce yet entitled by age and experience to be entrusted with the two-handed sword, by the use of which he had himself been so dreadfully distinguished.

At length, an English champion, one of the name of Foster, (if I rightly recollect,) had the audacity to send a challenge to the best swordsman in, Liddesdale; and young Armstrong, burning for chivalrous distinction, accepted the challenge.

The heart of the disabled old man swelled with joy when he heard that the challenge was passed and accepted, and the meeting fixed at a neutral spot, used as the place of rencontre upon such occasions, and which he himself had distinguished by numerous victories. He exulted so much in the conquest which he anticipated, that, to nerve his son to still bolder exertions, he conferred upon him, as champion of his clan and province, the celebrated weapon which he had hitherto retained in his own custody.

This was not all. When the day of combat arrived, the Laird's Jock, in spite of his daughter's affectionate remonstrances, determined, though he had not left his bed for two years, to be a personal witness of the duel. His will was still a law to his people, who bore him on their shoulders, wrapped in plaids and blankets, to the spot where the combat was to take place, and seated him on a fragment of rock, which is still called the Laird's Jock's stone. There he remained with eyes fixed on the lists or barrier, within which the champions were about to meet. His daughter, having done all she could for his accommodation, stood motionless beside him, divided between anxiety for his health, and for the event of the combat to her beloved brother. Ere yet the fight began, the old men gazed on their chief, now seen for the first time after several years, and sadly compared his altered features and wasted frame, with the paragon of strength and manly beauty which they once remembered. The young men gazed on his large form and powerful make, as upon some antediluvian giant who had survived the destruction of the Flood.

But the sound of the trumpets on both sides recalled the attention of every one to the lists, surrounded as they were by numbers of both nations eager to witness the event of the day. The combatants met. It is needless to describe the struggle: the Scottish champion fell. Foster, placing his foot on his antagonist, seized on the redoubted sword, so precious in the eyes of its aged owner, and brandished it over his head as a trophy of his conquest. The English shouted in triumph. But the despairing cry of the aged champion, who saw his country dishonoured, and his sword, long the terror of their race, in possession of an Englishman, was heard high above the acclamations of victory. He seemed, for an instant, animated by all his wonted power; for he started from the rock on which he sat, and while the garments with which he had been invested fell from his wasted frame, and showed the ruins of his strength, he tossed his arms wildly to heaven, and uttered a cry of indignation, horror, and despair, which, tradition says, was heard to a preternatural distance, and resembled the cry of a dying lion more than a human sound.

His friends received him in their arms as he sank utterly exhausted by the effort, and bore him back to his castle in mute sorrow; while his daughter at once wept for her brother, and endeavoured to mitigate and soothe the despair of her father. But this was impossible; the old man's only tie to life was rent rudely asunder, and his heart had broken with it. The death of his son had no part in his sorrow. If he thought of him at all, it was as the degenerate boy, through whom the honour of his country and clan had been lost; and he died in the course of three days, never even mentioning his name, but pouring out uninterrupted lamentations for the loss of his sword.

I conceive, that the instant when the disabled chief was roused into a last exertion by the agony of the moment is favourable to the object of a painter. He might obtain the full advantage of contrasting the form of the rugged old man, in the extremity of furious despair, with the softness and beauty of the female form. The fatal field might be thrown into perspective, so as to give full effect to these two principal figures, and with the single explanation that the piece represented a soldier beholding his son slain, and the honour of his country lost, the picture would be sufficiently intelligible at the first glance. If it was thought necessary to show more clearly the nature of the conflict, it might be indicated by the pennon of Saint George being displayed at one end of the lists, and that of Saint Andrew at the other.

I remain, Sir,

Your obedient servant,

THE AUTHOR OF WAVERLEY.

Printed in Great Britain
by Amazon

51091444R00131